THE LITTLE BOARD GAME CAFÉ

THE LITTLE BOARD GAME CAFÉ

Jennifer Page

An Aria Book

First published in the UK in 2023 by Head of Zeus,
part of Bloomsbury Publishing Plc

9 7 5 3 1 2 4 6 8

A catalogue record for this book is available from the British Library.

ISBN (PB): 9781804548363
ISBN (E): 9781804548349

Cover design: HoZ / Jessie Price

Typeset by Siliconchips Services Ltd UK

Printed and bound in Great Britain by
CPI Group (UK) Ltd, Croydon CR0 4YY

Head of Zeus
First Floor East
5–8 Hardwick Street
London EC1R 4RG

WWW.HEADOFZEUS.COM

For my lovely mum

Unlike Emily's mum, she can't cook, but she taught me to read and passed on her love of books, and for that I am eternally grateful.

Prologue

Most teenagers, if asked how they'd spend their ideal summer, would say surfing on a Cornish beach or backpacking round Europe or even just hanging out with their mates.

Not many would choose working as a waitress, especially not in the same café as their mother.

But Emily was having her best summer ever.

Mind you, she was looking forward to going back to school; she needed a rest.

She arrived home most evenings with an aching back, an aching head from adding up bills all day – the café needed a new till but that would have to wait until the owner got back – and aching feet despite wearing flat shoes. Granny shoes, she thought on her first day, hoping that none of her classmates would come in and see her. But Mum had been right to insist that she wore them; you definitely needed comfy soles in a job like this.

They'd forgone their usual fortnight in Devon. Dad hadn't minded. 'There'll be plenty more summers for family holidays,' he'd said, though he knew in his heart of hearts that wasn't strictly true; his little girl was growing up.

Mum had squeezed his arm. 'Are you sure you don't

mind?' she'd said. 'Only it'd be like a trial run. For the day when Em and I have our own place.'

'Of course I don't mind,' he'd said, smiling at her.

He probably did mind, thought Emily. He loved Sidmouth. He was less keen on the six-hour drive, the traffic jams on the M5 and the petrol prices at the service stations, but once they arrived, he was in his element. But he never refused Diane anything. It was a bit embarrassing sometimes, Emily thought, how he still looked at his wife. How they walked down Thornholme's high street, hand in hand like a pair of teenagers themselves. She'd even caught them snogging on the sofa when they thought she'd gone to bed.

'It's too good an opportunity to miss,' Dad had said to them both. 'You should definitely say yes.'

Mrs Benton, who ran Tricia's Treats, was going on a six-week cruise with a man she'd met through a dating agency. She'd asked Diane, Emily's mum, to run the café in her absence. The plan was for Diane to take over the kitchen – a move she'd been longing to make for years but Mrs Benton liked to do all the cooking and baking herself – whilst Emily did Diane's job waiting tables.

'Imagine if this were ours,' Mum had said as they'd opened up on the first morning. 'What would we do?'

'Fresh white tablecloths. Much classier than these wipe-clean things.'

'That's a lot of laundry, Em.'

'And a better menu. Steak and kidney pudding. Liver and onions.' She screwed up her face. 'I'd get rid of those for a start. Why does Mrs Benton serve that stuff?'

'Cheap, nutritious and the customers like it. Well, the older ones anyway.'

'And the walls are such a dull colour. How about sunshine yellow? Or pale blue?'

And so it had gone on. A whole summer of playing fantasy café owners together. If Emily had had a pound for every time one of them said, 'If this was our place, we could…' she'd have had far more money than the contents of the tips jar.

By the time the bushes down by the river were covered in juicy blackberries and the leaves in the park were yellowing, Em knew this was definitely, definitely what she wanted to do with her life. She and Mum would run their own café one day. Her parents both agreed that she should get some kind of qualification so she'd go to university first; do a business course perhaps, or marketing like her best friend Kate was intending to study. She had wondered about catering college, but her mum was such a good cook that they had that side of things covered. It wasn't as if they wanted to run an haute cuisine restaurant or anything; just a down-to-earth café for ordinary people like themselves. Somewhere that would be the beating heart of a community.

But she'd only been back at school a fortnight when everything changed.

Chapter One

'You're firing me? Seriously?'

Emily slumped back in the chair and folded her arms.

'I wouldn't say firing, exactly.' He pressed his hands together in a prayer-like pose under his chin and fixed her with a steely gaze. 'With regret, I am making you redundant.'

'With regret? That's what Lord Sugar always says in *The Apprentice*, when he *fires* people.'

'It isn't personal. We're having to let a few people go.'

She stood up. 'How? How can this not be personal?'

'Do you think you could keep your voice down a little, please? We don't want everyone to hear now, do we?' He stood up too and walked past her to the windows that separated his private office from the rest of the open-plan area. She turned to watch as he closed the venetian blinds, obliterating the view of Annie from Accounts who was staring, open-mouthed. Annie would probably put a glass to the wall if she thought she could get away with it. Not that you needed a glass with these walls; they were paper-thin.

He turned back to Emily, put a hand on her shoulder and pushed her back down into the chair. It was a cheap office chair with scant foam padding and she sat down with a bump. He returned to his side of the desk, to his deluxe leather chair, his own arse cushioned by precision-engineered springs and the down from three hundred small ducklings. It was a very nice arse, admittedly, but Emily didn't see why it was deserving of a softer landing than her own.

'Let's start again, shall we? I am in the very unfortunate position of having to let you go, but, as I said, it's nothing personal...'

She made an odd noise at this point, something midway between a harrumph and a snort. *He* was in a very unfortunate position?

'...it's nothing personal. You're just surplus to requirements.'

'Surplus to requirements...?' Her voice had reached a high pitch now, somewhere between wailing cat and warbling soprano.

'We're letting you go at the end of the month. You won't be entitled to much of a pay-out since you've not been here long – but there'll be something. I'll put that in writing.'

He'd put that in writing! And no doubt – since she did all his typing – she'd be writing that letter to herself.

'Fine,' she said, standing up again. 'I'd better get back to work then.'

'Look, I can see this has come as a shock. Why don't you take the rest of the afternoon off? Go home. Chill out. Put your feet up.'

'Thanks. I'll do that.'

She turned away from him and walked towards the door with as much dignity as she could muster. Which wasn't much. She placed a trembling hand on the handle and was about to open the door when he cleared his throat.

'One more thing, Em,' he said. 'Do you think you could pick up some semi-skimmed on the way home?'

Emily was outside on the pavement, underneath the enormous sign that read *Peter Ridley Engineering Ltd*, when the tears began to roll. On autopilot, she rummaged in her pockets for a tissue then realised she had no pockets. Damn. She'd left her coat in the office. There was no way she was going back in for it.

It was bad enough that she'd Just Been Fired in front of everyone. What made it worse, so much worse, was the fact that the man who'd fired her – or, as he insisted on calling it, 'made her redundant' – was her fiancé.

She hadn't even wanted to work at Peter Ridley Engineering Ltd and she'd never fitted in. The boss giving his other half a job – well, that move was never going to be popular with the workforce, was it? They were probably cheering now that he was letting her go.

It was chilly outside. Emily wanted to walk through the park to clear her head, but without her coat?

Oxfam, she decided. She needed a 'new' coat anyway.

She turned left towards the small centre of town. Essendale lay nestled in a little valley in the West Yorkshire Pennines. It mightn't have been quite as picture-box pretty as towns in nearby North Yorkshire, but it had its own quirky charm. A chimney still stood, towering over the town, though the mill it was once part of was long gone. Higgledy-piggledy terraced houses were tucked into the hillside below fields and tumbling drystone walls. Some of the cobbles had now been tarmacked over, but on sunny days, lines of washing crisscrossed the narrow streets between the houses. Not that there were that many sunny days; this was the Pennines. The skies were often grey, the valley often misty and if it wasn't raining properly, it was usually drizzling.

You never saw a policeman in Essendale – well, there wasn't much crime – but the town had its own super-vigilant neighbourhood watch: a group of somewhat aggressive white geese who patrolled the streets, held up the traffic on a regular basis and hissed at any dog who dared get too close.

They were gathered now outside the small library – only open on Tuesdays and Thursdays – so Emily steered around them, keeping her hands well above pecking height.

She'd only walked another hundred metres or so when her phone pinged, and then pinged again shortly afterwards. Peter probably. She ignored it and pressed on, passing Alessandra's, the only clothes shop in town, where her mother-in-law-to-be bought all her outfits. Emily couldn't afford their prices, but even if she could... Well, much as Peter would have liked it, she wasn't ready to turn into a mini version of his mother quite yet.

A man she vaguely recognised nodded and said, 'Eyup' to her as she passed him. Essendale was that sort of place; you greeted people even if you didn't know them. Although most people here did seem to know everyone else. Emily knew Peter, Kate and her old neighbour Marjory, plus all her soon-to-be-former colleagues from Ridley's and that was about it. She'd been here a few years and still felt like an outsider.

She passed the Red Lion, adorned with window boxes and hanging baskets, its sign promising real ales and a log fire. She and Kate spent many an evening there, mulling over the trials and tribulations of Kate's love life.

There were only a handful of shops in Essendale, and each bore an old-fashioned, hand-painted sign. No neon here, the local councillor liked to boast. Emily walked by the mini-supermarket, which Peter always referred to as the grocer's, the florist with its modest collection of potted hyacinths and daffodils on display and the Golden Wok, its windows now boarded up. She missed their chicken chow mein, though Peter wasn't fond of take-aways.

She paused for a moment beside Sweet Delights, the only café in town, peering at the cakes in the window, the bustling waitresses, the happy customers. One day, she thought, one day. Then she pressed on towards her favourite shop in Essendale: Oxfam.

She loved browsing in charity shops, but Peter had banned her from buying second-hand clothes. 'Mother says you'll bring moths into the house and they'll leave holes in all my cashmere,' he'd said. But if Emily chose diligently, he didn't notice that a new item of clothing wasn't actually new. And now she was officially joining the ranks of the unemployed...well, it was the perfect excuse. She would find a coat then go for a walk in the park.

But first, the books. A book would cheer her up. Emily loved the kind of books that made her feel inspired to take up a new hobby or go on an adventure. Of course, she never actually took up the hobby or went on the adventure, but she knew all about mixed media collage, glass painting and drying flowers. In her imagination, she'd wandered the streets of Montmartre, sipped coffee in a tiny café beside the Seine and sniffed the lightly scented roses in the Jardin des Tuileries. She'd dropped plenty of hints to Peter about her longing to go to the French capital, but he wasn't the most romantic of men and wasn't great at picking up on hints.

She'd seen most of the books on Oxfam's shelves already. In a small town like Essendale, the turnover in the non-fiction section wasn't very high. But she loved browsing. That was the fun part of charity shops. You could order what you liked from the internet, of course. Any book under the sun. But looking for books in charity shops was like digging for treasure; you were never sure what you might find. Some days there was nothing. Like a metal detectorist walking away after a day on the beach with only a couple of ring pulls from Coke cans for his troubles, she'd walk away empty-handed. Yet on other days, she'd strike gold. An out-of-print Peggy Porschen about cake decorating or a photobook of vintage bridal gowns. Books that would make their way onto the pile on her bedside table. You could always tell what Emily was interested in at any given time by looking at the titles by her bed.

A few years back, before she'd met Peter, there'd been several weighty tomes about how to be irresistible, how to meet and keep a boyfriend, and how to apply what somebody or other learned at Harvard Business School to the world of dating. All borrowed from Kate. You wouldn't have needed to be Sherlock Holmes or Inspector Barnaby to work out that Emily was looking for love.

The find-a-man self-help books had now been returned to their owner. In their place were how-to guides about creating hand-made wedding invitations, arranging bridal bouquets, cake decorating and making tiaras. She fancied being a 'DIY bride'. She didn't have the skills to sew her own dress, but had wanted to try her hand at making her own stationery and she could definitely bake her own cake. A three-tiered gooey chocolate cake, covered in a chocolate mirror glaze, decorated with red sugar-paste roses and shards of dark chocolate.

But Peter's mother had other ideas. She'd insisted on 'proper' save-the-date cards – someone from her Women In Business breakfasts ran a printing company so they'd got a discount – and she was adamant that her son and his bride should have a traditional wedding cake. Fruit cake. White icing with piped swirls. Made by a professional. She'd probably get her way. She usually did.

Emily thumbed her way through Oxfam's self-help section. What she really needed was *How to Stand Up to Your Mother-in-Law*, but if such a title existed, the charity shop was out of stock. Instead she looked for books on job-hunting, selecting one title about re-writing your CV and a second entitled *Surviving Unemployment*. She was wondering if there might be a section on how to cope if it was your own fiancé who'd made you unemployed, when a bright-red book with bold white writing caught her eye: *A Beginner's Guide to Starting Your Own Business*. Perhaps it was a sign.

With all three books tucked under her arm, she rummaged through the coat section. Several black and navy coats. A Barbour that had seen better days. Two red anoraks and a grey quilted thing that reminded her of a duvet. Eventually she settled on a lime-green woollen coat with a small collar, a fitted waist and large buttons. It was a brighter colour than she'd normally go for, but had hardly been worn and was a perfect fit. The employment gods mightn't be smiling down on her today, but the charity shop gods certainly were.

Behind the counter, a familiar face was waiting to take her cash. Emily knew most of the volunteers in here by sight, although not by name, and this one was her favourite. She always had an encouraging word or two and she didn't disappoint today.

'Your own business – that sounds exciting,' she said as she punched the prices into the till.

Emily smiled, tucking the books into her oversized handbag. 'It would be if I could pluck up the courage.'

'Just go for it. Sometimes you have to take a risk. Shall I put the coat in a bag for you?'

'No, thank you. I'm going to wear it now.'

When she'd paid and the assistant had snipped off the tag for her, Emily went out into the crisp spring sunshine, pulling on the lime-green coat.

In other parks in other towns at this time of year, crocuses and daffodils would be poking their way up through the soil, heralding the arrival of spring. Not in Essendale. The flowerbeds here were planted not with dahlias and pansies, but with herbs and fruit bushes. There was rosemary, mint and thyme for anyone to pick and, in the summer, strawberries and raspberries. It was the same in the churchyard and on the verges, and was another quirk of the little town that Emily loved. She paused to rub a stem of rosemary between her fingers, allowing the heady scent to transport her back to childhood for a moment, and the smell of her mother's roast lamb.

There were few people about today. One mother with a

pushchair, two dog walkers and an elderly couple walking hand in hand. Emily wondered if she and Peter would walk hand in hand through the park one day when they were that age. She couldn't picture it somehow. He wasn't keen on public displays of affection.

She sat down on a bench, wishing she'd thought to buy herself a take-away coffee from Sweet Delights. And then it hit her. She couldn't afford lattes and double chocolate muffins anymore. Not now she was about to be unemployed. The tears began to roll again.

It could have been far, far worse. She knew that. She wouldn't end up homeless. Or hungry. But she'd be dependent on Peter if she didn't find something else pretty soon and she didn't like the thought of that. There was that money from her mum but she tried not to touch it. Her mum had scrimped and saved to build up that little nest egg, and if Emily started dipping into it on a daily basis, it would be gone in no time. No, she wanted to save it, to do something special with it one day.

She watched a squirrel as it ran up a tree, an out-of-control terrier snapping at its heels. The dog owner came panting up behind, waving a lead. In the tiny play area, a giggling toddler was sitting on one end of the seesaw, his mother pumping the other end up and down. Would that ever be her one day with a little Peters? Again, Emily couldn't picture it, though she had no doubt that her fiancé wanted children. If only so he could change the sign to Peter Ridley and Sons Engineering Ltd.

She checked her watch. Ten past three. An afternoon off should feel like a treat, only it didn't. The time stretched ahead of her, empty, purposeless.

Sometimes her feet seemed to have a mind of their own. She stood up and walked, without thinking about where she was going. Back past the library, Sweet Delights and Ridley's. Left down the steps to the tow path by the bridge over the canal.

She stopped and watched as a bright-red narrowboat bumped its way into the lock. As one of the boaters closed the lock gates, she walked on, still not sure where she was heading. The rhythm of putting one foot in front of the other and the close proximity of water somehow felt soothing. Losing her job at Ridley's wasn't the end of the world. She'd find another job. Ridley's was the biggest employer in Essendale, but there'd be something, somewhere. Wouldn't there? Even if she had to look a bit further afield. Or perhaps now was the ideal time to... No, she was being silly. Best not to be overambitious. That was a pipe-dream. Another job. She'd get another job.

Emily began to feel calmer. At least she did, until a speeding cyclist forced her to jump into the bushes to avoid being mowed down. Cursing under her breath, she decided that she'd had enough of the towpath for one day. At the next bridge, she scrambled up a rough path onto the road.

She'd never been down this street before. Well, why would she? It was a road of stone terraces, much like any other. Except for one thing. As she walked towards the junction with the main road, there was a gap between the houses where a smaller, one-storey building stood. An unattractive building – more a shack really – constructed of breeze blocks painted an unappealing shade of mustard yellow with a flat roof. It had a shop window, but, from this distance, Emily couldn't make out what it was. Another charity shop, perhaps?

As she drew closer, she saw it was a café. Tatty-looking and dismal, it immediately made her think of the losers' café in *The Apprentice*, and the failed candidates sitting around a Formica table with their instant coffee in polystyrene cups.

According to the cracked sign above the window that had seen better days, this was Nico's. But according to the red and white estate agent's sign beside that, Nico, whoever he was, didn't want this little place anymore. It was for sale.

Chapter Two

Emily thought about Nico's as she walked back towards the centre of Essendale. She thought about that tatty sign and imagined herself perched precariously on tall stepladders, paintbrush in hand, lovingly painting 'Emily's' over that window.

Who was she kidding? She didn't have a steady hand and she didn't like heights. She'd have to get a sign-writer in.

And now who was she kidding? She wasn't going to buy Nico's. She was being ridiculous.

Although… a café…

It had always been the dream.

But that's all it was. A dream.

Nevertheless, as she passed Sweet Delights and peered in, she indulged herself with a fantasy about a chiller cabinet full of her chocolate eclairs – topped with real chocolate, of course, not that chocolate-flavoured icing that you got on supermarket ones that didn't taste of chocolate at all. Victoria sponge, made to her mum's recipe. Gooey brownies. Nutty flapjacks with the right ratio of crunchiness to chewiness. Fluffy scones oozing with fresh cream and home-made jam. Again, who was she kidding? She could bake a decent scone, but she'd never made jam in her life.

And savoury offerings too. An all-day breakfast. You couldn't beat a good all-day breakfast. Crispy bacon, sunny eggs, juicy tomatoes. Eggs Benedict. If she could get the hang of making hollandaise sauce. A bit more practise and she'd nail it. Fresh soups. Peter said her cauliflower cheese soup was the best and Emily liked to think that wasn't just because it suited his keto diet plan.

With thoughts of food swirling round her head, she'd barely noticed how far she'd walked and was surprised to find herself almost at home. Well, she tried to think of it as home, but this place still felt like Peter's home rather than hers.

She stopped outside the house and looked at it for a second. She knew she ought to be grateful to live in a place like this. Spacious. Modern. Warm. But it was sterile. Characterless. Red-brick with an ostentatious portico and ornamental urns, it was one of a small cluster of new executive homes built on the northern edge of the town. It had a gravel driveway with steel gates – the kind that you opened remotely with a little gadget as you drove up – and it wasn't very... Essendale. Only a few weeks ago, she'd given up her lovely stone-built terrace – well, the top floor of it; a lovely old lady called Marjory had the downstairs flat – to move in with Peter. Probably as well. Now she was going to be unemployed, she wouldn't be able to afford the rent.

Emily turned her key in the lock, praying that Peter wouldn't have come home early, and pushed the shiny black front door open. In the hallway, she took off her coat and shoes – cream carpets so no shoes allowed inside – and headed for the kitchen. It wasn't her sort of kitchen either.

It was almost clinical; the sort of kitchen where you felt you shouldn't make a mess. Stark-white units lined every wall. Everything hidden away. It had taken her ages to remember which door was the fridge when she'd first stayed here. She'd opened and closed practically every cupboard in search of a pint of milk the first few times she'd made a cuppa.

She opened a cupboard now, looking for a glass. Peter's glassware was incredibly organised. There were everyday glasses – small tumblers, highball glasses and wine glasses – then a whole array of crystal glasses for when his mother descended on them. What on earth were people meant to give as wedding presents when the time came? She selected a tumbler and filled it from the tap. There was mineral water in the fridge, of course. Peter never drank tap water, but Emily liked to do her bit for the planet so tap was fine with her.

She rummaged through her handbag in search of her phone, intending to message Kate to tell her about her impending unemployment, but when she found it, she saw that she'd had three texts from Peter.

At 14:17 – in other words, five minutes after she'd left the office and seven minutes after she'd Just Been Fired – he'd written, *Don't forget the milk.*

At 14:18: *Semi-skimmed.*

At 15:25: *You did get the milk, didn't you? Don't worry about cooking tonight. Let's eat out. My treat. Make up for today.*

You couldn't make up for firing someone by taking them out for dinner. But still, he was trying to be thoughtful. Peter always tried to be thoughtful.

She'd been working at Thorp's, one of Ridley's suppliers

in the neighbouring town of Hebbleswick, when she'd first met him. He'd come into the office one day to argue with Richard Thorp about the increased price of some component or other. She'd been wrestling with the printer; a sheet of A4 had got jammed in there for the fifth time that morning.

'Bloody thing,' she'd said, giving it a punch, which hurt her fist more than it did the printer.

'Allow me,' came a voice from behind. A deep male voice, with only the slightest hint of a Yorkshire accent. Emily turned to see who it belonged to.

A suited and booted, tall, dark and – she had to admit – rather handsome stranger, with hair so perfect it looked like the plastic hair on an action figure. Dark eyes. A shiny leather zip-up folder tucked under his arm.

He wasn't her usual type. She liked quirky men. Men whose ambition was to live on a narrowboat or who grew their own organic vegetables on their allotments. The sort of men who'd buy an old van and spend every spare minute converting it into a beautiful camper, and when it was finally finished, would drop everything to spend a month touring round the Highlands of Scotland. Geeky men who knew random facts like how far Jupiter was from Pluto or how many service stations there were on the M6. Men who collected unusual things like antique beer bottles or railway memorabilia. Men who wore interesting spectacles and their hair in a ponytail or had a mop of corkscrew curls.

Corkscrew curls. Emily sighed, remembering Greg.

Peter – she would learn later – wore a suit to work and jeans in the evening, drove a BMW and watched telly every night – documentaries rather than the reality-TV programmes like *Ramsay's Kitchen Nightmares* and *The Apprentice* which she preferred – and his idea of excitement was their bi-annual trip to his mother's second home in Cornwall.

'Allow me,' he said, putting the shiny zip-up leather folder down on her desk.

He deftly flipped open the lid of the printer, removed the offending sheet of A4 and fiddled around inside for a few seconds. She peered over his shoulder but couldn't quite see what he was doing.

'Aha, there's the culprit.' He held up a torn corner of white paper that had been stuck somewhere inside. 'Do you have a pen?'

She rummaged around in the general detritus on her desk and handed him her least chewed Biro.

He jotted something down on the tiny piece of paper, handed it to her, picked up his shiny zip-up leather folder and proceeded in the direction of Richard Thorp's office.

Emily looked at the paper.

Call me, he had written. And then he'd added his name and number.

She wasn't the kind of woman men normally handed their number to. She wasn't unattractive: dark-blond hair with fading highlights and a fringe that was always far too long and mostly ended getting tucked behind her ears (visiting the hairdressers was never top priority). She had pale-blue eyes and a chin that was a little bit too pointy in her opinion but Kate said it gave her that elfin look. Her best feature was her nose: she liked to think Nicole Kidman in *Bewitched*, but even more cute and buttony. But men didn't usually go for noses. Most men went for boobs and pouty lips, didn't they? And, let's face it, she was a bit lacking in those areas.

Men didn't go for the clothes she liked wearing either, but she'd no intention of changing. She loved dungaree pinafores: they were fun but practical and she had several in a variety of colours. They were suitable for most occasions and most seasons – with a plain or stripey t-shirt underneath in summer and a long-sleeved top, cardigan and woolly tights if it was cold. As it invariably was, living in the Pennines.

Emily stood there in the office, staring at that piece of paper, thinking, but this *never* happens to me. It happens to Kate with her sleek, dark bob, her come-to-bed brown eyes and her elegant, figure-hugging dresses, but not to me.

Later, despite all Kate's advice that she shouldn't be the one to call first, she did. After all, she had his number but he didn't have hers, did he?

Kate assumed it was his money that had piqued her interest. Emily wasn't a gold-digger or anything – she'd never been particularly interested in money – but in Kate's eyes, Peter's wealth was the only interesting thing about him. He was rather taciturn when Emily had first introduced them, disapproving almost.

In reality, the thing that had attracted Emily to Peter was that Peter was a grown-up. She'd never dated a man who was a grown-up before.

Greg, her first proper boyfriend, had been so young. They had met in the park in Thornholme when she was seventeen. She was taking a short-cut into town and he was walking his auntie's Labrador. She'd stopped to pat the Labrador and they'd started talking. Okay, not strictly true. She stopped to pat the Labrador because she'd spotted Greg's curly hair. She'd always been a sucker for curly hair. They'd been inseparable until... Well, she didn't like thinking about how that had ended. She'd behaved badly, she knew that.

And the man with the narrowboat? Well, he was never going to take out a mortgage on a three-bedroomed semi in Huddersfield and settle down. The man with the campervan? He'd gone on that Highland tour on his own when she couldn't get time off. He never came back. The man with the ponytail who collected antique beer bottles and knew everything there was to know about the universe was dating three other women at the same time as her and said he didn't believe in monogamous relationships.

Peter made it clear from the outset that he was looking for a Serious Relationship. He opened the passenger door of his car for her. He insisted on paying the bill. He always knew exactly which wine to order in a restaurant, was charming to the waiters and made sure to leave a hefty tip. On birthdays and Valentine's Day, he'd present her with a bouquet of flowers. Never roses. Always something a little more exotic: birds of paradise; anthurium; calla lilies. She always imagined he'd gone to great pains to choose those flowers especially for her, but when she started work at Ridley's, she heard him on the phone to the florist, ordering some for his mother, saying, 'Something a bit different. I'll leave it up to you as usual.'

Emily realised that she wanted what Peter wanted: stability; marriage; a lovely home; perhaps children one day. The narrowboat? The campervan? Pipe-dreams. A bit like running her own café.

Yes, Peter was definitely a grown-up. And she'd found that exciting at first. She liked that he booked restaurants and organised mini-breaks; the way his shirts were all lined up in his wardrobe with the hangers all pointing the same way; the way he always remembered to pick up his dry-cleaning and the respect with which he treated his mother. (Although it did sometimes border on subservience.) Peter made Emily feel secure and she loved that about him.

They'd dated then got engaged and he'd said it didn't look good for his fiancée to be working in the office at Thorp's.

'I want you to work for me,' he'd said. 'Be part of the family business.'

Emily was happy at Thorp's. Richard was a good boss and she liked her colleagues. She'd always promised herself that the only thing that would lure her away from there would be buying her own café. She'd stashed as much of her wages as she could manage in a savings account and, by the time she met Peter, she had quite a tidy sum. A few more months of scrimping and saving and, along with the money from her mum, she might have enough.

Peter sensed her hesitation. 'I was thinking you could do a part-time business course,' he said. 'Learn the basics. Accounts, marketing, that kind of thing.'

She never had done that business degree, opting for Modern Languages instead. Learning about accounts and marketing – well, that would come in handy when she did eventually pluck up courage to buy a café. Richard Thorp, lovely though he was, had never once offered her any training opportunities. Working for Peter was beginning to sound more appealing.

'A business course?' she said. 'That would be really useful when I—'

But she stopped herself. She'd never mentioned her café dream to Peter.

She had known back then that he wouldn't like the idea, and he certainly wouldn't like it now.

Chapter Three

Books by Emily's bedside: *Your Brilliant CV*; *Surviving Unemployment*; *A Beginner's Guide to Starting Your Own Business*.

'Would you like me to recommend a wine, sir?' the sommelier asked.

'Please,' said Peter.

As they debated the merits of the Château-What-Not 2009 versus the Cabernet Something-Or-Other 2013, Emily turned her attention to the menu. Hand-dived king scallops with candied lemon on a cauliflower puree. Roasted squab pigeon with celeriac and nasturtium. Rhubarb, hay and lemon verbena. Hay? Really?

She leaned over and peered under the table.

'What are you doing, Emily?' said Peter.

'Have you dropped something, madam?' said the sommelier.

She looked up to see them both staring. 'Checking I haven't got four legs. There's hay on the menu.'

'She's trying to be funny,' said Peter. Emily could have kicked him. If the sommelier hadn't been standing there, he'd have laughed.

'The Châteauneuf, I think,' said Peter, handing back the wine menu and scowling at her.

Peter had driven all the way to Leeds to bring her to this restaurant, but it wasn't her kind of place. Far too pretentious. If they had to come to a city, she'd have preferred a bar: the kind where you could order tiny plates of tapas with your glass of wine. She liked country pubs serving steak pie with rich gravy and the shortest shortcrust pastry, old-fashioned tea rooms where the cakes came on three-tiered stands, and cafés where you could buy an all-day breakfast with bacon, sausage and hash browns *and* toast and marmalade, all for under a tenner. That was the sort of café her mum used to dream of running. A place offering a warm welcome and simple, wholesome food. The kind of food she loved to eat. The food her mum had taught her how to make: hearty stews and hotpots made with real stock from the leftover bones; pan-fried plaice from the fishmongers at the local market; and roasts at the weekend with the lightest Yorkshire puddings.

The scent of dinner would greet Emily every day when she returned from school. Whilst other families had Birds Eye quarter pounders from the freezer, Mum would buy mince from the local butcher's and make her own. There was no sliced white in their house; Mum made sourdough long before it was trendy. Other children ate Rice Krispies and Frosties for breakfast, but Emily was sent to school on creamy scrambled eggs.

Diane, Emily's mum, spent years working as a waitress in Tricia's Treats, frustrated that despite her culinary talents, Mrs Benton insisted that she stayed front of house because the customers loved her. That one summer, when Mrs Benton had gone on her cruise, was the only time Diane had been allowed to do the cooking. 'I won't get to work in the kitchen again,' she said afterwards, 'unless I buy my own place.' But the dream hadn't materialised. She'd always promised she and her daughter would do it together one day but, of course, they never had.

Could Emily do it now? She wasn't a qualified chef but what she lacked in qualifications, she made up for in passion. She loved food and she loved cooking; her mum had taught her everything she knew.

Initially, she'd had a play kitchen, lovingly hand-crafted and painted by Dad, in the corner of their actual kitchen. She'd chopped Play-Doh carrots with a blunt plastic knife, whilst Mum chopped the real thing. She'd stirred imaginary sauces with a wooden spoon on her pretend stove, as Mum simmered broths and stews. She remembered how proud she'd felt when Mum had said she was old enough, sensible enough, to stand on a chair by the chopping board with a real knife to chop a real carrot; the first time she'd been allowed to stir and season the soup with Mum watching her like a hawk saying, 'Be careful, Em. It's really hot' and, 'Not too much salt. Taste it first.'

'Darling?' said Peter, and Emily realised he was waiting for her to answer.

'Oh, sorry.' She glanced down at the menu. 'I'll have the king scallops. Seeing as they're hand-dived.'

'I asked how your afternoon was.'

'How my afternoon was? Well, my boss fired me so it wasn't that great.'

Peter frowned. 'I meant, after that. What did you do? Apart from forget the milk.'

He smiled. He was trying to lighten the mood. He'd known all along that she wouldn't remember the milk – she could be a bit scatty sometimes – and had arrived home bearing a two-litre bottle of organic semi-skimmed.

'I browsed in…'

She'd been about to say Oxfam, but changed her mind. '…Alessandra's.'

He nodded approvingly. 'Mother loves that shop. Did you find anything?'

'A new coat. And then I went for a walk by the canal, and saw…'

The words 'a café for sale' were on the tip of her tongue but instead she said, '…a narrowboat going through the lock.'

The sommelier was back at their table now, holding the wine bottle out so Peter could scrutinise the label.

'Lovely,' said Peter. Emily wasn't sure if he was referring to the narrowboat or the Châteauneuf.

'I feel a bit awkward about coming into the office tomorrow,' she said when their glasses had been filled and the sommelier had departed. 'Everyone will be talking about it.'

Peter beckoned to a passing waiter, who was instantly at their side. He looked at her expectantly.

'The king scallops, please.'

The waiter nodded. It was the sort of place where they remembered your order rather than having to write it down. 'Very good, madam, and for sir?'

'Steak, medium rare. No sauce. And a mixed salad.'

His usual then.

That was the trouble with Peter. His predictability had

once made her feel secure, but now she longed for him to do something different. Something unexpected. Something to inject the pizzazz back into their relationship. Or was it unrealistic to have hoped that the initial excitement would last?

As the waiter disappeared towards the kitchen, Peter reached across the table and took her hand.

'I wanted to say, well, that…'

He wasn't usually lost for words. If they hadn't already been engaged, Emily would have thought a proposal was imminent. Perhaps, she thought suddenly, he was about to say that she was surplus to requirements in his personal life as well as in the office. But you didn't bring someone all the way to Leeds to dump them. He could have done that at home. Or down the local pub. And you didn't take their hand to do it.

'I love you, Emily,' he said. 'I know it mightn't seem like it after this week, having to let you go at work and everything. But we needed to streamline operations a bit, cut down the wages bill. And Mother felt that once we're married – not long to go now – that it wouldn't be seemly for my wife to be my typist.'

She might have known his mother was behind this.

'Typist! Admin assistant. No one says typist anymore, Peter. And what happened to me being part of the business? I mean, you sent me on that business course.'

'I know. Things have changed since then, Em. Margins are getting tighter. And it seemed a sensible option to make you one of the five.'

'You laid off five people?'

Peter let go of her hand. He picked up his knife, angled

it this way and that then polished it with his napkin before replacing it on the table. 'I did,' he said. 'It hasn't been a good day for me either.'

Or for them, she thought.

'Peter, don't you think it might have been better to give me a little warning? Perhaps tipped me off at home first?'

'With hindsight, yes. But I wanted to be fair to the others.'

'Or asked me to go? You could have let me resign. It's embarrassing. The thought of walking back into that office, and everyone knowing.'

'But there are four others. Frank, Tom—'

'Yes, but they're not engaged to you.'

She knew she was whingeing. Frank – well, he was getting on a bit and might never find another job. And Tom, she thought with a pang. Tom's wife had just had a baby. Emily was lucky really. Here she was in a fancy restaurant whilst they were probably wondering how to make ends meet. She couldn't bear to think about it.

Peter ran his fingers through his perfect hair. 'I'm sorry. But it is good timing.'

'Good timing? How d'you make that out?'

'With the wedding coming up? You must have tons to do for that. Finding your wedding dress, for a start.'

Emily was about to tell him that she'd already found her perfect dress, but was interrupted by the arrival of her king scallops. She lowered her nose towards the plate. They smelled heavenly.

'I've already bought my dress. And the wedding isn't for another eleven months.'

'You have a dress already? But Mother was looking forward to choosing it with you.'

'I chose it with Kate.' In the hospice shop in Huddersfield. But he didn't need to know that.

'I see. She will be disappointed.'

Emily shuddered at the thought of a shopping trip with her MIL2B. Heaven only knew what sort of a dress Florence would have made her buy. A meringue skirt, probably, with too much lace and a high neckline.

'Okay, so you've got the dress,' said Peter, 'but there must be loads of other things to organise. Don't all brides dream of having plenty of free time to attend to all the little details?'

'Your mother's been sorting all the little details. I haven't had much say.'

'Ah. Perhaps I should have a word.'

'No, leave it.' Emily cut into one of the scallops. 'I won't have much time for organising the wedding.'

'You won't have much time?'

She'd been about to say, 'I'm thinking of buying a café.'

Only something stopped her. There was no point upsetting him when it was just a pipe-dream. She didn't have the courage to buy a café, she knew that. So instead, she said, 'I'll be job-hunting. And perhaps making a few changes to the house – small ones, don't worry – so it feels more like home.'

'You will run them past...' He bit his lip. 'That sounds wonderful, Em. Absolutely wonderful.'

A week ago, she'd have been delighted to hear Peter say that he was happy for her to make the house more homely. But now, she realised suddenly, she wasn't bothered.

*

Later that evening, in an unusual act of rebellion, she took her clothes off and dumped them on the bedroom floor. Peter liked to put things away – either in the laundry basket or back in the fitted wardrobe. She watched to see if he'd notice, but he was busy hanging up his suit jacket on a padded coat-hanger and zipping it into a protective cover. She watched as he turned and clocked the crumpled pile of discarded garments. She silently dared him to pick them up; she knew he was itching to. He glanced at her, but left the clothes where they were and slid under the duvet beside her.

She turned her bedside light off, faked a yawn with almost Oscar-winning prowess, gave Peter a quick peck on the cheek and turned away from him. He'd be hoping for sex; it wasn't set in stone, but they almost always had sex when he'd taken her out for dinner.

But surely he couldn't expect sex with her on the day she'd been fired?

Fired. By. Him.

Yes, it seemed he could.

He put an arm over her and pulled her into a spoon. He nuzzled her neck, his fingers gently caressing her stomach and creeping up towards her breasts. He was interested in more than a cuddle. She normally wanted this. Normally no matter what mood she was in, she wouldn't be able to help herself succumb to his advances but tonight... Well, it turned out that being made redundant wasn't great for the libido.

'Not now,' she said. 'I've got too much on my mind.'

He sat up and turned on his bedside light. 'Talk to me.'

And that was another opportunity to tell him that she'd always dreamed of having her own café, and by a somewhat unbelievable coincidence, today of all days, hours after he'd fired her, she had stumbled across a café for sale right there in Essendale.

'Forget it, Peter. Let's go to sleep.'

Then she leaned across him and flicked his light back off.

Chapter Four

Word had clearly got round Ridley's by the time Emily and Peter walked into the office on Friday morning. No one said anything, but she could feel every pair of eyes upon them. They all knew she'd been fired. And there was probably a fair bit of speculation about whether she and Peter were still together.

Peter practically sprinted into his office, closing the door behind him. Annie raised her eyebrows questioningly at Emily, then turned round to look at Peter as he sat down on his deluxe office chair. He stood up again, walked over to the windows and closed the blinds.

Emily put her handbag down beside her desk and fired up her computer. There was a small pile of letters to type up, all in Peter's practically indecipherable scrawl. Who'd type his letters when she'd left, she wondered. Annie, perhaps. She'd waltz into his office and lean over as she handed them to him, affording him a perfect view of her cleavage. She was attractive, Emily thought grudgingly. Blonder hair, and straight too. Flawless make-up. Perfectly shaped eyebrows.

She typed up two of the letters, then limped into the small and ill-equipped kitchen area in the corner of the Ridley's office to make herself a consolatory mug of instant. There was no fancy coffee machine. There wasn't even a kettle. Someone – Peter, she guessed, or perhaps his mother – had installed one of those fancy taps that delivered boiling water on demand with an angry hiss of steam. You took your life into your own hands when you used it. Rumour had it that Annie's predecessor had had to go to hospital with third-degree burns.

Emily was sniffing the milk to check it was fit for human consumption, when Annie walked into the kitchen, blonde hair and hips swaying as she walked.

'I'm sorry to hear about your job,' she said, putting a beautifully manicured hand on Emily's arm. 'If you ever need a listening ear or anything. You know, I'm always happy to—'

'I'm fine, thanks.'

Emily couldn't imagine anyone she'd be less likely to turn to if she needed a listening ear. The MIL2B perhaps.

'So, are you and Peter…?'

'Are Peter and I what?' Emily pretended she didn't know what her colleague was angling to find out.

'Are you…?' Annie was usually pushy, but seemed reluctant to come straight out with it.

Emily picked up her mug of coffee with her left hand and took a sip. Her ring sparkled under the kitchen spotlights.

'Are we still together? Of course we are.' She smiled. 'Very much so. Why wouldn't we be?'

'Well, you know. With him making you redundant.'

'That was a business decision, Annie. Besides, when you have a bond like we do, it'd take more than a little thing like redundancy to break us up.'

'I'd hardly call redundancy a little thing,' she said.

She actually looked a little tearful. Odd. Emily had always suspected that Annie fancied Peter, but hadn't thought that the news that she and Peter were still together would upset the woman quite so much. She took her coffee back to her desk, slopping some of it down her pinafore, a pale-blue one that she particularly liked.

She was irritated. By the conversation with Annie. By ruining one of her favourite garments. And by the realisation that she hadn't clicked 'save' on the document she'd been working on and had somehow managed to lose it. Like the grit in an oyster that eventually leads to the production of a beautiful pearl, it was this irritation that made her put the rest of the letters to one side and google Nico's.

It didn't take long to find the little café on an estate agent's website. She was surprised at the price – pleasantly surprised. Over the years, she'd occasionally googled cafés for sale so had a rough idea what they'd cost – it varied from place to place, of course – but Nico's was less than she'd expected; within her budget, in fact.

There'd be rent to pay, of course, but even that was a reasonable amount.

Suddenly what had felt like an unattainable dream seemed like a real possibility.

And the synchronicity of it all…seeing an affordable café for sale right here in Essendale on the very same afternoon that she'd lost her job. Was the universe trying to tell her something?

No. Emily dismissed that thought. She didn't believe in that kind of stuff. It was just coincidence. Buying a café would be such a risk. All those years of saving up. The money from her mum. If things didn't work out, she could lose everything.

Sensible people in their thirties didn't spend thousands of pounds pursuing the dream they'd had as a teenager. She would get another job. That was the wise thing to do.

'Peter said what?' said Kate, grinning from ear to ear. You didn't expect the news that you'd Just Been Fired to make your best friend look like she'd won the lottery.

It was Tuesday evening and they were sitting in The Red Lion, Essendale's one and only pub. Kate was wearing one of her wrap dresses and looked far too alluring for a cosy little pub in a small Pennine town on a week night. Emily was wearing her brightest-red dungaree pinafore with a stripy red-and-white t-shirt; for someone who had just been fired by her fiancé, she was feeling rather cheery.

'That I'm "surplus to requirements",' said Emily, making inverted comma signs with her fingers.

'So you're single again? Yay!' Kate mimed punching the air. 'You can be my wingman. I have a new plan to meet—'

'We've not split up.'

'But you just said that he said…'

'I'm surplus to requirements at work. He's making me redundant. Not dumping me.'

'Oh.' Kate looked crestfallen. She took a sip of her Merlot.

'Crisp?' said Emily, pushing the Walkers towards her.

Kate's finger hovered over the open bag, but she didn't take one. 'Better not. I'm taking a leaf out of Peter's book actually, and giving keto a try.'

Great, Emily thought. She loved baking and now neither her fiancé *nor* her best friend would eat her cakes.

Kate tore the corner off a beer mat. 'So what are you

going to do, Em? Get another job? Or, better still, run your own café? You've been talking about it for long enough.'

'I've seen one for sale, but I'm not sure I'm ready.'

'Not ready? You're a fantastic cook. You know about running a business from that course Peter sent you on. And I can advise on the marketing.'

'I can rustle up a dinner party for six no problem, but cooking for an entire café full of customers when everyone's ordered different things? And that business course... Well, it only covered the basics. A bit of accounting. Profit and loss. How would I know how much food to order? Which dishes to prepare in advance and what to make fresh? And the regulations and food hygiene stuff and...there's so much I don't know. I don't even know *what* I don't know. The unknown unknowns. Who said that? Donald Trump, wasn't it? Donald Someone anyway. Duck?'

'Rumsfeld. Anyway, what are you going to do about Peter?' Kate took another sip of her Merlot, but her eyes never left Emily's face.

'Nothing. What d'you mean, what am I going to do about him? You've never liked him.'

'It's not that. He's a nice bloke. I just don't feel he's right for you. He's a bit... I dunno. Uptight. Well, isn't he?'

'I suppose.'

'And under his mother's thumb?'

'Yeah, well there is that.'

'And it's always seemed like he wants to mould you into someone else?'

Did he? Emily wondered. She'd have to think about that, but she nodded anyway.

Kate's face brightened a little. 'Perhaps this is the perfect excuse for you to end things. To move on.'

'I don't need an excuse. I don't want to move on.' Emily felt slightly disembodied as she said that, and heard her own voice as if it was someone else's. Someone who didn't sound too sure of what she was saying.

'Shame. I had this new idea. And I was rather hoping... I mean, I could do it on my own. But it'd be so much easier, so much better, so much more fun if you were to do it with me.'

Emily's heart sank. Kate and her ideas. They'd met at primary school, when Emily had been one of the little gang of girls Kate used to rope in to her projects. There'd been 'homework club' where each week, one of them – usually Emily – would do the homework and the others would copy the answers, with Kate insisting that they each changed one answer so as to fool the teacher. It always did.

Then there'd been that time when Kate had found a pair of waders in the charity shop. They'd taken it in turns to plunge into the pond by the golf course in Thornholme, where they grew up, in search of lost balls that they could flog back to the golfers. The waders had kept their legs dry enough, but their arms – and most of the rest of them – got soaking wet. And they'd only retrieved three balls.

A couple of years later, homework and money-making had given way to boy-finding schemes and Kate had insisted they befriend Liz from the year below at school; she had twin brothers in the sixth form. After over six weeks of buying huge bars of Dairy Milk for her with their pocket money and helping her with her homework, Liz had finally revealed that both lads were gay.

Emily wasn't sure she wanted to be part of yet another of Kate's mad projects.

Kate tore her beer mat in half, then into quarters. She picked up one of the quarters and began tearing that into the tiniest pieces. 'I'm sick, sick, sick of dating apps. All that time swiping left, swiping right. Or sending online winks. Or writing coy little messages.'

This was always the way it went when they met for a drink. No matter what else was happening in their lives, the conversation always came back to one thing: men. Although Emily had Just Been Fired and a little sympathy wouldn't have gone amiss, she didn't mind. She knew how much her friend wanted to meet someone. It was hard to see why she was finding it so difficult; Kate was attractive, funny and intelligent. Emily sometimes wondered if she was also too picky.

'Most of the time, it comes to nothing,' Kate said. 'I think most of the men out there just want some kind of pen pal. They don't want to go on an actual date. And then if you do get to meet them… God, it's awful. Sitting there in some random pub with a random stranger making small talk. You feel obliged to stay for an hour even if you know within the first five seconds that you don't fancy them. It's terrible. Occasionally you get a nice one. You think you've clicked. You think this could be it. And then you realise later he was using you for sex.'

'Thank goodness Peter only fired me. I'm glad I'm not single.'

Kate frowned. 'Well, personally, I think you'd be happier being single than being with him but—'

'Tell me your idea.'

'Right, yes. So instead of relying on the dating apps to

find me someone, I start getting out there. With you. Into the real world.'

'We're in the real world now. In the pub.'

Kate looked round. 'But do you see any eligible bachelors in here?'

There was a group of elderly men playing cards in the corner, but, other than that, they were the only people in the place.

'Now listen,' said Kate. 'We have to prioritise going to places and events where we might meet men. *Suitable* men.'

'We?! I already have a suitable guy, remember?'

'Hmmm.' Kate pulled a face that she often pulled, but despite all the years of knowing her, Emily never had been able to interpret. A look that hinted – perhaps – that she didn't agree, but knew there was no point in saying so. A look that suggested, 'You'll come round to my way of thinking in time.'

'You can come as my wingman. It'd be fun, Em. It doesn't have to be about meeting men. It'll help us both broaden our horizons, try new things, make new friends.'

Trying new things sounded good. As long as they weren't dangerous things like bungee jumping or sky-diving or roller-skating. She knew most people wouldn't consider roller-skating particularly dangerous but you could reach quite high speeds.

And perhaps she could get to know more people locally, put some names to faces. Improve her social life; apart from trips to the pub like this with Kate, it was pretty much non-existent.

'What sort of events were you thinking?' Knowing Kate, she already had a list.

'We should go for brunch – or at least a coffee – on Sunday mornings. There's a woman at work who met her husband in the queue in Costa.'

'We don't have a Costa,' Emily said. 'Don't tell me you want to hunt for Mr Right in Sweet Delights?'

'We could go into Manchester. Or Leeds.'

'All that way to have brunch? I'm unemployed now, remember. In any case, a trip to a coffee shop is hardly broadening our horizons.'

'How about skiing club?'

'Skiing? We live in the Pennines not the Alps! Can't you think of something cheaper? And less likely to involve a broken leg?'

Kate thought for a moment. 'Cookery classes.'

'I can already cook.'

'How about the running club?'

'Running? Me?'

'They do beginners' evenings and it has the added advantage of being good for us. Please, Em. Please come.'

'Fitness and me don't go together.'

'If you did more exercise, you could eat more cakes. And that would give you an excuse to do more baking.'

Emily had to admit that Kate had a point. In any case, if *she* wanted to go somewhere and needed someone to go with her, Kate would be the first to offer.

'I'll come once,' she said. 'I'm not promising to come every week.'

'Perfect. I'll get more drinks in.'

She watched Kate's back heading for the bar. What on earth had she let herself in for?

Chapter Five

Books by Emily's bedside: *A Beginner's Guide to
Starting Your Own Business*; *Surviving Unemployment*;
Running for Dummies. Kate had insisted on lending
her that last one.

On Thursday, Peter stayed late at the office, so Emily
found herself alone. She should probably have phoned
home, but her dad was a worrier and she didn't want to tell
him yet about losing her job. Instead, she made some toast
and sat on one of the bar stools in her fiancé's state-of-the-
art kitchen, googling cafés for sale on her phone.

Hebbleswick, a slightly bigger town than Essendale and
just three miles away, had four cafés, but none of them
appeared to be for sale. She broadened the search out to
Brighouse (even pricier) and Halifax (cheaper but not by
much), and then to the whole of West Yorkshire, but it was
the same story everywhere: very few places available and
those that were vacant were prohibitively expensive.

Nico's was the only affordable option, but was there a
reason it was so cheap? Location, Emily decided. It was
a little bit out of the centre. In all the time she'd lived in
Essendale, she hadn't even known it was there.

She could find empty premises and start from scratch, she thought suddenly, but a few Google searches later, she realised that wouldn't be as easy as it sounded; you needed planning permission for a change of use.

She flicked back to the estate agent's website and looked at the advert for Nico's again. It was a gloomy little place, but did it have potential?

Damn. It had gone half past. She was supposed to be in the park for the running club in only thirty-five minutes.

She didn't have proper running clothes, so pulled on leggings and a longish t-shirt and hoped they'd do. She didn't have the right shoes either; her old trainers would have to suffice.

She had to run to make it on time – only the last forty metres or so, but it left her struggling for breath. This didn't bode well for the evening ahead. Kate was already there. Her friend must have been shopping, judging from the brand-new running clothes and pristine white shoes. Everyone else was wearing the proper gear too, and some were already limbering up and stretching as if they knew what they were doing.

'I thought this was for beginners?' Emily hissed to Kate, nodding in the direction of a woman doing lunges on the edge of the group.

'It is.'

A woman with a clipboard approached them. 'Names?'

'I'm Kate. This is Emily.'

'I don't seem to have your form back, Emily,' she said. 'I have yours, Kate.'

'Form?'

'Yes, medical form. It's important that everyone declares

any medical conditions so we know they're fit to start running. Insurance and all that. Did you get it?'

Emily hadn't even realised she was supposed to fill in a form.

'I emailed it to you,' said Kate.

Emily shrugged.

'Never mind,' said the woman, reaching into her rucksack. 'I always bring paper copies. There's always one person who doesn't send it back.'

She handed Emily a pen and a sheet of paper as if it was an enormous effort and inconvenience.

'Not very friendly, is she?' Emily said to Kate, when the woman with the clipboard had moved on to 'greet' the latest arrivals.

'Never mind her. There are men.'

Sure enough, there were two reasonably good-looking men, one dark-haired, one slightly greying, but they were already surrounded by four very slim women, who looked like they were born in Lycra.

'Looks like those other women have beaten us to it, Kate.'

'Us? Does that mean you're looking?'

'Only on your behalf.'

'Perhaps we'll get a chance to talk to them later.'

The only other man in the group appeared to be in even worse shape than Emily. He was short, had a rather large belly – mind you, she wasn't in any position to judge – and was sweating already, even though it wasn't a particularly warm evening and they hadn't even started running. Had *he* filled in the medical form? Emily wondered. He looked awkward, on the fringes of the group, like he already knew he didn't belong. She knew how he felt.

'Let's say hello to that guy.'

Kate wrinkled her nose. 'Not my type. Too short, too fat and too sweaty.'

'Kate! Too judgmental. Anyway, you don't have to fancy him. We could go and be nice.'

'Suit yourself. I'll go and do some stretching in the eye-line of those other two.'

Emily left her to it and went over to the sweaty man.

'Hi, I'm Emily. Is this your first time too?'

'Rob,' he said. 'Second, actually. I came last week. Nearly killed me.'

Emily gulped. She'd hoped it would be easy.

Clipboard Woman had finished doing the rounds now and barked at everyone to get into a circle. Then she asked for the 'helpers' to join her in the middle. The two reasonably good-looking men and the four women they'd been talking to jogged over to her and introduced themselves to the group. They'd be running alongside the beginners, Clipboard Woman explained, and making sure that no one got left behind. The group would mainly stick to quieter streets, but the route would also cross a couple of busier roads, so everyone should be careful. But first, she announced, it was time for a warm-up.

She began by running gently on the spot, raising her knees up to waist height. Emily copied as best she could. Next, she had them all skipping sideways round in the circle, changing direction on her command. Emily felt like she was back in a PE lesson in primary school, and was grateful for her t-shirt and leggings. At least it was better than vest and pants.

When the warm-up was over and Clipboard Woman

was having some sort of discussion with her helpers, Kate elbowed Emily in the ribs.

'Aye, aye,' she said, nodding towards a clump of trees on the far edge of the park where a tall male figure was running over, dark, curly hair bouncing with every step. 'Your type.'

'He's not. Peter is my type.'

Kate harrumphed.

'Sorry I'm late. Overran at work. As usual.' The newcomer flashed the broadest smile at Clipboard Woman, who visibly softened. He held out his hand, and she slapped him playfully and laughed.

Kate nudged Emily. 'Bit of a charmer too.'

They set off. One of the women helpers came over and jogged alongside Emily.

'We need to have a conversation,' she said, 'so you can gauge if you're running at the right speed. If you can't talk as you run, you're going too fast.'

Making conversation with this svelte, Lycra-clad goddess proved rather difficult. For one thing, no matter how slowly they ran, Emily was out of breath. For another, they had little in common.

'What do you do for a living?' said the Lycra goddess.

It was like a first date, Emily thought. The small talk, bog standard questions and general awkwardness. Thank goodness those days were behind her.

Between pants, Emily told her companion that she'd recently lost her job – she missed out the bit about her fiancé being the one who'd made her redundant – and added that she wanted to run a café.

'You'll need to find a place where there's good football.'

'Football?...I don't...want...to run...a sports...café.'

'No, footfall. You know, plenty of passing trade.'

It seemed that running was affecting her hearing as well as her ability to hold a conversation. Fortunately, at that moment, Clipboard Woman, at the front of the group, suddenly slowed to a walk. Like dominoes falling, the change of pace rippled down through the group and, with relief, Emily slowed too.

'Two minutes of walking to catch your breath,' said the Lycra goddess.

They came to a road and the curly-haired man darted into the middle and held up his hand to stop the traffic so the group could cross safely. He mouthed, 'Sorry' at the waiting cars, but none of the motorists seemed to mind the interruption to their journeys; in fact, two wound their windows down and called good evening to him. Emily glanced at him as she panted by. He was very smiley. Wearing the proper running gear too, but old stuff. Not fancy. Still, it left very little to the imagination; there was hardly any fat on him. He wasn't muscly like a body-builder though. Just nicely toned.

She shouldn't even be looking. Not when she had a ring on her finger, soon to be joined by a second ring. But it was okay to read menus, wasn't it, even when you weren't actually hungry?

Two minutes of walking seemed to pass much more quickly than two minutes of running, and it was like that the entire time. Emily wondered how Rob was getting along, but he was behind her and she couldn't see. Kate was up near the front and her running companion, Emily noticed, was one of the reasonably good-looking men.

They continued alternating running and walking as they

crossed under the railway bridge then over a main road. Emily's companion sprinted ahead and helped the curly-haired man hold up the traffic – not that he seemed to need any help – and Emily was left running alone. She didn't mind. It was easier just to run, than to run *and* make small talk. The Lycra goddess didn't re-join Emily when the group had all crossed, but sprinted to the front and inserted herself deftly between Kate and the reasonably good-looking man. Within seconds, they'd dropped Kate, who followed a pace or two behind them.

They were on the canal towpath now, heading back towards Essendale. They passed a farm with a scruffy narrowboat moored alongside, went under a bridge and then, at a second bridge, took a set of steps up to the road. And suddenly there it was: Nico's.

It was an ugly building, Emily thought, incongruous amongst the stone terraces. But perhaps with a lick of paint and a bright sign over the top? A few cakes in the window to tempt customers inside? And a warm greeting as soon as they set foot...

And with that thought, she missed her footing and was suddenly sprawled on the pavement.

'Are you okay?'

She noticed the lightly tanned – and rather attractive – knees first. She'd never found a pair of knees attractive before but these definitely were. She glanced up to see who they belonged to, though she already suspected. The smiley, curly-haired man who had stopped the traffic was crouching beside her, only his smile had been replaced by a look of concern. He held out his hand and Emily took it, trying to scramble to her feet, but pain seared up her leg.

'Ouch. I'm not sure I can stand up. I think it's my ankle.'

'Stay there. Right or left?'

'Right.'

The next moment, she felt his fingers on her sore ankle and remembered she hadn't shaved her legs.

Kate was kneeling beside her now, stroking her hair. 'Poor Em. You should have opted for skiing.'

'I blame you for this,' Emily said, then, 'Ouch' as the curly-haired man turned her foot slightly.

A small crowd had gathered around them now, and Emily heard Clipboard Woman say, 'What's the verdict?'

'I'll run her to the hospital for an X-ray. To be on the safe side,' said the curly-haired man.

Emily sat up suddenly. 'No, thanks. I'll be fine. I'll see the GP in the morning if I'm not.'

'And the GP will send you to the hospital. I'd put money on it. And I'd definitely win.'

She had liked him up until this moment, but this seemed a bit cocky. She frowned at Kate, who shrugged.

'You can't know that,' Emily said.

'I can know that,' he said. 'I *am* the GP.'

Okay, not cocky then. Knowledgeable.

'But isn't Dr Pearson…?' Emily began.

'Retired,' he said. 'About a year ago.'

'I think you've been snookered there, Em,' said Kate. 'I know you don't like hospitals, but maybe you should—'

'I'm not going to the hospital, but I would appreciate a lift home.'

'I'll run you home,' said the GP, 'if you promise you'll come and see me in the morning. Or go and get an X-ray.'

'If it's still painful,' Emily said. 'That's my final offer. Deal or no deal?'

He smiled. 'Deal.'

Kate leaned over and whispered in her ear, 'Shall I stay, Em? Or will you be okay? I think I might have a chance to pull the guy in the red Lycra.'

'Go. I'll be fine.'

'And you might have pulled yourself.' She nodded in the direction of Emily's ankle where the GP was still prodding at her.

Clipboard Woman shouted, 'Right, everyone. Let's go.' The runners began to fall in line behind her as the GP helped Emily to her feet and put his arm around her waist. She put her arm around his shoulder and began to hobble towards the garden wall of one of the houses as the runners disappeared round the corner. It was weird being in such close proximity to a man who wasn't Peter. You're engaged, Em, she told herself. Do not let yourself get excited by the warmth of his body pressed against yours or the feeling of his fingers on your skin – her t-shirt seemed to have ridden up and his hand was on her bare flesh, above the top of her leggings. But it was difficult to ignore the scent of him: still fresh, even though they'd been running. With a hint of woody aftershave.

'You wait there,' he said, lowering her gently onto the wall. 'I'll fetch my car. I won't be long. It isn't far.'

He had settled her onto Peter's sofa before she realised that she didn't even know his name.

'I'm Emily. Em for short.'

'Ludek.'

'Unusual name.'

'My parents are Polish. Shall I make some tea?'

'Because it's good for shock?'

'No, because I'm thirsty. I came straight from work. Would that be okay?'

'Yeah, sure. The kitchen's through the hall on the right.'

She sat back against the cushions and listened to him filling the kettle then rummaging through cupboards looking for teabags and mugs, opening every single door in search of the fridge.

Her ankle was throbbing now. Perhaps he'd take another look at it before he left.

Then she heard a key in the lock. The door opening. Peter putting his briefcase down on the oak flooring. There was silence for a minute – he'd be swapping his shoes for slippers – before his head appeared round the door.

'Hello, darling,' he said, sitting down beside her. 'Why are you wearing leggings?'

And then Ludek appeared in the doorway carrying two mugs of tea saying, 'Blimey, your kitchen's tidy.'

Peter looked at the stranger and then at Emily and said, 'Oh? Who's this?'

'He's a doctor. I've sprained my ankle.'

Peter was looking at Ludek's outfit now. Emily had to admit that she found it hard not to look at it herself, given how it clung to every perfectly toned inch of him.

'I didn't know doctors did home visits these days,' Peter said.

She was praying that Ludek wouldn't come out with

something cheesy like, 'Only for very special patients.' Although that would have been kind of nice. In a way. But he didn't. He said, 'I'm with the running club so I was there when Emily fell.'

'The running club?' said Peter.

'Kate,' she said.

This seemed to satisfy Peter's curiosity; he looked relieved. 'I might have known this was Kate's doing. Well, thank you, doctor. Very good of you to bring her home. Shall I show you out?'

And before Emily could object, before Ludek could take even one sip of his tea, Peter had whipped the mugs out of his hands, placed them on the coffee table and was ushering him back into the hall.

Emily tried to get up, but winced as pain shot through her ankle. 'Thanks for the lift home,' she called as the front door closed.

Chapter Six

'Would it be a terrible inconvenience if I took today off?' Emily said to Peter next morning as he laid out his clothes on the bed. The bed she was still lying in. She felt even more reluctant to get up than she usually did.

'Yes, no problem. Is your ankle that bad?'

'No, it's not that. It's just...well, yesterday, everyone was staring at me. There's so much resentment in that office with the redundancies and I know I'm one of them but I'm also your fiancée. They've never really liked me and they like me even less now.'

'I'm sure you're just imagining that, darling.'

'And I want to look into a few possibilities, you know, for next month. When I finish at Ridley's.'

'Possibilities?' Peter stopped knotting his tie and looked at Emily in the mirror. 'What kind of possibilities?'

'I thought I might pop to Nico's.'

'Nico's? Is that the new art gallery in Leeds? Have they a vacancy?'

'No, it's a back-street caff. Here in Essendale.'

'Are you meeting someone?'

'No, I'm...' And then the words came out all in a rush,

before she could even stop to think if now was the right moment. 'I'm wondering about buying it.'

Peter had his back to her but she could see his reflection in the mirror. For a second he frowned, deep furrows wrinkling across his forehead. Then he fixed his smile back on and turned to her.

'Buying it? Now why on earth would you want to do that?'

'I've always wanted a café. Mum and I used to say we'd run one together one day.'

'You've always wanted a café? You've never mentioned that before. You know nothing about catering.'

'I can bake.'

'I've never seen you bake.'

'Well, no. But that's because you don't eat cakes. I'm rather good at baking actually.' She normally didn't like to brag, but in the face of his scepticism…

'Baking a few cakes is hardly the same as running your own hospitality business, Emily.' He straightened his tie, planted a kiss on her forehead and said, 'See you later, darling.' And with that, he was gone.

'Thanks for the encouragement,' she muttered under her breath as she heard his footsteps descending the stairs. A few minutes later, the front door slammed behind him and she rolled over and tried to doze.

It was barely ten o'clock when the doorbell rang. Emily ignored it. She knew exactly who it would be.

By now, she'd managed to make it downstairs; her ankle twingeing only slightly. She put her feet up on the coffee table and continued reading *A Beginner's Guide to Starting Your Own Business*, as she heard the key turning in the lock.

'Hello,' came a voice from the hallway. 'Only me. Anyone home?'

Emily stayed where she was. Her mother-in-law-to-be appeared in the doorway. She and Peter had had countless arguments about his mother letting herself in like this.

Florence looked pointedly at Emily's feet on the table. 'Well, at least you're dressed. Peter said you'd be having a long lie-in.'

She spoke with a plummy accent. Put on, of course. Peter had let slip once when he'd had a little too much Chablis that she'd grown up on a council estate in Barnsley. Emily never understood why people pretended to be something different from who they were.

'Hello, Florence. Are you here to pick something up?'

She looked flustered for a moment. 'Er, no, dear. I came to see you.'

'Lucky me,' said Emily, feeling anything but. 'I'll make some coffee, shall I?'

Florence followed as Emily hobbled into the kitchen and watched while she put the kettle on. Peter had a fancy coffee machine, of course, but Emily still didn't know how to use it. Besides, Florence was less likely to linger if she gave her instant.

'So, what did you want to see me about?' Emily asked. Though of course, she knew. Peter would have rung his mother in a panic the moment he'd got to the office.

'This café business,' she said, grimacing as if she had a nasty taste in her mouth. 'Peter is very concerned—'

'Concerned?'

'I mean, what will your role be? You won't be waiting tables, will you?'

'I imagine I'll be doing pretty much everything, Florence.' Emily put a heaped teaspoon of instant in a mug – knowing full well that Florence would have preferred a cup and saucer – and poured in the water. 'Cooking the fry-ups...'

'Fry-ups? It won't be some sort of builders' place, will it?'

'Cooking the fry-ups, waiting the tables, sweeping the floor. At least, until it gets going.' Emily handed her the mug. 'Perhaps eventually, I'll be able to employ someone to help. But it's a big responsibility employing staff. As I'm sure you know.' Florence and her late husband had run Ridley's before Peter took over.

'Yes, quite.' She took a swig of her coffee. 'Only, how will it look to everyone, the wife of a managing director of a prominent local company waiting on tables?'

'There's nothing wrong with being a waitress. My mum was a waitress.'

Emily's MIL2B wasn't often stumped for words, but she didn't know how to reply to that one.

'I'd offer you a biscuit, Florence, but we don't keep them in the house. You know, Peter and his keto diet. He won't touch them.'

Florence took another swig of the coffee, grimaced again and put it down on the worktop with a plonk. 'That's okay, dear. I have to be going anyway. I said I'd meet Sylvia for lunch.'

'At Sweet Delights?'

'No, we're going to a new place that's opened. Somewhere

near Otley. Or Ilkley. I forget which. Bit of a drive, but she tells me it's worth it.'

Emily had been intending to head to Nico's for lunch, to check the place out. But once Florence had left, it occurred to her that this was a golden opportunity to check out the opposition instead. She usually avoided Sweet Delights because her MIL2B and her cronies were often in there, but it would be her main competition – her only competition – if she did buy Nico's, and she needed to know what she'd be up against.

Wearing her new lime-green coat, she walked down the high street, wincing now and again at her grumbling ankle. She passed Alessandra's with its po-faced mannequins – okay, so mannequins didn't have proper faces, but if they did, the ones in Alessandra's would definitely be po-faced – and Oxfam with a tempting new display of self-help books in the window.

She stood outside the busy high street café, trying to see the place with fresh eyes even though she'd walked past it almost every day for the past few years.

It certainly had what Phil and Kirsty would call kerb appeal. A simple sign across the top read 'Sweet Delights'. It was an old-fashioned sort of sign, but perfectly in keeping with the style of Essendale's main street. A tall, wide window with a menu at one side and a small display of teapots, all brightly decorated. The tables inside were adorned with red-and-white-check tablecloths and small vases of red and white carnations.

The scent of freshly baked bread hit her as soon as

she opened the door. This place was a cut above a greasy spoon. Several cuts above. Simply decorated with powder-blue walls and framed oil paintings of local landmarks: the old packhorse bridge over the river; the towering folly on top of the hill; a ruined mill in the woods, now partially enveloped by greenery - Essendale's answer to Angkor Wat. The whole place hummed with voices: a mother with two sticky children munching on fancy cupcakes; three of Ridley's workforce, talking animatedly over cappuccinos and avocado toast, who either hadn't spotted her or were making a point of ignoring her; and an elderly couple in the corner holding hands. They let go of each other only reluctantly when their soup and sandwiches arrived.

Emily walked up to the counter to check out the cakes in the glass display cabinet. Generously filled chocolate eclairs, three types of scones, brownies, muffins, and the local speciality, curd tarts. All standard fayre, and probably bought in, but beautifully presented. A blackboard behind the counter announced today's specials: Wensleydale pie with chips and peas; local pork sausages and mash; Whitby mackerel fish cakes with a soft-boiled egg and salad. It would be hard to compete with this place.

'It's table service,' said the waitress somewhat abruptly. She was older than Emily, fifties she'd guess, with greying hair scraped up into a bun, and a name badge that read Peggy.

'Okay, sure, I was...' But Peggy had turned away already to make someone's cappuccino and the noise of the machine drowned out her words.

Emily took a seat at the only empty table in the room. It was still cluttered with the detritus from its previous occupants and she felt rather smug about that. The first fault she'd found. Well, the second; Peggy hadn't been exactly friendly.

Probably related to Clipboard Woman, Emily thought.

Peggy delivered the cappuccino to a neighbouring table, then came straight over to Emily, empty tray wedged under her arm and notebook at the ready. She glanced down at the dirty crockery, sighed as if the table not being cleared was Emily's fault and began to load the tray.

'Would you like to order?' she asked. 'Or are you waiting for someone?'

Emily had barely had time to read the menu. 'I'll have… er…eggs Benedict, please, and a glass of water.'

'The breakfast menu finishes at eleven-thirty.'

'I hadn't spotted that. Could you give me a few minutes then, please?'

'Sure,' Peggy said rather stiffly.

Emily always loved reading menus, but, today, there was an extra element of pleasure in it. She'd been playing Fantasy Café Owner for years, imagining what it would be like if she did have her own café. And now, it might – just might – become a reality. She looked at the breakfast menu: full English breakfast – with more local pork sausage; vegetarian breakfast; eggs Benedict; scrambled eggs. And there, in small print, '8 a.m. to 11:30 a.m. only'. In her café, Emily decided, she would serve breakfast all day.

She was intently studying the various fillings in the baked potato section and wondering if they were microwaved or baked properly in the oven, when she realised Peggy was by her side again.

A glass of water was plonked down in front of her. 'The

chef says you can have the eggs Benedict, but only on this occasion.'

That was fine. There wouldn't be a second occasion if this was how she spoke to customers.

As Emily waited for her food, four groups of people came in, saw there were no tables and left again. Only one couple decided to wait.

Emily had to admit that her eggs Benedict were delicious. It wasn't a huge portion though and almost as soon as she'd polished it off, Peggy was back.

'Anything else?' She was anxious to clear the table, and not just of her empty plate, Emily realised, but of her too. One person eating alone wasn't so profitable.

'A latte, please.' Her face fell, so Emily added, 'To go.'

'Come to the counter.'

As she waited for the bill, Emily scrutinised the cakes in the glass cabinet again. They looked delicious, but she could probably make cakes that looked as good. Well, almost. And she could certainly manage to smile at customers and make them feel welcome. And the eggs Benedict? Well, it had been tasty. There must be videos on YouTube showing you how to make Hollandaise sauce.

'Have you worked here long?' Emily said as Peggy handed her the bill. Still no smile.

'Twenty-three years,' she said.

'The boss must be nice.'

'I *am* the boss. I own this place.'

Emily eyed her, like a bull sizing up a matador. So this was who she'd be up against, if she were to buy Nico's. Not that she was really going to…but it wouldn't do any harm to arrange a viewing.

She paid for her lunch, collected her latte in its cardboard cup and turned to leave. The table where she'd been sitting a minute earlier was already occupied by a family of four.

Service with a smile or not, this café was popular. It was the place where everyone gathered. Peter had met clients here. Her mother-in-law lunched here at least twice a week. Kate had even had dates here. Admittedly Kate had had dates in almost every eatery within a twenty-mile radius.

As she opened the door to leave, another couple arrived in search of a table and turned away disappointed. There was definitely demand for café tables here in Essendale, Emily thought. Perhaps with a decent food offering, improved kerb appeal, a bit of marketing – courtesy of Kate – and a much warmer welcome than Peggy's, customers could be lured to walk that little bit further to the café near the canal.

Chapter Seven

Books by Emily's bedside: *The Art of Living
Your Dreams*; *Surviving Unemployment*; and still
in pole position, *A Beginner's Guide to Starting
Your Own Business*.

The estate agent had seemed surprised to get her call. Yes,
Nico's was still for sale. And yes, she'd be very welcome
to have a viewing. In fact, she could see it straightaway as
one of his other appointments had been cancelled.

Emily could barely contain her excitement. When other
little girls had played doctors and nurses or schools, Emily
used to seat her toys at the dining room table and serve
them imaginary cups of tea, and now here she was, one step
closer to serving real customers.

Nico's was, to Emily's surprise, closed. It had six tables,
well-spaced out but covered with dark, wipeable cloths.
There was a serving counter at the back, a professional-
looking coffee machine and a glass chiller cabinet for
displaying cakes and sandwich fillings. The floor was tiled
in black and white like a chessboard and the walls were

painted dark red. It had looked dark that evening she'd gone past with the running club, but even now, earlier in the day, with all the lights on, the overall effect was still somewhat dreary.

The estate agent handed Emily a sheet of paper with a fuzzy picture of the café, the price and some details about square footage, the number of covers and the kitchen equipment.

'And the monthly rent is...' He pointed at a figure at the bottom of the sheet. 'Very reasonable for this area. You do realise that you're buying the business, not the building. If the building itself was included, it would cost much, much more. A place like this could be worth a lot one day. Development potential and all that.'

Emily nodded.

'Have you run a café before?' he asked.

She shook her head.

'Then this place is perfect. It's a short lease. One year initially. Ideal if you're just starting out. So many people start cafés thinking it's going to be easy when actually it's a lot of hard work. Not that I want to put you off, of course. But you don't want to be tied in to a three- or five-year lease when you've never done it before.'

That seemed reasonable, although—

'But what happens when the year is up?' she said. 'Would I just renew?'

'You'd have to agree that with the landlord, but that would be the usual thing. Unless...'

'Unless...?'

'Well, you might be so successful that you'd need to find bigger premises.' The estate agent laughed. He looked,

Emily thought, a little shifty, but maybe that went with the job.

'And the current owner?'

'Mr Panagi? He's gone back to Greece.'

'He's left already?'

She hadn't realised that. Perhaps that explained why the whole place felt so gloomy. The owner had abandoned it.

The estate agent shifted from one foot to the other. 'He was hoping to find a buyer before he went back, but he couldn't delay. His mother's very unwell.'

'I'm sorry to hear that.'

A poorly mother hundreds – or was it thousands? – of miles away seemed like a reasonable reason to be selling up, but Emily had thought the business was being sold as a going concern.

'It seems a lot of money,' she said. 'I thought it was still operating as a café.'

'It only closed two weeks ago and I'm sure he'd be willing to consider a reasonable offer. It does include all the fixtures and fittings. An existing customer base. Goodwill.'

Goodwill? How did they put a price on goodwill? How could she tell if it was a fair amount to pay? Of course, as a businessman, Peter would know all this stuff but she felt disinclined to ask his advice. He'd only try to convince her that buying her own business was a bad idea.

She glanced around again, wondering what questions a prospective café owner was meant to ask. Mum would know. Emily wished she was here.

The menu, displayed behind the counter on a large whiteboard, listed a huge array of options: four different types of all-day breakfasts; about twenty different sandwiches, all of which could be served on ordinary bread or ciabatta; and six different types of omelettes. Not to mention the daily specials or the soup of the day. Mr Panagi had obviously never watched *Ramsay's Kitchen Nightmares*: in every episode, Gordon advised the hapless restaurant owner to pare back the number of items on the menu.

Mum would know exactly how to do that, how to work out which dishes to keep and which to ditch. She had an instinct for that, did Mum. A knack for working out what other people would enjoy. She always gave the right gifts at Christmas, things you didn't know you wanted but, when you peeled off the shiny paper, you couldn't understand how you'd lived without a pair of cashmere fingerless gloves for so long.

If Emily had had a bad day at school, it was as if she was psychic. Her favourite dinner would be on the table. This changed as she grew older – macaroni cheese when she was thirteen, Lancashire hotpot when she was fourteen, pan-fried plaice when she was fifteen – but Mum always got it spot on.

'Go and take a look in the kitchen,' said the estate agent. 'Get a feel for the place.'

She wandered into the kitchen. It wasn't quite the shiny, professional type that you saw on *MasterChef*, but then this was a back-street café in a small West Yorkshire town, not a Michelin-starred restaurant. What had she expected? It was half the size of Peter's kitchen. There was a hob with four burners – Peter's had six – and three microwaves. The oven was smaller than she'd thought it would be. Perhaps Mr Panagi hadn't baked his own cakes.

She wandered back into the front of the café. The estate agent was sitting at a table now, waiting for her.

'Have a seat,' he said. 'Would you like to see the accounts?'

Emily sat down, mentally kicking herself. Of course. The accounts. She should have thought to ask for those.

He brushed the table with his hand, knocking a few crumbs onto the floor, before opening a folder and angling it so that Emily could see. She wasn't an expert, but since the business course, she knew what she was supposed to be looking for. It seemed as if the café had been making a reasonable profit. Not a huge amount, but it had seemingly been quite popular despite being on a side street.

'I'll have to think about it,' said Emily.

'Of course,' said the estate agent. 'But don't think too long. There isn't another café for sale in the area, especially not at this price. It's sure to be snapped up.'

Emily walked home, weighing up the pros and cons in her mind, not even noticing her ankle anymore.

Nico's was well within her budget. She'd have a short commute. And it was a short lease: if running a café turned out not to be her thing after all, she wouldn't be tied in for years.

But it had a tiny kitchen. A back-street location too far from the high street. It had been closed for two weeks already: would it have lost some of its customer base during that time? And it was a miserable little place making some – but not much – profit.

It was a non-starter, Emily decided.

Although…

With a business like Nico's, she'd be able to make her mark. Give the entire place a make-over. Liven up the menu, putting the emphasis on quality not quantity. And Kate had offered to advise on publicity: surely the right marketing could ensure a steady stream of customers to her door, even if the place was a little off the beaten track.

If she were to buy a beautiful café that was already making plenty of money – *if* that was within her budget, which it wasn't – there'd be no challenge in it. She'd sign on the dotted line, hand over the cash, and carry on the business that someone else had established. If she could transform Nico's into the kind of place she and her mum had always dreamed of running, well, imagine the satisfaction. Just imagine.

Chapter Eight

Books by Emily's bedside: *Surviving Unemployment*;
Feel the Fear and Do It Anyway; and *How to Make
the Right Decisions*.

The alarm went off like on a weekday. Peter was out of bed immediately and straight into the shower, whistling away. In an especially good mood as he always was on a Saturday because it was his golf day. Emily rolled over, and tried to doze off again. Impossible with the rather out-of-tune version of Pharrell Williams' 'Happy' coming from the ensuite.

'Any chance of a coffee, Em?' he said, emerging with an off-white towel wrapped around his waist. All his towels had been hotel-white when she'd moved in. They were an assortment of shades now. Everything from grey to very pale pink. She ought to check the washing machine for stray socks before she put a load on.

With a sigh, she got out of bed, pulled on a dressing gown and went downstairs to put the kettle on. She popped some bread in the toaster, laid out his favourite high-protein, low-carb muesli and some milk – in a jug, of course, like his mother did. No milk bottles on the table in this house, thank you. As a tiny act of rebellion, she decided she wouldn't take his coffee up. He could come down for it.

By the time he finally appeared – 'I thought you were bringing a coffee up to me' – she'd already eaten her two slices of toast, smothered in creamy Irish butter, not the supermarket own brand she used to buy, with a generous dollop of marmalade.

'No news this morning?' he said.

'News? Oh yes. I have news. I've recently lost my job.'

'I meant…we usually have Radio 4 on.'

She stood up and turned the radio on. Amol Rajan's voice filled the kitchen. He was grilling a politician about unemployment figures.

'How appropriate,' Emily said.

She didn't like herself when she was like this, but couldn't snap out of it. She hadn't expected to feel this hostile towards him. It was business, after all. They were still together. Still engaged. They still loved each other.

Didn't they?

An airing cupboard.

There were lots of things that Emily didn't like about Peter's house, but today, her biggest objection was that, like many modern houses with their combi boilers and instant hot water, it didn't have an airing cupboard.

It wasn't that her clothes needed airing. Far from it. Peter had a tumble dryer for making sure that everything was 'cupboard dry'. Heaven forbid they should lower the tone in this fancy little estate by hanging their socks and knickers on a line in the back garden for the neighbours to see.

No, the problem was this: where was she meant to place her precious loaf of seeded dough for it to rise?

She had decided, after Peter had left for the golf club, that she'd do something she hadn't done in a very long time; she would bake.

She'd never made so much as a Victoria sandwich at his house. Since they'd been living together, she hadn't scratched her baking itch. Not once. Her cake tins, mixing bowl, wooden spoons and scales were all squashed into two cardboard boxes in the smallest of the guest rooms. He kept promising to make room for them in his kitchen cupboards, to move one of the high-tech gadgets that only got used once a year, if at all. But he hadn't got round to it yet.

Apart from butter and eggs – always plenty of those in the fridge for Peter's keto diet – there weren't any baking ingredients in his kitchen cupboards so she'd had to stock up in the corner shop. The supermarket would have been cheaper, of course, but the corner shop was closer and Emily had felt a real urgency to get started.

She flicked the radio in the kitchen to Radio 2, making a mental note to switch it back before Peter got home, then set to work. She'd decided to make the bread first. There was something therapeutic about all that kneading and she definitely felt as if she needed some therapy.

With aching arms, she put her precious mound of dough in front of the French windows in the lounge. Or, as Peter liked to call it, the sitting room. It was definitely the warmest spot in the house. Fingers crossed that it did the trick.

Emily was on a roll now – no bread pun intended – and decided to make brownies and apple crumble tarts.

She quickly knocked up a shortcrust pastry for the tart

bases and left it to chill in the fridge. She peeled the apples and put them on the hob to stew. She mixed flour with oats, sugar, butter and a little cinnamon for the crumble topping. She would bake that separately – the Raymond Blanc method – to ensure it was crunchy.

Then she made a start on the brownies, melting chocolate chips with sugar and butter in a bain-marie, and whisking the eggs. She gently folded the chocolate mixture into the eggs, and added a little flour.

When the oven had reached the right temperature, she put everything in, set two timers and waited. A chocolate-y aroma began to fill the kitchen, taking her right back to childhood days. She'd sit on a kitchen stool, cleaning out the mixing bowl with her fingers, savouring every delicious, sugary mouthful and counting down the minutes till the brownies would emerge, hot, gooey and oozing.

The first timer on her phone pinged. Emily took out the pastry cases, spooned in some apple and topped with the hot crumble mix, before putting them back in the oven. The brownies would take another few minutes. By now, the kitchen smelled completely different. Its usual scent was of Cif, she realised. Kitchens shouldn't smell of Cif. They should smell of roast garlic and cinnamon and freshly baked bread. Or brownies and apple crumble like this one did right now.

The second timer went off. She opened the oven door with all the excitement and trepidation of a finalist on *Bake Off*.

Her brownies were never quite as good as her mum's, but they weren't far off. They were the kind of brownies that made your fingers sticky, your tastebuds crave for more and your stomach say no, delicious though they were, that's quite enough richness for one day, thank you. The kind of brownies you needed to share.

She looked round Peter's normally immaculate kitchen. A small pool of melted butter had made the floor sticky. Flour had spread an inordinate distance across the black granite worktop. And a smear of chocolate had found its way onto one of the glossy white cupboard doors. How had that happened?

And how had she managed to use all those utensils? For one loaf, a few tarts and a batch of brownies?

Never mind. She would clear up the mess when she got back. There'd be plenty of time before Peter returned. He'd be hours on the golf course, as usual, then even longer at the nineteenth hole with his buddies.

Marjory's face lit up when she opened the door and Emily immediately felt a pang of guilt for neglecting her former neighbour. She hadn't been round for weeks. When she'd lived in the upstairs flat, they'd seen each other practically every day.

'Come in, come in.' Marjory bustled Emily into her tiny hallway, closing the door behind her as quickly as she could, as if she was afraid that Emily might change her mind and leave again.

Emily held up the tin of brownies.

'I'll get the kettle on,' Marjory said and disappeared into her kitchen.

Emily sank into the sofa. Peter's sofas were enormous, expensive things, deep and low. They looked inviting enough, but somehow contrived to be rather uncomfortable. Marjory's sofa was old-fashioned. Upholstered in a chintzy floral print, with curly arms and a high back, it didn't look stylish but as soon as Emily sat down on it, she felt all the tension of the past few days evaporate.

'How've you been?' said Marjory, placing a tea cup and saucer on the table in front of her and passing her a plate.

'I've been...' Emily didn't know where to start. 'Sorry I haven't visited in a while. How are you?'

'I'm fine, dear. A little lonely perhaps, but that's par for the course at my age, I think.'

Par for the course. Loneliness shouldn't be par for the course. At any age. If – and it was still a big 'if' – she did buy her own café, it would be a place that would bring people together. She could even have one of those tables with a sign that read, 'Sit here, if you'd like to chat.' The grown-up equivalent of the friendship bench in the school playground.

'Peter made me redundant,' said Emily suddenly, lifting the lid off the tin of brownies and handing them over.

'Oh dear. Lover's tiff?'

'Not at all. A business decision apparently. We're still together.'

Did she imagine it or did a frown pass fleetingly over Marjory's face?

'That's good,' Marjory said in a tone that suggested she didn't think it was good at all. She took a bite of her brownie.

'What do you think?' Emily said.

'I think it must be very difficult to be engaged to someone who has made you redundant. But I never got the impression you were happy at Ridley's. So maybe this is a chance to do something new.'

'I meant, what do you think of the brownie?'

'Delicious. But then, your baking is always superb, Em. Better than anything you can buy in any café or bakery for miles around. Have you never thought of setting up your own business?'

The BMW was already parked on the driveway when Emily arrived home.

She could sense the atmosphere the minute she walked into the house. She took her shoes off and placed them on the shoe rack, hung her lime-green coat in the cupboard and called out, 'Hi, Peter. I'm home.'

'I'm in the kitchen.'

Sod it. He'd seen the mess then.

'Hi, darling,' she said as she walked in. 'Did you have a good day? Get any birdies?'

Birdies? Was that the right word? She never usually asked much about his golf.

'What's been going on?' He gestured at the open packets of flour and sugar, the dirty mixing bowl, the spoons dripping chocolate on the worktops.

'Look, I'm really sorry about all this, and yes, I should have cleared up before I went out, but don't worry, I'll do it now,' she said, trying to keep her tone bright and upbeat. 'I've had the best day in ages.'

It was true. She'd felt so relaxed. Well, until now.

'I hope you aren't going to make a habit of this, Emily.'

He always said her full name when he was cross. It reminded her of her junior school teacher, Miss Styan.

Okay, so he had a point about the mess. She shouldn't have gone out and left the place in such a state, but she lived here too. And she loved baking. She'd missed it.

'Well, now I'm going to be unemployed,' she said, 'and will have time on my hands, I'm hoping to do more baking.'

'Here? In my house?'

And there it was. *My* house.

That one tiny syllable, that 'my' instead of 'our' was all it took for her to know that she was leaving him.

Hypocritical in a way, because *she* still thought of it as Peter's house but she hadn't realised that he did too.

Damn him. He'd practically forced her to give up the job she loved and come to work at Ridley's only to make her redundant. And then he'd talked her into giving up her little flat and moving in with him when she hadn't felt quite ready.

And now, not only was she about to become jobless, but homeless too. And buying Nico's was definitely out of the question. She'd never discover what it would be like to stand behind a counter as customers tried to choose between the apple crumble tarts or the gooey brownies.

'Freshly baked this morning,' she imagined herself saying.

'Yes, everything's made here on the premises.'

'The carrot cake and the lemon drizzle are gluten free.'

She snapped herself out of her daydream.

'Our house,' Peter was saying. 'I meant, our house.'

'It was never our house. And it never will be.'

Their eyes met. He knew exactly what she was saying without her needing to spell it out. She saw him bite his lip then wipe his cheek with the back of his hand. She looked away.

'I'm sorry, Peter,' she said. She wasn't sure if she was still talking about the mess in the kitchen or their relationship. 'Really, really sorry. I'll clean it all up, then I'll go to Kate's. I'll pack an overnight bag and come back for the rest of my stuff another time.'

'Sure,' was all he said.

She'd known this day would come. She'd been trying to pretend it wouldn't, keeping up the pretence of buying a wedding dress and moaning about how his mother was taking over all the arrangements, but deep down she'd known for a while now that she wouldn't be walking down that aisle. At least, not with Peter standing in front of the altar.

She thought she knew how he'd react too. He wouldn't shout. She didn't expect him to cry; his father had instilled in him the value of a stiff upper lip. She'd always imagined he'd try to cajole her to stay, to give their relationship another chance.

But he didn't. He sat down on one of the stools at the breakfast bar, with his elbows on the worktop, taking care to avoid the spillages, and put his head in his hands. He seemed resigned to the fact it was over. Almost as if he'd been expecting it too.

'I'm sorry,' she said again. She walked over to the sink, ran some water onto a cloth and began to mop up some of the mess.

Peter stood up and came over to her. She could sense him behind her. She froze, expecting him to put his arms around her, to hold her. Perhaps he was going to make that attempt to persuade her to change her mind. But he didn't. He tried to pull the cloth from her hand and said, 'Leave it, Em. The cleaner's coming on Monday. Just go. Please. Get this over with.'

She couldn't bear to look at him. She knew she didn't want to be with him, but she still cared about this man. Perhaps not in the way that Kate was besotted with each and every one of her boyfriends, but in her own quiet way, she had loved him. She let go of the cloth, rushed upstairs and packed hastily, shoving spare underwear and a spare t-shirt into an old rucksack.

Peter was standing in the hallway with puffy eyes, red cheeks and an air of resignation when she went back downstairs. Without a word, she handed him her keys, feeling strangely calm. As if she was going for a night away rather than leaving her fiancé.

Ex-fiancé now. Emily began to tug at the ring on her left hand, trying to ease it and cursing her chubby fingers.

'No, Em,' he said. 'Keep it. Sell it. Whatever. I don't want it back.'

'Okay, thanks. Because it isn't coming off.' She looked up, her eyes meeting his for a second, before she looked away again.

She could feel him watching her from the doorway as she walked across the gravel, the rucksack slung over her shoulder.

'Shall I give you a lift?' he called. 'What about your ankle?'

He could be kind, she thought with a pang of regret. Generous. Even at a time like this.

'No, thanks. It's not too bad now.'

'Em, don't worry about working out your notice. Take the rest of the month off. Otherwise...well, it might be awkward. You know. Under the circumstances. We'll pay you anyway.'

Emily had always been surprisingly efficient at extricating herself from relationships. There was no point prolonging the pain, after all. Might as well make it sharp and swift. Better for both parties in the long run.

So only minutes after Peter had been moaning about the mess she'd made in the kitchen, she was on Kate's doorstep with her rucksack full of spare knickers.

Chapter Nine

Books by Emily's Kate's spare bedside: *Single Again!*;
The Breakup Bible; *How to Heal Your Broken Heart*.
All Kate's.

Emily glanced around at her new abode. The room wasn't huge but it was, like the rest of Kate's house, tastefully furnished and impeccably tidy. There was a single bed with fresh white linen, a teal-coloured throw and matching cushion.

'I wish I could take break-ups as calmly as you do,' Kate said as she hastily cleared some space in the wardrobe of her spare room so that her best friend could hang up some clothes. 'Although…'

'Although?'

'Oh, it doesn't matter,' she said. 'Just a thought. I'm probably wrong.'

Kate no doubt had some explanation, gleaned from one of her self-help books, about why Emily found breaking up with boyfriends relatively easy whilst Kate herself was always distraught. Emily didn't enquire further; past experience told her that her friend's theory would be wide of the mark.

'I still don't get it,' said Kate later as they sat at the table, drinking endless mugs of tea. 'You split up over a messy kitchen? That's the kind of thing you have a row over, not a break-up.'

'I've always felt like a house-guest. He never once made me feel it was my home too.'

'But you could have talked to him about that?'

'I suppose. You've never liked him, Kate, so how come it feels like you're on *his* side suddenly?'

'It's not that I didn't like him. I just thought he wasn't right for you. But you said you loved him so I don't get why you'd walk away over this. It seems a bit...trivial.'

'Firing me wasn't trivial.'

'Aha, I knew it. This is cos he made you redundant.'

'I dunno. Suddenly I realised that I didn't want to be with him anymore. Perhaps his reaction to my baking was the final straw.'

'Maybe. Anyway, I'm surprised at how it ended, but I'm glad you ended it. I mean, it never worked, did it?'

'It did,' Emily said. 'Right up until the end.'

'Hmmm. But you never seemed that close. Even when you first told me about him. You never said, wow, I've met this amazing man. You never gushed about him. He didn't knock you head over heels.'

'Head over heels is a romantic fallacy. Designed to sell romance novels and Hollywood movies. You fall head over heels at least four times a year and where has that got you?'

'Thanks for reminding me,' Kate said primly.

'Sorry, I didn't mean that to sound so harsh. I worry about you. Anyway, are you up for having a house-guest for a while?'

'You can stay as long as you like. On one condition.'

Emily sighed. She knew what was coming: she'd have to accompany Kate on countless nights out as she hunted for the right man. For the last few years, Kate had been determined to find her life partner and the future father of her children, but she'd stepped things up a gear recently, now that she was in her thirties.

'Let me guess. You need a wingman.'

'Nope. Well, I do. But that's not the condition. Try again.'

'I have to keep the place tidy.'

'That goes without saying. Guess again. Third time lucky.'

'No idea.'

'Ah, come on, Em.'

'Tell me.'

'Don't just rush out and find yourself another job. Give your café idea some serious thought.'

'It's too risky, Kate,' Emily said. 'It was one thing considering it when I had a wealthy fiancé and a house, but now...'

'But it's your dream, Em. Some risks are worth taking.'

'The only affordable one is Nico's. The accounts don't look too bad, but it's a gloomy little place.'

'But could you transform it? Arrange a second viewing, Em. See if you could make it work. You're the person who can make a banquet from a few leftovers...'

'I learned that from Mum.'

Kate nodded. 'Exactly. I believe in you, Em. Okay, so the building isn't much but the inside? With a bit of imagination and a paintbrush, you could brighten it up. Turn it into the sort of place your mum used to talk about.'

*

That was the only proper conversation Kate and Emily had for the first few days they shared a house. Emily barely saw her friend; on weekdays, Kate left for work early – long before Emily got up – then popped in afterwards only to shower and change her clothes before heading out on yet another internet date, usually to Halifax or Huddersfield since she'd already exhausted the (supply of) men locally. When she returned – if she returned at all – Emily was already in bed.

Emily found life lonely in the little terraced cottage. Again, she could have phoned home – visited, even – but she knew she wouldn't be able to conceal the truth about her redundancy or her split from Peter and she didn't want her dad fretting. She'd go home when she had some good news to share. In the meantime, she spent hours in Kate's pristine kitchen with its oak cupboards, neat rows of spice jars and shelf of never-opened recipe books. Kate never cooked, living off omelettes and salad when she was at home, which wasn't often. Emily didn't cook here either, fearful of making her usual mess, but instead sat with her laptop at the table, poring over websites and gathering every last scrap of information she could find about running a café. She asked for advice on internet forums and scrolled through all the estate agents' websites, checking that no new (and super-cheap) cafés had come onto the market in recent days. She re-read all her old course notes about keeping basic accounts and genned up on the regulations around health and safety and hygiene in catering businesses.

And when she was too boss-eyed to focus anymore, she lay on the sofa, watching more episodes of *Ramsay's Kitchen Nightmares* and shouting at the telly.

'Don't serve him food that's been frozen. He'll notice. It's got to be fresh.'

'Clean out your fridge. He's bound to check it.'

'Your menu's too complicated. He always says keep it simple.'

She was sure she could do better than the hapless restaurant owners on the show. Only they'd had the courage to start a business in the first place, and she wasn't sure she did.

She perused Kate's selection of self-help books, hoping to find something on decision-making but instead found herself reading seven chapters of *Find a Man When You're Over Thirty* – just for fun; she knew she wasn't ready to meet anyone new. She also knew her time would have been better spent reading *A Beginner's Guide to Starting Your Own Business*, but she'd accidentally left that at Peter's.

Peter.

Emily wondered how he was doing. Perhaps she shouldn't have let their relationship drag on for so long. She'd ignored that nagging feeling that they weren't quite right for each other, even – she was ashamed to admit – as he slipped the ring onto her finger.

And now the relationship was over. But the ring was still on her finger. Firmly on her finger.

She'd pulled. She'd tugged. She'd wrestled.

She'd tried soap. She'd tried Vaseline. She'd tried butter.

She'd tried Google. Then dental floss (Kate's). Then some out-of-date lube that she found in the bathroom cabinet.

She'd soaked her hand in iced water until she couldn't stand the pain, but that platinum solitaire remained stubbornly in place.

And now she felt a sudden impatience to get rid of it. She didn't want it sitting there, reminding her that she'd agreed to marry someone then broken her promise.

If you couldn't remove a ring yourself, what were you meant to do? Ask the fire brigade to cut it off? Go to A&E perhaps?

Or…what about the health centre? Surely a GP would know how to get it off?

'And why do you need to see the doctor?' the receptionist said.

'I've tried and tried, but I can't get my engagement ring off.'

'Why do you want to take it off?'

Emily wasn't sure that was any of her business, but she didn't feel in a position to argue. 'I'm no longer engaged.'

'Surgery's over for the morning. The only appointments left this afternoon are strictly for emergencies. And it's hardly an emergency, is it? In fact, it's not a medical problem at all.'

'Perhaps tomorrow?'

'Emily,' came a voice from behind.

She turned round to see Ludek. 'Oh, hi,' she said, feigning surprise. 'It's you again. Essendale running club's favourite lollipop man.'

Oh god. Lollipop man? Why had she said that? It had sounded funny in her head.

But he didn't seem offended; his eyes were twinkling at her. 'Ha ha. You've forgotten my name.'

As if.

She hadn't forgotten. Not his name. Nor his perfect knees.

His smile. His beautiful mop of curly hair. He was wearing jeans today and an open-necked shirt, but she couldn't help thinking of him in that tight outfit that he'd worn at the running club.

'Of course not, *Ludek*.' She emphasised his name, raising her eyebrows, hoping she looked cheeky and fun, rather than just plain weird.

He laughed. 'What are you doing here? Is it the ankle?'

Damn. The ankle. That might have been a better excuse to come to the surgery. Although if she'd said her ankle was still hurting, he'd have insisted on her going to the hospital and that was never going to happen.

And she really did want that ring removing. It wasn't just an excuse. Not really.

'I was trying to make an appointment,' she said.

'Come through. I was going to buy a sandwich, but I can spare you a few minutes.'

Emily followed him down a long corridor. He opened a door, and stepped aside, letting her enter first. It was your usual doctor's consulting room with a desk, three chairs, an examination couch and a variety of posters extolling the virtues of a healthy diet, but a pair of fluffy dice – the kind you'd normally see suspended from the rear-view mirror of a car – hung at the side of the computer screen.

'How can I help you?' said Ludek, sitting down and gesturing for her to take a seat herself.

'I can't get my engagement ring off.'

She was hoping he'd ask – as the receptionist had – *why* she wanted to take it off. Then she could tell him that she and Peter had split up. That she was single. Available. But he didn't.

Anyway, it was too soon even to contemplate dating. Kate always advised giving it a month or two at least, after a major break-up, before getting involved with someone new, to allow time for a bit of emotional recovery. Not that Kate ever followed her own advice.

'Won't take long,' he said, then slid his chair nearer hers; it was one of those office ones with wheels, though not a fancy one like Peter had.

His sudden proximity made Emily's heart pound. Her mouth went dry, and the fact that Ludek would know exactly which hormones caused those things to happen made him seem even sexier.

Did it make her a terrible person, having this crush on another man so soon after she'd broken off her engagement?

He grasped the ring between his thumb and fore-finger and pulled it a little. 'That is a bit tight.'

She was thinking how long his eyelashes were, when he took hold of her hand.

For a split second, they sat there, her hand in his. She could feel his breath on her cheek, his skin against hers. She closed her eyes. Waited. Half-expecting – hoping – to feel his lips upon hers. Then he lifted her hand, raising her entire arm above her head. And he held it there.

How daft could she get? Of course, he wasn't going to kiss her. They were in the surgery, for heaven's sake. His workplace. And weren't there rules about doctors and patients? Although she could always change practices, register at Hebbleswick, three miles down the road.

She glanced up at his hand holding hers, and an image popped into her head of lying beneath him, with his hands holding her wrists as he...

'Hold it there.' He let go and wheeled himself back to his desk. 'So how are you, Emily?'

Was this a doctor-patient kind of 'how are you?' or a we're-casual-acquaintances-who-met-at-running-club kind of 'how are you?'?

'Fine, thanks.' Hopefully this covered both bases.

Emily glanced up at her arm again. She must look ridiculous with it above her head like this.

'Will we see you at the next running club? Since the ankle's better?'

'No. I've always hated running. I only went because my friend Kate wanted a...'

She couldn't say wingman. Kate would kill her if she told anyone they'd been there to meet men.

'...she thought we should get out more. Meet new people.'

Her arm was beginning to ache. She felt like a child in class, waiting forever with their hand up to answer a question, but never being chosen by the teacher.

'How much longer do I have to sit like this?' she said.

'A couple more minutes.'

He picked up a pen, tapping it on the desk. Emily shifted in her chair, wondering what to say next.

'I've been made redundant,' she blurted out. 'By Peter. My fiancé. Who is now my ex-fiancé.'

She scanned his face, hoping to glean if he was pleased that she was now single, but all she saw was an expression of concern. The same one he'd had when she was sprawled across the pavement outside Nico's.

'Hence the ring,' he said.

'Yep. Hence the ring.'

There was a moment's silence. Then Ludek said, 'What are you going to do? For work, I mean.'

'I'm thinking of buying a café. That's why I fell at the running club – I was distracted by the for sale board outside Nico's.'

'Ah, I see. Okay, I think that's long enough. Give me your hand.'

She lowered her arm – at last – and stretched it out towards him. He eased the ring off, with none of the tugging or wrestling that she'd had earlier.

'I tried and tried. Nothing would shift it.'

'Lovely ring.' He held it up and peered at it for a second before placing it in her palm and closing her fingers around it.

She stood up to go. 'Thank you, Ludek.'

'You're welcome.'

She was almost at the door when he said, 'Emily, I don't suppose…'

She stopped. Turned back to him. Heart pounding again. He was going to ask her out. Sod the hypocritic oath or whatever it was that doctors had to swear when they left medical school. She wouldn't tell if he didn't.

He paused.

Ask me, she willed him. Ask me out on a date.

'What are you doing on Friday evening?'

Yes! She could have punched the air, but Kate always said you shouldn't appear too keen.

'A group of us meet upstairs every week in the Red Lion. I thought you and Kate might like to come along. You know, since you want to get out more and meet new people.'

A group of us? Damn. Not a date then.

'Of course, it mightn't be your thing,' he said.

But meeting his friends? Having a drink and a chat? It was a start, at least.

'Why might it not be my thing?'

'Board games. We get together to play board games.'

Chapter Ten

'You had that second viewing on Nico's yet?' Kate said, popping her head into the lounge as she came home from work on Tuesday.

Emily shook her head. 'Not yet.'

She was about to tell Kate about Ludek and the board games group – it would have been lovely if the two of them could have gone along; she missed spending time with Kate – but her friend was racing up the stairs in search of a change of clothes before Emily could open her mouth.

On Wednesday morning, Emily got up to find a series of Post-It notes around the little terraced house: on the toilet seat; the fridge; the mirror in the hall; and the television. They all said the same thing. Arrange that second viewing.

On Thursday, Kate was clearly having a quiet day in the office as she texted Emily on the hour every hour. *Second viewing?*

When Emily replied to one of these texts asking how the dating was going, Kate didn't answer the question. She just wrote, *Not telling you till you arrange that second viewing*.

In the end, Emily decided to phone the estate agent just to get Kate off her back.

★

Emily said hello to three people as she walked down the high street. Dodged the geese who were hissing by the library. Stopped for a few moments to admire Oxfam's latest window display. Pressed her nose against the glass of Sweet Delights. Well, almost. She peered in to see how many customers they had in there (loads). Pressing her nose against the glass would have been a bit weird.

She'd always wanted to be one of those people who strolled through Essendalc saying hello to everyone and knowing their names. And now walking towards her was someone whose name she *did* know, but not someone Emily wanted to say hello to.

Annie.

Here she was, coming out of Ridley's – on her way to Sweet Delights, probably, for a late lunch – right at the very moment that Emily was trying to hurry past the office doors unnoticed.

'Hi.' The attractive blonde woman stopped directly in front of Emily, blocking her way.

'How are you?' said Emily, wondering if Annie had got her claws into Peter yet.

'All right. Under the circumstances.'

'Circumstances?'

'Peter made me redundant at the same time as you.'

'Shit, I'm sorry. I had no idea.'

Emily thought back to their meeting in the kitchen and Annie's red-eyes. Emily had assumed the tears were because she was still with Peter. Why hadn't she thought to ask if her colleague was okay? They'd never got on, but, even so, she could have checked.

'Two people on the manufacturing side are also going,' Annie was saying now. 'And the cleaner. Peter is using an agency instead. Must be cheaper.'

'That's terrible. Honestly, I didn't know.'

'Of course, you're the only one who hasn't had to work out her notice period.'

'I see. Well, that was more because of…us splitting up, you know. It would have been awkward.'

'It's caused a bit of resentment, to be honest.'

Emily nodded. She could see why – and she did feel bad about it – but it had been Peter's suggestion and she'd been relieved not to have to continue working there after the break-up.

'And there's no jobs to be had. I don't know what I'm going to do.'

Emily had told the estate agent she'd be there at two. She glanced at her watch, just momentarily, hoping that Annie wouldn't notice. No such luck. Nothing ever got past her.

'Well, I mustn't keep you. I can see you're in a hurry.'

'Yes, I've got an appointment. Look, Annie, I…'

Emily wasn't sure what she wanted to say.

'I…' she began again. 'Just take care of yourself, Annie, okay?'

Annie nodded. 'Yeah, you too.'

Emily watched the stooped figure walking away, feeling quite unnerved by the encounter. There were no jobs out there. Unlike Annie, she was in the incredibly fortunate position of being able to buy her own business, albeit a small one. Yes, it was a risk, but it seemed wrong not to take that risk. Someone like Annie would give their eye-teeth for such an opportunity.

Nico's was exactly the same as it had been a few days ago. Emily wasn't sure what she'd been hoping to see really, when she'd arranged this second visit. Yes, it was still dark and dreary, but did it have potential? How on earth was she meant to decide?

'I probably should let you know,' said the estate agent, 'that there have been other enquiries.'

Of course, she knew this was probably just a ploy intended to stoke her interest but it did the trick; his words sent her into a flat spin.

It was funny how you could be unsure whether you wanted something until you found out someone else wanted it too. And then, all of a sudden, you didn't just want it, you were desperate to have it. The last portion of sticky toffee pudding that the waiter was carrying to someone else's table. The polka-dot pinafore in Oxfam that another woman had picked up. And Kate once said it was the same with online dating. She hadn't been interested in Toby from Leeds until he'd said that he'd met someone else and then she'd been inconsolable for three weeks, convinced she'd lost the love of her life.

Emily glanced round the gloomy café but it was as if she was wearing a virtual reality headset; she didn't see the drab walls, the plastic cloths, the gloom. She saw the place as it could be. A few tins of white emulsion and better lighting would brighten it up no end. Fresh white tablecloths instead of those awful wipe-clean plastic things. Bunting, perhaps. Bunting had magical powers, transforming even the dullest of places. Well, it always seemed that way on Instagram.

Suddenly she was desperate to sign on the dotted line.

But she couldn't. Not yet.

She couldn't make such a big decision on her own.

She had been wondering whether to go to the board games group that evening. She'd been looking forward to it – well, to seeing Ludek really, although she wasn't averse to the odd game of Trivial Pursuit – but there was always next week. Kate wasn't free, in any case, and Emily didn't really relish the thought of walking into a new group of people on her own. And if there were other people interested in the café… Well, she needed to stop procrastinating and make that decision. Which meant she needed to talk to her mum.

Emily walked back to Kate's house, shoved a few things in her rucksack, and headed for the bus stop. She'd need to take two buses to reach Thornholme, the town where she'd grown up, and the journey could take anything between forty minutes and an hour and a half, depending on the traffic and how long she had to wait between buses. Today she was lucky: the second bus came within minutes of the first one dropping her off.

Thornholme had been an appropriate choice for her parents to set up home together. Dad was a proud Yorkshireman and Mum was a Lancashire lass. Lancashire and Yorkshire had long been rivals, enemies even, though these days the wars of the roses tended to be settled on the sports field rather than the battle field. Until the late eighties, the border between the two counties ran through Thornholme. Growing up, Emily had sometimes thought that it ran straight through their kitchen.

'I knew I shouldn't have married a man from the wrong side of the Pennines,' Mum would say after every argument.

The arguments were frequent but never serious; petty yet passionate squabbles about which teabags to buy (Mum liked Tetleys, Dad Yorkshire Tea) and which cheese (crumbly Lancashire versus even crumblier Wensleydale). It was best to stay out of the house if Yorkshire was playing Lancashire at Headingley or Old Trafford as one or other parent would sulk if their team lost. Emily had always wondered if that was why she didn't like sport. But they loved each other as passionately as they argued. Emily often had to leave the room in embarrassment as a teenager as they sat hand in hand on the sofa, sometimes rubbing noses, oblivious to her squirming. It was a wonder she wasn't as averse to sex as she was to cricket.

There was no one in when she reached home. Perhaps she should have phoned to say she was coming. She let herself in and ran upstairs to her old bedroom. Nothing had changed. The faded wallpaper was torn in places where she'd pulled posters off the wall over the years, swapping ponies for boy bands and, later, for arty French black and white photos. A framed picture of Mum and Dad on their wedding day took pride of place on her dressing table next to Belle, the rag doll with blue woollen plaits that had been her sleeping companion throughout childhood.

Emily wasn't sure where Dad would be. Not far away. That was for sure. The pub probably, or playing Bridge with his friends. But she knew exactly where she would find her mum.

It was lovely sitting outside in the early evening sunshine, just her and Mum. Once Emily started talking, she couldn't stop.

'Remember how we used to bake together when I was little? How I was never great at maths, but was ahead of the class when it came to weights and measures? And how our cakes – your cakes – were always the first to go at PTA events and we used to say we'd run a café together one day?'

In the excitement of telling her, Emily knew she was gabbling. 'There's a café for sale in Essendale and it's not exactly pretty, but I could make it nice. Couldn't I? And serve all the things you'd have served? Sandwiches with proper bread, not ready sliced stuff, and generous fillings. Baked potatoes from a proper oven, not microwaved. Hot chocolate with real chocolate and whipped cream and marshmallows. What do you think, Mum? Shall I go for it?'

She paused, waiting for an answer. A bird was singing in a nearby tree. Emily turned to see it but the sun was dazzling and she could only make out a silhouette. She reached into her bag for her sunglasses.

'Mum, what d'you think?'

She bit her lip, anxious to hear. If her mother thought she should buy it, she'd buy it. Otherwise…well, she'd be going to the Job Centre in Halifax on Monday morning and she didn't relish the thought of that.

'If buying a café will make you happy, you should buy a café.'

Emily could hear the words as clearly as if her mother had actually spoken. She reached over and ran her hand over the smooth, cold marble of the headstone. Then she stood up and looked around the graveyard; for half of her life now, she'd been visiting her mother here.

'Thanks, Mum. I was hoping you'd say that. That's all I needed to know.'

Chapter Eleven

It was next morning before she saw her father.

He was standing at the kitchen sink, staring out of the window, when she came down for breakfast.

'Morning, Dad.'

He turned round suddenly, feigning a heart attack.

'Jesus, Em. Shouldn't sneak up on an old fella like that.' He clutched his chest with the over-exaggerated, hammy acting of a player in the village panto.

'Stop it, Dad. It's not funny.'

'Sorry.' He straightened up. 'Did you sleep here last night?'

'Yes.'

'You should have told me you were coming.'

His hair was greasy and greying, Emily noticed, when once it had been dark and shiny. His jumper was one for the washing machine, if not the bin, and the skin on his arms and hands was flecked with liver spots.

Old. Her beloved dad was growing old.

She put her arms around him, drawing him in for a hug. He felt small – nowhere near as tall as she remembered – and thin, painfully thin.

And no wonder, she thought, as she opened the cupboards

in search of something to eat. There were sixteen cans of cat food, but nothing for humans. At least he was managing to feed Smudge.

The cake and biscuit tins which had always been full of home baking when Mum was alive were now empty. Dad didn't even buy supermarket biscuits. There was a loaf of bread in the freezer – heaven knows how long that had been there – and half a pint of milk, an old lettuce and a piece of mouldy cheese in the fridge.

'Oh, Dad,' she said. 'What are you living off?'

'I manage. No point doing a big shop when there's only me. I wander down to the corner shop most days. Buy a few bits and bobs. It gets me out of the house.'

'Why don't you come and stay with me for a weekend? You could have my room and I could sleep on the sofa…'

'The sofa? You've always said you and Peter had plenty of space?'

On the numerous occasions when Emily had tried to lure Dad out of Thornholme for a few days, she'd always emphasised what a waste it was having two spare bedrooms when nobody ever came to stay. But she'd omitted to tell him that she didn't live in that shiny executive home anymore and that she was dossing down at Kate's.

'I don't live with Peter anymore.'

'I think,' said Dad, 'that I'd better put the kettle on.'

'He said what?' said Dad, draining his mug of Tetley's. He'd made the switch from Yorkshire Tea after her mum had passed.

'That I was surplus to requirements.'

Dad stood up and began to pace around the kitchen. 'How dare he? How bloody dare he? After he made you leave your job at Thorpe's…'

'And then I made a bit of a mess doing some baking and he made it clear that I wasn't to do any more baking in his house. *His* house. That's how he saw it. Although to be honest, I did too.'

'That's a bit rich. Wasn't it his suggestion that you moved in?'

'It was.'

'Mind you, I have got *some* sympathy for him.'

Emily looked up at him, surprised. 'Sympathy?

He ruffled her hair. 'You always did make a terrible mess when you baked. Whereas your mother…such a tidy cook.'

'Thanks for that.'

'Perhaps it's for the best.'

'You never liked him.'

'I wouldn't put it quite like that. I think Peter is… a good egg. Probably. Just not the right egg for you. Pity you didn't stay with Greg.'

Emily winced at the mention of her first boyfriend. She took the lid off the teapot and peered in. 'Shall I make a fresh pot?'

'Or how about breakfast at the café in the garden centre? My treat?'

'Sounds like a plan.'

It wasn't far to Gordy's Gardens. They headed straight for the café as Dad was afraid it would be full if they loitered too long by the bedding plants. He was right to hurry, as theirs was the last table.

'What can I get you, Bill?' said the waitress with a smile.

'Two full English. Extra black pudding for me please.'

'And a large pot of tea?' she said.

He nodded. 'Yep, creature of habit.'

They'd been here before many times, but Emily looked round with renewed interest now that she was a Future Café Owner. At the table next to theirs, two children were colouring in whilst their parents looked at their iPhones. At another, an elderly couple were sharing a crossword and a Danish. A group of friends were chatting over the weekend papers and a woman sat on her own in the corner, engrossed in a novel.

'This is the sort of place I'm going to run,' Emily said.

'A garden centre? What do you know about gardening?'

'No, a café like this. Busy but relaxed at the same time. Somewhere you can chill out with a book or a paper and not feel awkward if you're on your own. The kind of place where the waitress knows your name.'

'Your mum used to go on about running a café.'

'I know. I'm going to make her proud.'

Dad took out a handkerchief and dabbed his eyes, just as the waitress brought over a tray with a large pot of tea, two mugs and a jug of milk.

'Shall we let it brew?'

Dad nodded. 'You know, Em, I never thought Peter was right for you. He's a nice enough chap. Impressive – owning his own company, even though he didn't actually start it himself.'

'So why didn't you think he was right for me?'

'I always thought he wanted to change you,' he said, 'into a mini-version of his mother. But it wasn't just that. You never seemed that – what's that modern phrase? You never seemed that into him.'

Emily was about to ask if he'd been borrowing Kate's self-help books, when the waitress arrived with their breakfasts and they turned their attention to the food: crispy rashers of back bacon, sunshine eggs, mushrooms with a hint of garlic, Bury black pudding and hash browns. Of course, the hash browns were the best bit, especially dipped in those egg yolks. Without being asked, the waitress brought some hot water over and Dad gave her a smile as he topped up the pot.

'I thought I'd buy some begonias for your mum's grave,' he said when she'd gone. 'What do you reckon?'

Whenever she visited Thornholme, Emily always stayed until Sunday teatime. Of course, this time, she could have stayed longer, given that she wasn't working, but she wanted to get back to Essendale so that she could go to the estate agent's first thing on Monday morning, before she lost her bottle. She spent the rest of the weekend batch cooking for Dad, determined that soups, stews, lasagnes and curries would fill his freezer by the time she caught the bus home.

Dad had always hated cooking. Not only hated it; he wasn't much good at it either. Family legend had it that even the neighbours' Labrador once refused to eat his custard. After her mum died, they'd lived on boiled potatoes, tinned peas and packets of stuff from the freezer. Findus crispy pancakes, Vesta curries and her own particular favourite

Birds Eye's boil-in-the-bag chicken and mushroom casseroles. All you had to do with those casseroles was put the bag in a pan of boiling water. Emily was reminded of them years later when she first saw one of the contestants on *MasterChef* cooking salmon sous vide. Who knew that boil-in-the-bag would one day become trendy?

After a couple of months, she'd taken over the kitchen, carefully recreating all Mum's favourite meals: the Lancashire hotpot with best neck of lamb topped with layers of sliced potatoes; the rich stew with its beefy sauce and chunky carrots; the chicken dinners with generous helpings of gravy and roasties. It was an improvement on the ready meals, but even though Emily knew her mother's recipes by heart, they never tasted quite as good. She could never get the outside of her ginger cake to be quite as crunchy, or the inside quite as sticky. Nevertheless, Dad was well-fed for his first few years as a widower, but Emily suspected he'd gone back to ready meals when she left home. Heaven only knew what he lived on these days.

'There's no need to go to all this trouble, Em,' Dad said, looking at the steaming Tupperwares all lined up, waiting to go in the freezer once they'd cooled.

'Isn't home-made better than supermarket ready meals?'

'Yes, it is. Nothing like a home-cooked meal.'

There was a pause. She knew what he was thinking, what he really meant. There was nothing like one of *Mum's* home-cooked meals.

'Mine won't be quite as good, Dad, but they're the next best thing,' she said gently.

She packed his freezer and cleaned up the kitchen before they said their goodbyes.

'You know, Dad, I would love it if you came for a visit. Essendale's only fifteen miles away. Two bus rides.'

Dad shook his head. 'I dunno, Em. Maybe one day. Perhaps when you've got your own place.'

She knew he wouldn't come. He had seldom ventured out of Thornholme since her mum passed. His world was limited to the house, a few local shops, the garden centre, the pub and his wife's graveside. He'd been to Peter's house only once, for Sunday lunch when they'd first got engaged. Nothing would persuade him to broaden his horizons even a little; God knows Emily had tried over the years.

In the early days, he'd barely left the house at all. He'd attended the funeral, of course, and had reluctantly gone back to work, when his boss said that he couldn't afford to give him any more compassionate leave. But back then, he never answered the phone or the door, and he'd let Emily do all the shopping.

Grief, her form teacher said when Emily told her she was worried, took people in different ways. Some people retreated from the world whilst others wanted to keep as busy as possible. The only thing she could do was to give him time.

So Emily gave him time. One month, then two. He didn't show up for parents' evening and said he had a headache on the evening of the end of year school musical. It was *Bugsy Malone* that year. Emily played one of the showgirls; it wasn't the biggest role, but she'd have liked him to be there nonetheless.

Emily felt bad leaving him to go to university. She felt even worse three years later when she didn't move back home, but the atmosphere in the house was so depressing.

Kate was already living in Essendale by then, and Emily had liked the idea of being close to her best friend so she'd taken the job at Thorpe's.

The bond between the two friends was stronger than ever. Kate knew what it was like to lose a mother: her own mum had left when she was sixteen, without even leaving a note. The circumstances were different but the suddenness, the shock, was the same. And when many young women would have been turning to their mothers for advice on men and periods, Emily and Kate relied on each other.

'Perhaps he's agoraphobic,' Kate had suggested when Emily told her how worried she was about her father.

'I think he's depressed. I never, ever want to be like that over anyone. Ever.'

'Personally, I think it's rather lovely,' Kate said.

'How the hell is it lovely?'

'To be so in love with someone that your world falls apart when they die.'

If that was Kate's idea of romantic, thought Emily, she could keep it.

Chapter Twelve

Books by Emily's Kate's spare bedside:
*The Café Owner's Handbook; The Daily Grind –
How to Run a Successful Coffee Shop;* and *Profit and
Profiteroles,* which Emily thought was another how-to
book when she ordered it from Essendale Library, but
which turned out to be a romance. Of the three, she
enjoyed it the most.

The estate agent seemed very surprised to find Emily on his doorstep on Monday morning. She was wearing her best pinafore dress – a smart navy-blue number – with a white t-shirt underneath. She'd actually ironed the t-shirt too – Emily normally avoiding ironing; life was too short – and she'd completed the outfit with a necklace of red glass beads. She'd felt overdressed on the bus to Huddersfield, but this felt like a special occasion. Besides, dressing up gave her more confidence somehow, and she badly needed a dose of that.

'I'm here to sign on the dotted line,' she said, acutely aware of the shake in her voice. 'I want to buy Nico's.'

Her hands were shaking too, but luckily there was no dotted line to sign on – not yet, anyway – as Emily wasn't sure she could have gripped a pen.

She should get the lease checked over by a commercial solicitor, the estate agent explained. The whole thing would take at least a couple of weeks, possibly longer.

It seemed a shame when Nico's was just sitting there empty, but Emily knew she could use that time wisely. She could think about the menu she'd offer, practise a few new dishes and upload some photos to Instagram to generate publicity.

Three weeks later, her big day finally dawned; the estate agent would meet her outside Nico's to hand over the keys. She'd officially become a café owner. She was so nervous that she could barely drink the coffee Kate had made for her, let alone contemplate any breakfast.

'Here's to your new venture, Em.' Kate clinked her mug against Emily's.

'Thanks, I'll tell you all about my first day later.'

'I won't be in this evening. I have a date with a guy called Freddie. And I've a feeling about him. He could be The One.'

Emily sighed. She so wanted this to be true, but had heard it many times before, only to watch Kate fall apart a few days / weeks / months and, on one occasion, years later. 'I hope he is, but be a bit careful. Don't fall too fast. I don't want to see you getting hurt again.'

'Don't be a killjoy. Good luck today with the café.'

'And good luck tonight with the date.'

Emily couldn't believe the state Mr Panagi had left the café in. She'd noticed how gloomy it was on her viewings, but not how dirty it was. She'd already decided to give herself a week to give the place a make-over, but she saw now that she'd be spending most of that time cleaning. It'd be touch and go if she would be ready to open next Monday as she'd planned. The grease on the cooker was baked on, the sink looked like it hadn't seen Fairy Liquid for years and the floor was so sticky that wherever she trod, she felt like an insect landing on a piece of flypaper. The dishwasher was full of dirty plates. He could have at least turned it on before he left. And she didn't dare look in the fridge.

One week to get the place spotless, paint the walls a lighter shade and fathom out how the coffee machine worked. Or even, *if* the coffee machine worked. She put the dishwasher on and emptied the kitchen of everything, piling every dish, pot and saucepan on the tables in the café so that the shelves and cupboards were clear. Then she set to work scrubbing.

She'd only shifted the grease from about three square inches of cooker when she heard a voice.

'Hello? Anyone in?'

She put her scouring pad down and peered through the kitchen hatch to see a small, grey-haired man standing in the middle of the café. His appearance was somewhat eccentric, with his chocolate-brown trilby, crimson bow-tie and foreign newspaper tucked under his arm. She glanced at her watch: eleven o'clock. She'd done two hours already and had barely achieved anything.

'I thought I'd locked the door,' she said.

'Good morning. You must be the new owner.'

'Yes, I am. But I'm not actually open yet. Not till next Monday.'

'I'll have a cappuccino and a pain au chocolat, please.'

Had he not heard her?

Honestly. She hadn't got time for this.

But then he smiled at her. A kind smile that creased his whole face, but there was sadness in his grey eyes, a loneliness that she recognised because she'd seen it in Dad. He looked about Dad's age too. Emily hated the thought of her father being turned away from the pub or the café in the garden centre.

'I've no pain au chocolat. Would a Chorley cake do?'

She had brought a Tupperware full of them, baked the previous evening at Kate's, to keep her going through the day. But, as Mum used to say, food was better shared. She could always nip out later and buy herself a sandwich.

'A Chorley cake would be lovely,' he said.

Emily couldn't quite place his accent. East European, perhaps.

She'd brought a pint of milk too. She took the top off and sniffed it just in case; it wouldn't do to give her first customer food poisoning by making their coffee with rancid milk. The milk was fine, but when she went over to the coffee machine, she remembered that she didn't even know how to turn it on.

Her customer – her first customer – was sitting at the only table that wasn't covered in pots and pans, waiting expectantly. She placed the Chorley cake in front of him. 'There's a problem. I don't know how to work the coffee machine yet. Would a cup of tea do?'

'I'll show you how.'

He stood up, stepped behind the counter and switched the machine on. Emily watched as he tipped some beans into the grinder. 'Don't grind too many. It's best to grind them fresh each day.'

'I'll need more than that when I open for all the other customers.'

'Don't grind too many.' He smiled and patted her arm.

Then he showed her how to measure out the right amount of ground coffee and frothed the milk.

'You need to check online for all the different ratios of milk to coffee. A latte is different to a cappuccino,' he said as he poured the milk into his mug – Emily had hastily washed one up – and finished the whole thing off with a sprinkling of chocolate. 'And I'm afraid I can't show you how to make those fancy patterns on the top. You'll have to use the YouTube for that. It's amazing how much you can learn on there. I've never looked back since I did the Silver Surfers course at the library. Anyway, you know how to do a cappuccino now.'

'If I can remember all that.'

'I'll order a second one then, and you can practise.'

She measured out the coffee, as he'd done, and frothed the milk, before mixing the two and adding the chocolate.

'Ta-dah!' Emily said, delighted that she'd made her first cappuccino.

'Since we have two cappuccinos,' said the customer, 'I think you might as well get yourself a Chorley cake and join me. You can tell me all about your plans for this place. I'm Stan, by the way. Stan Baranski.'

Mr Baranski told her he'd been coming to the café for several years. He called in every day after his morning stroll in the park and had a cappuccino and pain au chocolat whilst he read the paper.

'I'm happy to make it a cappuccino and Chorley cake from now on. These are excellent. Home-made?'

Emily nodded, her own mouth full of buttery pastry and juicy sultanas. You were supposed to use currants, but she preferred sultanas.

'The pain au chocolat were frozen things that Nico bought in anyway,' Mr Baranski continued. 'You can't beat home-made.'

When they'd eaten their fill of Chorley cakes and finished their coffees, he stood up, held out a ten-pound note and said, 'It's been lovely, Emily. See you again soon.'

She tried to wave his money away, but he pressed it firmly into her hand.

After he'd gone, she turned the sign to closed, double-checked that the Yale lock was on and studied the ten-pound note. Not to check if it was fake – though as a responsible business owner, she should probably have done that – but because it was the first money that her café had made. She felt like framing it. But there was work to be done, so she shoved it into her pocket, filled a bucket with hot soapy water and scrubbed the floor. She cleaned the fridge, washed every pot and pan in the place and scoured the cooker inside and out, removing every last speck of grease from the hob. Sustained by tea and Chorley cakes, she was still cleaning way after it grew dark. The whole place smelled fresher, but it was still gloomy. She would definitely need to paint the walls.

Emily had forgotten about Kate's date and was disappointed to find the little house was empty. It would have been lovely to tell someone about her first day in the café, and her first customer. She baked another batch of Chorley cakes that evening, rather than cooking dinner, and ate two, still warm from the oven, washed down with a glass of cold milk. Then she collapsed into bed.

The following day, Mr Baranski – sporting a purple bow-tie this time–- tapped on the door at two minutes past eleven. Emily put down her scourer and let him in, before firing up the coffee machine.

He arrived at the same time on Wednesday.

'Good morning, Mr B,' Emily said as she opened the door. She hoped he'd be okay with her calling him that. 'You've gone for blue today, I see,' she added, looking at his tie. 'Very smart.'

'Good morning, Emily.'

'Usual, is it?'

'Yes, please. And I'd love it if you would join me. You look like you could use a break.'

She washed her hands, made two cappuccinos and placed the Tupperware of Chorley cakes on the table between them.

'I've been living off these for the last few days. Been too tired to make dinner.'

'Emily, you've got to look after yourself,' said Mr B, his eyes full of concern.

On Thursday morning, Emily caught the early bus to Halifax – the nearest town with a DIY store – and selected two huge tins of white emulsion, along with a selection of rollers and brushes and a large plastic sheet to cover the floor. It was far too heavy for her to take on the bus, so she took an Uber back to the café. She pushed all the tables to one side, stacking the chairs and leaving one table tucked away in the corner for Mr B.

She had just finished putting the first coat of paint on the walls and ceiling when he arrived, at eleven on the dot, carrying a plastic bag.

A canary-yellow bow-tie this time, she noticed as she put down her paintbrush.

Emily made them each a cappuccino. As she placed the Chorley cakes on the table, he produced a Tupperware of his own.

'Your dinner,' he said. 'Man shall not live by Chorley cakes alone. Best put it in the fridge.'

She took off the lid to look and was hit by a familiar aroma: chicken soup. Real chicken soup made with proper stock from the carcass, the way her mum always used to. It didn't look like Mum's soup – there were noodles as well as vegetables – but it smelled so similar. Her eyes welled with tears and she scrabbled to find a tissue.

'Sorry,' she mumbled. 'It smells so delicious and it brought back memories. My mum—'

Kate knew about the accident, of course, and other friends back in Thornholme, but these days she never talked about what happened. Even Peter had known only the bare facts, not the details. But now she found herself telling Mr B about the worst day of her life.

Her mum had been standing on the corner of the high street, not far from the market where she'd been buying vegetables. She always went to the market on Thursdays, choosing the freshest ingredients, buying local produce that was in season long before it became trendy. A dog ran into the road and a lorry swerved to avoid it. It narrowly missed her mum on the pavement, but the stones it was carrying were not properly secured. Several tumbled off onto her.

A policewoman interrupted Emily's algebra lesson and drove her to the hospital. She barely recognised Dad. He appeared to have aged ten years in one morning and hardly uttered a word.

'Your mum wouldn't have felt any pain,' the doctor had said, but how could he be so sure? Emily had tried to picture the scene. She had so many questions. Whose dog was it? Why wasn't it on a lead? What did the driver look like? Was he upset? Was he sorry?

She'd imagined her mum lying in the gutter, bleeding, broken. A bag of vegetables by her side. A lonely swede rolling out into the road.

'She'd have laughed at the irony of it,' Emily said to Mr B. 'A proud Lancashire woman like her being crushed by a load of Yorkshire stone. You couldn't make it up.'

A knock at the door interrupted them. She hastily wiped her tears and looked over to see Ludek, peering in through the glass. Emily hadn't seen him since he'd removed her engagement ring at the surgery. She'd thought about him though – just a few times a day – and had wondered about going along to his board games evening, but Kate was never free and she'd somehow never managed to summon up the courage to walk in on her own.

Still trying to dry her cheeks, she went to let him in.

'Hi,' she said.

'I was passing.'

'Passing? It's a cul-de-sac.'

'I had a home visit. And I knew this place had been sold and wondered if you'd bought it.'

Emily nodded towards Mr B.

'Ludek, this is Mr B.'

Ludek held out his hand. 'Mr Baranski. How are you?'

Mr B beamed. 'Doctor, please call me Stanisław. Or Stan. Or Mr B, as Emily has nicknamed me.'

'Dobrze Cię znowu widzieć, Stan,' said Ludek.

'Wzajemnie, Panie doktorze.'

'So, Ludek, what can I get you?' she said. 'On the menu today are Chorley cakes and cappuccino.'

'No latte?'

'I haven't learned to make that yet. That's one of my many jobs this weekend. Along with stocking the fridge and baking loads of cakes, ready for the grand opening next week and the hordes of customers who beat a path to my door.'

Mr B opened his mouth as if he was going to say something, then closed it again and patted her arm.

'In that case, I'll have a cappuccino and a Chorley cake,' said Ludek.

'Coming right up.'

As she made the coffee, Ludek and Mr B chatted away in Polish. Obviously, she couldn't understand a word, but they glanced in her direction several times and she wondered if they were talking about her. Maybe they were admiring the café; the place was definitely looking brighter.

'Good cappuccino,' said Ludek, taking a first sip.

'I had a good teacher.'

Mr B smiled and got to his feet. 'I had better be going. It was lovely talking with you, Ludek.'

'You too, Stan.'

'The café's looking good,' said Ludek as the door closed behind Mr B. 'A lot fresher.'

Emily looked around, seeing her handiwork through new eyes: the light walls and the chessboard floor, sparklingly clean.

'It's been hard work. You should have seen how dark and gloomy it was.'

'I remember. Although last time I came down this street, I was rather distracted by an attractive woman I found sprawled on the pavement.'

Their eyes met. Her cheeks reddened. There was an awkward silence then Ludek said, 'Tell me about your plans. Are you going to change the menu?'

'Definitely.'

He glanced up at the whiteboard above the counter, still showing Mr Panagi's extensive selection of dishes. 'There's rather a lot of choice.'

'I'm going to pare it right down.'

'Sensible. Tell me your favourite five items to keep.'

Those twinkly eyes again, she thought.

'The all-day breakfast. Soup of the day...'

'And your favourite soup is...?'

'Home-made chicken and vegetable. A meal in itself.'

Ludek nodded, leaning forwards a little more. 'Delicious. Go on. Three more dishes.'

'My mum's Lancashire hotpot recipe. That'll be the special sometimes, not a regular thing. And it is *really* special. A ploughman's with chunky pieces of Lancashire cheese and thick-sliced honey-roast ham...'

'I'm sensing a Lancashire theme. Bit brave here in Yorkshire. And your final dish?'

'Baked potato.'

'Microwaved?'

'Of course not. Done in the oven so the skin is crispy.'

'Phew.' He mimed his relief, with an exaggerated gesture of running the back of his hand across his forehead.

Emily laughed. He seemed so enthusiastic about her new venture. Was he just being kind? Or was he genuinely interested?

'You might need to look at the prices too,' he said. 'Some seem a bit on the low side.'

'I know.'

Ludek looked thoughtful. 'Have you costed out each dish? Checked you'll make enough margin on everything?'

'You sound like you know your stuff.'

'*Ramsay's Kitchen Nightmares*. I'm an avid viewer.'

'Can't believe you watch that too.' She laughed again, then coughed, as a crumb of Chorley cake went the wrong way.

'I'm a sucker for reality TV.' He shrugged. 'Well, I have to do something on the long, lonely evenings when there's no running club or board games group.'

Emily couldn't quite believe it: a man who shared her love of reality TV. She knew she shouldn't compare, but it was such a change from Peter and those highfalutin documentaries he liked. Or at least pretended to like.

'Speaking of the board games group, you never did come along.'

He looked at her, his head cocked slightly to one side, his eyes gazing at hers. Slightly pleading, she thought. Spaniel eyes.

'Kate's always busy. And I didn't want to come on my own.'

'We're all very friendly,' he said. 'You could come along this week?'

'If I'm not too tired. I fell asleep on the sofa last night. And now I'll never find out whether Gordon managed to transform the beachside restaurant in Massachusetts.'

Emily thought he'd laugh, but he stood up to go. 'No problem.'

'Maybe another time,' she said. 'Next week, perhaps.'

'Sure.'

'Anytime you're passing…'

'Sure,' he said again. 'See ya.'

The door closed behind him and the café suddenly felt very empty.

She should have shown a bit more enthusiasm for his board games group. But she *was* tired and she didn't fancy an evening of answering question after question to win little coloured wedges or moving a tiny top hat round a board and saving up for a hotel on Park Lane. If he'd only asked her to meet for a quiet drink. Just the two of them. She'd have said yes to that.

She suddenly felt very alone. There was no one supporting her with her new venture. No business partner. No romantic partner. Kate was busy dating and Dad wouldn't leave Thornholme. And now she'd offended this lovely man who'd showed so much enthusiasm for her new business and whose company she enjoyed.

And she fancied the pants off him.

If I'm not too tired. Why on earth had she said that? Such a pathetic excuse. She'd obviously blown it.

Chapter Thirteen

By Saturday, the transformation was finished. Emily had bought pristine white tablecloths from the market in Hebbleswick and they gave the place a clean, fresh feel. The walls were adorned with four of her own photos of Lancashire: the ominous Pendle Hill covered in snow; the canal running past an old mill near Blackburn; the white windmill at Lytham St Annes; and the incredible Ribble Valley viaduct, stretching across a clouded landscape. She'd had them enlarged and mounted them herself using frames from the market. Her favourite bit was the newly erected sign outside bearing the café's new name. She hoped her customers would appreciate the humour: a café named *The Lancashire Hotpot*. Not something you'd expect in a West Yorkshire town.

'It's a bit of a risk,' Kate had said when Emily had told her.

'You're always telling me to take more risks,' she'd replied.

The café looked fantastic, even if she said so herself. Really inviting. Now all she needed was food and customers. A Sunday of baking and cooking and she'd be ready for the grand opening on Monday.

*

Only the grand opening turned out to be not so grand.

She'd baked and cooked till she dropped. Chocolate eclairs and vanilla slices sat temptingly in the chiller cabinet, Chorley cakes and scones under glass domes on the counter. The soup of the day simmered on the stove – Mum's chicken and vegetable soup recipe, of course – and she'd grated cheese and made coleslaw for baked potato fillings. There was bacon, mushrooms and a whole stack of hash browns for anyone who wanted an English breakfast – available all day – and fresh bread for sandwiches.

She took photos of everything – the food, the décor, even the salt and pepper pots sitting on the tables – and uploaded a few to Instagram.

On Monday morning, at nine on the dot, Emily turned the sign from 'closed' to 'open' and waited. She hadn't expected a queue of customers at the door, but it was a bit disheartening that by twenty to ten, not a single person had come in. Or even looked through the window. Or even walked past for that matter. Footfall, she thought suddenly, remembering the words of the Lycra goddess at the running club. There wasn't much footfall down this street.

She stood behind the counter, watching through the window.

A child on a scooter went past. They didn't so much as glance in the café's direction.

An old lady pulling a shopping trolley stopped outside the door for a second. Emily thought for a moment that she might come in. Then the lady swapped the handle of the trolley from one hand to the other and continued on her way.

Next came a man walking a dog. The man peered in through the window. The dog cocked its leg against the lamp-post outside and then they too were gone.

Ten to eleven. Still no customers.

She paced round the café, straightening all the chairs even though they were already straight.

She paced round again, moving all of the salt and pepper pots so they were in the exact centre of each table.

Finally, she sat down at one of the tables and pulled out her phone.

Eleven o'clock. Mr B arrived in a pea-green bow-tie.

'Good morning, Emily,' he said. 'The usual, please.'

Emily felt a stab of disappointment. 'Can't I tempt you with something different? A chocolate eclair? A scone? Or even a full English?'

'Cappuccino and Chorley cake, please. I'm a creature of habit.' He opened his Polish newspaper and began to do the crossword.

Emily fetched his order, made a latte for herself and sat down opposite him.

'You're my first customer,' she said. 'I mean, first customer since I opened. I was officially closed last week.'

'I'm very honoured. The café looks lovely. You've done a wonderful job.'

'Yes, and the fridge is well-stocked. Ready for the lunchtime rush.'

Mr B patted her arm and opened his mouth and closed it again. This seemed to be a habit of his. Emily wondered if it was a sign of dementia or something. Should she mention it to him? Or to Ludek, perhaps?

Later, Emily realised what he'd been about to say. He

was going to warn her that there'd be no lunchtime rush. He wasn't just her first customer of the day. He was her only one.

There was no one home when she got back from the café. She'd known that Kate wouldn't be able to get away from work to visit the café during opening hours, but had hoped that she'd be in that evening so Emily could at least tell her all about her first proper day. Not that there was much to tell. But the house was empty. Kate had been out every evening last week, only popping in to pick up some clean clothes, and she hadn't come home at all over the weekend either. Things were clearly moving fast with Freddie. And, much as Emily missed Kate's company, she was glad. Her friend had been dreaming of meeting the right man and having a big white wedding since she was a teenager.

But whilst Emily was pleased for her friend, right now she needed someone to talk to. Someone to commiserate with her. To reassure her that things would get better. To say that she should give it a little time. She phoned Dad.

'How did it go, love?' he said. 'Are the customers all raving about your cakes already?'

Emily paused. She couldn't tell him. Couldn't tell him what she was already beginning to suspect: that she'd wasted her inheritance; the money her mum had worked so hard to save up.

'Every single one of them,' she said. It was the truth after all. She'd only had one customer – Mr B – but he did seem to enjoy her Chorley cakes.

'That's grand,' said Dad. 'I knew they would.'

'I'd love it if you came along one day. I want you to see the place.'

'It's three buses, love. Bit of a trek.'

'Two buses. Or I could pay for an Uber?'

'Nah, you don't want to be wasting your hard-earned cash on me. Especially not when you're getting the place established.'

'It wouldn't be a waste, Dad. I'd love you to see it.'

'Maybe in a few weeks, then,' he said, but Emily knew he wouldn't come.

She fared slightly better at the café on Tuesday. Slightly. Mr B came as usual and then, mid-afternoon, the old lady with the shopping trolley appeared with a friend, also pulling a trolley. They struggled to drag them over the threshold, so Emily rushed to help, heaving the unwieldy things into a corner. The shopping trolleys, that is, not the ladies. The ladies themselves were rather trim. They ordered a pot of tea, inspected the cakes on display and ummed and ahhed, but didn't buy any. At five o'clock, Emily turned the sign to 'closed', ate three chocolate eclairs – well, they'd have gone to waste otherwise – and swept the floor. Not that it needed sweeping after only three customers, but it seemed like the sort of thing that someone who ran a café would do.

Kate was in when she arrived home. At least Emily hoped she was as she could hear the smoke alarm going off as she opened the front door. Either the place was on fire or Kate was making an omelette. Omelettes were all Kate ever cooked.

Sure enough, Emily found her in the kitchen, scraping charred eggy remains into the bin.

'Whoops,' Kate shouted over the noise of the alarm as Emily climbed on a chair to remove the batteries. 'My phone rang and I forgot all about the omelette.'

As the kitchen fell silent, Emily said, 'We must remember to put those back. If you're hungry, I've brought loads of lasagne home. Today's daily special.'

'Keto?'

'Sorry, no.'

'Why have you got so much left over? Did you make too much?'

'Only eight portions. I didn't sell a single one.'

Kate's face fell. 'Oh, Em. Are things not going well?'

Emily shook her head. 'Not well at all. Mr B comes in every morning, but I can't live off the profits from one cappuccino and one Chorley cake. Even though you aren't charging me rent.'

'You've had more customers than that, haven't you?'

'Two old ladies came in this afternoon.'

'Shit. Is that all? Three customers in an entire day?'

Emily nodded.

'You need to have a launch event,' Kate said. 'Put up some posters. Let everyone know there's a new place in town. Things will pick up then – you'll see.'

'A launch event? But I've already opened,' Emily said, putting two portions of lasagne into two bowls and popping them into the microwave. 'It's a bit late. Anyway, enough about me. How are things going with Freddie?'

'He's gorgeous, Em. We've been seeing each other rather a lot.'

'Yes, I had noticed. You're never here.'

Kate put on a mock frown. 'I've been neglecting you, haven't I? I'm so sorry, Em. Can you forgive me?'

'Course I can. I'm really pleased for you. I know how much you want to find The One.'

'And I really think he might be. Isn't that perfect, Em? I meet my dream man at the same time as you buy your dream café.'

Much as Emily liked her new little business, she wouldn't have described it as her *dream* café, exactly. It had more been a case of the only one she could afford. But she didn't want to dampen the mood, so she just smiled.

Kate looked wistful. 'We've been practically inseparable from the moment we met. Like you and Greg were.'

Emily ignored the mention of her first love and tried to put aside her growing unease about her friend's new man. Inseparable? After only a few days?

'Are you officially an item? Has he asked you to be exclusive?'

'Well, not exactly.'

The warning bells were ringing in Emily's head now, even louder than the smoke alarm had been a few minutes earlier. How could they not be ringing in Kate's? She'd only been seeing him for eight days, but had spent almost every spare minute of those eight days with him. And yet they weren't exclusive. Kate had been here before. So many times.

'Where's Freddie now?'

'A work thing. I'm meeting him in...' The microwave pinged and Kate glanced at her watch. 'Actually, I need to go. It's been lovely catching up.'

'What about the lasagne?'

'No time,' said Kate, picking up her handbag. 'And it isn't keto! Laters!'

And with that, she was gone. Emily spent the evening on the sofa alone, worrying about her friend, eating too much lasagne and watching *Ramsay's Kitchen Nightmares*. It didn't seem nearly as interesting now she was having a kitchen nightmare of her own.

Chapter Fourteen

On Wednesday, Emily opened the door with a heavy heart, but, to her surprise, she had a grand total of five customers that day. Five!

If anyone had told her when she first opened, that she'd be excited over five customers, she'd have thought they were crazy, but right now five customers – that was including Mr B – felt like a triumph.

The day would have been even better if she hadn't spilled the soup of the day – still chicken and vegetable – over one of those five customers, and then discovered that the toilet was blocked. Calling out an emergency plumber had blown five times her total takings in one fell swoop.

On Thursday, she felt a buzz of excitement every time the door opened. Who would come in? What would they order? Maybe this would be the person that ate a two-course lunch: the hot special then a pudding. They might even stay for a coffee. Maybe someone would have soup *and* sandwiches. Or even order afternoon tea, the full works. Might this next customer be the person who'd tell all their friends how marvellous her little café was so that gradually word would spread and people would be beating a path to her door?

But aside from Mr B, the only customers that day were a man wanting a bacon butty to take out, an older lady wanting a cup of tea to pass the time whilst she waited for her bus and a long-haired youth who plugged in his laptop and his phone for the entire afternoon, but only bought one lemonade.

Emily stayed late that evening, rather than returning to an empty house. She baked a batch of chocolate muffins, ever hopeful of a few more customers next day. She swept the floor even though there was virtually nothing to sweep. She wiped tables where no one had sat. She ate two bowls of the soup of the day; roasted red pepper and tomato now. Thank goodness she hadn't spilled that one on a customer or there'd have been dry-cleaning to fork out for on top of the plumber.

On Friday, her only customer was Mr B.

After he'd left, Emily found herself watching the door. Watching through the window. Every time someone came into view, her hopes were raised a little, then dashed again when they walked straight on by. Not that many people went by.

Three o'clock came and went. Hours on her feet and all she had to show for it was a paltry sum in the till, three Tupperwares of chicken soup for Kate's freezer and a tin of chocolate brownies. She hadn't sold a single one. She sat down at one of her own tables with a coffee and two cream scones; well, she hadn't had any lunch.

No wonder the café had been affordable. No wonder Mr Panagi had vanished off to Greece. Did he even have a sick mother?

Of course, she'd known it was on a side street and would

get little passing trade, but she'd hoped the photos she had put on Instagram would have drawn people in. It was time to face facts: she had bought a failing café. And if she couldn't turn things around – and quickly – she would be out of business when she'd barely started.

At five past five, she turned the open sign round to closed and headed back to Kate's. Friday evening. She'd only spoken to one person all day – Mr B – and tired though she was, she couldn't face another evening in front of the telly. She was single and in her early thirties, for heaven's sake. She should be out enjoying herself on a Friday night. Kate would no doubt be spending the evening with Freddie yet again, so Emily made a decision: she would go to the board games group.

She could smell burnt omelette as soon as she opened the garden gate. That could only mean one thing: Kate was home.

Emily pushed open the kitchen door to find her best friend standing over the bin again, and made a mental note: she'd put the batteries back in that smoke alarm once Kate had gone out, and then stock the freezer with a few batches of frozen omelettes that Kate could zap in the microwave.

'Freddie's on a boys' night out,' said Kate, closing the lid of the bin with a slam. 'Reckons he's been neglecting his friends since he met me. So I thought you and I could spend the evening together. What do you fancy doing?'

Perfect timing. Kate could be *her* wingman for a change. 'Actually, I was planning to go to the board games group.'

'Board games group?'

'Upstairs in the pub. It's a weekly thing, apparently.'

'Oh, come on, Em, we can do better than that.'

'No, seriously. I want to go. Come with me.'

'Not my thing. Remember when my dad made me join the chess club at school and I lost every week. The mere mention of board games triggers my PTSD.'

'Oh, come on, Kate, it'll be fun. I came to running club so you owe me.'

'Running club,' she said. Emily could practically see the cogs whirring in her friend's brain. 'I remember running club. You ended up face down on the pavement and were rescued by a rather handsome doctor. This sudden desire to play board games wouldn't have anything to do with him, would it?'

'Oh god,' Kate said. 'It's like a meeting of Geeks Anonymous.'

'Keep your voice down,' said Emily.

They hovered in the doorway. The large room was almost empty, except for three tables, all occupied by men. They were all wearing such similar clothes, it almost looked like they were in uniform: dark t-shirts with dragons on; jeans; the kind of cheap reading glasses you buy in Poundland; several beards and a lot of eyebrows that needed plucking. They were all hunched over, intently focused on the games in front of them. The room was dark but each table was illuminated by at least two Anglepoise desk lamps, attached to the wall sockets by a series of extension leads. There was no sign of Ludek.

'Come on,' Emily hissed to Kate, who was holding back. 'Okay, so they do look a *bit* geeky, but I bet they're really lovely blokes. And besides, we're here now. We might as well join in.'

'It's all Dungeons and Dragons.' Kate wrinkled her nose. 'Let's go back downstairs and have a drink.'

'You might enjoy it – we're the only women here. How many times in life can you say that?'

'Yeah, but I think there's probably a very good reason why we're the only women. I've never seen so many nerds and I went to Comic Con at the NEC with that accountant from Manchester.'

'You never did tell me what went wrong with him.'

'Like I said. We went to Comic Con at the NEC.'

'Oh, Kate. He was great guy. Anyway, I'm staying. And I did come to the—'

'Yeah, yeah, the running club. Okay, I'll stay. But only cos you fancy Ludek.'

'I don't.' Even to her own ears, her words didn't sound that convincing.

'Yeah, you do. He looks so like Greg.'

Emily decided to ignore this reference to the most shameful episode in her past. 'Anyway, I like board games.'

'Since when?'

'I dunno. We used to play Monopoly and Cluedo sometimes when I was little.' Okay, so it was limited to weekends in the Lake District when the weather was too wet to do anything else and Christmas Day once the Queen's speech was over.

'I don't see any Monopoly or Cluedo,' said Kate, looking at the tables.

Emily followed her gaze and realised she was right. No hotels on Mayfair or Professor Plums here.

'You made it,' came a familiar voice from behind.

They turned round to see Ludek wearing a t-shirt with a dragon on, but also an enormous smile.

That smile. There was something about that smile, Emily thought. Dungeons and Dragons? Bring 'em on.

'Lead the way,' she said.

As they wove a path through the room, Emily peered at the various game boards. She didn't recognise a single one: not only was there no Cluedo or Monopoly, there was no Scrabble, no Pictionary and no Trivial Pursuit. At one table, four bearded men sat playing a game with dragons – she couldn't see a dungeon – and on another, the players were constructing little railways across a map of America.

They looked up and said hello to Ludek.

'Ticket to Ride,' he whispered. 'They *always* play train games.'

They reached their table where two beardless men were sitting: a tall, grey-haired man with kind eyes and a slightly younger man in his late forties wearing a Star Trek t-shirt.

'Ludo!' said Star Trek man, standing up and shaking the doctor's hand.

'My nickname,' Ludek explained. 'Since school. Because I've always loved board games and—'

'And Ludo is a board game! Clever!' Emily said. She decided to ignore Kate's eye-rolling.

'Alan and Malcolm,' said Ludek, 'meet Emily and…'

'Kate,' said Kate.

They sat down opposite Alan and Malcolm, with Ludek at the head of the table. He leaned over and whispered, 'Don't mention insurance,' to Kate and Emily who looked at each other, baffled.

'What sort of games do you two play?' said Alan.

Kate said nothing.

'Cluedo,' said Emily. 'Trivial Pursuit.'

It was obviously the wrong answer and his face fell.

'We don't have those,' said Malcolm. 'We're into more serious games.'

Good job she hadn't said Operation.

'Serious?' Kate rolled her eyes. 'Aren't games meant to be fun?'

'Well, they're not all serious,' said Ludek. 'Shall we start with Can't Stop!?'

He took out a box, opened it and placed a diamond-shaped games board with columns numbered two to twelve. Seven was the middle column, and therefore the longest. On each turn, he explained, they'd roll four dice and advance their pieces up the columns according to the sum of the numbers on the dice.

'It's a push your luck game,' Alan said. 'You only have three pieces at a time, so if you're trying to move up columns six, seven and eight but you can't make any of those numbers with your dice, then you're out and you lose all the progress you've made that turn. If you roll one of those numbers, then you move your piece up and you can choose either to roll again, or to stop and keep all your pieces where they are till next turn. It's a game about taking risks.'

'Em'll hate it,' said Kate. 'She hates taking risks.'

It was true; Emily didn't like taking risks. She made reasonable progress on her first turn, advancing her pieces half-way up columns five, seven and eight, but then couldn't decide whether to stop or continue rolling.

'Go on,' said Ludek, 'just one more roll.'

'You can do it, Em,' said Kate.

She rolled the dice again, but couldn't make five, seven or eight with the numbers she'd rolled, so lost all the progress she'd made that turn. And it was the same *every* turn: either she played it safe and stopped rolling the dice too early, hardly rising up the columns, or she risked it and kept rolling, which invariably led to her losing everything. She was surprised to realise that despite doing so spectacularly badly, she had actually enjoyed the game.

Kate won, thanks partly to a streak of lucky rolls and partly to her willingness to take a gamble and keep rolling when the odds were against her. She glanced at her phone.

'I think I'm going to head off,' she said. 'You don't mind, do you, Em?'

'You can't leave now,' said Alan. 'Not when you're on a roll.'

'Good pun, Al,' she said, giving him a friendly punch in the arm. 'But I'm afraid I've got to go. Bit tired.' She yawned, but Emily knew when she was faking. 'Malcolm, Alan, lovely to meet you both. And to see you again, Ludo.'

They watched her go, then Malcolm said, 'Right, what are we playing next?'

'What do you normally do in your spare time, Emily?' said Alan.

'Cooking. Baking. Eating. Anything food-related. I've bought a café.'

'A café?' said Malcolm. 'I hope you've sorted your business insurance out. You need proper cover. Public liability insurance for a start in case anyone...'

'I know the perfect game for you, Emily,' said Alan. 'Ludek, I don't suppose you've brought A La Carte?'

'I have, as it happens.' Ludek reached down and unzipped a large rectangular bag, pulling out a box.

He took off the lid and Emily almost squealed with delight when she saw what was inside: small cardboard stoves and tiny frying pans, one for each player. They were like something from a doll's house. There were four miniature jars of ingredients: oregano (tiny green cylinders), lemons (tiny yellow ones), pepper (black) and paprika (red). In each jar, there were also little white cylinders representing salt. If too much salt got in the frying pan, the dish would be spoiled and no points would be scored.

Alan was right – this *was* the perfect game, Emily thought, as she took a tile with a recipe from the pile and placed it in her pan. She had to add two peppers and a lemon to make a tarte flambée which would score her three points. She didn't like to mention that those weren't the correct ingredients for a real tarte flambée; if only French cuisine was that simple. On her turn, she took the jar containing the lemon and opened it over her pot. It was against the rules to shake it. A salt fell out rather than a lemon. She had two more 'actions' so tried again but another salt fell out. For her third action, she rolled the dice, desperate to score three or more so she could raise the temperature of her stove a little - her dish needed to be cooked at between three and five on her little stove - but she only rolled a two.

'There'll be no customers in your café,' laughed Malcolm. 'Your food's still raw. And far too salty.'

Ludek gave him a hard stare.

It was Alan's turn next. He managed to get two paprikas and a pepper into his pan without getting any salt. What the game lacked in culinary accuracy, Emily thought, it made up for in fun. It was really exciting, though they must look ridiculous - four adults tipping tiny ingredients out of tiny jars. Play passed to Ludek and Emily realised she was actually holding her breath, as she watched to see if he could tip a lemon into his pan.

By the end of the game, Emily had managed to make four dishes and ruin another three, but she'd thoroughly enjoyed herself and didn't mind losing to Alan, who'd made the grand total of seven dishes.

After the game, she watched as Ludek began to pack it away, fascinated by how he meticulously sorted out all the pieces. Everything had its place: little plastic bags, one for each of the different coloured ingredients; perfectly sized compartments for all of the tiles.

Oh god, he was a tidy person, she thought as he put it back in the bag. Why did she always fall for the tidy ones, when she was so messy herself?

Hang on. Was she falling for him?

Malcolm saw her watching. 'He looks after his games,' he said, 'the way other people look after their children. Honestly, if his house caught fire – I hope you've got adequate contents cover, Ludo? – he'd try to save them all.'

Ludek shot him a withering look. 'Don't tell her that, Malcolm. She'll think I'm crazy. And we want her to come back next week, don't we? Expand our little group and get more people in Essendale into board games?'

He wanted her to come back next week, Emily thought, with a flutter of excitement.

Although…was that just because he wanted to expand his board games group?

Mind you, she *wanted* to return, and not just to see him,

but to play more games. There'd been loads of games in that bag of his, she'd noticed. It was like a whole new world. So many different ones to discover, all with different themes.

The Dungeons and Dragons guys all shook her hand as they left and said, 'Lovely to meet you.' They hadn't exactly met her, but it was a nice gesture. The Trainspotters, as she'd decided to nickname them, were a little more reticent, mumbling variations of 'See you next week.'

Later, when Malcolm and Alan had driven away in Malcolm's car, Emily and Ludek stood outside the pub.

'Did you enjoy the evening?' he said. 'I don't think your friend Kate reckoned much to it.'

'Yeah, it wasn't her cup of tea but I liked it. No, more than that. I loved it.'

He beamed. 'And would you come again? Next week, perhaps?'

'Definitely. I'll drag myself here no matter how exhausted I am. I knew running a café would be tiring, but I hadn't expected it to be *this* tiring. And that's without any customers.'

'There were no customers?'

'Not many. I'm beginning to wonder if I've made one giant mistake.'

Chapter Fifteen

Things slowly began to pick up. Mr B appeared at eleven every morning for his cappuccino and his Chorley cake which he ate whilst filling in the crossword in his Polish newspaper. The trolley ladies ventured in again. Several times, in fact. The second time they splashed out on two chocolate eclairs with their pot of tea. The third time they opted for all-day breakfasts. Emily was beside herself; the first customers to order her all-day breakfast. The fourth time they pushed the boat out ordering all-day breakfasts *and* slices of chocolate fudge cake. It was a wonder they could move after all that, but they disappeared off, their trolleys bumping along the pavement.

One morning, Marjory arrived. Emily had been longing for her to visit, but knew it was a little further from her flat than she normally liked to walk. She'd just sat down and was extolling the virtues of the lemon drizzle, when Mr B arrived for his morning coffee. He was looking especially dapper with a bright-red bow-tie and a matching handkerchief poking out of his jacket pocket. Marjory took one look at him, then looked at Emily, winking and nodding her head at him at the same time which made her look rather odd.

'Have you something in your eye, Marjory?' Emily said. She shook her head.

'Oh, I see. Mr B, this is Marjory. We used to be neighbours.'

'Delighted to meet you, Marjory. May I?' Mr B gestured at the empty chair at her table and she nodded.

'Usual order, Mr B?' Emily called.

'Yes, please.'

'More tea, Marjory?'

'Wonderful, dear,' she said.

After Mr B and Marjory had left, promising that they'd meet again the following day, same time, same place, Emily took advantage of the empty café to have a bowl of soup herself. Just in case she got the longed-for rush of customers wanting lunch. She'd barely lifted her spoon when the door opened.

She looked up to see Peter.

Emily didn't bear him any ill feeling; it was her fault their relationship had ended. Okay, so he had ~~fired her~~ made her redundant, but now she was a business owner herself, she could see that it had been a business decision. However, she didn't particularly want him in her café, especially when it was empty.

'Oh, Emily,' he said looking round. 'I'm so sorry. I was hoping Mother was wrong when she said you had no customers.'

'I do have customers. It's midway between the morning coffee rush and the lunch rush. That's why I was having lunch myself. Anyway, how would your mother know?'

'Her friends have been in.'

'Her friends?'

'Mrs Scott and Mrs Sinclair.'

'The ones with the shopping trolleys?' Emily couldn't think who else they could have been.

'That's them.'

Emily didn't think Florence would be friends with the kind of women who had shopping trolleys. She was more of an Ocado delivery kind of person.

'So do you want something? Or are you here to gloat?' she said.

'Don't be like that. I came along because…well, I thought you might need cheering up. I had an hour spare – a meeting got cancelled – so thought I might have an early lunch. Perhaps I could join you? That soup smells delicious. What is it?'

'Chicken and vegetable.'

'Lovely. Finish yours first though,' he said as Emily got up.

'No, it's fine. The customer comes first. Take a seat.'

She went through to the kitchen, put a second bowl of soup on a tray along with a freshly baked granary roll that he probably wouldn't touch, a pat of butter, a jug of water and two glasses. She carried it out to the table and set it down in front of Peter.

'Delicious,' he said, slurping a spoonful.

He ripped open the roll and began to smother it with butter.

'The bread isn't keto,' Emily said.

'I kind of gave up on that. After you left. So silly to live with someone who could bake amazing cakes and never once try one. After you'd gone, I troughed my way through boxes and boxes of Mr Kipling.'

'You never tasted my cakes so how do you know they're amazing?'

'Mrs Scott and Mrs Sinclair reported back to Mother.'

'They were spying on me?'

'Not spying exactly. Mother and I were worried about you.'

'Your mother was worried about me?'

'Yes, she's always liked you. She was really upset when we split up.'

'Your mother liked me?'

'Stop repeating everything I say. Anyway, that day. In my kitchen. The day you left. I could smell how good your cakes were. The whole house smelled of them. The bread was delicious too. I found the loaf proving in the sitting room so I baked it.'

'I'd forgotten all about that loaf.'

Peter put his spoon down and looked at Emily. 'Em, do you really have a lunchtime rush? And an elevenses rush? Or are you struggling?'

'I'm struggling.'

He glanced around.

'It's a bit…bare, Emily,' he said. 'Reminds me of the losers' café in *The Apprentice*.'

'Thanks for that. If you've come to criticise…'

She stood up.

'No, no, I shouldn't have said that,' he said. 'I was trying to make a joke. I know how much you love all those programmes. Honestly, Emily, I came here because I thought you might need cheering up. And I wanted to see if I could help in some way.'

She wondered what he was after. A reconciliation perhaps?

'Help? Are you planning to get behind the counter and start serving scones?'

'No, not that kind of help. Advice.'

'You've never run a café, though, have you?'

'No, I suppose not. But I do run a successful business.' He took another mouthful of soup. 'The trouble is, you've no footfall here. People don't pass by. Though even if they did, well, from the outside, it doesn't look particularly inviting.'

'I've done my best, Peter,' she said. 'I didn't exactly have unlimited funds or I might have been able to give it more kerb appeal.'

'And it's quite a walk from town.'

'Tell me something I don't know. I can't pick this place up and move it to a better location. I'm stuck with it. Either I make it work or I go bust and lose all the money Mum left me.'

'It needs a USP. You need to offer something that Sweet Delights doesn't.'

A USP. Perhaps he had a point. 'Such as?'

'I have an idea. Come out with me on Sunday afternoon.'

She knew it. He was definitely angling for them to get back together.

'Peter, I'm not sure that's a good idea. And Sunday's my only day off.'

'You know that programme you like where they go to a failing hotel and try to turn it around?'

'*The Hotel Inspector*.'

'That's the one. Well, they always take the hotel owners

to see a more successful hotel, don't they? Somewhere to inspire them to up their game.'

Emily was surprised he knew that; he'd never seemed interested in the programmes she liked watching.

'So…?' she said.

'So I'm going to do the same for you.'

'Peter the café inspector.'

'I'll pick you up and take you to the place I've got in mind. They've made it into a destination. People travel miles for their afternoon tea. You'll love it. Mother went last month and said it was out of this world. Even better than Fortnum's.'

'Peter, if you're hoping to get back with me…'

He held up his hands to stop her. 'It's not that, I promise. I still care about you, but I can see now that things weren't working between us. And I'm sorry that I wasn't more supportive when you broached the whole café idea. So let me make it up to you. Afternoon tea and business inspiration. My treat. This Sunday. What do you say?'

Perhaps she'd misjudged him. Perhaps he was just trying to be helpful.

'That's really kind of you,' she said. 'Sunday it is.'

Chapter Sixteen

On Wednesday, Emily closed the café early. Well, there were no customers so why bother staying open? She put the radio on, served herself a bowl of leftover soup of the day and wondered what the hell she was going to do.

There had to be a way of luring more customers in. She'd put more photos on Instagram, flyers in the local library and a home-made poster on the noticeboard in the mini-supermarket. What else could she do? Loyalty cards? Discount vouchers in the local supermarket? Some kind of special event?

A launch party, perhaps, as Kate had suggested. Bit late now though. The café was already open.

Perhaps the trip with Peter on Sunday would give her the inspiration she needed, but she doubted it somehow. Her new venture felt doomed.

She pulled off a piece of till roll and tried to calculate how much she needed to take each day in order to break even. And how much more she'd need to be able to pay herself some kind of wage. It was a depressingly large figure.

She'd been so naïve. This was the kind of thing she should have worked out *before* she bought a café, not afterwards when it was already going horribly wrong. She'd been so carried away with the idea of fulfilling her mum's dream that all sense of logic had flown out of the window.

Even more depressing was the next number she worked out: how many weeks she could keep going if trade didn't improve. It didn't bear thinking about.

She was sitting with her head in her hands when the door opened. Hadn't she locked it when she'd turned the sign to closed? She looked up, half-expecting it to be Mr B although he always came in the morning. But it wasn't. It was Ludek.

'Hi,' she said.

'I was passing.'

'Passing? It's still a cul-de-sac.'

'Okay, I wasn't passing. I was hoping you'd be here.'

He was hoping she'd be here. She pressed her palms together then realised it looked as if she was praying, so put her hands on her thighs.

'And if I hadn't been?'

'I'd have left a note.'

A note saying what? she wondered. Asking her out, perhaps?

She crossed her fingers under the table.

'I was rather hoping you might do me a favour.'

It turned out that the Red Lion was double-booked on Friday evening – some local boy turning eighteen which would obviously prove a lot more lucrative for the landlord than eleven middle-aged men nursing one pint – each, not between them – for an entire evening as they pushed pieces round their boards.

'We were wondering if we might play here?' said Ludek. 'Just for this week.'

'Sure,' Emily said. 'Why not?'

Well, it was certainly one way of getting a few more customers through the door. Even if they sat nursing one mug of tea all evening and didn't buy a single cake.

The Trainspotters arrived first, carrying an assortment of games boxes. All train-related, presumably. Just how many variations of building little railways across a map could there be?

The Dungeons and Dragons crowd were next. They nodded to the Trainspotters, then pushed two tables together and began to set up their board. Finally, Malcolm and Alan appeared.

'We're playing Agricola tonight,' said Malcolm, placing a games box on the table. There was a sheep on the front, Emily noticed, and an old-fashioned house.

'Is it food-themed?' she asked.

Alan opened the box. 'Well, there's food in it, but it's a bit complicated.'

'I can manage complicated. Is Ludek not here yet?'

'He'll be here soon. Running late at work,' said Alan.

'As usual,' added Malcolm.

Malcolm explained the rules whilst they were waiting. Alan hadn't been exaggerating when he'd said complicated; Emily wasn't sure she quite followed it, but it sounded intriguing. The game was all about farming. She was given two little wooden people – her 'meeples' Malcolm called them – and they lived in two rooms on her farm. Every round of the game, she would make one move with each of her meeples: ploughing a field to grow crops; fencing a pasture to breed animals; or playing one of the special cards she had in her hand, the point of which she hadn't grasped yet. Her meeples could have a family, which would be advantageous because it would give her more moves each round, but only if she built extra rooms on her house, and for that, she had to collect wood using one of her moves. What's more, every couple of rounds, she had to feed her meeples and their children, either by killing the animals that she'd bred or with the crops she was growing.

'Can't I just bake them a cake?' she said.

Malcolm frowned. 'You can bake bread, but not cakes.'

'She's joking, Malc,' said Alan gently. 'Now the important bit – point-scoring. At the end, you'll score points for how many animals and crops you have left, for the size of your meeple family and for the number of fields you've ploughed or fenced.'

Emily wasn't quite sure how she'd keep track of everything, but Malcolm assured her they'd help her through. She was just getting her head around it all and working out what she had to do, when Ludek arrived, slipping into the chair opposite her. She felt a flutter of excitement, but dismissed it. It was far too soon for her to be thinking about someone new, she reminded herself.

Wasn't it?

'Lovely to see you again,' he said, his brown eyes meeting hers.

Her game plan was to collect as much wood as possible to extend her house and fence pastures for her animals, but it had all been taken by the time it was her turn. She took a sheep instead: it would have to live in the house with her meeples until she could build fences for it. On her second turn, there weren't many options left, so she took some food tokens. If she didn't have enough food tokens, animals or crops when it came to feeding time, she'd have to take a begging bowl which meant negative points at the end of the game.

As things progressed, everyone forged ahead of Emily, building rooms for their houses and fences for their animals. Ludek was the first to have a child and the first to plough a field and sow crops. She managed to save up clay and wood and used it to build an oven in her house, which meant she could bake bread which was a more efficient way to feed her meeple family.

This was serious stuff, thought Emily, glancing round the table at her opponents. They barely said a word, heads bent over as they studied their cards, planning their strategies. Ludek was clearly planning his moves way ahead, and took ages over each turn, assessing what everyone else had done and calculating whether he was taking the right actions. He had a second child before she'd even managed to have a first, and had three fields towering with wheat whilst she only had one. Malcolm had clearly opted to specialise in animals and had three sheep and a pig, whilst Alan's farm was mostly arable.

'You need to have some children,' Alan said to her.

'I'd need to build more rooms for my house first and I don't have enough wood. Besides, my meeples are so wrapped up in love for each other that they don't want children. Maybe when the honeymoon period is over.'

'Meeples on honeymoon,' said Ludek, laughing. Her eyes met his; they were positively twinkling at her and Emily felt her cheeks reddening.

There was an awkward silence. Malcolm looked up – up until now, he'd been studying his cards, seemingly oblivious to the conversation.

Alan said, 'You need to have children, or you definitely won't win the game. The more meeples you have, the more turns you get each round.'

Emily realised she'd been holding her breath and let it out with a rush.

'Anyone fancy a cuppa?' she said.

'Tea break. Good idea,' said Alan.

'Milk, two sugars please,' said Malcolm.

Emily went into the kitchen and filled up two kettles. This was the first time she'd had to use more than one kettle at once; she'd never had this many people in The Lancashire Hotpot before. As she waited for the water to boil, she stared out of the hatch, enjoying the sight of the full tables. This. This was what she'd dreamed of. A full café – well, almost. Customers enjoying themselves. The buzz of conversation. She wished her mum could see it.

And board games. She loved them. She hadn't expected to, but she absolutely loved them. Even this complicated one with its farming scenario and its wood and its meeples and its baffling array of different cards, each offering a different benefit. No, make that *especially* this complicated one. She adored Agricola, even though she hadn't quite got the hang of it.

And the gamers themselves. She and Kate had dismissed them as geeky initially, but that was doing them an injustice.

She enjoyed their quiet, gentle company. Especially Ludek's. Obviously.

The kettles boiled. Emily snapped herself out of her reverie, made three pots of tea, one for each table, and carried them out on a tray with a jug of milk, a bowl of sugar, twelve mugs and some home-made biscuits.

When the tea break was over and play had resumed, Emily finally managed to collect enough wood to build an extra room for her house which allowed her meeple couple to have a child.

Two and a half hours after the game had started, they totted up the points. Ludek won with forty-three points and she came in last with a paltry twenty-two. Malcolm and Alan were somewhere in between, closer to Ludek's score than to hers.

As Ludek packed the game away, putting the little pieces into their little bags again – one for the sheep, one for the cows and so on – the three men indulged in a bit of post-game analysis; the kind of thing you'd see after a football match on the telly rather than after a board game.

Emily handed Ludek her little meeple family. He looked down at the three tiny wooden figures, sitting in his hand.

'I'm glad they finally had their honeymoon baby,' he said, raising his eyebrows, and she felt herself blushing.

Chapter Seventeen

On Saturday, Emily was in the kitchen, frying some bacon to make herself a butty for a late lunch, when she heard the door opening. A customer. At long last.

Mr B and Marjory had been in for their morning coffee and Chorley cakes as usual, and Mrs Scott and Mrs Sinclair, the two trolley ladies, had had their usual fry-up followed by scones and jam. Emily had wondered how they stayed so slim. And were they still 'spying' for Florence? Since they'd left, she hadn't seen another soul. Until now.

She turned the hob down to its lowest setting as no one wanted to smell burning bacon when they walked into a café and went to greet the new arrival.

Ludek.

'Hi,' she said, hastily wiping her hands on her apron. 'Just passing?'

He laughed. 'Hi. How are you?'

'Tired. A bit fed up. Not getting many customers. Last night was fun though.'

'Yes, that's why I'm here. I wanted to thank you. You really helped us out. It was great holding the games evening here.'

'Anytime.'

'I was wondering if...' He hesitated. 'I was wondering if you'd like to go out tonight. For dinner.'

Oh. He was asking her out.

'As a thank you,' he added. 'For hosting the games evening yesterday.'

Maybe not then. Just a thank you.

But that was okay; it was still too soon after Peter and she ought to be focusing one hundred per cent of her energy on her new business, not getting distracted by a man. They could be friends; she needed another friend now Kate was spending every spare moment with Freddie.

'Dinner would be lovely,' she said. 'About seven?'

'Curry okay?' said Ludek as she got into his car. 'I thought we could try the new place in Hebbleswick?'

'Curry would be lovely, thank you.'

Hebbleswick was larger than Essendale; a tourist hotspot, renowned for its lack of parking spaces, its hipster shops selling everything from tofu to tarot cards, and its plethora of artists' studios.

For once, they found a parking space quickly enough, but when they reached the Bengal Spice, there wasn't a table to be had; a birthday party had taken over the entire restaurant.

'Foiled by yet another birthday party,' said Emily.

'I can do you a take-away?' the waiter offered.

'Could we go back to yours?' said Ludek to Emily.

'Yes, or yours?'

'Yours might be better.'

Was it her imagination or did he look a little awkward?

'Sure,' she said.

She let Ludek order, salivating as he requested chicken makhani, lamb korma, bombay potatoes, pilau rice *and* a garlic naan. What a treat! She couldn't remember the last time she'd eaten carbs with a man.

On the very odd occasion when Peter had actually agreed to have a take-away, he refused to order chips or even rice. Whilst they waited for the delivery, he'd shove a cauliflower into the food processor to create carb-free cauliflower 'rice', then they'd both pretend it was as good as the real thing.

As Ludek pulled up outside Kate's house, Emily was surprised to see that the lights were on. The curtains were still open, and Emily could see her friend on the sofa, astride a blond-haired man – Freddie, presumably.

'Time for Plan B,' she said. 'Your house.'

Ludek frowned. 'I'm not sure that's a good idea.'

'Well, we can hardly eat in the car. You're not married, are you?'

'No, of course not.'

'Come on then. The food's getting cold.'

Ludek's house was in the older part of town. A large Victorian semi with pale-green window shutters. Some very round azaleas – either he had a gardener or he was handy with the secateurs. A crass joke about him having a well-trimmed bush popped into her head. Better not say that out loud.

Even the paving slabs on his driveway looked pristine;

not a weed in sight. Ludek was clearly a very neat and tidy person – well, she knew already that from the fastidious way he put his games away. They'd be totally incompatible.

He put his key in the lock, then hesitated.

'Look, er, this is a bit embarrassing. I wasn't really expecting to bring you here this evening. If I'd known, I'd have…'

'You'd have…?'

'Never mind. You'll see.' He opened the door, moving aside to let her in.

As soon as she set foot in the lounge, she understood why he'd been so reluctant to bring her to his home. There were so many board games: an entire shelving unit was devoted to them; two stacks of boxes towered up on the carpet; and although there were two sofas, you could only sit on one of them because the other was piled up with yet more games.

'It's a bit of a mess but have a seat,' said Ludek. 'I never bring anyone back here. Except for Alan and Malcolm and they know what I'm like.'

So he didn't do much dating. Interesting.

'It's fine,' she said, perching on the edge of the sofa. So he wasn't so tidy after all. Had she finally found a man who was messier than she was?

Ludek sat down beside her and something shot past her legs, past the stacks of games boxes which wobbled for a moment but thankfully stayed upright, and sprang onto his lap.

'You have a cat?' she said surprised.

'Yes, have you got pets?'

She shook her head. 'I'd never have a pet.'

'Too much commitment? Or too much mess?'

'Neither. Too much upset.'

'Upset? Pets bring so much joy. And, medically speaking, pets are great. They lower your blood pressure and there's good evidence that stroking cats can lower your cortico-steroid levels, thereby boosting your immunity. They're good for mental health too – they calm you down. Give you an overall sense of well-being. A sense of companionship. Almost as good as having a partner.'

Almost as good. But not quite.

'That's just it,' said Emily. 'You get attached to them, but unless you buy a giant tortoise they don't live for ever, do they? From the moment your eyes meet theirs in the rescue centre or the pet shop or wherever, and you decide they're the one, the clock is ticking. Dogs, rabbits, goldfish...you know you're doomed to lose them one day. The moment you become a pet owner, you're signing up for grief. Even with cats, and they've got nine lives.'

'Don't listen to her, Catan.' Ludek put his hands over the animal's ears.

'Catan? That's his name?'

'It's a game.'

She rolled her eyes, punching him playfully in the arm. 'I might have known.'

Catan began to purr really loudly as Ludek stroked him. Emily stretched out her hand to touch the soft fur, accidentally – well, not really – brushing Ludek's hand at the same time.

'Have you *never* had a pet?' he said.

'A rabbit. When I was little.'

Mum and Dad had bought Snowy for her when she was five. She'd lived in a hutch in the garden, but was occasionally allowed into the house. Emily had loved Snowy. As an only child, she couldn't wait to get home from school to see her. To whisper secrets through the wire netting. To poke through the carrots and lettuce leaves that she'd sneaked from the fridge.

The little white rabbit was Emily's best friend for about a year until, one morning, Snowy was gone.

'It wasn't fair to keep her caged up like that,' Mum had said. 'She'll have a much nicer life living in the fields with the wild rabbits.'

She would. Even as a six year old, Emily could understand that. But why hadn't they let her say goodbye first?

Later, when she was supposed to be in bed, but was actually sitting on the stairs as she often did, her face poking between two spindles, she overheard their conversation.

'Did you tell her?' Dad asked. 'About the rabbit dying? How did she take it?'

Dying?

'I said Snowy had gone to live in the fields with the wild rabbits,' Emily heard her mum saying. 'She seemed fine about it.'

She let out a sob, giving herself away. The living room door was flung open and Mum rushed to her side, gathering her up.

That was the first time. The first time Emily loved someone only to lose them. The first time her life was shattered by grief.

'What happened to the rabbit?' said Ludek.

'She died. Durr. That's exactly my point. When I was six. My parents offered to buy me another one but I said no.'

She stroked Catan again. For a moment, her eyes met Ludek's, then her stomach gave the most enormous rumble.

'The curry,' he said, standing up. 'I'll get the plates. You set the table. There are mats in the drawer of the sideboard.'

Emily opened the drawer. There were indeed mats. Along with six dice, a handful of the little plastic bags that he used to store his board games pieces, three tiny silver cubes and a green meeple. She cleared the table of two games boxes, and was laying out the mats as Ludek returned with the plates and cutlery.

He unpacked the bag, putting a dish onto each mat.

'What's your favourite food?' Ludek asked a short while later, between mouthfuls of korma.

'Too hard to say,' Emily said. 'I love most food. That's like asking you what your favourite game is.'

'Fair point,' he said.

'How about you?'

'Well, I do love a decent curry, but it would have to be Polish food. The sort of thing my mother cooks, but I don't get to eat that so much since she and Dad went back to live in Poland.'

'I don't think I've ever had Polish food.'

'Pierogi – they're a bit like dumplings. Usually savoury, but they can be sweet. Or pączki. Like doughnuts only better. Bigos. Barszcz. That's beetroot soup. Like Russian borsch, only never say that to my mother.'

After they'd eaten and Ludek had taken the plates and the leftovers – not that there were many leftovers – he said, 'I don't suppose you fancy a game, do you? Only I've bought one with you in mind.'

Emily had imagined they might sit on the sofa together

and chat some more, get a little closer perhaps, but playing another game was rather tempting. Especially if he'd bought it with her in mind.

With her in mind. So he'd been thinking of her then?

'Why not?' she said.

Ludek wiped the table, then pulled out a box.

'Ta-da,' he said. 'Wasabi!'

He peeled off the Cellophane wrapper and opened the box, pulling out cards, tokens and a square board with a grid. Like A La Carte, the game had recipe cards requiring different combinations of ingredients, only this time the aim was to make sushi and the ingredients were all shown on cards. There were no little cooking stoves or jars, but there were two tiny dishes shaped like the dip bowls in a sushi restaurant.

Emily picked them up. 'They're so cute. Is this another complicated one?'

'No, it's easy. Think of it like Scrabble, only the recipes are the words and the ingredients are the letters. You place the ingredients on the game board vertically or horizontally to make up each recipe. The longer the recipe, the more points you score.'

The game wasn't nearly as easy as Ludek had suggested because only one ingredient could be placed at a time. The skill lay in using ingredients that had already been placed on the board and Emily relished the challenge. Often, Ludek would use the rice that she wanted, thwarting her plans and, judging by his face, she foiled his a few times too. She finished her recipes first so was declared the winner.

'It's being in a kitchen all day,' he said good-naturedly.

'You're bound to be faster at making up dishes. Shall we play again?'

'Definitely. You know what we need?'

'What?'

'An Indian curry version of Wasabi! We could call it *Masala*.'

'Great idea. You can go into games design when you get bored of running your café.'

'Or when it fails and I go bankrupt.'

'Don't say that. You won't fail. I have every confidence in you. Come on, let's play again.'

After two more games of Wasabi!, Emily reluctantly decided she should call it a night. Working six days a week – and mostly on her feet rather than sitting behind a desk – was taking its toll and she was tired.

She watched as Ludek packed the game away, ensuring as he always did that every piece was accounted for, every card in the right place.

'You take very good care of your games,' she said.

'I do. It probably seems a little … extreme.'

'Perhaps a bit.'

'It's just … well, when we first came to the UK from Poland, my parents weren't very well off. We didn't have a lot of toys growing up, so I really treasure my board games.'

Emily nodded. It made sense now. And perhaps that explained why he had such a big collection; he was making up in adulthood for what he hadn't had in childhood.

'Thanks for a lovely evening,' she said, standing up, 'and a delicious dinner.'

'You're welcome,' he said.

They walked into the hall. Emily put on her coat but he made no attempt to open the door.

'I…er…' she began as he said, 'So I…'

'You go first,' he said.

'No, you. Please.'

'Okay, so, I was wondering…'

'Yes?'

She lifted her face up to his. Their eyes met. Was it her imagination or had he inched closer?

'Emily, I was wondering…'

She was conscious of her heart thudding in her chest. Her mouth went dry and she licked her lips a little in preparation for…

'I was wondering if the board games group could meet at your café every week?'

Chapter Eighteen

D *ress up*, Peter had texted. *It's quite a fancy place.*
Emily could have guessed that, given that his mother liked it.

'Dress up' was Peter-speak for wear a proper dress. Not jeans and not one of her beloved dungaree pinafores. For a second, she wanted to be a rebel, to put her jeans on and say to hell with him. She wasn't engaged to him anymore. He couldn't tell her what to wear. But he was trying to help her; it'd be a bit churlish to be awkward with him. Besides, she hated showing up somewhere only to find she was wearing the wrong outfit. She always felt that everyone was looking at her, judging.

He hadn't given her any clues about where this place was or what it was like. It could be anything, anywhere. A fancy new garden centre had opened about fifteen miles away and apparently the cakes at the coffee shop there were to die for. It was the sort of place Florence might frequent: she never got her hands dirty in the garden, of course – she had a gardener to do that – but she did like to select her own shrubs. Or there was that farm shop on the hills above Hebbleswick. Emily could imagine Florence going there, paying astronomical prices for organic beetroot and locally reared lamb, then, taxed by the stress and strain of having to carry her own shopping to a till, she'd be bound to visit the on-site restaurant for a cup of Darjeeling.

But you wouldn't need to dress up if you were going to a farm shop or a garden centre, would you? No matter how fancy it was.

Emily opened her wardrobe, rifling through her jeans and pinafores as if she expected the perfect garment to magically appear. She needed smart casual. She only possessed casual. Except for the figure-hugging poppy-red dress that Peter had bought her from Hobbs when they were going to the annual 'Businessman of the Year' awards dinner and he was under the illusion that he would win. He hadn't.

Perhaps she could go out and buy something. Would Oxfam have anything suitable? She'd need a smart outfit soon anyway for the job interviews she'd be attending in the near future; it was only a matter of time before the café went under. This afternoon with Peter wouldn't change anything.

Emily sighed. There wasn't time now. Not even to nip to Oxfam on the off-chance; Peter would be here in half an hour, chomping at the bit to get going. He was a stickler for punctuality.

She put on her navy pinafore as it was the smartest and paired it with a plain, long-sleeved white t-shirt and her red glass beads. The problem was shoes. The only smart shoes she had were the black stiletto heeled courts she'd worn to Businessman of the Year. She tried them on, but navy and black was obviously a no-go.

She went through to Kate's room. It would have been easy if they took the same shoe size. Kate had several pairs that would have worked with the pinafore, but trying to squeeze her chunky size 7s into Kate's narrow size 5s would, Emily thought, have been akin to the ugly sisters trying to shoehorn themselves into Cinderella's glass slipper. The two women weren't the same dress size either but maybe, just maybe, Kate might have something a little loose-fitting or with a lot of give that Emily might be able to squeeze into. Something that would work with black shoes.

She slid open the mirror door of Kate's fancy fitted wardrobe and peered inside.

One ripped seam later, and Emily decided that she would have to wear the Hobbs dress with the toe-pinching black shoes.

Twenty minutes later – Peter was early as per – Emily tottered down the stairs.

He stood on the doorstep wearing the smart purple-striped shirt that Florence had bought him from Ted Baker the previous Christmas.

'You *have* dressed up,' he said, looking her up and down. Emily wasn't sure if this was a compliment or not, and wished that the dress wasn't quite so low cut, and a little bit longer too.

When she climbed into his BMW, the dress became even shorter. Conscious of how much thigh she was exposing and not wanting him to get the wrong idea – he was her ex after all – she spent the entire journey trying to pull it down a little. And it was a long journey.

'Where on earth are we going?' she said.

They'd been in the car for almost an hour, mostly on A roads.

'You'll see,' said Peter, tapping the steering wheel.

After another ten minutes, Peter turned off down a track, passing a sign that said, 'Ingle Estate. Pedigree Limousin Herd'. A farm shop after all. She should have opted for the navy pinafore.

The car park was full. They had to circle four times before they finally bagged a space that had just been vacated by a Mini. After a bit of manoeuvring, Peter finally managed to squeeze the BMW in, but Emily couldn't open her door properly and had to slide over to his side of the car to get out. She must have put on weight during the journey. The dress felt tighter than before.

Peter led her through an arched gateway and into a courtyard surrounded by elegant Yorkshire stone buildings. In one corner, there was indeed a farm shop; there was also a pottery workshop, a quilting store and an art gallery, but no sign of a café.

'Come on,' said Peter, heading towards the art gallery.

In the window were three canvases, each depicting well-known features of the local countryside and a large sculpture of a young girl doing ballet.

He opened the door and stepped aside to let her go in.

The space inside was half art gallery, half café. If the Tate and Fortnum and Mason's had a love child, this would be it. Pale wooden floors. Pristine white walls hung with a mixture of local landscapes and strange abstracts with bold colours and gold leaf. Large white circular tables with clear Perspex chairs.

The far wall was completely taken up by a glossy shelving unit. The contents were sparsely arranged: jars of harissa paste and pesto; fancy packets of pasta; bottles of extra virgin olive oil and aged balsamic vinegar.

'Do you have a booking?' said a woman in a white jumpsuit with a chunky gold chain around her neck.

Emily saw her clock the red Hobbs dress.

She was overdressed, thought Emily. Damn.

'Peter Ridley,' said Peter.

'Of course, Mr Ridley,' said the woman in the jumpsuit, and they followed her to one of the tables in the centre of the room.

Emily sat down on her Perspex chair and glanced at what the other customers were wearing. Crisp white shirts. Perfectly ironed. Obviously. Thin cashmere sweaters. Tailored trousers. One woman was wearing jeans, probably designer.

'You said smart,' she hissed at Peter. 'I feel stupid now in this dress.'

'I said smart, not evening wear.'

'You know I don't do smart.'

'Just relax. Try and enjoy this. No one's looking at you. What do you think of the place?'

'It's lovely,' Emily said, still fretting about her outfit. 'But I know nothing about art.'

'I'm not suggesting you make *The Lancashire Hotpot* into an art gallery.'

'So why have you brought me here?'

'I'm suggesting you make it into a destination. This place was just a farm shop before. If you happened to be passing, you might call in for a few chops and some carrots. But then they added the quilting place and this art gallery, and suddenly people were prepared to go out of their way to get here. I was wondering if you could do something similar and entice people away from the town centre? Make them visit you instead of Sweet Delights?'

'I dunno. You're forgetting one thing.'

'And what's that?'

'Space. I haven't room for a quilting shop or anything like that.'

'I'm not suggesting that you try to *copy* this place,' he said. 'You obviously can't. You just need something to make customers go a little bit out of their way to visit you.'

'Are you ready to order?' A fresh-faced waitress was standing at their table now.

'I thought we'd have afternoon tea for two,' said Peter. 'Is that okay, Emily?'

She nodded.

'Any particular tea?'

'Darjeeling, please,' said Peter.

When their afternoon tea arrived, it was beautifully presented on a clear Perspex cake stand. There were tiny sandwiches, made with thinnest slices of white bread with the crusts cut off. Fruit scones with ramekins containing clotted cream, strawberry jam and butter. And a selection of delicate cakes.

'Looks amazing, Peter,' Emily said. 'Thank you.'

It tasted amazing too. The sandwiches were filled with lemony smoked salmon, tender strips of beef with horseradish sauce, and strong Cheddar with just the slightest hint of onion. Emily could make a decent scone, but hers were never this fluffy. And the cakes; the hazelnut macarons were to die for.

She bit into a raspberry mille-feuille, scattering shards of flaky pastry all over the immaculate white table.

'I wish I could make these,' she said, munching away. 'Who wouldn't walk an extra fifteen, twenty minutes to eat this kind of stuff rather than the bog-standard chocolate muffins at Sweet Delights? I'm sure they buy those in.'

'I knew you'd find this place inspiring,' said Peter. 'If you make The Lancashire Hotpot a bit more upmarket; offer moules marinière and pastels de nata instead of fried breakfasts and Chorley cakes, you'll attract a whole new clientele. My mother and her cronies would be in seventh heaven. They like somewhere a little exclusive.'

Emily refrained from saying that Florence's friends had been frequenting her establishment anyway and that she didn't want her café to be 'exclusive'; that *her* mother's vision was the exact opposite – a place where everyone was welcome. Including the woman who nearly became her mother-in-law. If she had to fake a smile and welcome Florence in for a strawberry meringue and a cup of Assam, then she would.

'This has been wonderful,' said Emily when they'd munched their way through everything. She glanced at her watch. 'A real treat. But it's ten to five, and I really need to get back. I've baking to do for tomorrow.'

Peter caught the waitress's eye and made a 'can I pay the bill?' gesture to her.

The bill didn't appear and, a few minutes later, Peter made the same gesture to a second waitress. It was quarter past five before he finally tapped his Visa on the card reader, batting away Emily's offer to pay half. They wouldn't get home till at least half past six at this rate; she was beginning to worry that she wouldn't get all her prep done for the following day. Although she only made a minimal selection of cakes for the café – well, there wasn't any point in making a lot since most of them didn't get eaten – she did want to ensure that there was a reasonable display in the chiller cabinet. It would be sod's law that the day the customers finally arrived was the same day she had little to offer them.

Thanks to a tractor, a set of roadworks and unexpectedly heavy traffic through Hebbleswick, it was almost seven when they pulled up outside Kate's house. Emily was about to thank Peter again for afternoon tea, when he kissed her. It was just a peck, but it was on the lips.

It took Emily by surprise. She put a hand on his chest to stop him, and he pulled away.

'Sorry, I shouldn't have done that. Habit,' he mumbled.

She couldn't undo her seatbelt fast enough. 'I've got to go. Thanks for the tea.'

She stumbled out of the car – these shoes were going straight to Oxfam on Monday – and came face-to-face with Ludek.

'Oh,' she said. 'Hello.'

Peter was suddenly out of the car and standing beside her, saying, 'Hi, haven't we met?' and holding out his hand to Ludek.

'Yeah, I brought Em… Emily…home when she twisted her ankle at running club. Peter, isn't it?'

'Do you want to come in for a cup of tea?' she said, looking at Ludek, all thoughts of the baking forgotten.

'That'd be lovely,' said Peter.

Ludek looked from Emily to Peter and then back to Emily. 'I'm fine, thanks. I was just… Well, I just wanted to give you this. I'll see you at board games on Friday. Bye, Peter. Nice to see you again.'

He thrust a plastic carrier bag into her hands, turned

and walked away. Emily looked after him and waved. She wasn't sure why she waved; he wasn't even looking.

'Do you really want tea?' she said to Peter. 'Only I've got baking to do…'

'No, it's fine,' he said. 'I should get off.'

But he stayed where he was, watching until Ludek had disappeared round the corner, before saying, 'Right then. I'll get off.'

When Peter had driven away, Emily didn't bake. Instead she put her feet up on Kate's sofa and reached inside the bag that Ludek had given her, pulling out a box. It had been a shoebox, but was now covered in photos of different curries, with the word 'Masala' written across the lid in black marker pen. She opened it; Ludek had made his very own version of the game Wasabi! that they'd played the night before, only in place of the maki, shrimp, tempura and scallops were Indian ingredients like coriander, mango chutney, naan bread, and paneer. He must have designed all the little cards and the two games boards on his computer; he'd even gone to the effort of laminating them.

He had made this for her. In just one day.

He liked her. He *definitely* liked her.

But how long had he been standing there on the pavement? Had he seen Peter kiss her? He must have. And now he was probably thinking she was back together with her fiancé.

Oh god. What a disaster. She'd always liked Ludek, right from the moment she first saw him, at the running club, a broad smile on his face, his curly mop of hair bouncing with every step. She liked the way he'd held up the traffic – pleasantly but assertively – and the way he was the first at her side when she'd fallen. But she'd never been sure – not one hundred per cent sure – that the feelings were mutual. Now, as she marvelled at the little ingredients cards, each one carefully printed, cut out and laminated by him, she was sure. He liked her.

But, looking back, she was also pretty certain that he must have seen that kiss.

Chapter Nineteen

Emily texted Ludek later that evening to thank him for the game. No reply.

She re-sent the text on Monday morning, just in case it hadn't arrived. Well, you never knew with technology. Still no reply. He was probably with a patient.

She gave up after that. She would see him at Friday's board games evening. And, in the meantime, she would focus on the café. Things were getting worse, not better. On Thursday, Mr B and Marjory were her only customers. She was propping up the business with the remains of her savings to the tune of... Well, she didn't like to think how much it was costing her each week to stay open. She put that figure to the back of her mind, along with the number of weeks – not very many – that she could continue if things carried on like this.

Her Sunday afternoon with Peter had been intended to inspire her to move forwards with her business rather than just setting back her love life, but she still hadn't come up with a way to transform the café's fortunes. The Lancashire Hotpot needed a Unique Selling Point, something that would make it a destination, to persuade people to drive miles out of their way to visit. Or, at least, schlep a few hundred yards from Essendale's high street instead of just going to Sweet Delights.

She walked past her rival café most evenings on her way home to Kate's. She'd always peer in through the window, trying to ascertain if they'd had a busy day by how messy the floor looked and how harassed the staff appeared. The floor was *always* messy and at least one of the waitresses *always* looked incredibly harassed. Business must be booming.

Emily saw Peggy the owner folding up her A-board one night.

'I know you, don't I?' the older woman said. 'You bought Nico's place. How's it going?'

Emily was loathe to admit that trade wasn't good. 'Brilliantly, actually. Plenty of customers.'

'Well, not for long,' Peggy said. 'Good luck though. Reckon we're both going to need it.' Then she hurried back into the café with the A-board, and bolted the door behind her.

Not for long? What did she mean by that? Had she some trick up her sleeve to lure all of Emily's customers over to Sweet Delights? Not that there were many customers to lure, but Peggy didn't know that.

Good luck though. Reckon we're both going to need it. What was the woman going on about? Was she hinting that Essendale wasn't big enough for two cafés to co-exist and only one would survive? Well, unless Emily pulled her finger out and thought of an idea pretty quickly, one thing was certain: it wouldn't be hers.

★

She had her eureka moment sitting in the bath that evening, thinking about what Peggy had said. There was a statue in Manchester's Vimto Park – yes, it really was called that – of Archimedes having his eureka moment, also sitting in the tub. She wasn't quite sure what his idea was – something to do with physics? – but he'd immediately sprung from the bath and run naked through the streets of – well, wherever he lived – shouting, 'Eureka' which was Latin or Greek or something for 'I've got it.'

Emily didn't think Essendale was quite ready for the sight of her galloping naked over the cobbles, and this was West Yorkshire and it was quite parky out. Besides, she'd only just run the bath and didn't want to waste the hot water.

She soaped her arms, mulling over her brainwave. She'd always wanted to go to Paris, to wander along the narrow streets and secret alleyways of Montmartre and sample the delights of all those lovely little cafés. The best cafés in the world, Mum used to say. It was where her parents had spent their honeymoon.

She would bring Paris to Essendale. She'd give the café a new name – she hadn't come up with it yet, but she would. She'd swap her Lancashire pictures for pictures of *Le Tour Eiffel* and *La Seine*. She'd put croque monsieur and croissants on the menu, and she'd learn the art of patisserie. How hard could it be?

The following day, Emily could think of nothing but patisserie. In the gaps between customers – and let's face it, there were a *lot* of gaps – she watched YouTube videos on how to create the most delectable mille-feuilles, make picture-perfect macarons and bake the lightest madeleines. The board games group arrived that evening, but she didn't join in with the games, opting instead to try her hand at a raspberry and vanilla Charlotte russe. Okay, so she *did* want to practise her patisserie skills, but her main reason for staying in the kitchen was to avoid any awkwardness with Ludek. They both avoided making eye contact when she took the tea through at half-time and she didn't dare ask why he hadn't replied to her texts.

Despite using shop-bought sponge fingers, her Charlotte russe didn't turn out that well. How did the contestants on *The Great British Bake Off* get things to look so neat? Perhaps they weren't distracted by the presence of a man they fancied just metres away. Or did they have coaching? Perhaps *she* could have coaching.

A quick Google and she found the solution: a patisserie course the following weekend. The website said there was one place left. There was just one snag: it was in London.

A week later, Emily arrived at the bakery school just off the high street in Chiswick a little bleary-eyed having caught the earliest London-bound train from Halifax. She probably should have travelled down the night before, but she'd had to open the café for the board games group – the atmosphere between her and Ludek had been decidedly frosty again. Plus the course had cost an arm and a leg and she couldn't afford a hotel on top. Not at London prices anyway.

Bleary-eyed and also late as she hadn't realised that the Piccadilly Line didn't always stop at Turnham Green, which was the nearest station to the school.

The class had already started when she walked in. She noticed the stainless-steel worktops, sparkling white walls and wooden floors, and immediately knew that the Lancashire Hotpot's kitchen would feel even smaller and even shabbier after this. She also noticed how smartly dressed the other participants were. She wouldn't fit in here.

The tutor, a tall, bald man with a curly moustache, was mid-sentence, outlining the plan for the day. He barely glanced in Emily's direction, but gestured to the one empty workstation at the back of the room where a stool and a pristine white apron embroidered with the cookery school's logo awaited her.

Emily wondered if she'd get to keep the apron.

'Through the desserts you create today,' the tutor said, 'you'll learn a range of skills that you can apply to make other things. We're beginning this morning with salted caramel profiteroles. You'll master the art of making a good choux pastry, learn how to create the perfect cream filling and top the whole thing off with a delicious salted caramel sauce.'

Great. Emily could already make choux pastry, she knew how to whip cream and a caramel sauce wasn't too difficult, salted or otherwise. She hoped this course wasn't going to be too basic.

'And then we'll break for lunch. You're welcome to eat your creations – assuming they're edible…'

A titter of nervous laughter ran round the class.

'This afternoon, we'll be tackling sugar dome fruit tarts. We'll begin by perfecting the art of shortcrust pastry – and, believe me, creating a good shortcrust pastry is much tricker than it sounds – and then we'll learn how to make a vanilla crème diplomat for the filling and we'll top the whole thing off with glazed fruit and a sugar dome.'

Emily was sure the website had mentioned making rough puff pastry and macarons too. All this way to learn to make two desserts? And desserts she could probably have made a fairly decent stab at anyway. Well, except for the sugar dome bit, but she could have taught herself that from YouTube.

The tutor began his demonstration. Emily joined the other participants, gathering around his workstation and watching as he gently heated butter, sugar and water in a saucepan until the butter had melted, then brought it to the boil. He then took the pan off the heat, added the flour and beat the mixture until it was stiff and glossy.

'Any questions?' he said, looking at the group.

Nobody said a word. The tutor looked a little disheartened.

Emily didn't like to disappoint him, so said the first thing that came into her head. 'Will all that beating get rid of my bingo wings?'

He looked aghast. 'I have no idea,' he said snootily.

'What if the dough isn't glossy?' asked a tall woman with blonde hair scraped back in a neat bun.

'Your pastry will be dense and dry,' he said.

'And why might that happen?' the blond woman said.

'Probably because you've got the eggs to flour ratio wrong,' said Emily before she could stop herself.

The tutor frowned. 'Too much flour or too little egg,' he added.

At eleven o'clock, the door opened and a girl appeared, wheeling a trolley.

'Ah, perfect timing,' said the tutor. 'Coffee break.'

The tutor left the room and Emily wandered over to the

trolley with the others. There was a large jug of filter coffee, a large flask of hot water for tea and a beautiful array of pastries: macarons; mille-feuilles; chocolate tarts; white chocolate eclairs.

She helped herself to an eclair and a mug of filter coffee and returned to her workstation.

'What do you do?' said the blond-haired woman who had asked all the questions, turning to look at her.

'I have my own café,' Emily said.

'Oh, we have a professional in our midst. No wonder you knew about choux pastry. Whereabouts is it? Would we know it?'

'West Yorkshire.' She suddenly felt as if every pair of eyes was looking at her.

'Goodness. You've come rather a long way for a course.'

'Don't you know all this stuff anyway,' said another woman, 'if you run your own café?'

'Most of it, yes. I was hoping the course would be a bit more advanced. Didn't they mention macarons and flaky pastry on the website?'

'Rough puff,' came a male voice from the doorway and Emily turned to see the tutor had returned. 'That's part two. Next Saturday. You can book on that as well if you like. We offer a five per cent reduction to returning students.'

Emily didn't remember seeing anything about a part one and a part two course on the website, but the tutor had such a steely gaze that she didn't dare argue. She'd have a look later.

The coffee break over, they placed their empty plates and mugs back on the trolley and the lesson began again.

At lunchtime, Emily wandered along the high street,

marvelling at the number of great charity shops. The garments on sale were a far cry from those on offer back in Essendale. Barely worn, many had designer labels. The prices though! Almost as expensive as buying new.

And so many cafés. Admittedly Chiswick had more inhabitants than Essendale, but imagine the stress of trying to run a café here, in the face of so much competition. The first two she went in were completely full – not a single table to be had – and she ended up buying a sandwich and eating it on a bench on the green.

After she'd finished, she took out her phone and googled the cookery school.

On our patisserie courses, the blurb read, *we teach you how to make different types of pastry including shortcrust, choux and rough puff, and a wide variety of desserts including profiteroles, fruit tarts, macarons and mille-feuille.*

On our patisserie *courses*. Not *course*.

She scrolled down and saw that there were six courses listed, ranging in difficulty from the easy one that she had selected to a full twelve-week diploma course. *This is the course to choose if you want to bake professionally*, the website said.

What had she been thinking? Of course it took longer than a day to bake to the level she'd need if she was going to transform The Lancashire Hotpot into a patisserie. How could she have thought any different?

Chapter Twenty

Emily scurried back towards King's Cross, tail between her legs and tears in her eyes.

This morning, she'd walked these same pavements full of hope and optimism, convinced that she'd master the art of patisserie then magically apply her newly acquired skills as she spent the weekend baking a whole batch of hand-crafted delicacies. She'd open on Monday to find a queue of people. Or at least a couple of customers whose names *weren't* Marjory and Mr B.

Okay, so she wasn't that unrealistic. She knew that patisserie wasn't easy. She knew it would take time and practice before she had anything good enough to offer to customers, and that even then, it might take a few days, weeks even, for word to spread of the new, improved offerings at The Lancashire Hotpot.

But that course hadn't taught her even a fraction of the skills that she needed and the fee had been astronomical. Money she could ill afford. A second course at a five per cent discount? Out of the question. Never mind the twelve-week professional diploma.

Emily wiped her cheeks on her sleeve, and weaved her way in and out, between businessmen in expensive Italian suits talking loudly on their iPhones and women with foreheads full of Botox and designer handbags full of… what did women like that keep in their designer handbags? She had no idea. They were obviously successful people anyway. Achievers. People who set out to do something and managed it. People who were the opposite of her.

It was a relief to reach the station, to look up at the information board and see the platform number for her train. She didn't venture into London often, but whenever she did, she always felt that she was already back home in Yorkshire the moment she stepped aboard the Grand Central at King's Cross. There was something very northern about those trains. The name for a start. 'That's grand!' was a phrase you often heard in God's Own County. All the staff had a Yorkshire accent and, once the trains had left London, they didn't stop again until they reached Donnie (Doncaster). Even ticket prices were designed to appeal to your average Yorkshireman (who was outdone, it was said, only by the Scots in terms of his reluctance to put his hand in his pocket. Emily thought this was a myth anyway; she'd met many generous Scottish and Yorkshire people in her time.) Anyway, it was the perfect route for a cash-strapped café owner from Essendale who'd already wasted far too much money on a useless patisserie course.

She walked along the length of the train, trying to find the quietest carriage. She needed to think. To work out what her options were now. The last thing she wanted when she was in this mood was loads of fellow passengers drinking wine from the buffet car and making lots of noise.

She finally decided on coach B. The seats were mostly arranged in twos but there were some groups of four with a table in between. She chose one of those, praying that no one would join her. Across the aisle, a pair of older women sat down, placing carrier bags from the National Gallery and the Tate on the table. She thought back to the art gallery/café where Peter had taken her. If only he hadn't. Then she wouldn't have wasted her time and money on this stupid trip to the capital. And Ludek wouldn't have witnessed that kiss.

She put her elbows on the table and her head in her hands, willing the minutes to pass and the train to depart. What was she meant to do now? Call it a day and admit that the café was a failure, do what she should have done all along and find herself another job? Peter was right: for the café to succeed, she needed to turn it into a destination but venturing into patisserie had been her one and only idea about how to do that. What else could she do? It was game over, unless she could come up with something else.

She looked at her watch. Two minutes and the train would be leaving and at least one bit of good luck: she had the table to herself. The carriage was filling up but was still reasonably quiet.

And then, a man came in. With two children. They rushed to her table and sat down opposite her. The man gave Emily an apologetic smile, shoved his two bags on the luggage rack above her head, then sat down beside her. Great. So much for her quiet journey.

Almost as soon as the train pulled out of King's Cross, the children were on their feet, taking off their coats which they shoved on the table, encroaching onto her half. The father stood up, put the coats onto the luggage rack and sat down again, flashing her a look which she took for an apology. He opened a book and began to read.

The little boy sitting opposite Emily swung his legs out, kicking her.

'Ouch,' she said. 'Do you mind?'

How was she supposed to concentrate on thinking up a new business plan with this going on?

'Sorry,' said the boy. The father didn't look up from his book.

Books! Could she have books? People could come in and borrow one to read whilst they drank their coffee. Or could she sell second-hand books perhaps?

She ferreted in her non-designer handbag, found a chewed Biro and an old receipt and wrote 'Books?' on the back of it.

'Can I have my bag please, Dad?' said the girl.

The father sighed, put his book down and reached up to the luggage rack. He put a small blue rucksack on the table. The girl rummaged around in the bag and took out a recorder. She began to blow.

The two older women stood up, picked up their bags and went off in search of another carriage. Emily wondered if she should join them – the noise was ear-piercing – but she stayed put and wrote down 'Live music?' on her scrap of paper.

The father said, 'Sorry about this.' He removed the recorder, placating the girl with a bag of crisps and handing a second one to her brother, who promptly opened it, scattering crisps everywhere. All over himself. The seats. The floor. And Emily.

'Sorry,' he said again.

Emily brushed herself down, wrote 'Children's parties?' on the receipt, then crossed it out. Too much hassle and mess.

'Can we play a game?' said the girl.

'We don't have a game,' the father said.

'There are games here,' said her brother, his mouth full of crisps. He gestured at the table in front of them.

Emily had been in such a world of her own – mulling over non-existent business ideas and astronomical amounts of money wasted on patisserie courses – that she hadn't noticed that the tables on the train were painted with chess boards and Snakes and Ladders. They looked pretty but weren't very practical unless you happened to be travelling with a chess set or dice and counters. Which Emily wasn't.

And nor, it seemed, was the children's father. 'We don't have any games pieces,' he said.

'Can I have my recorder back then?' said the girl.

'I'll play with them,' Emily said suddenly. Anything other than listening to a recorder for two and a half hours. Honestly, who'd be a music teacher? 'I can make some counters.'

She rummaged in her bag again, found three more receipts festering at the bottom and folded them up, fashioning three counters out of them.

'What about the dice?' said the boy.

Emily thought for a second. 'There might be an app. Hang on.'

There was an app. It took ages to download – the phone reception wasn't great and she couldn't make her ancient Android log on to the free WiFi – but eventually she managed to install it and they began to play.

Silence fell upon the carriage as the boy counted out five squares. He was utterly absorbed in the game, just as Emily herself always was at board games evenings. That is, when she wasn't distracted by the mere sight of Ludek.

It was her turn now. She 'rolled the dice' – in other words, clicked on the app – and scored a six, so had a second roll.

She moved her counter. The boy laughed as she went down a small snake and ended up almost back at the start.

His sister forged ahead by rolling a four and going up a ladder. They played on, rolling the dice via the app, moving their makeshift counters round the board, up ladders and down snakes. After three more games, the children asked if they could play on the other board.

'I don't think my origami skills are quite up to creating a chess set,' Emily said.

'Let's make up a game,' said the girl.

They were half-way through an elaborate game about dragons and witches, the rules of which she didn't fully understand, when the announcement came that the train was approaching Doncaster.

'Come on, kids,' said the father, closing his book and standing up. He pulled their coats and bags down from the luggage rack. 'Thank you so much for entertaining them. You're a life-saver.'

They waved goodbye as they left and Emily watched through the window as they emerged onto the platform and disappeared down a staircase into the bowels of the station. The carriage felt empty without them, but in the ensuing silence, Emily had her second eureka moment. She found the receipt she'd been writing on earlier and scribbled it down.

As the train journeyed on towards Pontefract, she jotted down more ideas. By the time the train pulled into Halifax, she had a complete plan. Admittedly, a plan written on the back of a receipt, but it was a plan nonetheless.

She was going to transform The Lancashire Hotpot from a very ordinary, back-street café into a board games paradise.

Chapter Twenty-One

Monday afternoon was quiet. Mr B and Marjory had been in for their elevenses. There'd been three tables occupied at lunchtime; Mrs Scott and Mrs Sinclair, of course – they came in at least three times a week now, their appetites for her all-day breakfasts seemingly unsatiable – but she didn't recognise the people on the other two tables. And then no one. Emily helped herself to a bowl of chicken soup and a roll and sat down at the table by the counter. Of course, it would be sod's law that the minute she sat down, she'd get a paying customer. But she didn't. Even sod's law didn't bring anyone to The Lancashire Hotpot that afternoon.

She finished her soup and decided she might as well shut up shop for the day and begin to put her plan into action.

She was going to get rid of those used-to-be-white tablecloths – she'd left a red sock in the washing machine – and paint her tables with different game boards like the ones on the train. As well as Snakes and Ladders and chess boards, she could do Scrabble and Cluedo. She could provide the pieces for each game in Kilner jars on the tables. She'd grabbed some sandpaper from Kate's DIY box that morning; Emily wasn't sure why her best friend had a DIY box, as the only screwdriver she'd ever seen in Kate's hand was of the cocktail rather than the B&Q variety. She turned the sign on the door to 'closed', whipped off one of the tablecloths and began to sand.

Sanding turned out to be even more arm-ache-inducing than beating choux pastry until it was glossy. It took ages to remove the stains and dark varnish from the first tabletop. Over two hours, in fact, but for a first-time attempt, she thought she'd made a reasonable job of it. The surface looked good and felt smooth enough to paint, but the entire café was now covered in dust. How could sanding one table produce so much? It was like when you knock over a mug containing just the tiniest amount of coffee and a huge pool of brown appears on the carpet. Emily knew this all too well. Messy person that she was, she had knocked over her fair share of mugs. And now she was covered with dust: in her hair; all over her clothes; and up her nostrils. She was sure she felt an itching sensation in her bra. At least she'd had the foresight to move all the food into the kitchen, but she should really have done the sanding outside.

She was wondering if this was such a good idea after all when she heard a knock. The door opened and Kate walked in. Damn. Emily had been hoping for ages that she'd come and see the café but hadn't wanted her best friend to see the place looking like this.

'Oh my god,' she said. 'What are you doing?'

'I'm sanding the tables.'

'Why?'

'To paint them. Instead of having tablecloths. I left a red sock in the washing machine and now my white tablecloths are all pink.'

'As are my white knickers.'

Emily grimaced. 'Sorry about that, Kate.'

'Seriously, Em. Buy new tablecloths. You can't do this. Look at the mess.'

She had a point. It was a ridiculous idea; Emily hadn't thought it through.

'I wish you'd warned me you were coming. I've been dying for you to see the café, but I didn't want you to see it looking like this.'

'Spur of the moment thing. I finished work a bit early but Freddie thought we should have a bit of a break from each other this evening – it has been pretty full on. And I got home thinking how lovely it would be to have a catch-up with you. Haven't seen you in days...'

'Weeks.'

'Okay, weeks. And then you weren't there and I guessed you'd be here. Is all this really because of the tablecloths going pink?'

'No, it's part of my grand plan.'

'Your grand plan?'

'To turn the café into a board game café.'

'A board game café? Why on earth...? Oh, don't tell me. Ludek. This is your grand plan to get with Ludek by proving to him how much you love his geeky hobby.'

'Too late for that. I've blown it with him.'

'Blown it with him? How?'

'It doesn't matter. It's over, Kate. Over before it even got started. The board game café idea is my grand plan to attract a few more customers through the door because if I don't, quite frankly, Kate, I can't keep going for much longer. And then I'll have lost everything. All my savings. My inheritance from Mum. And the dream I've had practically my whole life. And if I'm penniless I'll have to live at yours for ever, and, sooner or later, I'm bound to spill something on your cream carpets and then I'll lose your friendship too. And, by the way, board games aren't geeky. I love them.'

'Shit, Em. Are things that bad? I just assumed things would be going well. You checked the books before you bought this place, didn't you?'

'Of course I did. I'm not sure where I've gone wrong. Perhaps the last owner wasn't exactly honest with his figures. Or perhaps customers stopped coming here in the period it was closed, and never came back. Although it wasn't shut for that long. Whatever the reason, no one's interested in The Lancashire Hotpot so I'm planning to relaunch it as The Little Board Game Café.'

'Well, you know what you need for a relaunch, don't you? A marketing expert.'

'I can't afford you, Kate.'

'Don't be daft. I wouldn't charge you. Come home and let's make a plan.'

'I need to clear up. I'm opening tomorrow.'

'No you're not. You said it yourself. It's empty most of the time. Close the place. Draw a line under The Lancashire Hotpot right now. Set a date when you'll launch it as a board game café and get the transformation done behind closed doors. It'll be easier for a start. You can make as much mess as you want, if no one's coming in. And then generate publicity around re-opening.'

'I can't close it, Kate. Ludek's board games group meet here on a Friday. I'll change it little by little – buy some shelves and some games. Sand and paint the tables. Swap the Lancashire pictures for board games ones. Buy a new sign.'

'Nah, that's no good. A gradual change will go unnoticed. You *have* to close. The board games group can play in the pub again. Just for a week or two. Hang a sheet over the window so no one can see inside. Maybe even put a sign up saying, *Coming soon: Essendale's very own board game café*. That'd create a bit of intrigue.'

'Intrigue? Who with? Hardly anyone comes down this street.'

'Well, whatever. Decide how long you need to get everything ready, choose your date for the launch event – I'd suggest a Saturday – and I'll spend every spare minute doing your publicity. Well, every spare minute when I'm not at work or shagging Freddie's brains out.'

'That doesn't sound like a lot of spare minutes to me. If the last few weeks are anything to go by.'

'I'll create some time if you promise to close. Do we have an agreement?'

'Yes, okay. Thanks, Kate.'

'Come on, let's go home, open a bottle of wine and toast your new venture. And we can pop next door too; it'd be a lot easier with an electric sander and I think Gary's got one. I bet he'll let you borrow it.'

Emily should have known that Mr B wouldn't be deterred by a closed sign and one of Kate's old sheets hanging over the window. Next morning, she had almost finished her second table top – Kate was right; it was a lot easier with

Gary's electric sander – when the door opened and Mr B poked his head round.

'Sorry, Mr B, I'm closed today. As you can see, the place is rather a mess.'

He looked past her into the café. 'Make me a cappuccino. I'll be back in five minutes. Just popping back home for something.'

'But, Mr B, I'm not actually open,' she said, but it was too late. He had already gone.

She had started sanding the third table when he returned wearing bright-blue all-in-one overalls and carrying a cardboard box.

'We'll have these done in no time.' He opened the lid of the box and pulled out his own electric sander.

He had almost finished his first table when he suddenly said, 'What's all this in aid of?'

'Board games. I'm going to paint chess boards on the two small tables, Scrabble on two others. Cluedo on one and Snakes and Ladders on the other.'

'Good idea,' said Mr B, as if painting games boards on tables was something you saw every day.

'It's top secret. You can't tell anyone about this. My friend Kate says I have to create intrigue.'

'I see.'

'So where's Marjory today?'

'She's volunteering at the Oxfam shop. Mondays and Wednesdays. She wanted to get out a bit more. Meet some new people.'

'That's nice. I wish I could get Dad to do something like that. Get him out a bit more.'

Sanding was hard work. An hour or so later, Mr B stood up and stretched his back.

'Lunch?' he said hopefully.

Emily rustled them up some soup.

'What you haven't told me,' said Mr B, 'is why you're painting board games on the tables.'

'I'm transforming The Lancashire Hotpot into a board game café. There'll be the games on the table tops, but other games too. Though I'm not sure where I'll find the money to buy them.'

Mr B nodded. 'I could ask Marjory to keep an eye out for games in Oxfam.'

'That'd be great, thanks. Though I want some more unusual games too. The kind we play in the board games group. I don't suppose you'd find those in a charity shop. I'll try eBay.'

'And all this is in aid of impressing Ludek?' said Mr B. 'You must really like him.'

Why did everyone think this was about Ludek? Mr B had only seen them together once so Emily wasn't quite sure how he'd jumped to that conclusion.

'No, I'm doing this to attract more customers. And besides, I like board games.'

'Well, I hope it works. I worry about you going out of business.'

'You and me both.'

Mr B worked much more quickly than Emily did and, by five o'clock, all the table tops were sanded.

'Do you fancy some dinner?' she said. 'There's leftover soup from yesterday and I could make some scrambled eggs.'

'Yes, why not? But let's not eat here. It's too dusty. I'm only five minutes away. We can always come back afterwards and hoover up.'

She grabbed a box of eggs and filled a Tupperware with the previous day's soup of the day and they set off. On the doorstep, Mr B suggested dusting herself off a bit before stepping inside. 'We don't want to be cleaning my house as well as your café.'

Emily did as he'd asked, then heated the soup and scrambled the eggs in his tiny but immaculate kitchen. They ate at a small table in the corner. She was ravenous; all that sanding had really worked up an appetite. After they'd eaten, they both agreed that they felt too tired to clean up the café that night so she said goodbye to Mr B and set off for home.

The following day, Mr B was waiting outside the café when Emily arrived at five past nine. He was wearing his overalls again, and carrying a Sainsbury's bag.

They started work immediately, sanding the table legs this time. They were much more fiddly than the tops.

At around eleven, Mr B downed tools and said, 'It's cappuccino o'clock, Emily.'

She took the hint and fired up the machine. They sat down at one of the newly sanded tables and Mr B opened his bag. Instead of his usual Polish newspaper, he produced a Scrabble box.

'We can't play now,' Emily said. 'There's too much to do.'

'For reference purposes only.' He opened the lid and

unfolded the board. 'We need to work out what colours of paint to buy for our project.'

Since when had this become 'our' project? Emily didn't know, but she rather liked it. When she'd first bought the café, she'd felt so alone every day, standing behind the counter wishing someone would come in. And now Mr B was helping with the tables and Kate had promised to do the publicity. She felt as if she had a little team of people behind her, rooting for her, and it was a great feeling. If only Ludek were part of that team.

Together, Mr B and Emily figured out that they'd need two shades of green, two shades of blue, salmon pink and dark orange to recreate the Scrabble board on the table tops. Chess would obviously be easier: they'd need black and white. With the greens from the Scrabble and some sunshine yellow, they could make a Cluedo board. Mr B reckoned that they wouldn't need any extra colours for Snakes and Ladders – they could make do with what they'd got. They'd also need some paler shades, he suggested, as the base colours of the tables, and plenty of varnish to seal the end results and ensure a good finish.

They continued sanding the table legs until Emily's stomach told her it was lunchtime.

'There's still some soup,' she said to Mr B. 'Or I could make us scrambled eggs again?'

'Thank you, Emily, but I need to pop out for an hour or two. I'll see you a little later.'

It was after three when Mr B put in his second appearance of the day and suggested she made a pot of tea.

He had a shed, it turned out, and his two neighbours also had sheds. And in those sheds were lots of tins of leftover paint. Between them, he reckoned, they had most of the colours Emily needed. She would just have to buy a can or two of the base colour and the varnish.

'Of course, we'll have to sand the chairs before we start any painting,' said Mr B.

'The chairs?'

'The chairs have to match the tables, do they not? And you could probably do with re-covering the seat pads. They're very scruffy.'

This was going to take days.

Emily came home early on Wednesday. Who'd have thought that sanding could be so tiring?

She hadn't had a single text from Ludek since he'd seen her with Peter, but she needed to tell him that the board games group couldn't meet at the café for the next two Fridays at least.

She drafted a message with words to that effect and explained that The Lancashire Hotpot was becoming a board game café, hoping he'd be impressed. She told him there'd be a launch event and said she'd keep tickets for him and the members of the games group. She ended the text with, *Hope you'll all come*, then added two kisses then deleted them again. She'd just pressed Send when Kate appeared.

'No Freddie tonight?'

'I told him I'm busy.'

'Why? What are you up to?'

'Making a plan with you. We need to decide when the launch party's going to be.'

'Event,' Emily said. 'Rather than party. Calling it a party makes it sound like there'd be alcohol and I don't have an alcohol licence.'

'If you gave it away rather than selling it, you wouldn't need a licence.'

'I can't afford to.'

'Or do bring your own bottle?'

'I'll just do soft drinks. Ludek's board games group all prefer to keep a clear head when they're playing games. That's why they like playing in the café rather than the pub.'

'Ludek's board games group? They're coming?'

'Obviously.'

'But the launch is about attracting attention. Drawing new customers in. The board games group come to the café anyway.'

'Oh. I hadn't thought of that.'

'You've got room for how many?'

'Twenty people. Twenty-four at a push.'

'You need prominent people from the community, Em. The chair of the parish council. The local journalist. Prominent business people. Like Peter.'

'Peter?'

'He's the biggest business owner around here.'

Emily sighed. 'And he was supportive. In the end. Taking me to that art gallery place to give me some inspiration. I suppose I'll have to invite him. But with him and all the board gamers, and Dad – I'm really hoping I can lure him out of Thornholme – and you obviously... Well, there won't be room for many more people. I can't not invite my regular customers either.'

Kate shook her head.

'But there aren't many of them,' Emily said quickly. 'Just Marjory and Mr B and Mrs Scott and Mrs Sinclair.'

'We'll talk about this later. What I need from you now is a date. When do you think you can be ready? What do you still need to do?'

'Buy the games.'

'You've not ordered them yet?' Kate shook her head. 'Honestly, Em. You can't open a board game café without games.'

'I've been too busy.'

'Get them ordered. Do you think you could be ready by a week on Saturday?'

'A week on Saturday? That seems soon...'

'What else is left to do?'

'Apart from the board games? Shelves to put them on. A bit more painting. New pictures for the walls. A sign with the new name.'

Kate was jotting everything down. 'Let's go for a week on Saturday. You should prioritise ordering the games, and then finish the painting. I'll get on with the publicity. Invite a couple of prominent people. It's gonna be great, Em. You'll see.'

Once the sanding was finished, Emily and Mr B painted a base coat on the tables and chairs in a lovely shade of slate blue. They managed to get them all done in a day.

Painting the game boards on the table tops was a different matter. It was intricate work, requiring a level of detail and steady hand that she hadn't envisaged when she'd first come up with the idea, sitting on that Grand Central train. The chess boards were easy, but Snakes and Ladders, Cluedo and Scrabble were far more difficult. Mr B had made templates to scale using pictures from the internet and they painstakingly began transferring the designs onto the first two tables.

'It's going to take hours,' Emily said.

'Perhaps we could paint some of the table tops and leave the others plain.'

'But what if loads of people want to play the games? I don't want people fighting over where they sit.'

Mr B looked sad. 'Emily, I've wanted to tell you this since you first arrived. I've been coming here for years, and I've never seen more than three tables occupied at any one time.'

'But...the café was popular, wasn't it? I mean, I checked the books before I bought it.'

'I wouldn't like to accuse Mr Panagi of fiddling the books but...well, there were never many people here when I visited. Maybe at other times, but I doubt it.'

Had she been tricked into buying what basically amounted to a failing business? Perhaps so, but it wasn't going to be a failing business anymore. She was even more determined to turn things around.

Chapter Twenty-Two

These days, when Emily walked through Essendale, she could sometimes put names to faces. Not many, admittedly. Mr B could often be seen perusing the books in Oxfam's window or popping into the Red Lion for a quick half. She'd meet Mrs Scott and Mrs Sinclair, trundling up and down the high street with their trolleys. Of course, she didn't know which name belonged to which woman, but it was a start.

On Friday, she walked through the town, whistling to herself despite her exhaustion, breaking off her little tune to say good morning to a handful of people. Even one of the angry white geese taking a peck at her knees as she walked back couldn't dent her mood. The Little Board Game Café was almost ready for its launch.

Or should that be *her* launch? 'Its' sounded a bit impersonal. Ships were always referred to as 'she'. Why not cafés? Emily was very attached to her little café and was beginning to feel that it almost had a personality. Nico wouldn't recognise the place.

The Lancashire photos were now stacked up in her room at Kate's. She was planning to take them home for Dad; as a Yorkshireman, he'd be sure to appreciate them. In their place in the café hung huge canvases that Emily had had printed using photos from Google images: close-ups of meeples, dice, Scrabble tiles too and chess pieces; and an artistic shot of a Monopoly board.

She couldn't afford to hire a sign-writer as the canvases had cost more than expected and she'd splashed out on some salt and pepper pots in the shape of meeples – a bit of an unnecessary indulgence but they were cute – so, for the time being, she had ordered a stick-on one for the front window saying *The Little Board Game Café* with a pair of dice at each end.

Thanks to Kate's printer, Emily had new menus and had put posters up all over Essendale and Hebbleswick, advertising the launch event.

And thanks to Kate herself, there would be an article in the local paper the following week.

There was one thing that Emily still needed to do. The most important thing of all: buy the board games.

And that was where she hit a problem. She had hoped to buy twenty or thirty games to stock the shelves she'd bought for the café, but she hadn't realised how much they'd cost. At these prices, she could only stretch to one Ticket to Ride, one Settlers of Catan and one Carcassonne, and she bought them all second-hand. She had enough money left to buy a spare stable for Agricola, but not Agricola itself.

'Don't know what to do,' she said to Mr B on Friday morning. 'I can hardly run a board game café without board games.'

*

On Monday morning, she was beginning to worry about Mr B. It was twenty-five past eleven and he hadn't arrived; in all the weeks she'd been running the café, he'd never failed to appear by ten past at the very latest. Even when the café wasn't open.

The only visitor all morning was a dark-haired man with a large camera who told her he was from the *Gazette* and that, 'Someone called Kate suggested I dropped by. Said you're re-launching this place as a board game café.'

Emily struck various poses behind the counter with a teapot; he had wanted a shot of her standing beside a huge stack of board games boxes but that was out of the question since she didn't actually have any.

It was almost twelve o'clock by the time he left. Mr B and Marjory arrived a few minutes later, each balancing a stack of boxes.

Emily was relieved to see them. 'I was about to send out the search party.'

'I've been round all the charity shops in Halifax,' said Mr B, 'and found you these.' He placed his load down on one of the tables: three sets of Scrabble, two Cluedo, two boxes of draughts, a chess set, one Can't Stop! and a plain cardboard box.

'Can't Stop!' Emily said. 'That's the first game I ever played with Ludek's board games group.'

'And I went through the back room at Oxfam,' said Marjory, placing one Monopoly, a Trivial Pursuit and three sets of Buckaroo! beside Mr B's boxes.

'Wow, thank you. How much do I owe you?'

'There's no need. It's the least I can do. All those times when you were living upstairs and you popped down with cakes and stayed for a natter, even when you were busy. And I wouldn't have met this fella if it weren't for your café.' She gave Mr B's hand a squeeze.

Emily was surprised by this gesture, but, judging from Mr B's contented expression, he wasn't. Were they…? They couldn't be, could they?

She couldn't very well ask, 'Are you two an item?' so instead she said simply, 'That's fantastic, thank you. The Chorley cakes are on the house.'

'There's more,' said Mr B. He opened the cardboard box and took out six jam jars, full of games pieces with a printed label on each: Cluedo; Chess; Scrabble; and Snakes and Ladders. 'One for each of our painted tabletops.'

'Genius,' Emily said. 'Thanks, Mr B.'

'All you need now are the players,' said Marjory. 'And I gather from Mr B that there's one player in particular who you're rather keen to see coming through that door.'

Emily felt her cheeks reddening. 'I can't think who you mean.'

'He's going to be impressed,' said Mr B, 'when he sees your new board games.'

She wasn't so sure. Grateful though she was to Marjory and Mr B, this motley collection of second-hand copies of Buckaroo! and jam jars full of Scrabble pieces wasn't going to impress Ludek *or* entice serious gamers into the café. Or even ordinary families, for that matter. Who'd go to a board game café and spend their hard-earned cash if the games were the very same ones they had stashed in the back of their own cupboards? And even when her eBay orders arrived, well, three games weren't going to make much difference were they? She needed a lot more. An awful lot more.

And she needed them fast. The launch event was only a few days away.

She was suddenly aware that Mr B and Marjory were staring at her, waiting for an answer.

'Yeah, he will be impressed,' she said, 'although…'

'Although?' said Mr B.

'Well, I don't want to seem ungrateful. Because I *am* grateful. I appreciate all the trouble you've both gone to, but I need more games. I mean, this is a board game café.'

'Save the Children in Halifax had another Buckaroo!,' said Mr B. 'But I thought three would be enough.'

'No, I mean more variety. Ludek and his friends, they play games like…' She pictured Ludek's boxes, stacked high on his lounge floor. '…Azul, Codenames, Wingspan.'

'Never heard of them,' said Marjory. 'Where could you buy those?'

'That's the problem. I can't buy them. They're too expensive. I bought three second-hand off eBay, but I've already spent almost all of the money my mum left me, and I've got to keep some money back because… Well, I've got to live off something and I get so few customers in the café that I can barely pay myself anything, let alone a living wage.'

'I was afraid that was the case,' said Mr B, patting her arm.

'It's catch twenty-two. I need the board game café idea to take off, but I can't afford the board games to make it work.'

'Then borrow them,' said Marjory, 'from your friend Ludek.'

'We aren't really speaking at the moment. Peter – my ex – well, he was just dropping me off, but he leaned over and kissed me, and Ludek saw.'

'Ah,' said Mr B. 'That's very disappointing.'

'Anyway, he's very precious about his games. I'm not sure he'd want to lend them.'

'That's silly,' said Marjory. 'Like people who never use their best china for fear of breaking it.'

'Or people who have a heart but are afraid to love,' said Mr B.

Marjory was giggling at his words. Blushing slightly too. They were definitely more than just friends, Emily thought. And good for them. Marjory had been lonely for far too long.

Marjory's eyes lit up suddenly. 'I have a plan. This is a fantastic idea, if I do say so myself. We can kill two birds with one stone. The best way to a man's heart is through his stomach. Call me old-fashioned, but it worked on my Cecil, God rest his soul. You invite Ludek over for the evening and cook food like his mother would make. And he'll be so impressed with your cooking, that not only will he forgive you for kissing Peter…'

'I didn't kiss Peter. He kissed me,' Emily said.

'…but he'll offer to lend you his board games and fall in love with you as well.'

'That's a wonderful idea,' said Mr B.

Emily sighed. 'There's one snag there, Marjory. Ludek's mother is Polish. And I don't know the first thing about Polish food.'

'No, but I do,' said Mr B. 'I make the best pierogi in the Pennines.'

On Tuesday evening, Mr B's tiny kitchen became her classroom as he taught her the intricacies of Polish cooking, which involved rather a lot of dough. There was a sweet dough with yeast for the pączki, a type of donut, and a smooth dough of flour, eggs and water for the dumpling-like pierogi.

They rolled out the dough for the pierogi, then he showed her how to stretch it around the filling.

'Press the edges tightly together so none escapes during cooking,' he said.

'Okay.' It was harder than it looked.

'I think you mean, "Oui, chef",' he said.

'What?'

'On *MasterChef*, the contestants always say, "Oui, chef" to the head chefs.'

Emily threw a tea towel at him.

The pierogi were fiddly and time-consuming, but she grew faster the more she practised. Normally they'd be boiled, but Mr B said that his mother and grandmother had always preferred to fry them. They were tastier that way apparently, so she decided that was what she would do.

They made various fillings, testing them all out on Marjory – mushrooms and sauerkraut, sundried tomatoes with lentils – but settled on the traditional potato and cheese filling. That was the main course sorted.

For dessert, along with the pączki, she was making makowiec which was a poppy seed roll.

'Two desserts?' she said. 'Isn't that a bit much?'

'You can give him the leftovers to take home,' said Mr B.

'And save a few for us as well,' said Marjory.

With his eyes bright with excitement, Mr B opened the kitchen drawer and handed Emily a dog-eared piece of yellowing paper covered in spidery handwriting. Of course, it was all in Polish so even if she had been able to decipher the letters, she wouldn't have understood a word.

'My late wife Magda's makowiec recipe,' he said.

Making the makowiec meant making yet another dough, a rich buttery dough this time. Under Mr B's watchful eye, Emily covered it with a mixture of poppy seeds, chopped fruit, nuts and honey, before rolling it up like a roulade.

'Most people just fill it with poppy seeds,' Mr B told her, 'but I like this recipe better, and hopefully Ludek will too.'

She'd mastered the dishes – well, sort of – but there was still one part of Marjory's masterplan that she hadn't put into action: she hadn't actually invited Ludek to dinner.

She'd barely heard from him since she and Peter had returned from their trip to the farm shop. *No probs*, was all he'd replied when she'd texted to say that the board games group couldn't meet at The Lancashire Hotpot for two weeks. And then, when she'd gone to the board games group to tell everyone about her plans for the café and invite them all to the launch event, Ludek hadn't been there. 'I think he's working late,' was all Alan had said.

When Emily arrived home from Mr B's house, she texted him. *Haven't seen you in ages. Fancy dinner at mine tomorrow evening?*

His reply came quickly. *Sure, that'd be good. About seven?*

Fingers crossed, the plan was going to work.

She imagined how the evening would go. She'd have the desserts prepared, and the pierogi for the main course would need frying when Ludek arrived. She'd thank Ludek for the Masala game, and he'd say how he'd been embarrassed to intrude upon her and Peter and she would say, 'There is no me and Peter. He kissed me, but he shouldn't have. Peter and I are over, Ludek.' And then she'd fry the pierogi and he'd say how much it reminded him of his mother's cooking and how much he missed her. At that point, Emily would take his hand and say maybe they could visit Poland together one day. Then she'd serve the pączki and makowiec, and he'd say they were delicious, even more than the pierogi, but he wouldn't fall in love with her – not just yet; even in her daydreams Emily tried to be a realist – and then she'd explain about having no games for the café's launch and he'd say she could borrow his games.

'Keep them for as long as you like,' she imagined him saying. 'After all, they're meant to be played.'

And perhaps, before he left, they'd share their first kiss. Just a small one. A soft kiss. The kind of gentle, teasing kiss that leaves you longing for more.

Only it didn't quite work out like that.

Chapter Twenty-Three

Books by Emily's Kate's spare bedside: *A Guide to Modern Polish Cuisine*; *Authentic Recipes from Poland*; and *Perfect Pierogi*.

Emily took out every garment from her wardrobe, but none of them looked quite right. Her favourite dungaree pinafore – the bright-red one – seemed a bit garish somehow and the smartest one – the navy – seemed dull. She could wear jeans, but all of her jeans were tight and wearing tight clothes when she was about to eat a carb-laden meal didn't seem like a wise move.

She took out every garment from Kate's wardrobe too. Pointless really as she knew they were all too small, and she didn't want to tear another seam. Kate was being incredibly kind and tolerant letting her stay there rent-free for so long whilst she established the café; she didn't want to test her friend's patience by borrowing – and ruining – her clothes.

She settled on the jeans in the end, with a long t-shirt so that she could discreetly unfasten the top button should she need to after they'd eaten.

Make-up. Should she wear make-up?

She never usually wore much. She didn't have Kate's skill

at applying it for a start, so always claimed she preferred the natural look. But peering in the mirror, she realised she did look a little bit pasty and were those bags under her eyes? The stress and hard work of running her own business was definitely taking its toll on her appearance. Emily found her make-up bag and rummaged around, wondering what to use. The foundation was dried up, the mascara was lumpy and the green eye-shadow was just that little bit too green, Emily decided, if she wanted to keep things subtle. She sighed and wandered back into Kate's room.

Kate had a whole drawer full of cosmetics, so many that Emily didn't know where to start. She picked out a foundation and rubbed a bit on her cheeks with her fingertips, but Kate's complexion was darker than Emily's and she just looked ridiculous. As if she'd a bad fake tan. Emily borrowed some of Kate's make-up remover and scrubbed it off.

Au naturel. That was the look she'd go for. It wasn't as if this was a blind date. He'd already seen her at her worst, sprawled on the pavement outside Nico's. Then sitting in his surgery holding her hand in the air like a muppet. Emily grimaced. Yet still he'd seemed to like her. Or at least, he had. Till he'd seen her with Peter.

She looked at her watch. She needed to get on with the food. She'd left the dough for the pączki and the makowiec to rise a couple of hours earlier, but she needed to get on with making the dough and the filling for the pierogi.

With Mr B's help, making the three items hadn't seemed that difficult. A little time-consuming, perhaps, but Emily was confident she had enough time to get everything done. Without Mr B's help, it was a different matter.

The dough for the desserts hadn't risen. Emily couldn't fathom why; she was sure the yeast had been in date. Maybe the house wasn't quite warm enough. There wasn't time to start again; she'd just have to raid Kate's freezer for some ice-cream if Ludek had room for a pudding.

She had more success with the dough for the pierogi. She rolled it out, cut it into circles and added a generous teaspoon of filling to each. Then she folded the circles over and pinched the edges to seal the filling inside. Mr B had made this look easy, but it was incredibly fiddly and Emily was still finishing the last few when the doorbell rang.

Ludek was standing on the doorstep, looking even more beautiful than he usually looked; his hair curlier and his mouth more smiley. He was wearing beige chinos and a crisp white shirt. Emily looked down at her jeans, wishing she'd opted for a pinafore, and saw to her horror that her blue t-shirt was covered in flour. She must have inadvertently wiped her hands on it when she was cooking. Why hadn't she worn an apron? She always wore an apron in the café.

Ludek followed her gaze. 'What are you cooking?'

'It's a surprise.'

Emily led him through the hall and into the lounge.

'Wow, this is tidy,' he said.

'I do my best.'

So far, Emily was managing to be a pretty good house-guest, (almost) living up to Kate's high standards of neatness: the midnight-blue cushions in neat lines on the two pale-grey sofas; not a single dirty coffee cup on a small oak coffee table; nor a book out of place on the bookshelves, all aspirational titles arranged – by Kate – according to colour.

Emily knew for a fact that Kate kept her self-help, find-a-man books under her bed out of sight of any guests.

She went into the kitchen, poured them both a glass of Pinot Grigio and popped the pierogi into the frying pan.

When she returned to the lounge, Ludek was sitting on the sofa. She handed him the wine and he patted the seat beside him, indicating for her to sit down. Emily hesitated. She really ought to go back to the cooking, but the pull to be close to him was so strong. She sat down. Close but not too close. Close enough that her heart started to pound but not so close that their thighs were touching. She could imagine Kate saying, 'Don't look too keen. Be encouraging. Not desperate.'

'Cheers,' said Ludek, and chinked his glass against hers, just a little too eagerly.

A little wine slopped onto the pale-grey velvet.

'I'm so sorry,' he said.

'My fault,' she said, jumping up. 'I filled them too full.'

She found a tissue and began to dab at the fabric. 'I don't think it'll show,' she said. 'No harm done.'

She was about to go back to check on the cooking when Ludek said, 'I'm sorry about not replying to your texts. I just…well, to be honest, I felt a bit awkward. Intruding on you and…and then making you that game. I felt silly.'

'The game is brilliant. I love it. We should play it. And you shouldn't feel awkward…'

She was about to say that he hadn't been intruding, that Peter had just been helping with her business, when he said, 'Is something burning?'

Emily hared back into the kitchen to find one side of the pierogi was completely black. The pan was black as well.

Probably ruined. She never had got round to putting the batteries back in the smoke alarm.

She scraped the charred remains of the pierogi into the bin. She was a terrible house-mate – wine on the sofa and now a ruined pan. She filled the burnt pan with water, leaving it to soak on the off-chance she could rescue it; if not, she'd buy Kate another. Not that Kate ever cooked. She probably wouldn't miss it.

The plan to win Ludek's heart by cooking like his mother clearly wasn't going to work, but she could still rescue the evening and ask him about borrowing his board games.

'I think we might need to order a curry,' she said, going back into the lounge.

She opened some windows, to get rid of the smoke from the kitchen whilst Ludek phoned the order through to the Bengal Spice in Hebbleswick.

'It'll be twenty minutes.' Ludek tucked his phone back into his jeans pocket.

'Shall we play Masala! whilst we wait?' Emily said.

'Yeah, why not?'

As they made up the different curry recipes in the game, she marvelled once again at how much care and attention he'd lavished on the home-made ingredient cards; the hours it must have taken to find each picture online, print and laminate them and trim them all to the exact same size. He'd even rounded each one so there were no sharp corners.

They'd just finished the game when the doorbell rang. Emily sprang to her feet. 'That'll be the curry.'

When she went back into the lounge, the brown paper bag in her hand, Ludek was packing the game away, organising all the cards into separate piles and slipping each one into a small plastic bag as carefully as he would a shop-bought game.

'Thank you for making the game for me,' she said. 'It's really beautiful.'

'I enjoyed doing it. I used to make a lot of games when I was a kid.'

She recalled what he'd said, about how his family hadn't had much money, and suddenly she knew that she couldn't ask to borrow his games. Not for the launch party where there'd be food and drinks and people they didn't know. Something might get damaged.

Both her missions had failed; she hadn't won his heart with her Polish cuisine and she still had no board games for the launch.

Next morning, Emily was surprised to find Kate in the kitchen. She'd spent the night at Freddie's yet again, but had come home before work in search of a keto breakfast – yet more eggs - and clean clothes. The washing machine was already churning away.

'Hey, Kate. How's things? How's it going with Freddie?'

'He's great. Although we've still not had the conversation about being exclusive – but I'm hoping he likes me as much as I like him. How are things going with Ludek?'

'Well, I couldn't afford enough games for the café launch—'

'The café? Forget the café for a minute. Tell me about Ludek!'

'Give me a chance, Kate. So I decided to invite him round for dinner, sweeten him up a bit then ask him if I could borrow a few of his games. I burnt the pierogi so we had to have a curry.'

'Yes, I saw the pan in the bin.'

'I soaked it but it still wouldn't clean up. I'll buy you another.'

'Forget it, Em. Go on. How did it go once you'd finished burning down my kitchen?'

'Badly. I didn't ask him about borrowing the games. And that was one of the reasons I'd invited him in the first place. But those games are his pride and joy. He wouldn't want any of them in a café where there'd be members of the public. I'm not sure what I'm going to do about having enough games for—'

'Never mind the games. What about him? Did he snog you?'

'There was a moment when I thought he was going to, but then he didn't. He just left.'

Kate scratched at an unidentified splodge of something on the kitchen table. Emily clearly hadn't cleaned up as well as she'd thought she had.

'Perhaps you need to give him a bit more encouragement,' said Kate, 'without being too obvious. He's probably uncertain; you're only just out of a long-term relationship, so he probably doesn't want to rush you. Give him a bit more time.'

'You're right. And I didn't get a chance to tell him that Peter and me are definitely over.'

'You didn't explain about the kiss?'

'I was about to and then...' - no need to tell her about the wine being spilled on the sofa – '...Anyway, I should be focusing on the launch event. Not long to go now.'

Kate held up crossed fingers. 'Have you much left to do? Apart from finding the board games. You've finished the new décor? Sorted the food and drink?'

Bollocks. The food and drink.

She'd been so focused on the 'board game' part of starting her own board game café that the 'café' part had completely slipped her mind. No need to tell Kate that either.

'Yeah,' she said. 'All sorted. But I'm gutted because Dad says he won't come. I've sent him three texts – three! – but still he's saying no. I mean, I know he never leaves Thornholme but I was hoping that this would be the thing that finally persuaded him. And then if he came to this, he might be tempted to get out and about a bit more. It's been sixteen years since Mum died. And I still miss her too, but... Well, he's not coming and that's that. And it hurts, Kate, it really does. This event is important to me. I've ploughed everything into it. And I wanted all the people who matter to me to be there: Dad, Mr B, Marjory, Ludek. And you, of course.'

'Ah.' Kate bit her lip and frowned. 'The thing is, Em—'

'Oh, no. Don't tell me you're not coming either?'

'It's Freddie's brother's birthday and—'

'Shit, Kate. I can't do it without you.'

'You can. But if you really want me to, I'll tell Freddie I can't make it.'

Emily sighed. She couldn't do that to Kate. Not when she knew how important this new relationship was for her. Whilst Emily had always dreamed of running a café, Kate had dreamed of a husband and children.

'Don't be silly. You can't miss his brother's birthday. Being invited to meet the family is a biggy. The next step in the relationship. He must be serious about you if he's invited you to that.'

Kate held up crossed fingers again. 'Hope so. You sure you don't mind?'

'You let me stay in your house, don't charge me rent, advise on marketing, don't go apeshit when I ruin your frying pan. You do so much for me, Kate. I'd love for you to be at the launch. Of course I would. But you can't come and that's okay.'

Kate stretched across the table and put her hand over Emily's. 'Thank you. I really think that Freddie could be The One. I know I've said that before. But I really mean it this time.'

'I hope he is, Kate.'

'You'll have to take some photos to show me. Speaking of which, have you seen the paper?' Kate reached into her bag and pulled out a copy of the *Essendale Gazette*. And there, on the front, was a picture of Emily standing behind the counter brandishing a teapot. 'And I've made you a playlist.'

'A playlist?'

Kate picked up her phone and clicked a couple of times. 'There. I've shared a Spotify playlist with you – songs for the launch. You can borrow my Bluetooth speakers. Don't break them. And there's something else. Won't be a minute.'

She stood up, left the room for a few moments and returned with a parcel wrapped in brown paper which she plonked on the table. 'Go ahead.'

Tentatively, Emily tore off the Sellotape. Inside was a pinafore dress, only fifties style with a full skirt and a cinched-in waist, not the dungaree type that she usually wore. She stood up and held it against her. It appeared to be exactly the right size – how had Kate managed that? – but the best thing was that the fabric it was made from was printed to look like a Scrabble board.

'Thank you so, so much.' Emily put the dress down on the table and went to embrace her friend.

'Yeah, well.' Kate batted her away. 'I was sick of you rooting in my wardrobe, trying on my dresses and ripping the seams.'

'Oh. I'd forgotten about that. Sorry. But it was just the one seam.'

'Am I forgiven for not being able to be there?'

'Of course you're forgiven. And even without the front page, the playlist and the dress, you'd be forgiven. I know how important Freddie is to you, Kate. I get it. I do. I'll cross my fingers for you on Saturday night. And you cross yours for me.'

Chapter Twenty-Four

Books by Emily's Kate's spare bedside: *Men Are from
Mars, Women Are from Venus; How to Not Die Alone*
(cheerful title – and Emily thought *she* was a pessimist);
The Program. All left there by Kate and left unopened
by Emily. That last book was, according to Kate, the
bible when it came to dating.

As Emily opened the door to the café, the reality struck.
It was the day before the big launch event for her
board game café and she had hardly any board games and
she hadn't planned the food.

No board games + no food = no board game café.

'You look glum,' said Mr B, when he and Marjory came
in.

Marjory put her arm around her. 'What's up, Em?'

'Where do I start? Kate can't come tomorrow. Dad *won't*
come. I've not enough board games – the eBay orders
haven't arrived yet so I mightn't even have those – and I'd
completely forgotten that I'd need to serve food and drinks.
I run a café and I forget about food and drinks. I'm going
to cancel.'

Mr B slammed his hand down on the Cluedo table. 'Cancel? After all this work?'

The three of them looked around café. At the huge board games canvases adorning the walls. At the shelves laden with Scrabble, Monopoly and Trivial Pursuit. At the three sets of Buckaroo!.

'We can help with the food,' said Mr B at the same time as Marjory said, 'I thought Ludek was lending you the games.'

'I didn't ask him. Didn't want to put him in an awkward position. He loves those games – you should see how well he looks after them.'

'But if he loves you—'

'He doesn't love me, Marjory. He barely knows me. We fancy each other, that's all.'

'Did he like the pierogi?' said Mr B.

'I burnt the pierogi. He never even saw them. And I didn't manage to make any of the desserts. We got a take-away instead.'

'I see,' said Mr B. He had the same disappointed look on his face that Emily's dad used to have after every parents' evening. He sighed. He looked at Marjory. He looked at the board games tables that they'd worked so hard to paint. 'We can't abandon things now,' he said decisively. 'We'll go ahead with the games that we've got.'

Emily hadn't realised this was his decision to make.

'Everyone will think it's a board game café with a crappy selection of games. And then no one will come back. I'll end up with even less customers before.'

'I'll ring my sister in Leeds,' said Marjory. 'See if she can't find a few more unusual games in the charity shops there.'

'Great idea,' said Mr B.

'And we can make the food ourselves. Stan and I will help.'

'We will, and I have the best idea,' said Mr B, his face brightening a little. 'Since Ludek didn't get to taste your Polish food on Wednesday evening, we'll serve it tomorrow instead. Pierogi, pączki and makowiec. Perfect finger food.'

'Won't that seem a bit weird? I'm launching a board game café, not a Polish café.'

Mr B's face fell again.

'Perhaps…' Emily didn't want to disappoint him so racked her brains for reasons why it might be a good idea to serve Polish snacks when launching a board game café. 'Perhaps people will be more likely to remember the evening if the food is a bit unusual.'

'Exactly,' said Marjory. 'It's a genius idea, Stan.'

'And,' said Mr B. 'I could do a slideshow in the coffee break. Polish wildlife. I haven't had my slides out in years. I hope my projector still works.'

Pierogi and pączki. Beavers and board games. An odd combination if ever there was one.

Emily was about to say that there wouldn't actually be a coffee break – she would welcome everyone, serve drinks and snacks and then everyone would play games till they went home – when Marjory elbowed her in the ribs.

'That's a great idea, isn't it, Em?'

Emily looked at Mr B's hopeful face. She couldn't disappoint him. He was her most loyal customer. Some days, her only customer. And he'd painted all those tables, traipsed round charity shops in search of games, supplied her with home-made chicken noodle soup and heaps of encouragement. The least she could do was let him have his slideshow.

'Brilliant idea,' Emily said. 'Thanks, Mr B. I think we'd better start cooking.'

Making a few pierogi had been tricky enough, but assembling a hundred of them – it took hours. Even with three pairs of hands and even though Emily had decided to keep things simple and stick to one filling.

At half past twelve, they were interrupted by a knock at the door.

'I'll go,' Emily said.

She washed the flour off her hands. A woman was waiting outside. She was probably early forties, Emily would guess – and well-groomed with smart jeans, newly coiffured hair and manicured nails.

'Oh hello,' she said as she tried to peer past Emily into the café. Perhaps Kate had been right and the sheet across the window had created a bit of intrigue. 'I wondered if there were any tickets left for tomorrow evening. My husband and I would love to come along.'

The café was small: only twenty-four seats. By the time she'd allocated places for Mr B, Marjory, Ludek and his friends from the board games group, there'd been only a handful left, and, to Emily's surprise and delight, they'd been bagged very quickly after the article had appeared in the paper.

She shook her head. 'None, I'm afraid. Sorry.'

'Oh, that's a shame. My mother's offered to babysit our boy George and well... Well, that's quite a rare event, to be honest, so we wanted to make the most of it. Do something a bit different.'

'Your boy George?' Emily had a vision of a small child with braided hair, a black hat and a lot of eye make-up singing *Karma Chameleon* over and over to his increasingly fed-up granny.

'Don't worry. We should have booked sooner.'

The woman turned away. It seemed a shame. After all, Granny didn't often offer to babysit and Emily still had the two tickets she'd put aside for Kate and Dad, didn't she? She reached into her jeans pocket. Yes, there they were. 'Hang on,' she said. 'I've got these two, but they're a bit tatty. You're welcome to them.'

'Wonderful, thank you,' George's mother beamed. 'See you tomorrow.'

The pączki and makowiec were ready. The pierogi sat waiting to be fried; they were all slightly different shapes and sizes, leaving her with even greater admiration for those contestants on *The Great British Bake Off* who managed to produce batches of cakes and pies that looked identical. She wouldn't be entering that any time soon.

The sheet had been removed from the window, Emily had slipped into the Scrabble pinafore and placed a bouquet of helium balloons – another gift from Kate – outside the door. The stage was set.

She opened up at five to seven to find a young couple already waiting outside. Her mouth was dry with excitement

– or nerves? – as she welcomed them, directed them to Marjory who was in charge of drinks, and pressed 'play' on Kate's playlist, praying her phone would connect to the Bluetooth speakers. The unmistakable tones of Abba's 'The Name of the Game' filled the café. Emily laughed. Even in her absence, Kate was managing to make her presence felt. What else was on that playlist?

Ariane Grande's 'Monopoly' began to play as more people arrived. An older couple, friends of Mr B, Emily guessed, seemed confused when they saw the board games shelves and asked Emily if they were in the right place for the Polish evening.

Then Peter appeared, his mother on his arm. He looked Emily's Scrabble dress up and down. 'You look good, Em. That dress – well, it's such a good fit.'

Emily felt suddenly self-conscious. If only Kate hadn't got the sizing quite so spot on; it showed off her figure perhaps a little too much.

Peter still couldn't keep his eyes off the dress and Emily wished she hadn't felt obliged to invite him. 'Rather unusual fabric,' he added.

As they moved away, she heard Florence hissing to him, 'She always did have terrible taste in clothes.'

'Go and fry the pierogi,' Mr B whispered to her. 'Marjory and I will look after everyone.'

Emily had rather envisaged herself as the host of the evening, but she could hardly expect him to do the cooking, so did as instructed, headed for the kitchen and put two large frying pans on the hob. She turned away from the stove to reach for a spatula and saw that Ludek was there in the doorway, watching her. He was wearing his beige chinos again, and a tailored navy-blue shirt. He had the faintest hint of stubble on his chin, which gave him a slightly rugged air, Emily thought with a flutter.

'Lovely dress,' he said. 'Although... Scrabble? You couldn't find an Agricola one?'

'Kate had it made for me.'

'Brilliant! Is she around? I haven't seen her. I thought she'd be helping out.'

'She couldn't make it.'

'In that case, can I help?'

'Can you fry pierogi?'

'Is the Pope Catholic? I'm Polish, aren't I? Pierogi are practically the only thing I can cook.'

Suddenly Emily felt hot and sweaty. With all the last-minute preparations, there hadn't been time to go home and shower. Motorhead's 'Ace of Spades' was blaring – couldn't someone turn it down? – and her beautiful new pinafore had flour on it already. And her hair! It must look awful, scraped back behind a nondescript hairband. She hadn't even run a comb through it.

'Why pierogi?' asked Ludek as he placed a batch of the little dumplings in one of the pans.

'Mr B's idea. I didn't like to say no.' Emily wondered whether she should tell him that she'd learned to make Polish food in the hopes of impressing him. Perhaps not; Kate would no doubt caution against laying her cards on the table like that, and Kate was the dating expert. Instead, she said, 'There's going to be a slideshow of Polish wildlife too.'

'Random.'

'Yep. It certainly is.'

'I'll fry these,' Ludek said. 'You go and greet your guests. And perhaps turn the music down whilst you're at it.'

Emily wiped her hands, flashed him a grateful smile and went out into the café. She was instantly showered with compliments: for the new décor, her dress and the delicious non-alcoholic raspberry and pear cocktail she'd rustled up.

When Ludek appeared with a huge plate of pierogi, he was instantly mobbed by the boardgamers who helped themselves to generous handfuls; you'd think they hadn't eaten for days.

'I'll go and fry some more,' he said, leaving the plate on a table and heading back into the kitchen.

Boy George's mother – Emily didn't know her name – and her husband took one each.

'This is wonderful,' she said to Emily, and then to her husband, 'I might go outside and give my mother a quick ring. Check he's behaving.'

Her husband put a hand on her arm. 'Leave it, Julia. They'll be fine.'

It was only then that Emily noticed. The games shelves. They were full. Agricola. Ticket to Ride. Carcassonne. Caverna. Marjory's sister must have bought them all in Leeds, but god knows what they'd have cost – even second-hand – and how on earth was Emily going to pay her back?

Queen's 'Play the Game' began as Mr B walked past her, munching on one of the pierogi.

'Mr B, all these games,' she said. 'How on earth did Marjory's sister find them all?'

'Ludek brought them.'

'You asked him?'

'No. He brought them off his own bat.'

Emily was on her way back to the kitchen when Alan stopped her.

'Fantastic selection of games, Emily,' he said.

'I hope they're all insured,' Malcolm added.

'They're Ludek's,' she said.

'Ludek's?' Alan almost choked on pierogi. 'But Ludo never lends out his games. He must be – excuse my language –shitting himself. What if someone spills something? Or pieces get lost? Where is he anyway?'

'In the kitchen doing the cooking.'

'He can cook?' Alan shook his head in disbelief.

As Emily went back to the kitchen, she heard him saying to Malcolm, 'She's got him twisted round her little finger already.'

She stood in the doorway. 'Ludek, your games. I can't thank you enough, but what if something happens? I mean, food, drink, strangers. They could easily get damaged.'

'It's a risk I'm willing to take, Em.' He looked up from the frying pan and his eyes met hers. 'For you.'

She felt her jaw drop. She stood there for a second, then remembered to close her mouth. Gawping wasn't her best look.

Marjory poked her head round the kitchen door at that moment and called, 'Service please!'

'What?' said Ludek, turning to her.

'I said, service please. We need more pierogi out here.'

'No,' said Ludek. 'It's the chef who says, "Service please" when the food is ready and the waiting staff then come and collect it. The waiting staff don't tip up and say it when they want the food. You've got it the wrong way round. I'll send some out in a minute.'

'I don't think she watches enough *MasterChef*,' he added as Marjory disappeared. He plated up another pile of pierogi. 'Here you go.'

Take That's 'Patience' was playing as Emily left the kitchen. Honestly, Kate must have spent hours finding all these games-themed songs. Emily bit her lip, wishing her friend was here. She was pleased that Kate had met someone, but she did miss her.

'Good choice of song,' said Mr B suddenly, appearing at her side.

'I can't claim credit. Kate made a playlist.'

'You know, this song spent longer in the top ten than any other Take That song until the release of "Rule the World".'

'I didn't have you down as a Take That fan, Mr B.'

'You don't know everything about me, Emily. Far from it.'

When everyone had had their fill of pierogi, Ludek emerged from the kitchen.

'Big hand for the chef, everyone,' said Emily. The café erupted into spontaneous applause and Ludek gave three bows, and then, as an afterthought, a curtsey. She glanced at Peter. He wasn't clapping. She wondered if Ludek had noticed; she'd have to find a quiet moment to explain to him why she'd felt obliged to invite her ex along this evening. She didn't want Ludek thinking there was still something between them.

Take That gave way to 'Quit Playing Games with My Heart'.

'The Backstreet Boys,' piped up Mr B. 'Another good choice.'

And with that, he picked up two empty plates and disappeared into the kitchen.

'I never had Mr B pegged as a boyband expert,' Emily said to Marjory.

'He isn't. My grand-daughter visited last week and she's been listening to all her mother's old CDs.'

'I might have known,' Emily laughed. 'Ludek, shall we start getting the board games out now?'

She turned the music down slightly as everyone sat down and Ludek began to suggest games to different groups of people. Mrs Scott and Mrs Sinclair, she noticed, were playing Scrabble with two of the Dungeons and Dragons crowd; Emily wondered if they'd only make words like curse, weapon and elves. One of the Trainspotters was playing the Scandinavian version of Ticket to Ride with Florence and Peter, and Mr B and Marjory were attempting Azul with Malcolm and Alan. Her tiny café was full of happy people.

'Room for one more,' said Ludek, beckoning her over to the table where he was sitting with Julia and her husband, about to embark upon a game of Stone Age.

She slipped into the seat beside him as he finished explaining the rules. Abba was playing again. 'The Winner Takes It All'. Emily glanced around the café to double-check again that all her guests were okay. Ludek saw her. 'Relax, Em. Everyone's enjoying themselves.'

He reached across the table and rubbed her hand, scattering two of Julia's meeples onto the floor.

'Sorry about that,' he said, as Emily bent over to pick them up.

Her fingers had just grasped the furthest one, when

the door of the café opened. Through the jungle of table legs, chair legs and people legs, she saw two pairs of shoes entering: one man's, one woman's. Black slingback courts with fake diamond detailing on one side. She'd have known those shoes anywhere.

Kate.

She sat up so suddenly that all the blood rushed from her head and she felt slightly sick.

Beside her friend was a tall, blond-haired man with model looks. He must be Freddie. No wonder Kate had been a bit obsessed.

He took a swig from the can of lager he was carrying, then staggered slightly as he took a step further into the café. Kate linked her arm through his to steady him, though she didn't seem that stable herself. She had a drink in her hand too, Emily noticed. Some kind of alco-pop.

'Em,' she called as she spotted her. 'Em, this is Freddie.'

Emily got up and went over. 'I thought you weren't coming.'

'Freddie and I wanted to support you, didn't we, darling?' Kate was slurring her words.

'Where's the bar?' said Freddie. 'You said it was a party, Kate.'

Emily frowned. 'It's not really a party. More an evening of board games. And er... Polish culture and cuisine.'

'Oooh, culture and cuisine,' he said, mocking her accent. 'Very fancy.'

'Freddie,' said Kate reproachfully. She made an apologetic face at Emily.

Emily was aware that the whole café had fallen silent now, listening to this interaction. This was awkward. She couldn't think what to say, and ended up coming out with, 'I haven't got enough chairs.'

Peter, Mr B and Ludek instantly sprang to their feet.

'Board games!' Freddie sneered. 'Who plays board games?'

'Freddie!' said Kate again.

'Kate, I so wanted you to come but you're both drunk,' Emily hissed. 'Go home. Please. Don't ruin my evening.'

In her heart of hearts though, she felt they'd already ruined it. It had all been going so perfectly until now. She had no idea that the worst was yet to come.

Chapter Twenty-Five

'The dress looks fantastic on you, Em.' Kate gave a hiccup, as if to underline the fact that she was very, very drunk. 'Did she tell you,' she continued, addressing the entire café, 'that I had that dress made for her? Shpecially for this evening.'

'Kate, please…'

Kate held up her hands in surrender. 'Okay, okay, I get the message. We'll go. Don't want to lower the tone.' She glanced round the room. 'But first, I have to say hello to Ludo.'

Before Emily could stop her, Kate made a bee-line for him, staggering past Malcolm who was still trying to explain the rules of Azul to Marjory. Kate put a hand on the back of Ludek's chair, lent over him and said, 'What are you playing, Ludo?' and, at that moment, Freddie came up behind her, slapped her bottom and the bottle in Kate's hand splashed all over the game.

'Shit,' said Ludek, jumping up and rummaging through his pockets for a tissue.

Alan sprang to his feet, proffering a handful of napkins.

'Kate,' said Emily. 'You know how he feels about his games. I told you.'

'He knew it was a risk, Em.'

'He knew...' She was putting two and two together now. 'You asked him to bring them?'

'Yeah, well. Someone had to. And you wouldn't.'

Emily looked at Ludek. He was trying to salvage some very soggy cards now, seemingly oblivious to the stain down his chinos that made him appear as if he hadn't made it to the gents in time.

'Kate, I think you should go now,' Emily said. 'Back to Freddie's sister's birthday party.'

'Brother's.'

Emily was unsure whether the message she wanted to convey should be said in a firm and school-mistressy tone or a pleading and desperate one. She opted for the latter. 'Please go home and sober up. Please.'

'Okay, we're going. Come on, Fred.'

Kate linked her arm through his again and the whole café watched as they left. Well, the whole café except for Alan and Ludek, who were still frantically mopping.

'Ludek, I'm so sorry about your game,' Emily said.

He smiled, but it wasn't his usual warm, overflowing-with-happiness kind of smile; it was a what-can-you-do? kind of smile. Resignation.

Emily was suddenly aware that the rest of the café was still listening in on the conversation; no one had resumed their games. She caught Mr B's eye.

'Turn the music off,' he mouthed.

Emily clicked 'stop' on her phone, bringing 'Tumbling Dice' by The Rolling Stones to an abrupt end and Mr B clapped his hands together before addressing the room. 'If I could have everyone's attention, please. I think this might be the perfect moment for us all to enjoy a cup of Emily's excellent coffee, along with some pączki and makowiec – donuts and poppy seed cake to the non-Polish speakers amongst you – and this evening's slideshow which is entitled, "Wildlife in the Białowieża Forest". You can play the music again now, please, Emily.'

As The Beatles' 'Ticket to Ride' began to play, a queue formed at the counter. Mr B and Emily set to work, making lattes and cappuccinos and the odd espresso. Marjory handed round the pączki and makowiec, people began to chat again, and the hum of conversation filled the room.

When everyone had been served, Mr B set up his projector and Ludek put a folding screen in place.

Emily decided that she ought to say a few words as she hadn't officially welcomed her guests. She turned off the music – they were partway through Bruce Springsteen's 'Roll of the Dice' – and banged a teaspoon against a mug to get everyone's attention. She would keep it short, she decided. She wasn't accustomed to public speaking and was doubly nervous for some reason as she felt Ludek's eyes upon her. 'I'm so sorry about the interruption earlier. I'd like to welcome you all to The Little Board Game Café which I hope is going to be a popular venue here in Essendale for many years to come. You can come in to play a game or have a coffee, but I'm very much hoping you'll want to do both. I hope you've all enjoyed this evening's special Polish food...'

'Yeah, and the entertainment!' someone quipped.

Emily waited whilst a couple of people laughed. '...and I want to thank Mr B for teaching me his Polish recipes and Marjory for all her support. And, of course, Ludek for helping me in the kitchen this evening and loaning his games. Now, if anyone has room for seconds, I've put the remaining pączki and makowiec' – she took extra care over her pronunciation and saw Ludek smiling in approval – 'on a plate on the counter so help yourselves. In the meantime, I'll hand over to the wonderful Mr Stanisław Baranski, who will share his photos of the Bia...Bia...Białowieża Forest. Phew. I managed that one.'

There was a titter of laughter as she flicked off the lights and slipped into her seat beside Ludek, who had a plate with two pączki on his lap. He offered her one, but she shook her head.

Mr B's slides began with a landscape scene: tall trees around a river. He gave a short explanation; the river had apparently been dammed by a family of beavers.

'Well, I'll be damned,' whispered Ludek.

Emily smiled. She was still mulling over the events of earlier. This really wasn't how she'd wanted the evening to go.

'Next slide, please,' said Mr B and Marjory dutifully pressed a button on the projector. A small black and white bird appeared on the screen, unremarkable to Emily's eyes but apparently it was a three-toed woodpecker.

'How many toes do woodpeckers normally have?' whispered Ludek, before biting into one of the paczki.

Emily smiled again, and held up her hands to gesture that she didn't know. Bless him, he was trying to cheer her up. It was working too; she could feel herself beginning to relax.

'Next slide, please,' said Mr B again and a lone wolf trotting down a tree-lined road replaced the woodpecker.

The photos continued: some unusually shaped fungi; cobwebs strung across conifer branches catching the early morning sunlight; a herd of shaggy beasts with frighteningly large horns.

'There are about eight hundred bison living in the forest,' said Mr B. 'They're the heaviest land animal in Europe.'

'I'll be taking that title,' said Ludek, 'if I keep eating your pączki.'

Emily bit her lip to stifle a laugh. And then a yawn. She closed her eyes.

The warmth of the room and Mr B's calm tones must have lulled her to sleep. In her dreams, she was frying a never-ending mountain of pierogi when raised, anxious voices roused her. Her head was on Ludek's shoulder. She hoped she hadn't drooled all over him, but he sprang up before she could check. What was going on?

Marjory was standing up and was clearly struggling for breath. A heart attack? Oh god, not Marjory. Emily couldn't bear to lose Marjory.

Mr B was by her side. 'She's choking,' he said. 'Breathe, Marjory. Breathe. Ludek, do something.'

Ludek was behind the elderly woman now, talking to her in a gentle, but firm, voice.

'Shall I call an ambulance?' asked Peter.

'No need,' said Ludek. 'You'll be fine, Marjory. Try and relax.' And then he put his arms around her. What was he thinking? Emily thought. Her friend needed medical help, not a hug. But then it all happened so fast. Emily wasn't sure quite what he did, but something flew out of Marjory's mouth and she gasped and the next minute she said, 'I'm fine. Honestly, everyone. I'm fine.'

'Thank goodness you were here, Ludek,' said Mr B and began to clap.

The rest of the café joined in. Even Peter, Emily noticed, albeit a little grudgingly.

As the applause died down, Marjory addressed the room. 'I'm sorry, everyone. I feel very silly. A nut got stuck in my throat, that's all. Can't we get on with the evening? Next slide, please.'

But if any of them had ever had any interest in looking at slides of the Białowieża Forest, they hadn't now. A couple of people stood up, glanced at their watches, and said they had to go. Others then began to drift away and the café emptied in minutes.

'Rather a dramatic evening,' said Peter to Emily. 'I think perhaps I'll take Mother home.'

'Thanks for coming.' Emily kissed her former MIL2B on her cold cheek, then reached up and kissed his too. She watched them go before turning to look at the empty café. Only Ludek, Mr B, and Marjory were left.

'Well, that went well,' she said. 'I bet none of them ever come back.'

'Oh, Emily, I feel so awful,' said Marjory.

'No, I do,' said Mr B. 'If we hadn't put nuts in the makowiec, this would never have happened.'

'You put nuts in the makowiec?' said Ludek. 'My mother just puts poppy seeds.'

'My late Magda's recipe,' said Mr B.

'Fair enough,' said Ludek.

'Anyway, it was me who chopped the nuts,' Emily said. 'I must have missed one of them. I'm so sorry, Marjory. You could have...'

And the next minute, she was in a crumpled heap on the floor, tears streaming down her face.

'Leave her to me,' she heard Ludek saying to Marjory and Mr B. 'I'll take care of her. She'll be okay.'

Marjory bent down, kissed her on the cheek and then had to be helped up again by Mr B. 'It's my knees,' Emily heard her saying. She felt a hand on her shoulder as he said, 'Don't worry, Em. The customers won't be put off by a little thing like this.'

And then they were gone. Ludek sat down on the floor beside her and pulled her in for a hug. 'It's okay. Marjory's fine.'

'But she could have died,' Emily blubbed.

'But she didn't.'

'But she might have. Everyone dies.'

And then suddenly, from nowhere, she found herself telling him about her mum. About the dog and the lorry swerving and his unsecured load. About the life support being turned off.

'Oh, Emily,' he said. 'I never realised. Seeing Marjory this evening… Well, it must have brought it all back.'

'I feel like I'm a jinx,' she said. 'Things get broken. Drinks get spilled. The people I love have accidents…'

'And people you *don't* love have accidents.' Ludek brushed a stray hair from Emily's wet cheek. 'I did a few months in A & E when I was training. You're not a jinx, Em. Accidents just happen. Every day.'

He handed her an already-soggy tissue from his pocket. Judging by the smell of it, Emily thought, it was one he'd used earlier to mop Kate's spilled alco-pop off the Stone Age board.

He cupped her face in his hands and gently kissed the tip of her nose. Somehow the music had started again – she must have been sitting on her phone – and the unmistakable tones of Amy Winehouse filled the café: 'Love is a Losing Game'. She closed her eyes and felt Ludek's lips brush against each of her eyelids. She sighed as they worked their way down towards her lips, but then they stopped.

She opened her eyes. He appeared to be looking past her, at something in the far corner of the café.

'What's the matter?' she said.

'I think one of my meeples is under that table.'

Chapter Twenty-Six

When the stray meeple had been retrieved, Ludek announced he was walking Emily home.

'I'll pick up my games another day,' he said. 'Let's get some fresh air.'

They walked along the canal, back towards the town centre. The geese were asleep on the towpath, their usually vicious beaks tucked under their wings. Emily and Ludek headed through the small park, deserted now, and along the high street.

As they passed Sweet Delights, he nodded across the road to the boarded-up shop which was once The Golden Wok.

'Any idea what's happening there?' he said. 'There've been shopfitters in this week.'

'Not a clue. I hadn't even noticed. I walk past every day but I've been so preoccupied with the launch that I hadn't spotted them. Fingers crossed for another Chinese. Or an Indian. Save traipsing all the way to Hebbleswick every time we want a curry.'

As they reached Kate's house, Emily was relieved to see that all the lights were turned off. She loved her best friend to bits, but didn't want to see her this evening, not after what had happened. And besides, she was hoping that

Ludek might come in for a cup of coffee, that they might resume where they'd left off before he'd spotted the meeple.

She opened the gate and stepped onto the path, assuming he'd follow, but he held back.

'Goodnight, Emily,' he said.

'Would you like to come in for...' she began, but he cut her off, saying, 'Perhaps not tonight. I...I think I should probably head home.'

And then, against her better judgment, against all the advice Kate had ever given her and all the words of wisdom in those find-a-man self-help books, Emily did what you were apparently never supposed to do: she made the first move. She put her arms around Ludek's neck, pulled him towards her and practically clamped her lips onto his.

At first, he didn't respond, but then he began to kiss her back. Gently at first. Teasing her lips with his tongue, then more firmly. More insistent. Urgent almost.

But then he pulled away.

Emily scanned his face, trying to read his expression. His cheeks were flushed. He looked down at his feet. He seemed awkward, unsure of himself. Not unlike how he'd appeared on their very first date. It seemed so long ago now.

'It's been a big day,' he said.

'Yeah, it has.'

She wondered if she should ask him in, but he'd already declined once. And there was no need to rush things, she thought. Better to take it slowly.

'Goodnight, Ludek.'

'Goodnight, Em. I'll talk to you soon.'

'And thanks again. For the games. The pierogi frying. Saving Marjory.'

And kissing me, she wanted to add. For kissing me and making my insides melt.

'You're welcome.'

She walked up the path and found her key – which seemed to take an absolute age as it had worked its way down to the very bottom of her handbag and was hiding under a load of detritus. She knew he was watching her, as she unlocked Kate's front door. He was being chivalrous, making sure she got inside safely, before he walked away.

She closed the door behind her and leant against it, like women always do in films, contemplating the kiss. But then the back of the letterbox began to dig into her back, so she relocated to the sofa.

That kiss.

She couldn't quite decide if he'd wanted it too.

He hadn't responded.

At least not initially.

Then he had responded. Really responded.

But then again, he'd pulled away.

And before that, he had declined to come in for a coffee but perhaps he was being thoughtful. Considerate. He knew she'd been working flat-out to prepare for the launch event and he'd seen how upset she'd felt afterwards. Ludek wasn't the type who'd take advantage and seduce an exhausted woman in an emotional state. Even if he really wanted her. And Em loved that about him.

Although… Well, it would have been nice.

Perhaps not seduction. Not yet. But she would have liked him to hold her some more.

Next time, she decided. She would invite him over for dinner again. And this time, she'd light some candles.

Although board games, alcohol and candles? Perhaps not a good combination. Could result in yet another spillage, or, worse still, a fire. Board games were mostly cardboard. Highly flammable.

Anyway, she was sure Ludek liked her. He'd hardly have lent his board games to her café if he didn't, would he? Perhaps candles wouldn't be necessary.

Emily lay awake, reliving the evening's events, both the highs – Ludek lending his games and frying the pierogi, the unforgettable sight of her little café full of people enjoying themselves and that kiss, the highlight of the entire night - and the lows. She shuddered recalling Kate and Freddie's interruption and Marjory choking on that nut. She fell asleep just as it was beginning to grow light, and awoke late, to a soggy Yorkshire Sunday. It didn't pour with rain and it wasn't dry either. But it kind of matched her mood. Now that the launch event was over, she felt flat. Incredibly flat.

Kate wasn't home. Emily wasn't surprised by this; her friend was hardly ever home and Emily imagined she'd be sleeping off her hangover at Freddie's. With nothing else to do, Emily decided she'd go to the café.

She put the key in and the door swung open, but she stood on the threshold, shocked by the sight that awaited her. She'd forgotten what a state she'd left the place in; dirty plates and cups everywhere. The projector was still plugged in, but must have turned itself off. That was one piece of luck anyway. She might have arrived to find the café had burnt down because the projector had overheated. Or might that have been a relief? She'd be rid of the café then and could claim on the insurance. Malcolm would be proud.

On autopilot, she collected the crockery and stacked the dishwasher, remembering Ludek's face when she kissed him. Had he wanted that? She didn't know anymore.

As she straightened all the tables and chairs, the other events of the evening played on a constant loop in her mind. Kate and Freddie coming in. The angry exchange of words. The pool of liquid on the game board. Leaving the makowiec on the counter and telling everyone to help themselves. Mr B's soporific commentary. Drooling on Ludek's shoulder – that would have been bad enough in itself without what happened next. Marjory's stricken face as she struggled for air.

And if she'd died, well, it would have been Emily's fault. She was the one who hadn't chopped all the nuts properly. How did anyone live with themselves if they were responsible for someone else's death? The guilt. The shame. The thought that you'd deprived another human being of life itself. How had the driver whose stones had fallen on her mum coped with the knowledge that he'd killed her?

Emily sat down at one of the tables, her head in her hands, overwhelmed by the images in her head of both the previous evening and that day all those years ago. She had never longed for her mother more than she did right now.

The door rattled and Emily looked up, hoping it was someone coming in. Okay, so her mum would never walk into the café, but she craved company right now. If only her dad would appear, apologising for his absence yesterday. Or Kate, apologising for her presence. Or Ludek, pulling her into his arms for a hug. But the door rattled again, and Emily realised it was just the wind.

Emily didn't expect Kate to be home that evening, but was still disappointed to find the little terraced house was empty. In all their years of friendship, yesterday had been the closest they'd ever come to an argument. Emily tapped out a text: *Hope you're not too hungover. Can we catch up tomorrow? Xx* Then she pressed send, and hoped she wouldn't have to wait too long for a reply.

The following morning, at five to eleven, Mr B arrived in a salmon-pink bow-tie and sat down at his usual table.

'No Marjory? Is she okay?'

'She's fine, Emily. I think a kind of delayed shock about what happened – or nearly happened – has set in and she needs a rest.'

'I blame myself. She could have died. And your slideshow was ruined.'

'It was an accident, Em. Not your fault at all. And I'm not sure there was much interest in my slides. I'm told one person even fell asleep.'

Emily studied his face; she couldn't tell if he knew that person had been her. 'Perhaps I should go over and see her?'

'I think I'd leave her for a day or two, Emily. Let her rest. Maybe send her some flowers?'

★

When Mr B had left, she baked some rich, nut-free brownies. Once they'd cooled, she boxed them up, along with a pot of double cream and some fresh raspberries, took a blank sheet of paper from her notebook and wrote, *I'm so sorry for what happened. I can understand if you never want to eat my baking again, but these brownies are nut-free, I promise. Emily xx.*

She tucked the paper inside the box, popped a sign in the window saying 'Back in ten minutes' and closed the café. Then she headed to the local florist.

On the way, she passed Ridley's. She prayed that no one she knew would emerge from the double doors and see her. She didn't want that conversation. The one that went, 'What are you doing now?' Especially not today of all days. But she was in luck. The doors remained firmly closed as she hurried by, keeping her head down.

She closed the florist's door behind her with relief and chose the biggest, most expensive bouquet that they had. Which wasn't actually that expensive given that this was the florist in Essendale and not the posh one in Hebbleswick that Peter always used.

'Can you deliver it here, please? And drop off these at the same time?' She handed over the box of brownies and the slip of paper with Marjory's address.

'Delivery is another three pounds,' said the florist. 'Why don't you do it? It's only round the corner.'

'She'd feel obliged to invite me in. And I've been told she needs her rest today. Besides, I need to get back to my café.'

'Are you from The Little Board Game Café?' she said. 'We wanted to come to your launch event, but we couldn't get a babysitter. But I heard great things.'

'You've heard great things? I thought it was a disaster.'

'Everyone enjoyed it.'

'Good to know. Please spread the word. I need all the help I can get. I don't get many customers, to be honest.'

'And you must be worried about Costa.'

'Costa?'

'Yeah, opening soon. Where the Chinese restaurant used to be. The signs have just gone up this morning.'

Emily practically sprinted from the shop, across the road and over to where The Golden Wok used to be. A sign in the window announced that the florist had been right: Costa Coffee would be opening here in three weeks' time.

Had Nico known, perhaps? Was that why he'd sold up? Could she have found this out somehow before she'd bought that café? She thought she'd looked into everything. Had there been planning notices up that she'd missed? She never read those notices; maybe she should start. Although did you even need planning permission to open a coffee shop in a former restaurant? Probably not.

Costa. That was all she needed. It was bad enough having Sweet Delights as her competitor – they were better positioned in the centre of town, even if the service did leave a lot to be desired – but being up against a brand-new Costa as well? It felt like The Little Board Game Café was doomed to failure from the start.

There was a small queue outside the café when Emily returned. Only five people, but Emily felt a small frisson of excitement. Her first queue. Maybe things would get better after all.

Or maybe not. She couldn't compete with Costa.

The five people wanted lunch – two soups of the day, two all-day breakfasts and a baked potato with beans and cheese – and then Florence arrived with Mrs Scott and Mrs Sinclair and they ordered afternoon tea for three with cakes and sandwiches and everything, and began a game of Scrabble.

When she'd served them all, she should probably have gone back into the kitchen and started clearing up because in her haste to serve up five lunches and three afternoon teas, she'd managed to make the place look like a bombsite. Some butter had melted on the worktop and dripped onto the floor, there were breadcrumbs everywhere and she'd managed to spill some soup when she dished it up.

But she didn't feel inclined to clean up the mess yet. She stood behind the counter, staring at the awesome sight of eight paying customers sitting in her café and trying to resist the urge to go over to them every two minutes and say, 'Is everything okay? Can I get you anything else?'

The five people who'd had lunch left, and she watched from a distance as Florence thrashed Mrs Scott and Mrs Sinclair at Scrabble; there was some kind of dispute about a triple letter score. And then they packed up the game and left. Emily had just decided that it was about time she cleared up when she heard the door opening again.

She went back into the café. The new arrival was Ludek.

'Aren't you at the surgery?' she said. A daft thing to say. Clearly he wasn't.

'Lunch break.'

'It's after three.'

'Late lunch break. Most days, I don't even get one. But I wanted to talk to you. To apologise. Saturday night. I shouldn't have kissed you. I got carried away and I shouldn't have. It was a mistake.'

Chapter Twenty-Seven

'A mistake? I thought...' Emily bit her lip, fighting back tears. She scrutinised his face, but couldn't read his expression. 'I thought you liked me?'

'I do like you.'

'But not in that way? You don't fancy me?'

Oh god. Had she misinterpreted the signs?

Had there been any signs?

Yes, she was sure there had been. Holding her gaze for a little too long. Inviting her out to dinner. Creating that Masala! game for her. A hand-made gift and now he was saying that kissing her had been a mistake?

'You'd better take your games back.' She gestured towards the shelves.

'No, Emily. Please. Don't be like that.'

'I feel like a fool. I practically threw myself at you on Saturday, because I thought you liked me. And now you're telling me you don't find me attractive?'

'No. Yes. *Yes.*'

He said that last 'yes' rather emphatically. Almost shouted it.

Confusing. He found her attractive but kissing her was a mistake?

'You do fancy me then?'

'Very much so.'

Emily didn't understand. She opened her mouth to say that, but the café door opened. Julia, the woman who'd taken the last two tickets for Saturday's launch event, appeared with a sulky-looking boy of about nine or ten, wearing a maroon school blazer and grey trousers. Presumably this was Boy George.

She had longed for customers so many times, but now she wished they would turn around and go away.

'Hang on,' she said to Ludek, then she fixed a smile on her face and went over to George and his mum and said, 'Lovely to see you both. Do take a seat. Anywhere you like.'

They sat down at a corner table and Emily fetched her notebook. She wanted to serve them as quickly as possible, so she could go back to her conversation with Ludek.

'What would you like?' Julia said to her son.

George looked Emily squarely in the eye. 'A mint choc chip Frostino and a Gimme S'mores cake.'

'Please,' Julia added.

Emily had no idea what a Frostino was. Nor a Gimme S'mores cake either. 'I'm afraid I don't have either of those.'

'When Costa opens,' said George, 'they'll have Gimme S'mores cakes and Frostinos.'

Costa. She was trying to forget about bloody Costa.

'But they won't have board games,' Emily said. 'I even have Buckaroo! Three sets in fact. You could bring your friends in. Organise a Buckaroo! tournament.'

She could feel Ludek's eyes upon her. 'I've no idea what a Frostino or a Gimme S'mores cake is, but I will google them and learn how to make them for your next visit. In the meantime, how about a chocolate milkshake and a rocky road?'

'I suppose it'll do,' he said grudgingly.

'We had a lovely time here on Saturday,' said Julia.

'Did you? Honestly?'

'We did. Though it was a little unfortunate the way the evening ended. Do you know if that lady was okay?'

'She's fine, thanks. Now what can I get you?'

'A latte for me, please.'

'I'll bring them over. Help yourself to games.'

She glanced over at Ludek, who had edged over to the door. Feeling torn between the need to attend to her customers and her desire to talk to him, she went over to him and said, 'Can you give me a minute? I'll just serve these people and—'

'Don't worry, Em. I can see you're busy and I need to be getting back. We'll catch up another time. I presume the board games group can meet here on Fridays again?'

'Absolutely. I'd be upset if you didn't.'

'Perfect,' he said. 'And Em?'

'Yes?'

'Keep the games for as long as you need them. Till you've built up a collection of your own.'

And with that, he was gone.

When George and Julia had left, she closed up for the afternoon. Takings wise, it was her best day so far, but she still felt deflated. Even if she took this much every day, she couldn't pay herself the minimum wage.

★

Kate was sitting at the kitchen table when Emily got home from the café that evening.

'No Freddie?' Emily said.

'Well yes, I'm going over in a few minutes, but I wanted to see you first. To apologise. I'm so sorry about Saturday night. I don't know what I was thinking. What we were thinking.'

'I'm sorry too. I didn't exactly make you welcome.'

'We were drunk, Em. And it wasn't that kind of event. We shouldn't have come. Is Ludek furious about the game?'

'Probably. I dunno.'

'Look, give him this. To buy a new one.'

She scrambled around in her handbag, pulled out her purse and held out a note.

'A tenner? If those kinds of games only cost a tenner, I wouldn't have needed to borrow his in the first place. I'd have bought my own.'

'Oh yeah. Sorry.' She handed over two twenties. 'Will that be enough?'

'I should think so.'

'So was the event a roaring success after we left?'

Emily could hardly bring herself to tell her. 'It was awful, Kate. During Mr B's slideshow…'

'I knew that slideshow was a mistake.'

'No, it wasn't the slideshow itself that was the problem. Marjory choked on a nut in the middle of it. I thought she was going to die. Thank god for Ludek. He did the…what's it called?'

'Heimlich manoeuvre.'

'Yeah, that's it. And she was fine. But everyone drifted off then. And then I threw myself at Ludek. Full-on snog. And he couldn't leg it fast enough.'

'You should have waited for him to kiss you, Em. Have I taught you nothing?'

'No. This is the twenty-first century, Kate. Women *can* make the first move. Anyway, today he came to see me. Said he regretted kissing me.'

'You see. This is *because* you made the first move. You've scared him off.'

At this, Emily swallowed her tea the wrong way, then spluttered, showering her friend, herself and the table. She coughed to clear her throat. One choking incident in a week was quite enough.

'That's ridiculous, Kate. I don't buy into all that play-hard-to-get stuff.'

Kate dabbed her top with a piece of kitchen roll. 'I think you should forget about Ludek. He's lovely, but the games obsession…it's a bit geeky. I've never liked geeky men.'

'We're talking about me here,' said Emily. 'Not you. I'm quite partial to a geek…'

'Yes, I 'spose. Greg was a bit geeky, come to think of it.'

Emily frowned at the mention of her first love and hastily moved the conversation on. 'And I like the games. I run a board game café, remember?'

'Okay, so play games with him. See him as a friend. But forget about any romance. He's made it clear he isn't interested. Take him at his word and move on.'

On Tuesday morning, Emily walked down the high street on her way to the café. The shopfitters at Costa were carrying materials inside, whilst dodging the hissing white geese on guard outside the door. Emily couldn't help hoping the geese would stay there when the coffee shop opened for business. They'd be sure to deter a few customers from going in.

She crossed over the road to peer into Sweet Delights. It was business as usual, a queue already forming at the counter.

She spent a couple of minutes perusing Oxfam's latest window display, then ambled along the towpath to The Little Board Game Café, still wondering about Ludek. It was all very well for Kate to tell her to forget him. That was easier said than done.

She'd loved Peter, of course she had, but when they'd first met, he hadn't set her pulse racing the way Ludek did. He didn't occupy her mind every waking minute. She didn't walk round town hoping to catch a glimpse of him. She'd only felt this way once before. With Greg. Emily stumbled over a tree root, and narrowly avoided falling. Greg. She didn't want to think about him.

By the time she reached the path up to the street, she was running late. Only a few minutes, and what did it matter anyway? Her first customer of the day would be Mr B, and he never arrived before eleven.

But she was wrong. A group of workmen were standing outside the café.

They stepped aside as she approached, allowing her to open the front door.

'Morning,' she said. 'Sorry I'm a little late.'

She flicked the lights on, fired up the coffee machine and put some water in one of the kettles.

'What can I get you?' she said, smiling at the first man in the queue. They all requested bacon or sausage butties and extra strong tea. One of them seemed familiar, but Emily couldn't think where she'd met him before. He asked for two hard-boiled eggs and some grilled bacon instead of the butties that the others ordered.

'I'm on a keto diet,' he said.

Not another one, she thought. First Peter, then Kate and now … no, she really couldn't place him.

'Haven't seen you lot in here before,' she said.

'We used to go to the burger bar in the layby – you know the one. Between here and Hebbleswick.'

Emily nodded though she didn't. There'd been a burger bar? She'd never noticed.

'Yeah, we've tried that Sweet Delights place, but there's always a queue and the owner doesn't seem to like scruffy customers.'

Emily looked at their paint-splattered overalls. She could imagine Peggy's face when they walked in. 'Well, I'm very glad to have you.'

After they'd left, the café was quiet for over an hour until Mr B and Marjory arrived for their morning coffee. Then there was a small crowd for lunch, including Florence, Mrs Scott and Mrs Sinclair. Emily still didn't know which one was which. Florence ordered soup of the day with a roll and, much to her disapproval, Mrs Scott and Mrs Sinclair had their usual all-day breakfasts.

'Don't you worry about all that saturated fat?' Emily overheard her saying as she fried their bacon.

They argued their way through two games of Scrabble and had only just left when George and Julia returned with another mother and son.

'George has admitted that your chocolate milkshakes are better than McDonald's in Halifax,' Julia whispered, 'but don't tell him I've told you.'

By the time Emily turned the sign to closed, she was exhausted, although delighted to be counting notes as well as coins for once.

And then she remembered the money that Kate had given her for Ludek; two crisp twenty-pound notes still tucked away in her purse.

When she'd finished cleaning up, she decided, she would go over to his place and ask him outright why their kiss had been a mistake. It would be better to know. Then she could put all those distracting thoughts of romance with him to the back of her mind and focus on her business. She needed to build it up as much as possible in the three weeks before Costa opened, in the hope of weathering the storm once it did.

Cleaning up took an age, as usual, and by the time she'd finished, she felt sure he'd be home. She felt a few spots of rain as she locked the door of the shop behind her. She looked up at the ominous grey clouds; a heavy shower was definitely on its way. She had no umbrella and her coat didn't have a hood.

She hurried down the street, hoping to get to Ludek's house before the rain arrived and her hair turned to rat's tails. She almost broke into a jog, as she neared his road, reaching his door just as the heavens opened.

He looked surprised to see her. 'Oh, hi.'

'Hi. Kate asked me to give you this.' She held out the notes to him.

'Come in out of the rain,' he said, 'It looks a bit dodgy

for the local GP to be accepting money off someone on the doorstep.'

Emily slipped off her damp coat, then followed him through the obstacle course that was his hallway, and into the lounge.

'Have a seat,' he said, gesturing towards the one empty sofa. 'Cuppa?'

'No, I'm fine, thanks,' she said then realised how dry her mouth was – nerves, probably – and added, 'Yeah, go on. Some tea would be lovely. Thanks.'

He disappeared off to the kitchen. She sat down and put Kate's money on the coffee table. Catan jumped onto her knee and curled up.

Emily wondered how she'd phrase it.

Why don't you want to go out with me?

No, too direct.

You said our kiss was a mistake and I was wondering why.

Slightly better. Could she say that?

Ludek returned with a tray which he put down on the coffee table, on top of the two notes.

'Say thank you to Kate,' he said. 'Though there was no need.'

'She felt bad about your game being ruined. We both did.'

'Hungry?' He picked a plate of chocolate biscuits off the tray and offered them to her. 'Only shop-bought, I'm afraid. Not as good as your baking.'

'I'm sure they're delicious.' Emily took one. 'Thanks.'

He smiled. It had only been a few days since she'd seen him, but she looked at him as if for the first time. His dark, curly hair. Long eyelashes. The t-shirt he was wearing wasn't quite as tight as the one he'd worn at the running club, but she could still see the outline of his pecs. And that smile! He was gorgeous. Just gorgeous.

But for some reason, he didn't want her.

Suddenly she decided that she'd rather not know what that reason was. It was humiliating enough that she'd flung herself at him like that. It would be even more humiliating to ask him to explain why their kiss was a mistake.

He'd turned her down and perhaps that was a good thing. She ran Essendale's only board game café. He ran Essendale's only board games group. And his group played in her café every week. It would be far simpler if the two of them were just good friends. If they had embarked on a relationship and then it didn't work out... Well, it could get awkward. Messy. It was awkward enough now after just one kiss.

'I wanted to apologise,' she said, 'for the way I behaved on Saturday night. I shouldn't have thrown myself on you. It was just a heat of the moment thing. It's probably better if we forget all about it. Don't you think?'

She picked up her mug of tea and dunked the chocolate biscuit in, before lifting it to her lips and licking off the melted chocolate. That was the good thing about deciding you were just going to be friends with a man; you could risk getting a chocolate moustache in front of him.

Ludek paused as if he wanted to say something, but wasn't sure he should.

'You're right,' he said. 'Let's forget it ever happened.'

Chapter Twenty-Eight

It's probably better if we forget all about it.

Why the hell had she said that? She *couldn't* forget all about it.

As she crossed through the park on the way to the café, she remembered the first time she'd seen him, running along, dark curls bouncing with every step, how Clipboard Woman had melted before their eyes, instantly forgiving his tardiness. Kate had said he was a charmer, but that wasn't quite true. Men who were charmers, in Emily's experience, tended to use their charms to impress or manipulate others. Ludek wasn't like that; he was just kind and smiley and people warmed to him easily.

As she unlocked the café door, she remembered the fall when she'd twisted her ankle, how quickly he'd come to her aid and how reassuring he'd been. The first time his skin had touched hers as he assessed what the damage was. The scent of him as he'd put his arms around her and helped her to his car.

Images of Ludek seemed to flood her brain, whatever she did. Flicking the coffee machine on – him chatting away to Mr B in Polish as she made him a latte. Writing the soup of the day on the blackboard above the counter – him asking if she planned to pare down the menu and confessing that he watched *Ramsay's Kitchen Nightmares*. Packing the leftovers in Tupperwares and putting them into the fridge at the end of the day – him fastidiously packing away his games.

Was he struggling to put her out of his mind too? she wondered. Was he sitting in his consulting room, picturing her with a ring stuck on her finger and her arm in the air? Was he reminded of her every time a patient came in with a twisted ankle?

Probably not. She sighed. Men had that famous ability to compartmentalise, didn't they? How did they do that?

The best course of action, she decided, was to distract herself. She would keep busy, throw herself more than ever into the business.

Emily took photos of the café from every conceivable angle. She took photos of every dish she made. Between customers, she uploaded these to Instagram and Twitter, with strings of appropriate hashtags. She cleaned until the worktops shone and you could practically have eaten your dinner off the floor; even Kate would have been impressed by how spotless the place was. She worked late in the evenings, experimenting with new recipes, costing out every ingredient to work out the margins.

Ludek. That was what he'd suggested, back when she'd first bought the café.

It was no good; she couldn't *not* think about him.

But whilst her strategy was unsuccessful at distracting her from thoughts of Ludek, it worked wonders for her business. There a steady stream of new customers through the door. Two men in dark-grey suits who looked slightly incongruous in her quirky café, but later peered at the board games shelves on their way up to the counter to pay. A family with two sticky-looking children who played a game of Snakes and Ladders as they waited for their early lunch of soup and sandwiches. Emily made a mental note to wash the dice and counters. A woman who sat in the corner breast-feeding. She looked exhausted. She only ordered a coffee, but Emily took her a free slice of cake.

The regulars came too, of course, and Emily could now count the workmen amongst them as they arrived every morning for their breakfasts.

It wasn't until Friday when they visited her little café for the fifth time that Emily realised that the man on the keto diet was the sweaty, overweight man from the running club, the one Kate had so rudely dismissed. No wonder she hadn't recognised him initially; he was now completely transformed.

'Rob, isn't it?' she said.

'I knew you'd remember me eventually.'

'Sorry. You look so different.'

'No need to apologise. The running club's worked wonders,' he said, 'plus getting this job. Lots of lifting. And the diet.'

A little later, Mr B arrived with Marjory and spent an hour trying to figure out the rules to Carcassonne. Emily would have explained them, but she had far too many other customers waiting for her to take their orders, and a backlog of coffees to make.

Soon after Mr B and Marjory left, having given up on

Carcassonne for the time being, Florence, Mrs Scott and Mrs Sinclair appeared.

'I'm afraid I'm out of all-day breakfasts,' Emily said.

'Not to worry,' said the taller one of Florence's friends. Emily thought she was Mrs Scott, but she didn't honestly know. 'We all fancy trying your Lancashire hotpot. Assuming it's on today?'

'It is, as it happens. And a pot of tea?'

They all nodded.

'Now, Emily,' said the shorter woman. Mrs Sinclair? 'Have you bought Frustration? Scrabble is great, but we'd like more variety.'

More variety? This from the woman who, until today, ordered the same meal every time she visited?

'And we're sick of Florence beating us,' added Mrs Scott.

Ah. So that was the real reason.

'Not yet. I've had rather enough actual frustration in my life of late.'

They all laughed. Emily wasn't sure she'd ever heard Florence laugh; she had certainly never laughed at any of her ex-DIL2B's jokes before.

'Anyway, I have lots of new games now. Why don't you take a look?'

Florence took off her reading glasses and glanced towards the shelves. She shook her head. 'I think we'll stick with Scrabble.'

By the time Julia and George arrived, with a large group of mums and children, Emily was on her last legs and had run out of the soup of the day – Cullen skink – for the first time ever. She'd even sold six Lancashire hotpots. Six! There was hardly any bread left and the cake display was looking rather depleted. The publicity surrounding the launch of the Little Board Game Café and her recent efforts on social media had done the trick; trade had definitely improved. Emily just hoped things would continue once Costa opened. Only two weeks to go now.

The mothers had pulled two of the tables together and were sitting in one big group, gossiping away, completely oblivious to the four-letter words their boys were spelling out on the Scrabble tables when Emily went over to take their order.

They wanted so many coffees, all different types. And the boys all wanted milkshakes. She'd struggle to make all these in a reasonable time.

She was frantically frothing the milk for two oat lattes when Julia appeared at the counter. 'You look like you could use some help,' she said. 'May I? I used to work in a café.'

'Really? Are you sure?'

But Julia was already behind the counter, washing her hands. 'This place is getting too busy for you to run single-handed.'

'It's not always like this. Some days, I've sat around for hours on end without any customers. Twiddling my thumbs. I've wiped tables that didn't need wiping. Just for something to do.'

Julia laughed. 'I have a feeling those days are over. There's a good vibe in here. Word is starting to spread.'

'You mean, you've started to spread the word?'

'Perhaps,' she said. 'Have you thought about taking someone on?'

'Are you hinting? Looking for a job?'

'God, no. Not me. But seriously, you might want to get some help.'

'It's too soon. A week or two back, I couldn't afford to pay myself. Things might go quiet again.'

Julia looked thoughtful. 'I don't think you need to worry on that score.'

Emily glanced around the café. The children all engrossed in their games, fingers sticky with chocolate brownies and gingerbread meeples. The mothers equally engrossed in their conversations. Yes, it was busy now, but that might easily change.

When all the mums and children had finally left and Emily turned the sign to closed, she was dead on her feet. Not long now and the board games group would arrive for their first Friday- night session in The Little Board Game Café.

The board games group. Ludek.

Emily glanced at her watch. Quarter past five. She'd been so busy that she hadn't thought of him for thirty-nine minutes. A new world record.

And she'd be seeing him soon.

Her back was aching. Her feet were aching. And was that a headache coming on? She felt terrible and was pretty sure she looked terrible too. A hot bath. That was what she needed. She'd head back to Kate's.

On the way, she passed Sweet Delights, already closed for the day. Unusual. Normally they were still clearing up after a busy day when she went past. She glanced at Costa: its dark-maroon sign was up now. Emily wished she'd been able to afford a proper sign for her café, rather than the stick-on thing. One day soon, she promised herself.

She stopped by Oxfam and peered in the window. She hadn't been in once since she opened the café; there hadn't been time. Maybe Julia was right. Maybe it was time to employ someone to help. Then she could occasionally take an hour off.

'Nice dress, isn't it?' said a voice beside her.

Emily turned to see Annie from Ridley's. The woman she'd never clicked with. The one who'd set her sights on Peter. At least, she had until he'd laid her off at the same time as he'd made Emily redundant. Bet Annie didn't fancy him after that.

'Yeah, nice dress,' Emily said, though in truth, the little black number hanging in the window was a bit formal for her liking. 'How's it going, Annie?'

'Not great.'

'How come?'

'I lost my job, remember?'

Emily nodded. 'Sucks, doesn't it?'

'You must have got a bigger pay-out than me, Emily. I suppose that figures. Sleeping with the boss.'

'A bigger pay-out?'

'You bought your own café.'

Anger began to bubble up inside Emily. 'Not with my pay-out. I'd been saving up for years. Since I was a teenager, in fact. And I had a small inheritance. My mum was killed in an accident when I was sixteen. So if you think Peter or money from Ridley's paid for that café, well, you'd be wrong.'

'Oh god, Emily. I'm sorry. I didn't know about your mum. I feel terrible now.'

'It doesn't matter.'

'No, it's… Well, I'm so fed up. I lost my flat soon after Peter laid me off – I couldn't afford the rent. And now I'm sofa-surfing with friends and I'm not sure how much longer they'll put up with me. I don't know what I'm going to do.'

'I'm sorry to hear that, Annie,' Emily said, and she meant it. She'd never warmed to the woman when they worked together at Ridley's, but she wouldn't have wished that on her. 'Look, I've got to go. But if I hear of any jobs, I'll let you know.'

'Great, can I give you my number?'

'I'm not sure I've got a pen.'

Annie pulled out a battered iPhone. 'Tell me your number and I'll give you a missed call.'

Emily felt reluctant to give her phone number to her former colleague, but she wanted to get home for her bath, so she reeled it off, then said, 'Look, I've got to go. Good luck with everything.'

She could feel Annie's eyes boring into her back as she hurried away, her phone ringing in the bottom of her bag.

It wasn't until later, as she sat in the bath in Kate's pristine bathroom, that it occurred to her: she could employ Annie.

No, that wouldn't be a good idea.

For one thing, they didn't get on.

For another, what if this week was a one-off? In a few days, Costa would open and the customers might stop coming.

It didn't bear thinking about.

She put Annie and Costa to the back of her mind and inevitably found her thoughts wandering back to Ludek.

Soon she'd be face-to-face with him for the first time since they'd agreed just to be friends. And just being friends was the last thing she wanted. This would be awkward. Super awkward.

Chapter Twenty-Nine

We're just going to be friends, we're just going to be friends, Emily repeated to herself in time with the rhythm of her footsteps as she walked back to the café to open up for the group. It was her new mantra. She resolved that she wouldn't indulge in any daydreams about him; she mustn't stoke that flame. She wouldn't allow seeing him again to stir up her feelings.

In the end, it was surprisingly simple. All she had to do was avoid looking at him. If she didn't catch sight of his curly hair, his long lashes or his smile – and he didn't smile much that evening anyway, she noticed when she did steal a tiny glance at him – then she could almost believe that she didn't fancy him at all, that she didn't long to run across the room and fling her arms around him.

And, of course, it helped that she'd joined the Trainspotters for a game of Ticket To Ride.

'I need to sample a wider variety of games,' she'd told them. 'It helps when I'm chatting to customers.'

Emily tried to avoid making eye contact with him, but he hung back in the break, after the others had taken their mugs of tea.

'Is something wrong?' he said. 'Have I offended you in some way?'

'I'm just tired. The café has been busy this week. So busy that I'm wondering if I need to take someone on.'

'You must make sure you have employers' liability insurance,' said Malcolm, returning to the counter and helping himself to a second biscuit.

Employers' liability insurance? Emily hadn't thought of that. And there'd be National Insurance to pay too - what a minefield! Still, not something she needed to think about just yet.

Alan joined them. 'Are you worried about Costa opening, Em? The impact on business?'

'Of course I am,' said Emily. 'I can't think of anything else.'

Her eyes met Ludek's.

Anything else. Except you.

The number of workmen coming in each morning seemed to have multiplied.

'We've been spreading the word,' said Rob as Emily served up his keto breakfast and his mates' rolls stuffed with bacon and sausages, all dripping with ketchup. When they went back to work, she did a quick stock-take: she'd have to start ordering more food.

There was a steady stream of customers in the café every day. Emily found it exhausting; trying to take orders, make coffees, serve up food and clear the tables afterwards, but she was determined to enjoy it. Only ten days now until

Costa opened, and then everything might change. What if her customers decided that the chain's coffee was superior – it probably would be – and that her café having a few board games didn't really make up for that?

Not everyone played the board games, she noticed. Some people just ordered coffee and cake as if it was an ordinary café; they barely looked at the games shelves. And, of course, there were others who'd borrow a game, order one pot of tea and sit playing for three hours, without buying so much as a piece of shortbread. Thankfully they were in the minority. And Emily didn't mind, not really. It gave her a thrill to see the café full of happy people, to see children's faces when they came in for the first time and saw the tables painted with Snakes and Ladders boards, to hear the little place buzzing with conversation and laughter.

She thought back to her first visit to Nico's, to how she'd thought it was like the losers' café in the Apprentice. It was full of winners now.

If only her mother could see this, could see how she'd transformed the dreary little building. Food brings people together, Mum always used to say. And board games do too, thought Emily.

Saturday. Five days to go. Costa had a picture and a headline in the *Gazette* far bigger than Emily's had been. The local MP *and* a celebrity were coming to the opening. She should have thought of that for *her* launch event. Not the MP – she wasn't bothered about him – but a celebrity would have been nice. It might have boosted her social media following for a start. Too late now though.

★

Four days to go. Emily walked past Sweet Delights on the way home and saw Peggy staring out of the window, an anxious look on her face. Sweet Delights had been there for years, she thought, and had a loyal clientele. Surely Peggy didn't have anything to worry about.

Three days to go.

'What are you working on at the moment?' Emily asked Rob as she served his workmates their breakfast butties and handed him his keto bacon and boiled eggs.

'A barn conversion. Once that's finished, we've two extensions lined up. There's always building work round here. People wanting extensions. Renovations. And newbuilds too. Such a demand for homes in this valley.'

Emily nodded. Sooner or later, she'd have to think about getting a place of her own. She couldn't impose on Kate for ever. She'd look for somewhere in the next couple of months. Assuming Costa's opening didn't completely decimate her business and put her out of a job.

Two days to go.

Emily had her busiest day ever. She couldn't quite believe the amount in the till at the end of the day, and the tips jar was pretty full too. There hadn't been an empty seat in the place at four o'clock. Coming in for coffees, cakes and milkshakes on the way home from the school run had become a daily thing now for Julia and her crowd of friends.

Emily wondered how they could afford it, but she wasn't complaining. She just hoped it would continue and that the Frostinos and Gimme S'mores cakes in Costa wouldn't be a bigger attraction for the children than the games were.

One day to go.

'Are you worried?' asked Mr B when he and Marjory arrived for their usual cappuccinos and Chorley cakes.

'No,' said Emily. 'I'm hoping the games are enough of a unique feature to keep drawing people in, and our little town will prove to be big enough for two cafés *and* a Costa.'

She sounded much surer than she felt.

Thursday morning.

A huge arch of balloons in Costa's trademark shade of maroon towered in front of the new shop's door, reminding Emily that today was the day. Not that she needed reminding. The windows were now sparkling clean, she noticed as she walked down the high street, and a large sign proclaimed: 'Free coffee for the first fifty customers'.

Great, Emily thought. Fifty free coffees? That was sure to affect her trade.

She crossed over the road and peered in. A brand-new glass-fronted counter. Wooden floors and tables. A maroon banquette along the entire length of one wall and huge pictures displaying a variety of tempting offerings: a latte with the froth shaped like a coffee bean – Emily still hadn't got the hang of that despite watching several YouTube videos; a chocolate milkshake topped with a perfect swirl of whipped cream; a selection of golden pastries.

It looked inviting, she had to admit.

'But it doesn't have board games,' she said out loud as she walked on. 'It *doesn't* have board games.'

An anoraked man with a greyhound gave her an odd look. Emily glanced across the road to see Peggy watching her. Emily felt a sudden wave of sympathy for her; the new Costa just a few metres from the front door of Sweet Delights. She held up her hand and waved, but the rival café owner didn't wave back.

The workmen arrived for breakfast as usual.

'You didn't fancy a free Costa coffee then?' she said.

'Nah,' said one of Rob's friends. 'No one makes a bacon butty like you, Emily.'

She was on edge all day. It reminded her of those early days when the Little Board Game Café was The Lancashire Hotpot, when she watched the door all day, praying for customers. But this time, she needn't have worried. The free coffee at Costa might have lured a couple of people away, but not many. By closing time, her feet were aching as usual.

'I think everything will be okay,' she said to Kate later, when her friend had dropped in to pick up another change of clothes.

'That's a relief after all your hard work.'

'Why don't you just keep more stuff at Freddie's? You're practically living there.'

'I suggested that. He went a bit quiet.'

'That's odd. I thought he was really keen?'

'So did I. But we haven't even had the discussion about being exclusive.'

'Seriously? After all this time?'

'Seriously. Not one word about it.'

'Perhaps,' said Emily, 'he doesn't feel you *need* to have that discussion. I mean, you spend almost every night there. Neither of you has time to be seeing anyone else.'

'Actually, you've got a point there, Em. And how about you? Isn't it about time you started dating again?'

'It's too soon after Peter.'

'Really? Or are you still thinking about Ludek?'

'No. We've agreed we'll just be friends and I'm focusing on the café. If Costa doesn't affect my trade too much, I'm going to take someone on.'

To Emily's relief, Friday was just as busy as Thursday. All her regulars came in as usual, plus a couple of people she hadn't seen before and takings were up on the previous day.

At the board games group, that evening, Emily decided she'd had enough of trains and developed an urge to try Dungeons and Dragons.

'Really?' said Ludek, baffled. 'I wouldn't have thought it was your cup of tea?'

'It's very popular,' she said.

The Dungeons and Dragons guys were lovely, trying to explain the rules to her, whilst clearly being a little confused at her sudden desire to join their table. They were partway through a campaign, they said, but she could be an elf and help them fight off various monsters.

Ludek held back again during the break, waiting till the others had returned to their tables before coming up to the counter for a mug of tea.

'You enjoying fighting the dragons?' he asked.

Emily lowered her voice. 'Not really. You were right. It's not my kind of thing at all.'

'Perhaps you might come back to our table next week? We've missed you.'

Shame he'd said 'we' rather than 'I', Emily thought.

'Perhaps,' she said.

'How has trade been? Has Costa had much of an impact or is it too early to tell?'

'Far too early. But so far so good.' She held up crossed fingers. 'It's been busier since I launched as a board game café and I've not noticed any difference since Costa opened.'

'Fabulous news, Em. We need to celebrate.'

'Celebrate?'

'Of course. Dinner at my place? Tomorrow night?'

Chapter Thirty

Books on Emily's Kate's spare bedside: *Friends to Lovers; Get Out of the Friends Zone; He's Just Not That Into You*. All (reluctantly) borrowed from Kate's bookshelves.

Emily took every item she owned out of the wardrobe in Kate's spare room but still couldn't decide what to wear.

Ridiculous. This was just two friends getting together.

But it wouldn't hurt to look her best. Just in case.

She managed to ladder three brand-new pairs of tights and didn't have any others. Wearing one of her usual pinafores was no longer an option; it was too cold for bare legs. Her best jeans, Emily decided. They were a little too tight – scoffing her own cakes at the café wasn't doing much for her waistline – but they'd have to do.

'Come in,' said Ludek, opening the door. He had a huge grin on his face. He ushered her into his lounge. 'Take a seat. Glass of wine?'

'Please,' she said. He disappeared into the kitchen. She

sniffed. The house smelled clean and fresh. She couldn't smell anything cooking. He had said dinner, hadn't he? Perhaps he would order a take-away again.

He reappeared carrying a glass of white wine for her, and a glass of what looked like water for himself. Emily wondered why he wasn't drinking; perhaps he was planning to drive her somewhere, to take her out to dinner. Shame she'd worn jeans.

His face was full of excitement. 'How would you fancy dinner in Paris?'

Wow. She hadn't seen that one coming.

'Tonight?'

'Why not?'

A million thoughts flashed through her mind from the practical – did she know where her passport was? – to the romantic – if he was taking her to Paris for dinner on the spur of the moment like this, he had to want more than friendship, didn't he?

How on earth were they going to get there in time for dinner? The closest airports were Manchester and Leeds but they were both at least an hour's drive away. Was that why he wasn't drinking?

Ludek was looking at her expectantly. 'What do you think?'

'That'd be amazing.'

Dinner in Paris! It was definitely a shame she'd worn jeans. Still, she'd need to nip home for that passport, so perhaps there'd be time to change.

She took a sip of wine as Ludek pulled a game from his shelves.

'Ta-dah,' he said. 'Dinner in Paris.'

The picture on the front of the box showed a Parisienne square, with brightly lit cafés under coloured awnings. In the background, the spires of Montmartre were silhouetted against a vibrant sunset.

'I bought it with you in mind, Em. Thought you'd love it. It's all about setting up cafés and restaurants.'

She tried to smile, but obviously wasn't quick enough as he said, 'You thought I meant dinner in actual Paris.'

Emily felt her cheeks reddening. 'Only for a second. This is wonderful.'

And it was. He had bought another game with her in mind.

'Would you really have come to Paris with me? On the spur of the moment like that?'

'I dunno. Maybe. Probably. But the game sounds great. I'm starving though. We couldn't play after dinner, could we?'

'Sure,' he said. 'I've made pierogi. But if you're sick of pierogi, we could order a take-away.'

He had made pierogi.

He had bought Dinner in Paris especially for her *and* he had cooked for her.

He had to want more than a friendship. Didn't he?

After they'd eaten – Emily had to admit that his pierogi were far better than hers – Ludek set the game up. Okay, so perhaps a game wasn't quite as good as a trip to Paris, but the tiny little buildings with their signs saying 'boulangerie', 'fritterie' and 'pizzeria' were delightful. Even so, as they raced to collect ingredients, build their restaurants and add terraces in front of them, her mind kept wandering to what it would be like to fly to France with Ludek at her side.

To sit down on real terraces, rather than placing cardboard ones on a games board. To order café au lait from a little back-street café and buy bread from a boulangerie.

The game ended and they totted up the scores. Emily won by a couple of points.

'Great game, Em,' said Ludek. 'Might have known you'd win. You had the advantage after all.'

'Because I was first player?'

'No, because you run a café, so you know what you're doing.'

'I wish,' said Emily. 'Most of the time, I don't have a clue.'

Their eyes met across the board. Emily's legs turned to jelly. They didn't say a word and she was suddenly aware of every sound: the hum of something electrical in the room, a DVD player perhaps; a car passing by outside; her breathing, so fast that she was half-expecting him to diagnose her with something.

And then he stood up, walked round to her side of the table and pulled her to her feet. He brushed a loose strand of hair from her face, and gently, ever so gently, touched his lips against hers.

'I have wanted to do that all evening,' he said.

'I thought kissing me was a mistake?'

He took a step back. 'I'm sorry. I didn't mean that. It was Peter.'

'Peter?'

'Well, you hadn't long split up from him. And I'd seen you getting out of his car and then he was there at the launch. I thought you might still have feelings for each other.'

Peter? So that was the reason? She'd intended to say something, to explain why she'd felt obliged to invite her ex to the launch, but with all the drama at the launch event, it had slipped her mind.

'There's nothing romantic between Peter and me. Not anymore. He took me out for the afternoon, to give me some business ideas, but that was all it was. Well, all it was on my part anyway. And then I had to invite him to the launch because he'd been supportive. Well, since we split up, he has. When we were together, the last thing he wanted his fiancée doing was running a café.'

'So it's definitely over?'

'It's over.'

'And there's no chance…?'

'None whatsoever. I can't speak for him, but I definitely don't want to get back together with Peter.'

'I've been hurt in the past, Em. A woman who hadn't long come out of a long-term relationship. I fell in love. She went back to him.'

'Oh, Ludek, I'm sorry. But don't let what's happened in your past hold you back in your present.'

He took a step forwards, put his arms around her and pulled her into him, pressing his lips against hers, still gently but with more urgency than before. It didn't take long at all before he was leading her up the stairs.

Was this too soon? she wondered.

But it felt so right. She wanted him so much. So she followed him into his bedroom and was pleasantly surprised to find that it wasn't full of board games. In fact, she noted as they tumbled onto the bed together, there wasn't a single game in sight.

Chapter Thirty-One

Afterwards, Ludek wrapped his arms and legs around her, clinging to her body like one of those little koalas you see sometimes in toy shops that grips on the top of a pencil.

She felt safe. Protected. Reassured by his presence. Bathing in the blissful afterglow of sexual hormones. She nestled into him. His skin felt smooth against hers, his body warm.

He was asleep in seconds. Not in a callous 'man who doesn't care' way, but in a contented way.

She lay there for a few minutes. Mulling over the events of the evening.

She expected to drift off to sleep, but she didn't. She couldn't. She wanted to roll over – she always slept on her side but didn't like to move. He looked so peaceful, like a baby almost. It would have been a shame to disturb him.

But she couldn't sleep on her back. She tried to focus on her breathing, to employ those mindful techniques that she'd heard on meditation apps, but she was aware only of his breathing. The beating of his heart against her ribs. His nakedness pressed against hers.

Eventually she gave in and turned over. He sighed but didn't wake, obligingly rolling away from her, onto his back.

She lay on her side, facing him. Still, she couldn't sleep. She stared at him, marvelling at his prominent but rather distinguished nose, the loose curls of his hair splayed on the pillow, those long, dark eyelashes. She found him beautiful, attractive, arousing. She loved his company. He was interesting, funny, entertaining. And she'd now discovered he was pretty good in bed. She should have been elated. Excited. This could, after all, be the start of something. He didn't strike her as the type to have a one-night stand.

And yet, somewhere deep within her there was a growing sense of unease. She wanted to get up. To leave.

She couldn't fathom why.

He'd done nothing wrong. The sex had been great. He was a gentle, generous lover.

But...

But what exactly?

She imagined herself pulling on her clothes, tiptoeing out of his room, creeping down the stairs to the front door. He'd wake next morning to find an empty space where he'd expected to find her. She pictured him running his hand over the sheet where she had lain, like they did in films. Sitting up, puzzled. Wondering if she was in the bathroom, perhaps. Discovering that she wasn't.

And her heart wanted to burst for the abandoned Ludek of her imagination because she knew he'd be disappointed, knew he'd be hurt and that was the last thing she wanted to do to him.

Yet still, that urge to leave.

And not only to leave his bed, to remove herself from his life.

Why, why, why? When she had spent weeks longing for this man?

She didn't get up. She didn't move. She watched his sleeping form beside her, feeling such a strange combination of emotion. The desire to love. The desire to leave. How was it even possible to feel both of those things at once? It didn't make sense.

Commitment phobia. Perhaps that was it.

But that couldn't be it. She wasn't afraid of commitment; she'd been engaged to Peter, for heaven's sake. She'd never felt this way with him.

Or maybe, it *was* too soon after Peter. Had Ludek been right to be wary of her?

No, that wasn't it either.

A fear had been triggered, a faded memory stirred; something deep in her subconscious that she couldn't quite access. She replayed the evening in her head, remembering how he'd led her upstairs, undone the buttons on her shirt, kissed her neck. Where had this inexplicable desire to run away come from?

She was torn. One voice in her head was whispering, 'Leave. Leave.' Another was urging her to press her lips up against his, to run her fingers over the silky, downy hair on his oh-so-flat stomach, to wake him and be pulled back into his arms.

But her leg was out of the bed, her foot touching the carpet, seemingly without her making a conscious decision. The voice saying 'leave' had been that little bit louder, that tad more persuasive.

Her bra and knickers were somewhere in the bed. Gently, she lifted a corner of the duvet and retrieved them. Ludek didn't move. She pulled on her socks and struggled into the jeans, grabbed her top and crept to the door, praying it wouldn't creak as she opened it. It didn't.

On the landing, she pulled on her top, then, feeling like a cartoon character, she tip-toed down the stairs, pausing after every step to listen for stirrings from Ludek's bedroom. Nothing.

In the hall, she picked up her coat and was about to open the front door when she stopped. She wanted to leave and yet…sneaking off like this. Well, it didn't seem like a kind thing to do. And he was lovely. Didn't he deserve better?

She turned and glanced up the stairs. Ludek was standing at the top, wrapped in a navy dressing gown.

'I'm er… I couldn't sleep. I thought maybe… my own bed…'

'Look, the spare room's made up if you'd prefer to sleep there. I'd have to move a few games boxes…'

She hesitated. 'I'm being silly. Sorry.'

'Or you could come back to my bed? Let me hold you.'

That did sound inviting.

He held out his hand, she took it and for the second time in two hours, he led her back upstairs, back into his bedroom and closed the door behind them.

'Catan will come in otherwise and wake us at the crack of dawn, probably with an unsavoury gift.'

He didn't undress her this time. He took off his dressing gown and got back under the sheets. She peeled her clothes off, feeling self-conscious, wondering if he was watching her. As she unhooked her bra, she glanced over at him, but he was lying on his side, eyes closed.

She left her knickers on, and slipped into bed beside him, immediately rolling onto her side. He pulled her into a spoon and nuzzled her neck with his face.

'What happened, Emily? Did I take things too fast?'

'No. Yes. I don't know.'

Tears were rolling down her cheeks now. She didn't want him to know she was crying. Didn't want him to ask questions she couldn't answer. So she made no attempt to brush the tears away, leaving them to soak into the pillow and a damp patch to form under her cheek.

Her breathing must have given her away, as Ludek said, 'Emily, are you crying?'

'Yes,' she whispered.

'Why?'

'I don't know. I can't explain.'

She could feel him moving behind her. The bedside light came on. She turned to see he'd sat up. She sat up too, pulling the duvet over her naked breasts.

'Emily, you did want this, didn't you? I mean, I would never have forced you.'

'You didn't. I wanted it. I can't explain. It doesn't make sense. Not even to me. I like you, Ludek. Really like you. But afterwards, I felt...fear, I think. But I don't know what I felt afraid of. And I had this urge to leave. And I honestly don't know why.'

And that was the truth. She couldn't explain it. Not even to herself.

Chapter Thirty-Two

'I'm sorry if I rushed things,' he said next morning. 'I didn't mean to make you want to run off.'

Emily felt her cheeks reddening as she remembered sneaking downstairs. She took a sip of coffee. This was awkward. The morning after the night before. She wondered how Kate did it; all those internet dates; those nights she didn't come home. She must have had so many mornings like this. An awkward breakfast with a stranger. Tottering home in her heels and the previous evening's clothes. No wonder she'd been so excited to have found Freddie.

At least Ludek wasn't a stranger. Although she felt strangely distant from him now.

'Do you want something to eat?' he said.

'No, I'll grab something at the café. Speaking of which, I should get going.'

'I thought you didn't open on a Sunday?'

Was it Sunday? Yes, she supposed it must be.

'Stock-take,' she said.

He nodded.

She drained her mug and hopped off the bar stool. Should she kiss him goodbye? On the lips? Or the cheek?

Or should she just say, 'See you at board games on Friday'
as if nothing had happened?

'I guess I'll see you at board games on Friday,' he said as
if he'd read her mind.

'Yes, okay.'

'I think perhaps we should stick to just being friends
after all.'

Again, she felt a strange mix of disappointment and
relief. In equal measures.

'Okay, I...' She wasn't sure what she wanted to say.
'Perhaps I need a bit more time. Maybe the break-up
affected me more than I thought. Perhaps you were right –
steer clear of women who are on the rebound.'

'I will in future.'

But she didn't think that being on the rebound was the
problem. Actually, she was sure that it wasn't.

She was surprised to find the front door of Kate's house was
unlocked. She knew she'd locked it the previous evening, so
this could mean only one thing: her friend was home. Odd.
Weren't Sunday mornings for long lie-ins and shagging
Freddie? Or had they reached the Sunday papers, filter
coffee and croissants stage of their relationship?

Neither, it seemed. Emily found Kate lying face down on
the sofa. She was fully dressed, and, judging by her outfit,
she'd been there all night – that tight black dress was hardly
Sunday morning attire. As Kate looked up, Emily saw that
her friend's eyes were red raw.

'What's happened?' Emily said, though she could guess.

She'd seen this so many times before. Kate flung herself headlong into a new relationship. Fell in love. Decided this was The One. Ploughed all her energy into him. And then things ended and she fell apart. Emily didn't understand why she didn't take things more slowly.

Yes, okay. A bit rich given how she'd leapt into bed with Ludek the previous night.

'Freddie said ...' Kate sniffed and Emily handed her a tissue. '...just a bit of fun...time we call it a day...before we develop feelings...' Kate blew her nose. 'Only I had *already* developed feelings. I love him. And he doesn't love me.'

'I know, Kate, I know,' Emily said, putting her arms around her friend and rocking her.

Usually they didn't reach this stage quite this quickly. Often Kate would be with them for a few months. On one occasion, it was two years. But the end result was the same.

Emily made a pot of tea and they sat on the sofa, Kate sniffing and sobbing her way through the Kleenex, Emily stroking her back and her shiny dark hair and wondering how many times she'd have to do this before Kate either met the right one or stopped letting herself become quite so smitten with the wrong ones.

This was normally an evening thing – well, perhaps it had been an evening thing and Kate had come home last night to an empty house. Emily felt a pang of guilt for not being there. On previous occasions, by the time the cardboard oval was ripped off the second box of Kleenex, it would be time to open the wine. But it wasn't even nine a.m. Bit early even by their standards.

After another pot of tea, the conversation followed its usual course. As quickly as she'd fallen in love in the first place, Kate went from loving the man in question and despairing that she'd never see him again to snorting with laughter as she regaled Emily with a long list of his faults. Freddie was lambasted for snoring, banging on about the cricket scores and miserliness when it came to tipping in restaurants.

The trick, Emily knew from experience, was to stop her here, because soon she'd be tearful again, imagining how beautiful their babies would have been, then howling because her biological clock was ticking and she'd never meet anyone else in time to have children, beautiful or otherwise.

Emily had never experienced a break-up like this. From the outside looking in, it resembled grief. No one had died, but you'd never guess that looking at Kate with her puffy eyes and her snotty nose. Emily thanked her lucky stars that she wasn't the kind of woman who fell so hard when she met a man. All her break-ups had been relatively untraumatic. Yes, it was sad when something came to an end. She was sad this morning, after what had happened with Ludek – really sad – but she'd pick herself up and life would go on.

Whereas Kate would be miserable for weeks now. Were those few weeks of excitement and happiness when she'd first met Freddie worth the heartache and agony that followed? Surely not.

'So where were you last night?' Kate asked.

'Ludek's.'

'Good one. I knew he was your type the minute I saw him. So, you two are an item now?'

'Not exactly,' Emily said. She didn't intend to tell Kate what had happened, but as they went into the kitchen to make yet another brew and find some breakfast, it all spilled out.

'You idiot,' Kate said, pouring some berries into a bowl and adding yoghurt and a sprinkling of nuts. 'Why the hell would you want to leave?'

'I don't know. I like him but…it was a feeling. An instinct almost.'

'Was he crap in bed? Because if he was, that could be fixed. I've got a book you could…'

'No, it wasn't that.'

'And now he assumes you're not that keen on him so says you should just be friends. Bit of a pattern here.'

Emily shook some cornflakes into her own bowl. 'I've no idea what you mean.'

'One word,' Kate said. 'Greg.'

Greg had been Emily's first love. She'd lost her virginity to him – she was a bit of a late starter in the sex department – and for three months, they went everywhere together. He'd proposed, presenting her with a cubic zirconia ring bought from Argos and promising to replace it when he got a better job.

'You're supposed to spend a month's salary,' he said. 'And, believe it or not, my wages are so low that almost was a month's salary for me. But I'll work my way up, buy you a proper one.'

Emily didn't doubt it for a minute. Greg was a grafter. Even Dad was impressed with him.

She read bridal magazines. She and Kate spent their Saturday shopping trips trying on designer white wedding gowns in posh shops where you had to make an appointment to go in, instead of rummaging through the sales rail at Topshop. She spent ages in front of the bathroom mirror, straightening her hair, curling her hair, putting her hair up, putting half her hair up and leaving strands of it dangling down the sides of her face, trying to work out what was the best look for her big day.

And then, one Saturday, she got back after another marathon dress-trying-on session to find her dad ashen-faced.

'You'd better sit down,' he said, handing her a cup of tea.

She took a sip and almost spat it out.

'Why've you put sugar in?' she said, but she knew. They'd given her sweet tea when Mum died. Sweet tea meant something bad had happened. Something really bad.

Greg had collapsed on the football pitch. It was his heart. He was okay, Dad said. The ambulance had reached him in time. Dad would drive her over to see him in the hospital when she was ready.

'But he's only twenty-four,' Emily said.

'I know, love. It doesn't make sense.'

Hypertrophic obstructive cardiomyopathy, the doctor said. It was, if she understood correctly, the way his heart had developed as he was growing up. He'd need to take medication to prevent it happening again.

Again? It could happen again?

'Might want to go easy on the football pitch for a while,' the doctor said.

Things were never the same after that. And Emily did the most shameful thing she had ever done in her entire life; she ended things. Told him she wasn't ready, that she was too young, that things had moved too quickly between them. Greg said he would wait; that given time, they might rekindle their relationship. But after three months, he'd met someone else and Emily didn't see him much after that.

Dad still saw his aunt sometimes in the park with the Labrador. Probably a different one by now. Apparently Greg was now happily married with four children.

'That was different with Greg,' Emily said to Kate. 'I was too young.'

'Too young? You didn't feel too young until he had a heart problem and then you couldn't get out of there quick enough. Why would you leave someone you loved because you found out they were ill? It was mean, Em, and you're not a mean person.'

'I didn't leave him because of that. Things changed. *He* changed. It felt different. It made me think about things. Made me realise I was caught up in the romance of it all – the ring, the dresses, the thought of a big wedding. But the reality – the whole "til death do us part" stuff. I suppose it scared me.'

'Yet "til death do us part" didn't scare you when it came to marrying Peter?'

'That was different.'

'You're right. It *was* different. When you talked about Peter, your face never lit up the way it did when you talked about Greg. Or the way it lights up now when you talk about Ludek. I never saw Peter make you laugh till you almost wet yourself like Greg did. When you told me Greg had proposed, you were glowing. You were very matter of fact when you told me about Peter.'

'I'm not sure what point you're trying to make. Greg was my first love. I was older when I met Peter. It was a...more mature love.'

'Okay, don't listen to me. I'm not an expert...'

'No, you're not.'

'...but you seem to steer clear of getting too emotionally involved.'

Emily was irritated. Who on earth did Kate think she was, with her amateur psycho-babble? That gift subscription to *Psychologies* magazine last Christmas had been a mistake.

They sat in silence for a few minutes. Kate had no right to tell her that she hadn't been in love with Peter. No right to bring Greg up after all these years. She didn't know what she was talking about.

'I would love,' Kate said suddenly, 'would absolutely *love*, to meet someone who makes my face light up when I talk about them. I've been looking for that my whole adult life. I watched you walk away from Greg and now I'm watching you walk away from Ludek. Twice you've had a shot at the kind of relationship I'd give anything for. The kind of relationship your parents had.'

'Yeah, and look how that ended? Not exactly a happy-ever-after for Dad, was it?'

'And *that's* the problem,' she said. 'You're scared. You watched your dad fall apart when your mum died – and he's never recovered, has he? – and now you're scared that if you love someone the way he loved her, you might end up losing them too. I didn't much like Peter, but I felt sorry for the guy. You always kept him at arm's length.'

Arm's length? How dare she?

And bringing Mum's death into this? Who did Kate think she was?

'Okay, Dr Freud.' Emily stood up. 'Interesting though this has been, I've got to go to work.'

'You don't open on Sundays.'

'Stock-take. I need to do a stock-take.'

Chapter Thirty-Three

She stomped down the high street, then stopped dead in her tracks.

There was a 'for sale' board outside Sweet Delights.

Had the competition with Costa Coffee proved too much for Peggy?

Emily didn't like the woman, but it seemed a shame. Someone had once told her there'd been a café there for over sixty years; it had been Peggy's mother's and grandmother's before her. Perhaps the new owner would keep it as a café, but Emily doubted it somehow. It'd be a brave person who took that on with one of the UK's biggest coffee shop chains practically next door.

She closed the door of the Little Board Game Café behind her with a bang, thinking about Kate again. She put her bag down, unsure of what to do now she'd got here. There was no need for a stock-take. She already knew what was in the fridge and the freezer. She made herself a pot of tea though she wasn't thirsty – not after all the tea she and Kate had drunk – and took a pack of playing cards from the shelf.

And then, sitting at one of her own tables in her own, empty café, she began a game of Solitaire.

What a crap weekend this was turning out to be. She'd screwed things up with Ludek, then fallen out with Kate. Why had sleeping with Ludek made her panic so much? Could Kate be right? Was she afraid of falling head over heels with someone for fear she might lose them? Because of the brutal way she'd lost her mum?

And what was it she'd said to Ludek? Oh, the irony. *Don't let what's happened in your past hold you back in your present.*

She felt bad about walking out on him like that, and now she felt bad about Kate too. She shouldn't have abandoned her either, not when she was upset about Freddie.

Where would she be without Kate? She'd been staying in that spare room for weeks now. Rent-free.

Emily suddenly thought of Annie. Hadn't she said she was sofa-surfing? That her friends were getting sick of her? Emily thought of their conversation outside Oxfam, how Annie had been admiring that awful dress but probably couldn't afford it, not even at charity shop prices.

An idea popped into her mind; maybe if she did something good this morning, she'd feel a bit better about things. And Julia was right: she could use some help in the café. The new Costa opening didn't seem to have had much impact upon trade.

She scrolled through her phone and found the missed call from Annie and, on the spur of the moment, without doing any calculations to see if she could afford to employ someone, sent her a text offering her four hours a day, Monday to Friday. Twelve till four. Minimum wage. Which admittedly wasn't much, but was more than she ever managed to pay herself.

Annie would probably turn it down anyway. It might interfere with her benefits or something. Working twenty hours a week wouldn't be worth it.

Emily put down her phone and picked up the cards again. When they were all sorted into their respective suits, she played another game. And then another. And then she decided that Solitaire wasn't that exciting – not compared with the games she usually played with Ludek – and she might as well open up the café if she was going to be here all day.

It was almost three o'clock when her first customer came in, a tall woman in a tweed skirt who somehow made Emily think of libraries. She ordered a pot of tea and a brownie, donned a pair of reading glasses and sat in the corner, absorbed in a paperback.

About fifteen minutes later, more customers arrived: a fair-haired woman wearing a tie-dyed dress with a dark-haired little boy in some kind of smock.

'We wanted to know what the fuss was about, didn't we?' The woman ruffled his hair.

'The fuss?'

'Insta. This place has loads of great reviews.'

Perhaps that was why it had been so busy recently. Social media was working its magic.

They sat down in the window table and requested an americano, a glass of milk and a banana. 'He only eats *natural* sugars,' said the woman.

Once Emily had taken their order over, she glanced at the other customer, who was happily pouring a second cup of tea from the pot. With no one to serve, Emily pulled out her phone, and checked out Instagram. There was a whole heap of pictures she hadn't seen. Snaps of her rocky roads, brownies, lemon drizzle and even a Chorley cake. She'd never noticed any customers taking photos of her food. This was unexpected. Flattering though.

A sudden crash interrupted her reading. She looked up. The little boy was standing by one of the empty tables and the menu, the sugar bowl and the meeple salt and pepper pots lay on the floor at his feet. Luckily nothing had broken. His mother said nothing.

The boy squealed and ran to another empty table, swiping everything onto the floor again and laughing loudly. Before Emily could stop him, he'd rushed to a third. The librarian-like customer closed her book, pulled on her coat and left. Half of her brownie lay uneaten, her tea cup was still half full. Emily was about to take them away, when there was another crash as the boy swept more items onto the floor.

Stay away from the board games, Emily prayed.

'Excuse me,' she said, walking over to his mother. 'Could you please ask your child to stop doing that?'

'Nothing's broken. I don't know what your problem is.'

She spoke too soon. The boy shoved the remains of the abandoned brownie – so much for his sugar-free diet – into his mouth and pushed the teapot onto the floor. He laughed as it smashed into pieces.

'He could have been scalded,' the mother said in an accusing tone as if it were her fault, as if making tea with boiling water was a serious health and safety breach rather than something that happened on a daily basis in homes and cafés up and down the country.

'Scalded? He ought to be *scolded*.' Emily was struggling to keep her voice calm. 'I should charge you for that teapot.'

The boy picked up the tea cup and threw it onto the floor.

'Accidents happen,' said his mother. 'Things get broken. Surely you have that all the time when you run a café.'

Deep breath, she told herself. Take a deep breath. 'It wasn't an accident though, was it? He broke that cup deliberately.'

The cup and teapot lay on the floor in a puddle of tea. The child's rampage continued, onto yet another table where the menu and salt and pepper pots once again ended up on the floor. Emily started picking things up, still praying he'd keep away from the games shelves, and cursing under her breath as she discovered that one of the meeples salt pots was cracked. She put everything back on the tables, but this only added to his game and he followed her round the café, swiping them onto the floor again.

'Please,' said Emily. 'Get your child under control.'

She made no attempt to sound calm this time and the mother looked furious. 'My husband and I don't believe in saying "no" to Charlie.'

For a second, Emily thought they were cocaine addicts, but then realised she was referring to the little boy.

'Clearly,' she said under her breath.

To Emily's relief, the mother was gathering her things now, coats and bags. Finally, she grabbed the boy's hand and said, 'Come on, darling, we're not staying in this dreadful little place a moment longer.'

And they left, letting the door slam behind them. Emily turned to survey the damage. The only breakages were the teapot, the cup and the cracked meeple salt pot. She cleared up as quickly as she could, not wanting any customers to come in and see the mess. In her haste, she cut her finger on one particularly sharp shard and dripped blood all over the floor. Having put on a plaster, Emily mopped the floor, then put back all the menus and salt and pepper pots. Order was resumed. You couldn't tell anything had happened. But she was still seething that someone could allow their child to run riot then make her feel that she was to blame. She didn't know there was worse to come.

Monday was quiet. The workmen still came for their sausage butties but there seemed fewer of them. Mr B never missed his Chorley cake and arrived at four minutes past eleven wearing a polka-dot purple bow-tie, but Marjory wasn't with him.

Then, at ten to twelve, Annie appeared.

'I wasn't sure what to wear,' she said. 'Is there a uniform or anything? I don't have chef whites, I'm afraid.'

'Chef whites?'

'To wear in the kitchen.'

'I thought you'd wait tables whilst I cook.'

Hang on. Emily hadn't even known that she was accepting the job, let alone that she'd be starting today.

'I thought I'd bake the cakes. I'm brilliant at baking. Isn't that why you offered me a job?'

Emily opened her mouth but said nothing. What could she say? *I felt sorry for you. I only offered you a job because I was feeling guilty about having fallen out with my best friend and the man I fancy – no, make that love – and I wanted to do something nice for someone to make myself feel better.*

Or, *I was dog-tired last week and thought I needed help but actually it was quiet this morning so perhaps I don't after all.*

And then her mouth opened again and she said, 'Yeah, baking would be great.'

'I thought I could make cube-shaped sponge cakes and decorate them to look like dice, rectangular biscuits that would be dominoes and gingerbread meeples.'

Emily was so surprised by these brilliant ideas and by the fact that Annie knew what a meeple was – she hadn't; not till she'd met Ludek – that she found herself saying, 'Yes, that all sounds amazing.'

The next minute Annie was in the kitchen, wearing Emily's apron and searching through her spice selection looking for ginger and Emily was standing behind the counter feeling redundant in her own café.

Only two people ventured in for lunch, ordering soups of the day. As Emily ladled out the creamy mushroom into two white bowls, and put two crusty rolls and two pats of butter on the side, she couldn't help but notice the baking smell in the kitchen. It was heavenly.

Florence, Mrs Scott and Mrs Sinclair didn't appear which was unusual as they always came in for lunch and Scrabble on Mondays – other days too sometimes, but always on Mondays. When the two customers had gone, Emily wandered into the kitchen to see what Annie was doing.

'You don't have many mixing bowls,' she said. 'Could you wash that one up for me please?'

Emily did as instructed, washing and drying the bowl and handing it to her new employee.

'Thanks. Could you measure out eight hundred grams of self-raising flour?'

'Yeah, sure.'

Emily measured out the flour, thinking that she should be the one giving the orders. And then Annie needed eggs whisking, so she did that too, all the while wondering why she'd decided to take the woman on in the first place.

By half past two, Annie had turned out perfect batches of dice sponge cakes, domino biscuits and gingerbread meeples. There was no one there to eat them yet, but Emily was sure they'd go down a storm with the mums and kids crowd.

Half past three came and went. School must have finished but not one mum or child ventured in.

'I'm grateful for the job,' said Annie, 'but I don't understand why you needed to take someone on. It's not exactly busy.'

'It isn't always this quiet,' Emily said. But who was she kidding? It *was* usually this quiet. She'd just had one busy month and jumped to the wrong conclusion: that her fortunes were changing because of the board games theme.

Annie left on the dot at four. Emily turned the sign to closed, bolted the door and cashed up. As she already suspected, takings were down significantly on the previous week. Just when she'd thought she was finally beginning to get somewhere. What the hell had happened?

Then it dawned on her. That fair-haired woman with the badly behaved child had said she'd come in because she'd read about the place on Insta. She'd probably left a review of her own. A quick search and Emily found it: a very ordinary-looking photo of the glass of milk and banana that she'd ordered for Charlie, with a damning review underneath.

I had high hopes when I visited this café, drawn by all the excellent reviews. Honestly, I cannot see what all the fuss is about. It's very ordinary. The cakes and coffee aren't bad but their nothing special. But the worst thing is the woman who runs it – she's so rude. She actually told my child off when he was only playing. This is not the place to go if you have children. She needs to be more tolerent if she's going to run a café.

The post had thirty-seven likes. Thirty-seven! She hadn't had more than half a dozen on any of the pictures that she'd posted in recent weeks.

Emily clicked on her reviewer's profile: over nine thousand followers and most of her posts were reviews of cafés and restaurants.

Bloody social media. It was so unjust. She slumped into a chair, her head in her hands. Was this why the school mums hadn't shown up? Solidarity amongst mothers?

She should have kept calm.

She *would* have kept calm if she hadn't already been in a bad mood because of her lack of sleep the previous night and her argument with Kate.

Of course, there could be other reasons why she hadn't had many customers today. It could be… What exactly? No, it had to be that review.

She'd blown it. After all her hard work. If she'd just

been patient for a few minutes longer, the woman would have finished her coffee and taken her naughty child away. She wouldn't have written her appalling review and Emily would still have customers and a business that was well on the way to being successful.

And now she was back to square one. No, worse than square one. When she was at square one, the café didn't have a reputation. Now it had a bad one.

Chapter Thirty-Four

Books by Emily's Kate's spare bedside: *Overcoming Setbacks*; *The Bounce Back Book*; *What to Do When You've F***ed Up*.

Next morning. Some customers. Much to Emily's relief. 'This place needs a proper sign,' said Rob as he waited for his breakfast. 'It says Lancashire Hotpot over the front and The Little Board Game Café in the window.'

'I can't afford a sign-writer.'

'Can I have a crack at it? I wouldn't want paying. I love doing things like that. Helps me relax of an evening.'

'Would you? That'd be wonderful.'

'I'll pop in for it later, on my way home. Can you do me a rough sketch of what you'd want it to look like?'

'Thank you, yeah. I will. Bacon butties on me today, guys.'

She kicked herself when they'd left. She couldn't afford to be giving food away, even for a new sign. She'd be out of business soon and, let's face it, a new sign wasn't going to change that.

But was there anything she could do? How about taking to social media again herself? With the café empty, she took photo after photo, trying to get the perfect shot. The jam jars full of Scrabble tiles. The table tops. The canvases. The shelves of board games, mostly Ludek's. She shuddered, thinking how much damage Charlie *could* have done. She'd have to return them.

She flicked through the photos, trying to decide which one to use first, finally settling on a photo of a coffee mug with one of Annie's dice cakes in the foreground, taken from a low angle so you could see two of the canvases in soft focus in the background. She uploaded it to Instagram, tagging it with #boardgames, #boardgamescafé, #Essendale, #deliciouscakes.

Mr B arrived for coffee with two of his Polish friends. Instead of Chorley cakes, they ordered three domino biscuits.

'You've surpassed yourself with these, Emily,' said Mr B. 'I love your Chorley cakes but these are out of this world.'

Emily decided not to mention that she hadn't actually baked them.

The men began a game of Scrabble in Polish, but gave up after ten minutes; apparently there weren't enough 'z' tiles in the English set for the words they wanted to make.

On Wednesday, Mr B and Marjory both ordered dice cakes, proclaiming them divine, before embarking on a game of Ticket to Ride.

'I still prefer Scrabble,' Mr B said. 'These other games are...'

'...a bit complicated for the likes of us,' said Marjory. 'But we like the new games-themed cakes. So imaginative. And they taste great. Your baking's getting better and better, Emily. You should go on *The Great British Bake Off*.'

It had definitely been a mistake taking Annie on: not only would she have to raid what remained of her savings to pay her wages if trade didn't pick up by Friday, but Annie's superior baking was showing Emily's up.

On Thursday lunchtime, the door opened and the familiar little black wheels of a shopping trolley appeared in the doorway. Emily rushed over to help, grabbing the door as Mrs Sinclair and Mrs Scott came in and sat down at their usual table as if they'd never been away.

'You haven't been in for a few days,' Emily said, as she went over to take their order.

'Half-term, dear,' said the taller one. 'I went away for a few days with my son, daughter-in-law and their four children and I'm exhausted. Baby-sitting every single evening so they could enjoy themselves. I'm saying no next year.'

'And you, Mrs...?' Emily hesitated. 'Have you been somewhere nice?'

'No, but I didn't want to come in without Sylvia. I can't handle Florence on my own. She insists we play Scrabble and she's very argumentative. Last week I made the word "check-in" and she said it was hyphenated, and I didn't have a g to make it into "checking" and she said I had to miss...'

At that moment, the door opened and Florence appeared.

Mrs Scott – or was she Mrs Sinclair? – looked slightly guilty and said, 'I think I'll have the hotpot again please, dear.'

Her former MIL2B greeted her with a kiss on both cheeks and said, 'I'll have one of your delicious hotpots too, please, Emily.'

Emily went to the kitchen, marvelling first at how friendly Florence had been and secondly at the fact that their absence had had nothing to do with the bad review. School holidays! It hadn't occurred to her. Did that explain Julia and George's absence too?

On Friday, Julia and George appeared, but there were no other mums with them.

'Julia, can I ask you something?' Emily said, placing their order on the table.

'Fire away.'

'It's just... I haven't seen you for a while.'

'Centre Parcs,' she said. 'I'm exhausted.'

'Nothing to do with the review then?'

'Review?'

'A customer left me a bad review on Instagram,' Emily said. 'And she posted it on TripAdvisor and Facebook too. Then you stopped coming in and a couple of other people too. I was worried I'd lost my best customers. Thought I'd go bankrupt.' She laughed to make it sound as if she was joking.

'I don't know anything about a review.' Julia took a sip of her americano. 'God, I needed that. You're a nightmare in the school holidays, aren't you, George?'

George was looking at the games shelves, dithering between Carcassonne and Ticket to Ride.

'Show me the review,' said Julia.

Emily found it quickly and handed over her phone.

'Blimey, that is bad.'

George arrived back at the table with Ticket to Ride. He nuzzled up to his mother so he could see her phone screen. Emily went to peer over her shoulder, although she knew it practically word for word by now as she'd read it so often.

...The cakes and coffee aren't bad but their nothing special. But the worst thing is the woman who runs it – she's so rude....She needs to be more tolerent if she's going to run a café.

'Mum would never, ever take any notice of that,' said George. 'There are spelling mistakes. It's tol-er-ant. And they put "t-h-e-i-r" when it should have been "they're" with an apostrophe.'

'*No one's* going to take any notice of this,' said Julia. 'It's a bit of a rant. I don't think you need to worry about it.'

'That's good, because I took your advice and I've found someone to help with the café. Annie. I used to work with her at Ridley's. She's doing the baking.'

'Ah,' said Julia. 'I was hoping you wouldn't have done that quite so soon.'

Chapter Thirty-Five

Julia waited until Annie had gone home at four o'clock before she explained.

'How long did you sign the lease on this place for?'

'A year initially. Normally they'd want you to sign for longer, but less commitment felt like less risk. I thought that was a good thing. You know, in case it didn't work out? And if it did work out, I could just renew it.'

'Yeah, I can see why you'd think that. You haven't seen the planning notices, have you?'

'Planning notices?'

'On the lamp-posts outside.'

There were always notices in Essendale – as Rob had said, there was a shortage of homes in the valley and people were always wanting to build new ones, or extend existing ones – and Emily never stopped to read them. They never seemed that interesting.

She stared down at the table, barely able to take in what Julia was saying. '...outlying planning permission... demolish...block of flats ...'

'So, they mightn't get planning permission?'

'You could fight it, of course. Get your customers to object. I'd be happy to write something, although I doubt the council will listen. There's such a demand for homes here.'

'But...but...what about Annie?'

'Yeah, I know. And what about you?'

'I'll be okay,' Emily said. 'I'm staying with Kate. She doesn't charge me rent. Although, well, we had a bit of an argument, but she'd never turf me out. But Annie was hoping to save up and get her own place again. Not that I pay her enough for that, but a job is something, isn't it?'

'It certainly is. Being unemployed isn't exactly good for the self-esteem.'

'God, poor Annie. Laid off twice in the space of just a few months. First by my fiancé – well, ex-fiancé – and now by me.'

'My fault for encouraging you to take someone on. I was hoping I'd get a chance to tell you before you found anyone.'

'It was a spur-of-the-moment decision. I bumped into her outside Oxfam and felt sorry for her. I can't believe it. Do they really want to demolish this place?'

'Seems so.'

'But I've decorated it. Bought canvases. What will I do with all the tables? Mr B and I spent hours painting all them. Days, in fact.'

Julia put her hand on Emily's. 'Perhaps you could start again. Set up a new board game café. Isn't Sweet Delights for sale?'

'Yeah, but I couldn't afford it. I blew all my money on buying this place. Surely they can't just do this – let you spend thousands buying a business then kick you out when you've barely got started.'

'I honestly don't know, Em. You'd have to ask a lawyer.'

'I *had* a lawyer. When I bought this place. Shouldn't he have pointed this out? That it was a risk?'

Julia shrugged. 'They probably hadn't applied for planning permission then. But I'm not an expert. You'd have to ask someone.'

'Another lawyer?'

A tear ran down Emily's cheek. George, who'd been playing on his mother's phone, pulled a grubby tissue out of his pocket and offered it to her.

'Er, thanks, George, but I think I'll pass on that,' said Emily. She stood up and went to find a napkin. 'And Rob offered to paint the sign. It was going to look so great. But I guess I won't be needing that now.'

On the way home, she walked past Sweet Delights, its red and white for sale board still firmly fixed above the door.

Essendale had two independent cafés, but soon it would be left with none. Just a Costa Coffee. Not that Emily had anything against Costa Coffee or any of those coffee chains. But that was the point. They were chains. Big chains moving in would change the whole high street; one by one, the small businesses would close. It had happened in so many other towns and now it was happening here.

Unless…unless she bought Sweet Delights like Julia had suggested.

Nah. Emily didn't need Google to know that it'd be out of her price range. She didn't even have a price range. Buying Nico's had wiped her out. Her café dreams were over.

★

It was probably best, she decided on Monday morning, to tell Annie straight away. Get it over and done with. Tell her that fabulous though her baking was – admittedly Emily was still a bit sore about that – the café would be closing soon. She had phoned the landlord to double-check, but Julia was right: the rumours were true.

'I don't suppose,' he'd said, 'you'd like to shut up shop sooner rather than later. Save yourself a few months' rent. The developers will be chomping at the bit to get started as soon as the planning permission comes through.'

Saving herself some rent sounded good. If she was going to have to close anyway once her lease was up, what was the point in carrying on now? She could limit her losses. Move on from the place as soon as possible. Draw a line under the whole sorry episode.

But then…he was kicking her out for heaven's sake. Did she really want to roll over and say, 'Yes sure, here are the keys.'

She could at least make him wait for her answer.

'I'll think about it,' she said.

On Monday morning, she was on autopilot. Her heart wasn't in it as she served up the bacon and sausage butties to Rob and his mates.

'Thanks for offering to do the sign,' she said. 'But I changed my mind. I don't think I need one.'

'Suit yourself,' he said frowning. 'Gift horse in the mouth and all that.'

'What's up with you?' said Marjory later as she and Mr B tucked into their gingerbread meeples. 'These are delicious. We thought your Chorley cakes were good, but these...! Sublime, aren't they, Stan?'

'Nothing's up,' Emily said. It wasn't fair to tell them before she told Annie.

Annie was in a very cheerful mood when she arrived at twelve o'clock. She rolled her sleeves up and said, 'Right, what needs baking?'

'Can you do Gimme S'mores cakes?' Emily said remembering how she'd promised George on his first visit. Might as well honour that promise before she closed the doors on the Little Board Game Café for the final time.

'Sure,' she said, 'but you'll need to buy marshmallows.'

'I'll pop out and get some. Before the lunchtime rush.'

Emily set off for the corner shop. She didn't need Gimme S'mores cakes. Didn't need to buy marshmallows. This was a delaying tactic on her part, putting off the awful moment when she broke the bad news.

The café was full when Emily returned with the last three bags of marshmallows from the shop. Full. Mrs Scott, Mrs Sinclair and Florence were finishing off plates of Lancashire hotpot. There was a table of four in the corner scoffing all-day breakfasts, two tables with soup and sandwiches, two tables waiting for their orders and Annie was in the kitchen, whistling.

Annie thrust two plates of sandwiches into her boss's hands. 'Deliver these to table four, please, Em.'

'Which one's table four?' She had never numbered the tables.

'The couple playing chess. In the corner.'

She'd just delivered the sandwiches when Annie bobbed her head through the hatch and called, 'Service, please.' Emily scurried back and collected two bowls of soup, with rolls and butter. You couldn't fault Annie; perfect baking and efficient to boot. And she was nothing like the person Emily had thought she was, when they'd worked together at Ridley's. Emily felt even more awful at the thought of telling Annie the bad news.

'Table six,' Annie said.

'Which one's...?'

'By the window. Scrabble.'

Emily delivered the soup. As soon as everyone had gone, she would tell her.

When the last of the customers had left, Emily locked the door so they wouldn't be interrupted. She headed for the kitchen. It was stiflingly hot in there. Annie was doing her best impression of Martha and the Vandellas, singing 'Heatwave' at the top of her voice as she cleared up. Not that there was much to clear up; the place was pristine. It would have been an entirely different matter if Emily had had to prep lunch for six tables.

'Oh, Em, I've got something to tell you,' said Annie. 'I'm so excited. I've been offered...' She did a mock drum roll on the worktop with her knuckles.

Emily said a silent prayer. Please let her hand in her notice. Say she'd got another job.

'...a caravan.'

Emily wasn't expecting that. 'A caravan? Are you planning a holiday?'

'No. To live in. It's in a field on a farm between here and Hebbleswick. I'll be able to walk to work along the canal towpath. Oh, Em, it's such a relief because my friend wants her sofa back. She said I had to find somewhere by the end of next week and I've been so stressed about it. I can't thank you enough for giving me this job, because I couldn't have afforded the rent on the caravan without it. Although it is quite low rent because they want me to bake cakes for the farm shop. But I won't let that affect my work here, I promise.'

'A caravan,' Emily said again. Oh god, she couldn't tell her now, could she?

Peggy was pulling her A-board in as Emily walked past Sweet Delights that evening.

'Any buyers?' Emily asked.

'No, why? Are you interested? I hear your place is doing very well. You're going to need bigger premises soon.'

She was going to be *out* of her premises soon, but she didn't want Peggy knowing that. Not yet. She mustn't tell anyone until she'd told Annie. 'No, I'm happy where I am, thanks.'

It was true, Emily realised. She had been happy. She'd had the best few weeks, running her little café. Trying out that dream that she'd shared with Mum for all those years. True, she hadn't had many customers at first. And she'd lost money rather than making it. And there'd been many lonely hours standing behind that counter longing for some customers to come in, and the awful incident with Marjory choking on a nut and that dreadful child running round smashing things. But she'd made new friends – Mr B, Julia and George – and she'd learned to cook Polish food and even her former MIL2B was being nice to her these days because she liked playing Scrabble in the café. It had been good while it lasted.

'Why are you selling up?' Emily said.

'The competition,' she said. 'I'm losing customers.'

'I couldn't believe it when I heard Costa was opening.'

'Not Costa, Emily. You. Everyone prefers your place to mine these days. I blame those wretched games.'

'Me? You're selling because of me?'

Emily felt dreadful. She had wanted her business to be a success, but not at the expense of someone else's.

And Peggy looked miserable. Devastated.

Emily had to tell her. She couldn't let her rival sell the café that had been in her family for decades. Not when The Little Board Game Café was closing soon anyway.

'Peggy, please don't mention this to anyone – I haven't told Annie yet that she'll be out of a job – but you won't have competition for much longer. I'm closing my business. The building's being demolished.'

'Oh, Emily. Come here.'

The A-board clattered onto the pavement as Peggy pulled Emily in for a hug. 'I'm so sorry. I know how hard it is running a café and I bet you've poured your heart and soul into that place, haven't you?'

'I have. Mum and I always wanted to run a café. She was killed when I was sixteen and I used my inheritance to buy it. And I've lost that now. It's worthless.'

'Buy my place.'

'I can't afford it. I've got nothing left. And anyway, you needn't sell now. Your customers will be back. Most of my games are borrowed, but you can have the ones that aren't. Turn Sweet Delights into a board game café.'

'Nice idea, but I don't think so. I've rather set my heart on retiring to Spain. My daughter lives out there. I just need a buyer.'

'I'm sure you'll find one soon. Good luck, Peggy.'

'And good luck to you too, Emily.'

The following morning, Annie arrived in an even more cheerful mood than she'd been in the previous day. She clearly didn't read the planning notices on lamp-posts either, Emily thought. Thank goodness. She had to break the news before word got round.

'Look what I found in Oxfam.' Annie reached into a plastic bag and pulled out a pale-blue cushion decorated with an appliquéd cupcake. 'For my new caravan. I'm moving in on Friday.'

'That's wonderful news.'

Emily looked at the cushion and decided. She wouldn't let the landlord have his building back yet. The Little Board Game Café would stay open, until the last possible moment, to give Annie time to find another job so she could still rent her caravan. Emily would search the internet for her, write glowing references, whatever it took. Her mind was made up.

At least it *was* made up. Until her phone rang.

'Hello, is that Em?' said a familiar voice. A voice she hadn't heard in a long time.

Chapter Thirty-Six

Richard Thorp had heard about the café. Apparently, news travelled fast along the Essendale and Hebbleswick business network's grapevine.

'It's marvellous timing, Em,' he said.

'It doesn't feel like it to me.'

'No, no, that was tactless of me. Obviously, it's sad for the café. I heard you were doing well. But we miss you here at Thorp's and your replacement has just given in her notice. The job's yours if you want it.'

She had enjoyed that job. She'd never have left if it hadn't been for Peter. She wasn't sure she'd enjoyed it as much as running a café though. Still, that wasn't an option anymore.

'Could you wait two months, Richard? I could join you then.'

'No, I need someone sooner. By the end of the month ideally. To have a handover period with Sally.'

Emily wasn't sure she needed a handover period for a job that she'd already spent several years doing. But Richard was insistent. Either she took the job now. Or she didn't take the job at all.

*

Annie cried when Emily broke the news.

'I really wanted that caravan,' she said.

'I feel terrible. How about I pay the rent on it? I've got a new job. Kate doesn't charge me rent so I could pay yours. A kind of pay-it-forward thing. At least until you get another job.'

'But I'd never be able to pay you back,' said Annie.

'You needn't. You could find a way of paying it forward yourself. Help someone else out somehow. When you're able to. It needn't be money.'

'It's kind of you, Em, but I can't let you pay my rent. I'll think of something. Don't worry about me.'

Emily found an auction where you could sell second-hand professional kitchen equipment. She went to watch. You could spot the new café owners a mile off – it was the hope on their faces. Perhaps they'd fare better than she had. Her stuff didn't make much, but she insisted on Annie taking what she did make. Annie argued, of course, but finally gave in.

Emily returned all of Ludek's games and told him the café had closed.

'Your Friday-night games group will have to go back to playing in the pub,' she told him.

'Oh, Em, I'm so sorry. I hope you'll still be joining us.'

'I don't think so, Ludek. I'll see you around.'

She was through with board games. She'd loved them, almost as much as Ludek did, but playing games would always remind her of what she had lost. She took all the ones she owned – the chess sets, the Scrabble and the three

Buckaroo!s – to Oxfam. She kept just two: Masala! as she could hardly give that away when Ludek had taken so much trouble to make it; and Can't Stop! which she kept as a reminder that risks were never worth taking.

She'd never wear her Scrabble dress again, so she donated it to the hospice shop in Hebbleswick, rather than to Oxfam in Essendale. The volunteers in Oxfam would only have put it on a mannequin in the window, and Emily didn't want to see it there every time she walked past: a reminder of her failure.

Mr B insisted on storing the tables in his shed. 'Because you never know,' he said.

He hadn't got room for the chairs, so Emily gave those away on Facebook.

She took him and Marjory a large Tupperware full of Chorley cakes and owned up that she hadn't baked the domino biscuits, dice sponges or gingerbread meeples. 'They were Annie's. She was a better baker than me by far.'

She went to watch the day they began to demolish the café. She debated asking if she could keep the old Lancashire Hotpot sign, but what would be the point?

She'd imagined a controlled explosion and then The Little Board Game Café falling to the ground, like you saw on the news when they demolished a power station. But it was far less dramatic. The bulldozers moved in and they kind of chipped away at it. There wasn't even one of those giant balls.

She went back a few days later. The whole place had been reduced to a pile of bricks. If this were a film, Emily thought, there'd be a solitary meeple somewhere, lying in the dust. She would pick it up and keep it for ever to remember the café by.

But it wasn't.

There may well have been the odd meeple, playing card or dice lurking in the rubble, but Emily didn't stop to look. She turned away and went to Costa for a hot chocolate and a Gimme S'mores cake to cheer herself up.

Chapter Thirty-Seven

It was as if she had gone back in time.

Every morning she would go to work at Thorp's. She'd type Richard's letters and make his coffee. At five-thirty, she went back to her little flat, the upper floor of a terraced house very much like the flat she used to rent before she moved in with Peter. This flat was above a hairdresser's rather than above Marjory's so there was no one downstairs in an evening if she wanted to share a cuppa.

Kate was grateful to have her house to herself again, but they were still friends and always would be. They'd patched up their argument over a bottle or three of Sauvignon Blanc in the Red Lion one Friday evening. Emily wondered if the board games group were upstairs but if they were, she didn't see them.

Occasionally Kate would rope her into being her wingman and drag her along to some awful event. Speed-dating. Salsa dancing. A 'golf for beginners' day at Peter's club.

'As long as you never expect me to go to running club,' Emily said. 'I'm not doing that ever again.'

'It wasn't my thing either,' Kate admitted.

One day Peter arrived at Thorp's for a meeting with Richard. It really was like old times. He and Emily even laughed about whether there was paper stuck in the printer. She half-expected him to ask her out again.

'Mother says hello by the way,' he said.

'Say hello back from me.'

'She says to tell you that she misses your cooking. She and Sylvia were asked to leave Costa last week because they were arguing too loudly over a game of Scrabble.'

'That sounds like your mother.'

The following day, a huge bunch of red roses arrived for Emily at Thorp's. There was no card. They had to be from Peter, she thought, although red roses were never his style. But she'd had the feeling that it had been on the tip of his tongue to ask her out again the previous day as they'd joked about the printer. And who else would they be from?

But she didn't want Peter back, and she didn't want his roses.

She was going to Thornholme straight from work that evening. She still hadn't told her mum about the café dream being over. She hadn't been able to face it. On her way out of the office, Emily scooped the flowers up, intending to put them into the first bin she saw on her way to the bus stop but she didn't pass a bin.

'I brought you some flowers,' she said, placing them down on the grave. Peter had been thoughtful enough to buy the ones that come with their stems in a plastic bag filled with water. The bouquet was a little top heavy, but Emily balanced it against the headstone.

'Red roses! Dad'll think you've got an admirer. He'll probably be jealous.'

Mum would have laughed at that.

'Dad will be jealous of what?'

Emily looked up to see her dad standing above her.

'I didn't know you were coming this weekend,' he said. 'That's a lovely surprise.'

She hadn't actually been intending to stay. But then again, she had nothing better to do.

'I wanted to talk to Mum. I've something important to tell her.'

'You know, Em, you can talk to me too. I'm always here for you.'

Emily stood up. 'Okay, well, I can tell you both. The dream that Mum and I always shared – that one day we'd run our own café – well, it's over. I tried. I failed. The Little Board Game Café has gone. Demolished.'

'Demolished? That's a bit dramatic. What did you do? Burn the all-day breakfast and set fire to the place? I thought that was more Kate's style than yours.'

'The landlord wanted the building back. He's sold it to a developer. They're building flats there now. I didn't do enough research. Do you think Mum's looking down on me, furious that I've lost my inheritance?'

At that moment, the roses toppled over.

'That's her saying no,' said Dad. He bent down, setting them upright again. 'Your mum would never be furious. She'd be proud of you for giving it a go. Let's go and have a cup of tea.' He lowered his voice. 'I've gone back to Yorkshire Tea. Don't tell your mother.'

And at that, the flowers toppled over again.

★

Dad filled the kettle. 'I thought things were going well for you.'

'Not at first. I had no customers. Then things went well for a month or so, until I heard that the landlord wouldn't be renewing my lease and there didn't seem much point after that. I still wish you'd seen it.'

Dad ignored her last comment. 'Why didn't you get many customers?'

'It wasn't a great location, to be honest. No passing trade. People tend to stay in the town centre. That's why I turned it into a board game café. I thought I could lure them in by offering something extra. My USP. It worked for a bit.'

'Why didn't you buy in a better location?'

'It was all I could afford.'

'You could have borrowed some money.'

'Too much of a risk.'

'That's the problem with you, Em. Always afraid to take a risk.'

'Said the person who never leaves Thornholme.'

Dad frowned and sipped his tea. 'We're talking about you, Em. Not me.'

'Yeah, but ...'

'So what are you going to do now?'

'I'm working at Thorp's. Luckily for me, my old job came up at exactly the right time.'

'Pity that,' said Dad.

'How is it a pity?'

'You're going to go back to where you were a few years ago. Same old, same old.'

'Said the person who never leaves Thornholme,' Emily said again.

Her dad ignored her. 'Next minute you'll be telling me you're back with Peter. Or is there someone new? Please tell me you've found someone new.'

'There was someone, but that didn't work out either.'

Dad rolled his eyes. 'Okay, let's sort out what we're going to do about this café dream of yours, and then we'll discuss your love life.'

There was no café dream. Not anymore. But nor did she want to discuss her love life with her father so she decided she'd indulge him and talk about the café.

'I shouldn't have bought a café on a back street in a town where Costa Coffee was about to open. Not that I knew it was. But maybe if I'd done more research. Even Sweet Delights has been struggling and that's in a great position on the high street. That's for sale now.'

'Well, there's your answer.'

'My answer?'

'You buy Sweet Delights.'

'I can't, Dad. I've no money. Buying Nico's wiped me out. And don't tell me to borrow the cash because no one would lend to me – not with my track record in business – and, as you pointed out, I don't like taking risks.'

'I have the money.'

'*You* do? Since when?'

'Your mother's life insurance. I never felt right about spending it. Sometimes wondered about buying myself an Austin Healey one day. That's always been my dream. But what's the point? As you say, I never go anywhere.' He sighed.

'But you can't give me your money, Dad. What if I lost it? I've already made a complete mess of one café. I'm quite capable of screwing up another.'

'All successful entrepreneurs have their failures, Em. It's how they learn. Look at Branson. Before he started Virgin Records, he... Actually I'm not sure what he did, but I'm sure he had the odd failure or two. On Monday morning, you're going to find out how much Sweet Delights is going for.'

'No, Dad. Thanks, but no.'

'Okay, *I'll* buy the café. And you can run it. How does that sound?'

'Dad, no. I can't let you do that.'

'I *want* to do that. I listened to your mother chattering on about running a café for years and it's beautiful that you share her dream, Em. I'd like to be part of it.'

Well, when he put it like that, it would be kind of churlish to say no. And he looked so hopeful. Like this was what *he* really wanted.

'But what about *your* dream? Your Austin Healey?'

'It's only a car, Em. Perhaps one day, I'll get to sit in one. Have a little ride in it even. Let's buy a café together. Father and daughter. Not quite as good as mother and daughter, but it's the best I can do.'

'On one condition, Dad.'

'Name it.'

'You have to come and visit.'

'Fine,' said Dad. 'You've got yourself a deal. Now, that's the café sorted. Tell me about this man of yours. What's he called?'

'Ludek. But he's not mine. It's over.'

'And it's over because…'

'It's hard to explain. I had strong feelings for him, but then I kind of panicked.'

'I've noticed over the years that you always seem more comfortable with men if …' He hesitated, looking at her face, as if he was unsure whether he dared say it.

And Emily wasn't sure she wanted to hear it, but she said, 'Go on.'

'You always seem more comfortable with men if you can keep them at arm's length.'

'Have you been talking to Kate?'

'No, why?'

'That's what she said. *Exactly* what she said.'

'Well, maybe there's something in it then,' he said. 'I've known you all your life. She's known you for most of it. If this is something we've both picked up on…'

'I'm not sure what you mean by "keeping them at arm's length"?'

'Well, look at Peter. I mean, he's a decent guy and everything, but you shouldn't marry someone you can live with. You should marry someone you can't live without. That's how I felt about your mum.'

'And then she died, you *had* to live without her. And you've never, ever seemed happy since.'

'That's true,' he said. 'You bring me a lot of joy, but I've never felt truly happy since I lost your mum. Not deep down.'

'You're not making a very good case for the "can't-live-without-them" kind of love.'

'We're back to taking risks, Em. The "can't-live-without-them" love brings such joy. I can't describe how I felt the day she said yes to me. The day she told me we were expecting you. Watching her breast-feed you. Seeing her face full of pride the day you sang that solo in the school nativity. I felt so happy that I wanted to burst. But when you allow yourself to feel great love like that, you risk great heartbreak too. Like when they came to tell me at work about the accident. Seeing her in the hospital…words can't describe the pain I felt. And it's never gone away. It's changed, perhaps, over time. But it's still there. I miss her every day.'

'Oh, Dad,' Emily said, reaching across the table and stroking his hair. 'I miss her too. And I never, ever want to miss anyone like that ever again.'

'Then you'll never experience the kind of love your mother and I had, Em. And I feel very sad for you.'

He stood up, took the kitchen roll from the worktop, tore off a sheet and dabbed at his eyes. Then he placed the roll on the table in front of her. He filled the kettle and flicked it on.

'Tea,' he said. 'We need more tea.'

Her dad opened the cupboard and rummaged through the mugs. He selected two, put a teabag into each and got the milk out of the fridge. He stood gazing out of the window whilst he waited for the tea to brew.

'Remember when your rabbit died?' he said as he placed two mugs on the table. 'You said, "I never want another pet ever again."'

'And I've never had another pet.'

'And you've missed out. I don't know what I'd do without the cat. Some days, she's the only person I speak to.'

Smudge chose that moment to appear through the cat flap and wind around Emily's legs. Emily reached down and stroked her fur, listening to the loud purrs. She had to admit it was soothing, comforting.

'If you don't allow yourself to really love someone,' said her dad, 'then yes, you protect yourself from the pain of losing them one day. But you also miss out on all the good things. If I could put the clock back, if I'd chosen Joan or Elfrida or that woman from the Co-op – they all had their eye on me, you know – I'd still be with her now. I'd have spared myself the heartbreak of watching your mum's life support machine being switched off. Of watching my little girl sobbing her heart out. They were dreadful times, Em. You know they were. But they were worth it for the good times I shared with your mother.'

Emily had never heard Dad make such a long speech. Let alone such a long, impassioned one. It was a lot to take in.

'I...'

'Let me finish, Em,' he said. 'I'm on a roll.'

He took a sip of his tea then continued. 'My grief means I never leave Thornholme. I should, I know, and I can't quite put my finger on why I don't. It's as if by staying here... Well, your mother's still close to me somehow. Your grief means you keep men at a distance. You avoid getting too attached. I have no idea if Ludek is the one for you. But I've promised I'll pluck up the courage to come and visit your new café, Em. If I can do that, the next time you get a chance at love, proper head-over-heels, can't-live-without-them love, promise me you won't shy away.'

'I dunno, Dad...'

'Promise me, Em.'

'Okay. I promise.'

Chapter Thirty-Eight

Books by Emily's bedside: *Recipe for Success –
How to Run A Profitable Café; Good Grief – Positive
Ways to Heal After Bereavement; Swipe Right – A
Guide to Twenty-First Century Dating.* (That last one
was a flat-warming gift from Kate; Emily wasn't sure
she'd bother to read it.)

Emily drained her glass of rioja. 'Kate, I need a wingman.'
'A wingman?'

'Yep. We're going to the running club.'

'The running club? Seriously? Ah, I get it. You want to see Ludek again.'

'No. I could go to the board games group to see Ludek, and I wouldn't need a wingman for that. Perhaps it's not a wingman I need exactly. More moral support. Clipboard Woman was really scary.'

'Why the sudden interest in running? Are you wanting to get fit?'

'Nah, don't be silly,' said Emily. 'I like cake too much for that.'

*

Clipboard Woman didn't remember them.

'Welcome,' she said, almost smiling. 'Always nice to see new members.'

'I've brought my medical form,' Emily said, handing it over. 'Kate, d'you have yours?'

When Clipboard Woman had gathered all her forms from the new arrivals, she instructed the group to form a circle around her, called her helpers into the middle and introduced them.

Damn. He wasn't here. This evening was going to be a complete waste of time. He was the only reason she'd wanted to come.

'Right, warm-up,' said Clipboard Woman. 'Jogging on the spot. Knees high.'

Emily could see why it was called the warm-up. She was hot and sweaty within about thirty seconds.

'Who are you looking for?' said Kate.

'No one.'

'It's Ludek, isn't it? I knew this was about him.'

'No, not Ludek. I don't think he helps with the beginners—'

Kate nudged her. 'He's rather nice. Look!'

Emily followed her gaze and saw him sprinting over the grass. He joined Clipboard Woman and the other helpers in the middle of the circle. Not a wasted evening after all.

He caught Emily's eye and gave a little wave. She gave a bigger one back.

When the warm-up was over and they began to run, he came straight over and ran alongside her and Kate.

'How are you, Em?' he said.

She was already beginning to pant. 'I'm good, thanks. You?'

'Yeah, good. Didn't think this was your thing?'

Couldn't they slow down a bit?

'No. But I didn't…know how else…to get in touch… with you.'

Kate elbowed her at that point. Emily knew what she was angling for: an introduction. Her friend still hadn't sussed that she'd met this guy before. 'Kate…meet Rob,' Emily said.

Rob nodded at Kate, then looked back to Emily. 'You wanted to get in touch with me? How come?'

'Well, actually… I wanted…to ask you if—'

Thankfully at that moment, Clipboard Woman slowed to a walk and then the whole group slowed.

'Two minutes walking,' she shouted from the front of the group.

'What did you want to ask me?' said Rob.

Emily stopped walking. Put her hands on her knees and tried to catch her breath. Kate and Rob stopped too and people began to overtake them.

When Emily stood up again, the running group were a little way ahead.

'I was wondering if your offer still stood.' Emily put her hand on her chest. Her breathing was becoming a little more normal now. 'I need someone to paint me a sign.'

'Why d'you need a sign, Emily?' said Kate just as Rob said, 'What d'you want the sign to say?'

Emily wiped a drop of sweat from her forehead. 'The (Not So) Little Board Game Café. Dad and I have bought Sweet Delights.'

*

Emily had the strongest sense of déjà vu ever as she stood at the top of a dodgy stepladder, wielding a paintbrush loaded with pale-grey emulsion. Not so long ago, she'd been doing this in Nico's. And now here she was: proud new owner – well, co-owner – of Sweet Delights, which was about to become Essendale's second board game café. Not the original, but it was definitely going to be the best.

'More tea?' said Marjory, emerging from the kitchen. She was giving it a deep clean, though Emily wasn't sure why as Peggy had left the place spotless.

'Definitely,' said Mr B, putting down his paintbrush.

'Another tea break?' Emily said. 'There's only ten days till the launch.'

The front door opened and Annie poked her head round. 'Anyone need sustenance?' she called.

'Great timing, Annie. Marjory's putting the kettle on,' said Mr B.

They sat at one of the tables, drinking Yorkshire Tea and eating Annie's latest creation: cupcakes with huge swirls of icing, a bright green snake and a tiny ladder poking out of the top of each one.

'How's the caravan, Annie?' said Marjory.

Annie had been the first person Emily had told when they'd signed the deal on Sweet Delights. Annie was going to bake all the cakes for the new café, do some of the cooking and she'd even suggested she could do the accounts – she'd always done them at Ridley's so it seemed like a sensible idea. The promise of a job had been enough to secure the caravan and she'd moved in pretty much straight away.

'You've no idea how good it is to have a place of my own again. Quite a few people live on the farm – there's a couple of converted vans in the yard and a narrowboat moored next door on the canal. I've got a bit of company in an evening, when I want it. It's ideal. I'm making cakes for the farm shop too. They're selling like…'

'Hot cakes?' said Mr B.

'Yeah, hot cakes. People love them. We could put some flyers for the café in the farm shop if you like, Em. Get a bit more publicity?'

'That'd be great. Thanks, Annie.'

The door opened again. This time it was Kate. She had a bit of a knack for showing up soon after Annie had arrived with a box of cakes, her keto diet conveniently forgotten.

'Mmmm.' Kate helped herself to a cupcake and took a bite. 'Delicious, as usual.'

She munched on the cupcake whilst walking round the café, casting a critical eye on the new paintwork.

'I'm not sure about this colour, Em. It's a bit…dull.'

'I chose it,' said Mr B. 'And it isn't dull. It's neutral.'

'I think something bolder would make more of an impact.' Kate walked over to the table where they were all sitting and took a second cupcake. 'Perhaps a midnight-blue feature wall along here…' – she gestured, waving the cupcake around in her hand – '…and then the canvases from the old café could go on that wall there.' Some crumbs flew off onto the floor and, without a word, Marjory fetched a dustpan and brush and began to sweep.

'I think it looks perfect as it is,' said Mr B. 'Why don't you stick to the marketing and let me get on with the décor?'

Kate and Mr B glowered at each other, neither one willing to back down. Emily mentally added 'peace-keeper' to the list of roles that she had to perform as a café-owner.

'When are we going to meet your new business partner, Emily?' asked Marjory, sitting down again. 'All that time of having you as my neighbour and I never once met your dad.'

Emily shrugged. 'Soon, I hope.'

But she wasn't that hopeful. For all his promises when he'd persuaded her to take a risk and buy Sweet Delights – well, it was him taking the risk as it was his money – he hadn't yet set foot outside Thornholme, let alone caught the two buses between there and Essendale.

There was always an excuse.

'I'm feeling a bit under the weather today, Emily.'

'I've got an appointment at the optician's.'

'It sounds like you've got a lot of helpers at the café already, Em. I don't want to get under your feet.'

Or her personal favourite. 'Tomorrow. I thought I'd come over tomorrow.'

And, of course, he never did.

She wanted her dad to see her new venture, to squeeze her hand as they opened the doors to customers for the first time, to meet all her friends as they toasted the café's success. Surely he'd be happier if he broadened his horizons a little? Became something of the man he used to be?

There was another man whom Emily was desperate to see, stepping through that café door. Ludek. Persuading Dad to come over was proving tricky but Ludek? Surely all she had to do was invite him?

There was no time like the present, she thought later that afternoon, when she and Mr B had finally washed out their paintbrushes and hung up their overalls.

It was growing late. Might Ludek be home by now? She'd pass his house on the way back to her new flat. Well, almost. If she took a diversion down St John's Street, cut across the park and walked an extra three-quarters of a mile. That was on the way, wasn't it?

The extra exercise would do her good anyway, she decided. She knew she'd put on a bit of weight after she'd bought Nico's – all that slipping an extra bacon rasher in the pan for herself when she fried up an all-day breakfast for a customer; all that dipping her finger into the cake mix to 'double-check it's okay' – but her second visit to the running club had shown her that she was even more unfit than she'd thought.

She hesitated as she reached his street. Was it a little intrusive to be knocking on his door, uninvited? Did she know him well enough to do that? Was it a bit stalker-ish even? You spend one night with someone. They decide they want to cool it, then show up on your doorstep over two months later. Yes. Decidedly stalker-ish. But they had been friends, hadn't they?

Emily was almost there when she saw a woman, just a few metres away, leaving Ludek's house. She was slim – she would be, wouldn't she? – and smartly dressed with long dark hair tied back in a ponytail. She pulled his front door shut behind her, took out a key and locked it.

Emily watched as she unlocked Ludek's car – she had his

car key too? – and climbed into the driving seat. Then the car sped off. Emily stood frozen to the spot.

His girlfriend? Must have been a whirlwind romance to have reached the 'have a set of my house keys' stage already. It wasn't that long since he'd spent the night with Emily and she was sure he wasn't with anyone then; there'd been no evidence of another woman at his house and he wasn't the type to cheat. She was certain of that.

But now he *was* with someone else.

A man approached with a dog on one of those extending leads. He went one side of her, the dog went the other and the lead wrapped itself around her legs. She tried to step over the lead as the man came back round behind her, tugging at the dog, and the lead somehow became entangled round one leg. Tears began to roll down her cheeks.

'Get a grip,' said the man, finally unwinding the lead. He swore under his breath as he went on his way.

And still she stood there, in the middle of the pavement, outside Ludek's house. The house where they'd shared curry and played Wasabi! and Dinner in Paris. The house where he'd kissed her gently then led her upstairs, undressed her slowly and made love to her, looking into her eyes the entire time, making her feel as if she was the only woman he'd ever want. Why the hell had she walked away from all that?

Chapter Thirty-Nine

The following morning Marjory arrived at the café with a printed sheet, which she proudly Blu-tacked to the wall.

'Marjory!' said Mr B. 'We've painted that. It'll leave a mark.'

'It's important,' she replied. 'I'll put the kettle on.'

Emily and Mr B hurried over.

Marjory had printed out a list of jobs.

The (Not So) Little Board Game Café – Roles, she had written.

Emily – Manager. Annie – cake designer and head chef. Mr B – interior designer. Kate – publicity / chief cake taster. Marjory – head cleaner.

'Now everyone's clear,' she said. 'And there'll be no more arguing.'

Emily wished Dad's name was on that list, but she could hardly have expected Marjory to have included him, when he was never there.

And Ludek's too. *Health and Safety Manager*, Emily

imagined it saying. Appropriate she felt, given his job and the way he'd leaped to Marjory's rescue in the old café.

Kate was doing all the publicity but she had given Emily one task: to go to the board games group and invite all the players to the launch. Emily suspected that this was Kate's attempt to get her back together with Ludek; she'd never told her best friend about the woman she'd seen leaving his house a few days earlier. Kate would say that it was her own fault; that she should never have run away from him the morning after they'd slept together. And she'd be right.

Emily longed to see him again, but, at the same time, she dreaded it. Seeing him – smiling as he caught sight of her walking in, carefully unpacking his little games pieces from their Ziploc bags, getting excited with Alan over the rules to a new game – would stir something in her, something she needed to suppress. He belonged to someone else now. In many ways, it would be easier if she never saw him again, if she forgot he existed.

But she couldn't avoid him for ever. She was starting a board game café – again – in a small town where he ran the local board games group. Their paths would inevitably cross.

The atmosphere in the upstairs room of the Red Lion was a little more subdued than normal, and there was no sign of Ludek. The Dungeons and Dragons crowd were in the corner, engrossed in some campaign against the forces of evil. Some train game – not Ticket to Ride, but one she hadn't seen before that appeared to involve trains and, of all things, cows – was underway on the Trainspotters' table.

One of the players looked up and called, 'Hi, Emily! Lovely to see you!' And then the others all looked up and waved.

On the table where she'd first met them, Malcolm was poring over some games rules and Alan was laying out a board and arranging the pieces ready to play.

'May I join?' she said.

Malcolm patted the chair beside him. 'This chair has your name on it.'

She sat down next to him and looked at the unfamiliar board: a map of Europe, major cities marked out with lines connecting them.

'Powergrid,' said Alan. 'Do you know the rules?'

Emily shook her head.

'I'll explain,' said Malcolm.

They would each build a network of cities across the board, Alan told her. The aim was to supply electricity to those cities by buying power plants. Some of the power plants were green – wind turbines mostly – so worked out cheaper to run. For the others, you had to buy coal, oil or uranium.

Emily glanced at the door. Still no Ludek.

'Cities, power plants and fuel all cost money,' said Alan. 'How much money do we have to start with, Malcolm?'

Malcolm began leafing through the rules book to find out, then handed each of them a few bank notes. Pretend ones, obviously. The fourth chair at the table remained empty, Emily noticed, and Malcolm hadn't put any notes there ready. Perhaps Ludek wasn't coming.

She was about to ask where he was when Malcolm told her to choose a city where she'd start building her network. She opted for Paris, not for tactical reasons, but because she still dreamed of visiting there one day. That probably wouldn't happen any time soon; not with a new business to run.

Next came the auction of power plants. There was a choice of coal, oil or renewable power. She would have liked to go green, but Malcolm outbid her and she ended up with the cheaper coal plant. Even so, she paid far too much money in the auction and forgot to save any to buy fuel. Paris would be in darkness for the time being. She would get more money at the start of the second round. The more cities you supplied power to, the more money you accumulated.

Games like this required calculation and concentration but Emily was too distracted by Ludek's absence, too busy wondering where he might be. He hadn't been at running club either. Maybe he didn't go running anymore, but she'd never known him miss a games evening.

Perhaps now he had a girlfriend, board games group was out and Netflix, take-aways and snogging on the sofa were in. The thought of Ludek snogging made it impossible for her to figure out how much money to bid in the auctions and which cities to buy next, whilst still leaving enough for the fuel she needed and the pipelines to connect the cities. Board games usually absorbed all her attention but her mind kept wandering. Back to Ludek.

'Come on, Emily, catch us up a bit,' said Malcolm.

But already, she was too far behind. She managed to connect Paris to Reims and Amiens, but she'd need a whole twenty notes to link Dijon into her network. She couldn't afford another power plant so, even though she had three cities, she could only supply power to two so earnt less money than Malcolm and Alan, which gave her a disadvantage in the next round.

She was trying to calculate if she should swap her coal plant for oil, when Malcolm said, 'I wonder if he's got critical illness cover.'

'Insurance is probably the last thing on his mind right now,' said Alan. 'I'll bid thirty on that nuclear plant.'

'I'll pass,' Emily said. 'Think I'll stick with coal.'

'I'll pass too,' said Malcolm. 'But it might come in handy if he can't work for a few weeks.'

'Who can't work for a few weeks?' Emily was curious now.

Alan paid his notes and reached over to take the nuclear power plant card. 'Ludo.'

'Why can't Ludek work for a few weeks?' said Emily.

'Well, we don't know it's a few weeks,' said Malcolm. 'I was hazarding a guess. Maybe he'll never be able to go back to work…'

Might never go back to work? She was panicking now.

'What's happened to Ludek? Why isn't he here?'

Was no one going to tell her?

Alan put his hand over hers. 'Oh, Emily, I'm so sorry. I thought you knew. He was in an accident. Hit and run.'

'When he was out running,' said Malcolm. 'So more, run and hit and run.'

'Not funny, Malcolm.' Alan shook his head.

'And how is he?' Emily was distraught now.

Alan shrugged. 'He's in hospital. That's all we know.'

'It's all my fault,' Emily said to Kate. 'Everyone I love dies. Mum. Gran. Snowy.'

'Snowy?'

'My pet rabbit. Died when I was six.'

'Your gran was ninety-two,' said Kate. 'I don't think her death had anything to do with you. And your mum – well, that was a terrible accident. And how long do rabbits live? Probably not that long. Anyway, Ludek isn't dead.'

'No, but he could have been. It could be serious. Hit by a car... I can't bear to think about it.'

'I thought Alan said he was recovering,' said Kate.

'No, just that he was in hospital.' Emily looked at her watch. 'Will you drop me off? Alan said visiting hours finish at half past eight and it's almost quarter to now and I really, really want to see him. See with my own eyes that he's okay. Assuming he is okay.'

'Come on then.'

She grabbed her handbag whilst Kate found her car keys.

Emily's anxiety levels rose with each mile. Kate took every corner at speed, went through every amber traffic light. And possibly a couple that had just turned to red. Emily gripped the door handle and tried to hit the brakes with her right foot, like a nervous driving instructor, only they weren't in a dual control car. Unfortunately.

And it wasn't just Kate's driving. She was desperately worried about Ludek's injuries – Alan hadn't known much – *and* she felt awkward about seeing him again. She'd only seen him once since the morning after they'd slept together – when she'd returned his board games – and that had been decidedly awkward. And now he was seeing someone else...

Oh god, how badly was he injured? What if he didn't pull through?

Kate pulled up outside the main entrance with a screech

of brakes. Emily wiped her sweaty palms on the skirt of her pinafore.

'Are you going to be okay, Em? You look awfully pale.'

'I'm fine,' she said, but as she opened the car door and tried to get out, she realised that her legs were shaking.

'This is the first time, isn't it?'

Emily nodded. She knew what Kate meant; the first time inside a hospital since the day she went to see Mum for one final time before her life support was turned off.

Emily had spent her whole adult life avoiding hospitals. That bad gash from a kitchen knife that probably needed stitches? Steri-Strips from the pharmacist. That bang on the head when she was stepping aside to avoid the hissing geese and walked into a lamppost? Well, she was only unconscious for a minute or two. That dodgy ankle when she tripped outside Nico's? So lucky that Ludek had been there.

Ludek. She had to see him.

Her mouth was dry. A wave of nausea rose up from her stomach. She was half in, half out of the car, still gripping the door handle. Another vehicle beeped from behind.

'Em, you don't have to do this,' Kate said. 'We can ring the ward, see how he's doing. Send flowers or something.'

'I don't think they allow flowers on hospital wards any more, do they?'

'Grapes then. Interfruit.'

Emily managed a small smile. The car behind sounded its horn again.

'I'm going to have to get out of his way, Em. Are you getting back in the car? Or braving it?'

'Braving it. Please can you wait for me?'

She slammed the car door and walked towards the entrance, trying to take deep, steady breaths. Behind her, she heard Kate drive away, revving the engine way too much as usual. The automatic doors opened as she approached and willed her legs to take her inside.

She wasn't sure she could do this.

Chapter Forty

The smell hit her as soon as she was inside. That all-too-familiar smell: Costa Coffee. Since when did hospitals have a Costa in the foyer?

It had taken them twenty minutes to drive to the hospital, but it took her at least another ten to find the right ward. When she eventually opened the double doors, Emily spotted her – Ludek's girlfriend – before she spotted him.

The dark hair was loose now and she looked even more attractive with it lying on her shoulders. She was wearing a navy shift dress. Emily looked down at her own outfit, the old pinafore she'd been wearing all day; there was a splash of paint on the skirt. Well, whoever this woman was, she didn't need to worry about Emily. There was no competition.

And then it hit her. Why would Ludek want to see her when he had this gorgeous creature by his bedside?

She started to turn away again. It was becoming a habit now. She'd see the dark-haired woman, turn on her heels and flee. But then she heard her name.

'Emily?'

She turned back to the ward. The dark-haired woman was heading in her direction.

'Emily, isn't it? You're not leaving, are you? I'm sure Ludek would love to see you.'

Great. So not only was she beautiful, she was nice as well. But he deserved it; he was the loveliest guy. Emily sighed. She looked over at him lying in the bed. He lifted his hand and gave her a little wave.

Her heart gave a little leap. He was well enough to wave.

'Come on,' the dark-haired woman said. 'Come and say hello. He's been through a hell of a lot this last week. He needs his friends more than ever.'

His friends. His girlfriend was marking her card. Telling her firmly which category she belonged in.

Still, friendship was better than nothing. She wanted this man in her life, one way or another.

'I'm Rachel, by the way,' the dark-haired woman said.

Emily shook her offered hand, the other woman's skin cool and smooth against her own clammy palms. Then she followed Rachel over to Ludek's bedside, wondering what on earth she was supposed to say.

Sorry you got run over.

Sorry I ran away after I slept with you.

Sorry you're with someone else now.

Ludek stretched his hand out to her. The one that wasn't attached to a drip. Emily looked at his bruised face, his pale complexion.

'How are you, Em?' he said, but all she could hear were the sounds of the ward: monitors beeping; the swish of curtains being pulled around beds; someone calling, 'Nurse.'

The last time she'd heard those sounds…

She bit her lip. Pulled herself together. 'Never mind me. How are you?'

'I've been better.'

'How on earth did it happen?' The words were out of her mouth before she could stop herself. She didn't really want to know; knew the memories it would trigger.

'I was out running and this car came from nowhere. He must have been speeding. I was lucky really. My injuries could have been far worse.' He glanced at Emily. 'Oh god, Em, I'm sorry. I didn't think.'

The tears were streaming down her cheeks. Rachel handed her a tissue.

'No, I'm sorry. It's just everyone...'

She'd been about to say 'everyone I love dies'. But she could hardly say that in front of his girlfriend, could she? And besides, he *hadn't* died. Nearly died, maybe. But he was still here, living, breathing. Right in front of her.

'Everyone at the games group is very worried about you.' What she really meant was, *I'm very worried about you.*

'Yes, Alan was in earlier,' he said. 'Although he didn't look that worried. He brought Catan in.'

'Are cats allowed in hospitals these days?' Emily sniffed.

'The game.'

'Oh,' she said. 'Who won?'

'Alan. I'm not thinking straight – I blame the painkillers. He told me about your new café. It sounds wonderful, Em. I can't wait to see it. As soon as I'm out of here...'

Emily felt a stab of annoyance that Alan had told him her big news. She'd wanted to do that herself. But that wasn't important. Not really. The main thing was that Ludek was okay.

'Any idea when that'll be?'

'They think the day after tomorrow,' said Rachel, smiling at Emily and then at Ludek.

'If you're home by the eleventh, you could come to my launch party,' she said. 'Probably a good idea if you do come, actually, given what happened last time. Though I'm not serving anything with nuts in this time. And Marjory's promised to put her teeth in.'

'She didn't have her teeth in?'

'Course she did. That was my attempt at a joke.'

He laughed. A bit late. But he laughed.

Rachel probably had a razor-sharp wit. If she didn't work as a... Well, Emily didn't know what she did, but no doubt she was so hilarious that she could have done stand-up for a living.

'And you're very welcome too, Rachel,' she added. 'Do you like board games?'

'I can't stand them.'

Emily could see that Rachel and Ludek made an attractive couple, but if she didn't share his favourite hobby...? And games were more than a hobby to Ludek. They were his passion. This was like her and Peter, wasn't it? Him not sharing – or even appreciating – her love of cooking and baking. Wanting to watch documentaries on National Geographic when she wanted to watch *Ramsay's Kitchen Nightmares*.

Would Rachel be insisting that Ludek's stacks of boxes were all relocated to the garage sometime soon? Was there a glimmer of hope?

'I will definitely be there,' said Ludek. 'And I'll talk Rachel into coming along too.'

Perhaps not.

Rachel glanced at her watch. 'I ought to go.'

'Could you please bring me some pyjamas in tomorrow?' Ludek said to her. 'I hate wearing these things.'

He pointed at his hospital gown, standard issue, blue and white, in the thinnest of fabrics. Such weird things, hospital gowns. So undignified. Emily hated the way they gaped open at the back. Although… a sudden image of Ludek's arse came to mind, which seemed so very inappropriate with him being injured and his girlfriend standing right beside her.

'I'd best go,' she said. She had to leave first; she didn't want to be there to witness them kissing each other goodnight.

'If you're at a loose end tomorrow, Em,' said Ludek, 'I'd welcome another visit.'

'Yeah, sure,' she said and her heart gave a little flutter. He was still keen to see her, even though he was dating Rachel.

As a friend, she reminded herself. He just wants you as a friend.

She said goodbye, then turned and left, without a backwards glance. Down the long, antiseptic corridors. Past Costa Coffee. Out through the double doors. Past the smoking shelter where several patients in wheelchairs and on drips were puffing away, and towards the car park where she guessed that Kate would be waiting.

Emily saw her friend as soon as she turned the corner. She was leaning up against her car. Even from forty metres away, Emily could see her pose was provocative, her gestures flirtatious. The hand through the hair. The head on one side.

She was talking to a man on crutches. It was only as Emily drew closer that she realised who *he* was.

'Kate,' she said.

'Emily, look who I've found.'

'Hello, Rob,' said Emily.

'Shame,' said Kate, putting the car into first gear. 'We could have given him a lift home, but he said his mate was picking him up. How was the hospital? Did you cope?'

'Just about. It was hard to keep a lid on the memories. I'm glad you were here to meet me.'

Kate pulled out of the hospital car park, turning left onto the main road. 'And how was Ludek?'

'He's okay. Recovering. His girlfriend was there.'

Kate stole a sideways glance at Emily. 'He has a girlfriend? Oh, Em. Are you okay?'

'Yeah. I suppose. I already knew about her. I didn't tell you, but I saw her leaving his house.'

'Oh, Em. You should have said.' Kate glanced in her rear-view mirror. 'I think that's Rob in the car behind. Can you believe how much he's changed?'

'I can, actually. I watched it happen.'

Kate turned to look at Emily.

'Keep your eyes on the road,' Emily warned as they narrowly missed a parked car.

'You watched it happen?'

'Yeah, he used to come into the old café. He started work as a builder. Guess that helped get the weight off.'

'You might have mentioned him.'

'You dismissed him,' Emily said. 'Sweaty, fat guy, you called him.'

'Hmmm. Bit judgy of me.'

'*Very* judgy of you. And he's on a keto diet. Imagine the low carb dinners you could share.'

'I've given up on that. Annie's cakes have proved my downfall. Anyway. Back to Rob. I'm so embarrassed that I didn't recognise him at running club. Why didn't you tell me?'

'I didn't realise it was such a big deal.'

'He looks like that, Em, and you didn't realise it was a big deal?'

Mr B and Kate were arguing again about the colour of the walls in the toilets when she arrived the following morning.

'White would look fresher,' said Kate.

'And need repainting sooner,' said Mr B. 'Besides, the grey matches the walls in the café.'

'But...' began Kate.

Annie appeared carrying a freshly baked batch of croissants, Marjory hot on her heels with a large cafétiere of coffee.

'Kate,' said Marjory, 'I think it's important we stick to our assigned roles.' She gestured at the list which she'd now moved to the side of the chiller cabinet.

'We're not changing anything now, anyway,' Emily said. 'Everything's ready for the grand opening. Let's sit back and enjoy it.'

The café looked amazing: a mixture of the tables that she and Mr B had painted for The Little Board Game Café with some of the tables from Sweet Delights painted to match – although they'd decided not to paint any more game boards on the table tops since they now had such a fantastic selection of games to choose from.

Dad had paid for the café, but Emily had paid for the games. She'd sold her old engagement ring, the ring that Peter had bought – she'd asked his permission – and that Ludek had prised off her finger. The brightly coloured boxes of Azul and Agricola, Puerto Rico and Powergrid, SpaceBase and Steam were now stacked on her shelves, along with quite a few others. She wished Ludek was here to see them; wished he'd been part of all this preparation. After all, he was the one who'd introduced her to board games in the first place.

Each table had a set of meeple-shaped salt and pepper pots and a menu. The menus – all designed and printed by Mr B who'd learned Photoshop at his Silver Surfers Club at the library – had dice going all the way round the edges. Kate had even found napkins with hearts, spades, clubs and diamonds on Etsy. Emily suspected they'd cost a small fortune and she'd be resorting to plain ones once they ran out.

'I've got you a new dress, Em,' said Kate, 'since you gave the Scrabble one to the hospice shop.'

'I feel bad about that. I was going to buy it back.'

'Nope. New café. New beginning. New dress. You're going to love it. Drumroll, please.'

Mr B, Annie and Marjory obliging drummed on the table top, so hard that the meeple salt and pepper almost jumped up and down, and Kate handed Emily a parcel, wrapped in the same brown paper that the Scrabble dress had been wrapped in.

Emily pulled off the Sellotape and folded the paper back. Inside was a pinafore, in exactly the same style as her Scrabble dress.

'Ta-dah,' said Kate. 'I managed to find some meeples fabric. You're going to look wonderful, Em.'

Posters were up all over town. An article had appeared in the local paper with a picture of Emily sitting at one of her tables with a huge pile of board games and a mug of coffee. Thanks to Rob, the sign above the café was freshly painted. The guests were all invited and only a few still had to confirm. One of those being Dad.

'There'll be loads of people there,' he said when Emily phoned for the eleventh time to remind him about the event. 'You won't need me.'

'I need you more than I need any of those other people, Dad. What was it you said? That it was beautiful that I shared Mum's dream and that you'd like to be part of it. Of course, you've got to be there.'

'I'm not sure, Em. It's a long way. Three buses.'

'Two,' Emily said, but she knew it wasn't the number of buses. Dad was never going to leave Thornholme.

At half past two, Emily grabbed one of the games from the shelves, and she and Kate left the others to it.

'I could have taken the bus to the hospital,' Emily said as they drove away. She didn't fancy another white-knuckle ride.

'No, I needed to get out of there. Mr B and Marjory are

driving me nuts. That list of roles! Honestly. Anyway, I've taken it down. It's in my handbag.'

Emily reached behind her and pulled the bag off the back seat. 'May I?'

Kate nodded, so she opened the bag and took out the list.

'Might keep this for my memory box,' she said. 'So one day, when I've a chain of board game cafés all over West Yorkshire, I can look back and say, "This is where it all began."'

'All ready for the big launch?' said Ludek. 'Preparations going smoothly?'

'Yes, all ready. And yes, pretty smoothly. Except for Mr B and Kate arguing over paint colours. Marjory made this.'

Emily pulled the now-crumpled list out of her bag and handed it to him.

'Shame I'm not on there,' he said. 'I'd have loved to help.'

'Hang on.'

Emily took the paper back, fumbled in her handbag and pulled out one of her chewed Biros. She wrote 'Ludek' on the bottom and added a role. 'How's that?'

'Health and safety? Er…thanks, Em. Are you being ironic?'

'Ironic?'

'Well, I'm currently in a hospital bed due to being run over.'

'Oh god, no. Ludek, I didn't mean that. Although…'

'Although?'

'Well, it *is* a bit ironic, now you mention it. Essendale running club's favourite lollipop man being run over.'

Ludek laughed and shook his head.

'But,' she added, 'what I meant was with you being a doctor, it was apt to put you in charge of health because that's your expertise.'

'But not my *only* expertise.'

Was he being suggestive? Emily wondered, remembering his skill in the bedroom. She felt her cheeks beginning to redden.

'Is there a reason why hospitals are always so warm?'

He shrugged. 'Patient comfort? Maybe cos lying in bed for long periods makes you feel colder. Give me that list.'

Emily handed it back.

'Pen?' He held out his hand.

Ludek scribbled out 'Health and Safety' and wrote 'Board Games Consultant' in its place, before handing the sheet back.

'Perfect,' she said. 'You're the official games consultant of The (Not So) Little Board Game Café. Now, I've brought Patchwork with me. Do you fancy a game?'

'Love it. Most people bring grapes or flowers. You bring a game. And one designed by the great Uwe Rosenberg at that.'

'Don't think you're allowed flowers in hospitals anymore. And I didn't know if you liked grapes.'

'Speaking of flowers, I never asked...did you get mine?'

'What flowers?'

'The roses.'

Of course, the roses. Emily had thought it was odd; roses weren't Peter's style. Why hadn't it occurred to her that they might be from Ludek?

Did this mean...? But what about Rachel?

'Yeah, they were lovely. I should have thanked you, but...'

'You didn't realise they were from me.'

Emily looked down at the sheets on Ludek's bed. Straightened them. Brushed away an imaginary crumb. 'No.'

'You thought Peter had sent them?'

She nodded, still avoiding his gaze. 'Possibly. I wasn't sure...it didn't occur to me. Anyway, thank you for the flowers.'

'You're welcome.'

God, this was awkward. Change the subject.

'Ludek, could I ask your professional advice?' She looked up at him. 'It's about my dad.'

'Go on.'

'Since Mum died, he won't leave Thornholme. He goes to the shops, the library, the garden centre. But that's it. He used to be so adventurous. I thought the launch party might persuade him, might be the catalyst that finally lured him out but I don't think he's going to come. Is it normal for grief to last this long? Do you think there's any kind of quick fix, hypnosis or anti-depressants or something, that might work before next Saturday?'

'Bit of a tall order, that one, Em.'

'Yeah, I know.'

Ludek looked thoughtful. 'Look, this isn't medical advice and it mightn't work in time for the launch, but is there something your dad has always wanted to do? Like a bucket list thing?'

'I dunno. Well, there is one thing. He's a bit of a penchant for Austin Healeys...'

'Lovely cars.'

'...and he's always wanted to go in one.'

'Bingo. You could hire one.'

'That's an idea. If I hired one and drove over in it to pick him up and brought him over for the launch, it might just work. Although, well, I should stay at the café on Saturday in case there are last minute things to do.'

'I'd offer, but I don't think I'll be up to driving. Not on these painkillers.'

Emily glanced at the shape of Ludek's body under the bedcovers. He hadn't said much about his injuries and she hadn't liked to ask.

'Does it hurt a lot?'

'It's getting better.'

'I was worried you'd...'

'No vital organs were damaged.'

He raised his eyebrows and Emily felt her cheeks reddening again.

Get a grip, she told herself. 'So your heart's okay? Your liver and...kidneys?'

'They're fine. It could have been far worse. I might have a limp for a while. And I probably won't be at running club for a few months. Now, is there someone else who'd drive over to your dad's in an Austin Healey?'

'I know. Peter. Peter would do it. He'll probably know where I could hire one too.'

Ludek frowned at the mention of the name and Emily realised how excited she'd sounded. She wanted to explain that excitement wasn't about her ex-fiancé, but about the possibility of her dad coming to her new café.

But she said nothing. What was the point? Ludek had a girlfriend. And, right on cue, here was Rachel now, striding down the ward, her perfect smile on her perfect face and they hadn't even opened the Patchwork box.

Chapter Forty-One

'I presume it's okay if I bring a date to the launch,' said Kate.

'Please tell me it isn't Freddie.'

'It isn't Freddie.'

'Then who?'

'You have to wait and see.'

But Kate's mystery date was the last thing on Emily's mind. She was too busy worrying about how the event would go and whether Ludek would be well enough to be there and whether the chance of a ride in an Austin Healey would persuade Dad to come. In that order. No, not in that order. The thing she wanted most was for Dad to be there. Or Ludek? No, she needed all three things: a perfect launch party with both Dad and Ludek in attendance.

There was someone at Peter's golf club who had a business in Manchester that hired out classic cars, so, despite the short notice, a cream-coloured, open-top Austin Healey with burgundy leather seats had been hired for the day for an eye-watering amount. 'And that's with mate's rates,' Peter had said as Emily handed over her credit card. It had better be worth it. Dad had better come.

★

She smoothed down the fabric of her new meeples pinafore and pressed Play on Spotify. Abba's 'The Name of the Game' began to play, just as it had when she'd launched her first board game café. She paused for a moment, remembering how she'd filled that gloomy little building with happy customers. If only for a few short weeks. She crossed her fingers and looked out of the window at the sky.

'Say a prayer for me, Mum, if you're up there,' she said, 'and please make Dad come.'

A small queue had already formed outside, so Emily opened the door, greeting her guests one by one – she was surprised to discover that she knew almost everyone's name – and ushering them towards the counter where Annie was serving drinks.

Once everyone had arrived, she circulated, handing out meeple-shaped cookies. Julia and George were inspecting the selection of games. Richard Thorp and his wife – there'd been no hard feelings when she'd handed in her notice for a second time – were talking to Florence.

'But have you got a fully comprehensive policy?' Malcolm was saying to Mrs Sinclair. Or was that Mrs Scott?

Emily tried to mingle, tried to be the perfect hostess, but she couldn't keep her eyes off the door.

Every time it opened...but no. It was the Dungeons and Dragons crowd. Then more of Rob's colleagues, the workmen who always came for breakfast in the old café, then George's friends and their parents.

Where was Dad? Where was Ludek?

And where was Kate?

The plan has failed, Peter texted. *Your dad's not at home.*

Please could you look for him, Emily replied. *Shop? Library? Garden centre? He never leaves Thornholme. Thank you.*

The door opened. Emily looked up anxiously. It was Kate. With Rob. And they were holding hands.

But she didn't have a chance to think about that because Rob had suddenly dropped Kate's hand and was holding the door open for someone. Dad? Emily wondered for a moment, but then she saw it was Ludek. The next best thing.

He was walking slowly, holding onto someone's arm. Not Rachel, but a shorter man with the messiest hair Emily had ever seen and jeans that looked about three sizes too large for him. She went straight over to greet them all.

'Kate, Rob. Lovely to see you.' Emily flashed Kate a look intending to convey, 'Since when?' but Kate flashed one back that said, 'Obviously I can't tell you now.'

'Come on, Rob. Let's go and get some drinks,' Kate said.

Emily turned to Ludek and his friend. 'I'm so glad you made it, Ludek.'

'I wouldn't have missed it for the world. Em, this is Rasmus. He's going to be my locum for a few weeks. Longer, maybe.'

'Pleased to meet you, Rasmus. Do you like board games?'

'I'm a bit of a Scrabble addict, as it happens,' said Rasmus.

'Perhaps we can broaden your tastes,' said Emily. 'Is Rachel not coming?'

'She's out with her husband,' Ludek said. 'Wedding anniversary.'

He was seeing a married woman? She wouldn't have

thought it of him. And in such a small town. Word would soon get round, if it hadn't already.

She left them to peruse her new games collection and sidled over to Kate.

'She's married,' she hissed.

'Who's married?' said Kate.

'Ludek's girlfriend. The woman who was visiting him in hospital when I went.'

'She mightn't be his girlfriend.'

'She had the keys to his house. I saw her coming out one day.'

'Even so...there could be another explanation. Don't turn round but...I said *don't* turn round, but he's looking at you now. A man doesn't look at a woman like that unless he's seriously interested.'

Rob came over then bearing two glasses of Emily's virgin cocktail mix. He planted a kiss on Kate's nose. Emily left them to it and went to help Marjory behind the counter. There was quite a queue forming.

Her hands were trembling with excitement as she served the growing line of customers. There was a buzz in the air. Mum would have loved it. She'd never heard of the concept of a board game café, of course, but she'd have loved the way this place was bringing people together. Emily wished her dad could see this.

The door opened again and her stomach lurched, but it was one of Annie's friends.

Ping! Another text from Peter. *He's not at the library, shop or garden centre. Went back to the house. Still no sign. I'll drive round the town one more time, then is it okay if I head back to Essendale? I don't want to miss your launch.*

That's fine, Emily replied. She had to accept it; there'd be no Dad at her launch party. The plan hadn't worked. He'd never even seen the Austin.

Half an hour later, she was wondering if she should invite everyone to play some games, when the door opened again. Peter poked his head round and beckoned her to come outside.

He hadn't found Dad, Emily thought, but he wanted to break the bad news in private, knowing she'd be upset.

She hurried to the door. As soon as she stepped outside, she saw the real reason Peter had summoned her: the Austin was parked right outside the café and there was someone in the passenger seat.

'Dad!'

She rushed over and flung her arms around him.

'Get in, Em. Peter is taking us for a ride.'

'But the café…? The launch…?'

'Ten minutes. Fifteen at most,' Dad said. 'Today is the day that you fulfil yours and your mother's dream, and I get to fulfil mine.'

'Where did you find him?' said Emily as Peter helped her into the cramped back seat. There was barely room for her legs, so she kicked her shoes off and tucked her feet up.

'At the bus stop.' Peter got into the driving seat.

'At the bus stop? Really?'

'I was on my way.' Dad turned to look at her. 'I'd have got here hours ago, but two buses were cancelled – shortage of drivers. It was lucky Peter came along.'

A small crowd had left the café now and were watching

from the pavement. Peter turned the key and the engine began to purr. 'Hold onto your hats,' he said as they drove away.

Emily waved at the people watching, feeling almost like royalty, and shouted, 'I'll be back in a minute.' It probably wasn't 'good optics' as Kate would say, driving away from her own launch event, but they wouldn't be long and Dad leaving Thornholme was every bit as monumental an occasion as opening her new café.

Dad leaving Thornholme. And of his own volition? Emily couldn't get her head round the fact that Peter had found him at the bus stop.

'So, Dad, you were coming here anyway?' she said. '*Before* Peter picked you up?'

'Of course.' Dad turned to look at her. 'A promise is a promise. I've kept mine and now you've got to keep yours.'

'What was your promise, Em?' said Peter, glancing at her in the rear-view mirror.

Emily shrugged. 'I don't remember.'

What had she promised exactly? Something about the next time she got a chance at love, she wouldn't shy away.

She'd cross that bridge when she came to it. Probably wouldn't be for ages. Ludek was with Rachel, and Emily couldn't imagine feeling about someone else the way she felt about him.

'I hope Smudge will be okay today,' said Dad as they turned left, up a narrow lane that led to the moor. 'She's not used to being without me for more than an hour.'

Peter skilfully negotiated several hairpins – Emily was glad that Kate wasn't driving – and the Austin chugged its way up the steep gradients until finally they were on the open road, speeding across the purple moorland.

Marjory ran out to meet them later as they pulled up outside the café.

'I've always wanted a ride in one of those open-top Jaguars,' she said.

'It's an Aust...' Emily began, but Dad interrupted her, 'Come on, then. What are we waiting for? Chauffeur?'

Peter laughed and doffed an imaginary cap. 'Your carriage awaits, sir. Madam.' He helped Marjory into the back of the car.

'But, Dad, the café?' Emily said. 'You're supposed to be here for the launch.'

'One short spin,' said Dad. 'Then I promise you, I'm all yours.'

Emily watched them drive away, then went back inside. She gazed over to where Ludek was now talking to Alan.

And then she had another eureka moment. Once again, she decided not to do an Archimedes and streak down the high street; that probably wouldn't be good optics either, though it might get her some publicity. She was thinking about what Dad had said – *I hope Smudge will be okay today; she's not used to being without me for more than an hour* – and it suddenly occurred to her. Who had fed Ludek's cat when he was in hospital? When exactly had he had his accident? Was it before that evening when she'd walked round to his house?

She sidled over to him, hovering as he and Alan debated the merits of Agricola versus Caverna.

'I think the mines bring that extra something to Caverna,' said Alan.

'There's too many options though,' said Ludek. 'It feels less strategic.'

Emily didn't quite know how to wangle her way into the conversation. In the end, she said, 'Agricola's the better game. Caverna's cruel – the donkeys get sent down the mines. Ludek, who fed Catan whilst you were in hospital? It's just occurred to me.'

They both looked at her as if she was mad.

'Rachel,' he said. 'Why?'

'And she used your car?'

Ludek looked baffled. 'Yes, just to make it easier. She lives out of town.'

Emily nodded. She was about to leave them to it, but then she thought sod it. Why not ask him? She had nothing to lose and she wanted to be sure. 'So you and Rachel aren't... you know...seeing each other?'

'What? She's married, Em. I told you. *And* she's a colleague. So no, we're not seeing each other. Why would you think that?'

Her cheeks were beginning to burn. 'Because she had your keys.'

'She knew I kept a spare set in my drawer at the surgery. She's got three cats of her own so when I had my accident, she thought she'd better feed Catan. Mind you, he'd have been okay anyway. I think half the neighbourhood feeds him behind my back.'

'Oh,' Emily said. 'I see.'

What an idiot she'd been. Kate had been right; there *had* been an innocent explanation. Alan and Ludek were both staring at her. Her cheeks must be scarlet by now and she couldn't think what to say next, so scurried back towards the counter.

She served a few more customers; Annie's snakes and ladders cupcakes were going down a storm and there were hardly any gingerbread meeples left.

'Could we have two glasses of your special punch please, Em?' Julia and her husband were standing in front of her.

'Coming right up,' she said. 'Anything for George?'

'No thanks. He's fine. He's playing with your friend.'

She nodded over to the table in the window where George was now playing Wasabi! with Ludek.

'He's a sweet guy,' whispered Julia. 'Are you two…?'

'No, we're not. Not yet anyway.'

'He was so kind to George, explaining all the games rules. He'd make a great dad.'

Emily bit her lip. Julia was right; Ludek would make a great dad. And a great boyfriend, come to that.

Perhaps the time had come for her to keep her promise – to stop shying away from love –much sooner than she'd thought.

Chapter Forty-Two

Emily was watching through the café window as the cream Austin Healey pulled up outside the café for a third time.

Dad climbed out of the passenger side, and held the door open for Marjory. He ushered her into the café. Emily walked outside to see Peter.

'Thank you so much. It means so much to me having Dad here.'

'You're welcome. Though you didn't need me in the end. He'd have got here on his own. Late, but he'd have got here. Anyway, I've enjoyed myself. It's a gorgeous vehicle. I can see why he's always wanted one.'

Peter locked the antique car and they walked towards the café.

'It seems a shame to make Dad sit in the café when he'd probably rather be driving round in that car,' said Emily. 'But then, the whole point of hiring the car was to get him to be here for the launch.'

Peter put his hand on the door, but he didn't open it. 'How about later?'

'But you've got to return it. I only paid for four hours.'

'You did. But I paid for the rest of the weekend.'

'Really?'

'Yeah. I was going to ask you to come out for the day with me tomorrow. I'd planned a picnic. Bought the food and everything. I thought we might rekindle things but I can see now that's not going to happen. I've seen the way you look at Ludek. You've never looked at me like that.'

'Peter, I'm so sorry…'

'No, Em, it's fine. Perhaps you and I were never meant to be. Looking back, I always felt that you held me at arm's length somehow. That you liked me but you weren't head over heels in love with me.'

Arm's length? Not head over heels? He was beginning to sound like Kate and Dad.

'I know Mother's a dreadful old battle-axe at times,' Peter continued, 'and when Dad was alive, he was a little… Well, shall we say henpecked? But you should have seen the way she looked at him. Pure adoration. If I'm going to marry someone, I'd like them to look at me that way too.'

'You deserve that, Peter. You really do.'

They were still standing on the doorstep. Peter's hand was resting on the handle. Emily glanced into the café and saw Annie laughing as she handed a snakes and ladders cupcake to little George.

'I know,' she said. 'Why don't you take Annie out for a picnic tomorrow?'

'Annie?'

'Why not? She's always liked you.'

'Annie has?'

'Yeah. I mean, she's never said anything. But when we both worked at Ridley's, I always suspected she did.'

'Annie.' Peter shook his head. 'I've never thought of her in that way. Annie.'

'She's lovely, Peter.'

Peter opened the door to the café and stepped aside to let Emily in first.

Always the gentleman, she thought. She hoped he would find someone who adored him.

'I might ask her out for a drink,' Peter said. 'Keep it, you know, a bit casual. But we hired the car for your dad, didn't we? How about I take him and Marjory out for the day? They seem to be getting on well together.'

He nodded over to the table in the window where her dad and Marjory were drinking punch together. Her former neighbour's hand was on his arm; she was looking at him almost coquettishly. Emily wasn't having that. She went straight over to them.

'Marjory, could I have a word in the kitchen please?'

'Sure, Em.' She stood up then leaned towards Dad and whispered, 'Won't be a minute. Stay right where you are.'

Honestly, thought Emily. Brazen. Pensioners these days.

In the kitchen, Annie was arranging some more cupcakes onto a plate.

Emily shut the service hatch so they wouldn't be overheard. 'Are you flirting with my dad, Marjory?'

'He's a lovely man.'

'Yes, but you're with Mr B. I don't want Dad getting his hopes up and then being hurt.'

'I'm not with Mr B,' said Marjory. 'It's true, we have had a little...dalliance. But he was just my back-in-the-saddle man as your friend Kate would say.'

Her back-in-the-saddle man? That was one mental image Emily could have done without.

'What about Mr B? I don't want him getting hurt either.'

'I think you might find that Mr B also has his eye on someone else.' Marjory opened the hatch and nodded in the direction of the table in the corner, where Mr B and Florence were playing what seemed to be a rather intense game of Scrabble. There was obviously an argument going on, but they both looked to be enjoying it.

Now that everyone had had a drink and something to eat and no one was off galivanting round the Yorkshire countryside in the Austin, Emily banged a teaspoon against a glass.

'A huge welcome to you all,' she said, 'at this, the launch party of The (Not So) Little Board Game Café. I hope you've all enjoyed the punch and Annie's delicious cakes and biscuits but now I'd like to invite you all to take a seat, if you haven't already. It's time to pull off the shrink wrap and open the boxes: we've a whole heap of brand-new board games waiting to be played.'

There was a smattering of applause, a flash as the photographer from the local paper snapped her picture and an exchange of smiles between Emily and Ludek.

'Oh, and if you wouldn't mind washing your hands if you've got sticky fingers,' she added as an afterthought. Ludek gave her a thumbs up.

The experienced boardgamers strategically placed themselves at different tables, so they could suggest suitable games to people who were more accustomed to Cluedo and Monopoly, and explain the rules. Emily sat down with

Mrs Scott and Mrs Sinclair and wondered for the umpteenth time which one of them was which.

'Have you bought Frustration yet?' one of them asked.

Emily shook her head, kicking herself for forgetting. She made a mental note to order it on Monday.

'There's plenty of other games, Mrs...er... Actually, this is ridiculous. How many times did I serve you in the other café? And I still don't know which of you is Mrs Scott and which of you is Mrs Sinclair.'

'It might be easier if you call us Sylvia and Helen,' said one of them.

'Okay, I will,' said Emily. Then it dawned on her that she was none the wiser: which one of them was Helen? And which Sylvia? She'd have to ask Florence later. 'So what would you like to play, Helen? Sylvia?'

'Cluedo,' they said in unison, before one of them added, 'We're not sure about those new-fangled games you've got.'

'Not sure they're our sort of thing,' said the other.

It didn't take them long to work out that Colonel Mustard had done the dirty deed in the dining room with the dagger.

'Shall we try something else?' Emily suggested. 'How about Carcassonne? You have to build a map. It's no more difficult than doing a jigsaw. And it's based on the famous French city which is a UNESCO Heritage site.'

She knew that was bound to impress them.

Having finally persuaded them to try something new, she laid out all the little tiles face down, stealing a glance at Ludek. He was at a neighbouring table, with George and his parents, playing Scotland Yard. The three adults were hunting George, who was 'Mister X', across the city of London.

As Helen – or was it Sylvia? – debated where she should place a tile with a crossroads on, Emily glanced round the café – round her café – and counted the faces she *could* put names to. Six months ago, she'd walked round Essendale wishing she knew more people. And now she knew Malcolm and Alan, Rob and a couple of his colleagues, George, Julia and her husband Steve. She knew that George's best friend was Jack and that Jack's sister was called Alice. The Trainspotters were Harry, Tom, Simon and Martin and that the Dungeons and Dragons crowd were Mike, Andy, Dave and Freddie. She knew Mr B. And, of course, she knew Ludek. All these people had come into her life either because of board games or because of the café. These days, she couldn't walk down Essendale's high street *without* seeing someone she knew. And she suspected – hoped – that over the next few months, as her business grew, she'd come to know more names still. And they would know hers.

The games had all finished by ten forty-five and most people had drifted away. Julia and Steve dragged a very tired George home to bed. Peter was driving Marjory home with the promise that he'd 'go the long way round'. True to his word, he'd arranged to pick both Dad and Marjory up again in the morning and planned to take them to the shores of a nearby reservoir for a picnic; he was still plucking up courage to ask Annie out for a drink later that week.

Kate had given Rob a chaste kiss goodnight, then sent him on his way. 'I'm not rushing it this time,' she'd said to Emily. Then she gestured towards the corner table where Mr B and Florence were arguing over yet another game of

Scrabble. 'Our Mr B is a bit of a Romeo, isn't he? Hats off to him.'

'I thought you didn't like him. All that arguing over paint colours.'

'Course I like him. He's a wonderful chap. We argued because we both wanted the same thing: everything at the café to be one hundred per cent perfect, Emily. We want you to succeed because we both love you.'

'Oh, Kate.' Emily's eyes filled with tears and she wiped them away with the heel of her hand.

'Your dad and Annie are tidying up the kitchen, and Ludek's packing away your new board games as carefully as if they were his own. All for you. And now, I suggest you go and help him whilst I go and clean the toilets. Someone's got to do it and I look rather good in a pair of Marigolds.'

Kate gave her a firm nudge in Ludek's direction and went off to find the Domestos. Emily walked over to the table where he was sorting through the games, checking each and every one for missing pieces.

'Shall I help?' Emily said.

'Sure.' He handed her Wasabi!

She began to count the cards of ingredients.

'This place is brilliant, Em. You're right on the high street, you've all the games and your excellent baking...'

'Annie's excellent baking.'

'Your cakes are delicious too. Oh, it appears we've lost a Carcassonne tile and a green meeple.'

Emily got down on her hands and knees – well, he was still injured – to search for the missing pieces, fortunately locating both within a couple of minutes.

'Sweep the floor whilst you're down there,' Annie called to her through the hatch.

Emily clenched her fist around the meeple. She owned this place but Annie was still giving her orders. But when she looked up, Emily saw Annie was peering through the hatch, smiling at her.

'Ludek's right,' she said as Emily scrambled to her feet and popped the missing pieces into the box. 'This place is brilliant. And I'm going to do everything I can to support you with it. I owe you. Big time. I'm never going to forget that.'

She turned away and began to clatter about in the kitchen. Ludek glanced at the hatch to check that Annie wasn't still listening, then over at Mr B and Florence. They were completely engrossed in their game. He cleared his throat. 'I was wondering...if you...' He cleared his throat again. 'Would you like to come over to mine next Saturday? Come for lunch. We could spend the day together.'

There was something about the way he asked her – the hesitation; the throat clearing; the hopeful look in his eyes – that made her realise that this wasn't just one friend inviting another over for lunch and a few board games. This was a man asking her out.

But she couldn't possibly leave the café for a day. Not so soon after opening.

'I'd love to but I can't. I've got this place.'

'I can manage all the cooking,' came Annie's voice from the kitchen. Emily might have known. Still listening in.

'And Kate and I will do front of house, won't we, Kate?' said Mr B, without looking up from his game.

'Yeah, sure,' said Kate, poking her head out of the toilet door. 'What could possibly go wrong?'

Florence seemed to be the only person in the place who wasn't eavesdropping on their conversation. 'You can't play that,' she said to Mr B. 'It's a proper noun.'

Dad was in a cheerful mood the next morning, whistling as he popped some bread into the toaster, smiling to himself as he made a pot of tea. He had spent the night in Emily's bed, whilst she had slept on the sofa.

'You know, Em,' said Dad. 'This change of scene has done me a power of good. I feel...alive again.'

'And this is nothing to do with Marjory?'

'Maybe a little. She's a lovely woman, Em. No one can replace your mum but, well, I could use a friend. And Peter taking us out for a picnic. How kind is that?'

'Dad, I hope you aren't thinking we might get back together.'

'Not at all. I rather like Ludek.'

'Glad to hear it. But it's early days.'

Dad spread his toast with a thick layer of butter. 'I'm expecting you to keep that promise, Em. Don't shy away from him.'

Emily smiled. 'I'll try not to.'

'Do you have any marmalade? You know, I always thought there was only one thing that could ever lure me out of Thornholme.'

Emily reached into the fridge and pulled out a jar of Golden Shred. 'And what's that?'

'Grandchildren. Right, I think I'll go and have a shower. Can I use your shower gel? Want to smell my best for Marjory.'

Chapter Forty-Three

'How about this?' Emily said to Kate, holding up the navy dungaree pinafore with a chunky necklace of red beads.

'Not chic enough.'

'Chic? I'm only going to Ludek's house for lunch.'

'Hmmm,' said Kate. 'Even so...'

'Okay, how about your black dress? You could lend me that.'

'Not after seam-gate. Anyway, you don't want to look like you've made too much of an effort. With men, it's important not to appear too keen.'

'I can't win. The pinafore's not chic enough, but your black dress makes me look too keen. Anyway, Ludek and I...it's probably just a friends thing. Isn't it?'

'We'll see.' Kate rummaged through Emily's wardrobe. 'I think jeans. Your smart jeans. The tight ones. And a plain white t-shirt. And the chunky necklace. And comfortable shoes.'

'All my shoes are comfortable. I don't do heels, remember?'

It took another hour of pencilling in her eyebrows, straightening her hair and squeezing herself into her jeans before Kate finally deemed Emily smart enough – but not too smart – to head over to Ludek's.

She walked over the perfect flagstones, past the neatly trimmed bushes and rang his bell with a trembling hand. Why was she so nervous? This was just lunch, she reminded herself, wondering if he'd be cooking. Or would it end up being another take-away?

He opened the door and Emily stepped into the hall. There was a rucksack sitting on the floor.

'Oh, are you going away somewhere?' she said.

'Yeah. No. Er…come in.' He took her jacket, hanging it over the stairpost. He glanced at his watch. 'Do you fancy a quick coffee?'

A quick coffee? Were they in some kind of hurry?

There was something a little odd about him this morning. Emily couldn't put her finger on it. Perhaps he was nervous too.

She followed him into the kitchen.

'What's for lunch?' she said as he put the kettle on. She couldn't see any signs of cooking.

He opened a Sainsbury's carrier bag that was sitting on the table to reveal two bottles of water, two pre-packed sandwiches and two bags of Walkers crisps.

'Meal deal,' he said. Didn't know if you'd prefer ready salted or cheese and onion so I got one of each.'

'I'd prefer ready salted.'

'I love cheese and onion so that's perfect.'

A meal deal? Had he seriously asked her to leave her beloved café, her brand-new business, in the hands of Mr B, Kate and Annie on its second Saturday of opening for a quick coffee and a meal deal from the supermarket?

Perhaps it was churlish of her – after all, he was still recovering from a serious injury – but she'd been hoping for a little more than this.

They sat down with their coffees at his dining table. To her surprise, he made no attempt to get out a game.

'Aren't we going to play something?' she said.

'Not yet. We're going on a surprise trip.'

'A trip? Where to?'

'If I told you that, it wouldn't be a surprise.'

From outside, she heard a car horn beep. Ludek looked at his watch. 'That must be our taxi. Bit early. Come on.'

He grabbed the rucksack as they went out, but Emily took it off him, mindful of his injuries, and refused to hand it back. She was surprised at how heavy it was; what the hell had he got in there? She let him carry the bag with their meal deal.

They were heading for Halifax, Emily thought, as the taxi wove its way along the main road. But why?

'Are we going to the Piece Hall?'

'Nope.'

'The Minster?'

'Nope.'

The taxi pulled up outside Halifax station. Leeds or Manchester then, Emily thought as they made their way down onto the platform. Knowing Ludek, it had to be something games related. A new board games shop perhaps?

She looked up at the sign indicating the next train. 'London? Are we going to London?'

Ludek shrugged, but when the Grand Central train pulled into the station, he said, 'This is us. Coach C.'

'Wow,' he said as they sat down. 'The table tops have board games on.'

'I know. That's what gave me the idea for my board game café. I went on a patisserie course in London and on the way back...'

'Hang on. I thought I gave you the idea. When I brought the board games group to play at The Lancashire Hotpot instead of the pub.'

''Fraid not. It was definitely these tables. Although, come to think of it, if you hadn't got me into board games in the first place, maybe I wouldn't have come up with it.'

'I'll drink to that.' Ludek reached down into his rucksack, stashed under his seat, and pulled out a bottle of champagne. 'I brought this to wash down our Sainsbury's sandwiches. What d'you reckon?'

It seemed rather decadent to be popping a champagne cork on a train when it was barely lunchtime. But by the time they reached Dewsbury, the bottle was empty.

'Why are we going to London?' Emily said.

'You'll have to wait and see. Like I said, it's a surprise. Fancy playing a game?'

Emily looked down at the table top. 'Draughts or snakes and ladders? Oh. But we don't have any games pieces.'

'That's okay. I make it a rule never to travel without a board game in my bag.'

She might have known. He reached down into the rucksack again, and pulled out a box. No wonder that bag had been heavy. A bottle of champagne *and* a board game. Heaven only knew what else he had in there.

Ludek placed the box on the table.

Emily peered to see what it was. 'Great. I love Dinner in Paris.'

'Can you set it up?'

Odd. He always set up the games.

She opened the box – carefully, of course, knowing how he liked to keep his games in pristine condition – and took out the rules leaflet. Underneath were two sheets of printed paper. Without looking at what they were, she handed them to Ludek.

'Not sure how these got in there,' she said.

He handed them back. 'You might want to read them.'

She looked at him, puzzled, but he just raised his eyebrows and nodded at the paper in her hand. She glanced down and couldn't quite believe the first word that caught her eye.

'Eurostar?'

'Eurostar.' Ludek smiled and nodded.

She looked at the sheet again. 'To Paris? Today?'

'If you'd like to? A short walk from King's Cross to St Pancras and off we go. We're not going to play Dinner in Paris; we're going to *have* dinner in Paris. I've booked a lovely restaurant near the Seine.'

'As in dinner in actual Paris? In France?'

'As far as I know, there isn't another Paris. And then tomorrow...'

'Tomorrow?'

'Tomorrow, we're going to explore all of Montmartre's finest little cafés. How does that sound?'

'But what about *my* café?'

'Kate...'

'Kate knows about this?'

'I had to let her in on my plan.'

Kate had known they were going to Paris? No wonder she'd told Emily that she had to look chic.

'Kate, Annie and Mr B are going to cover the café until we get back,' said Ludek, 'so you don't need to worry on that score.'

Emily was amazed; they were all going to so much effort. For her. But there was one snag.

'I don't have my passport.'

'No, but I do.' He reached down into the bag for a third time and pulled out one of his Ziploc bags, containing two passports. 'And I've got a change of clothes for you too.'

She had a sudden image of him breaking into her flat and rummaging through her underwear drawer. The thought of him seeing her greying collection of knickers. Her period pants. That stupid red feathery thong she'd once bought on a whim. Or worse still, the Spandex all-in-one that Kate had talked her into buying, saying that it would give her a better shape.

'Don't worry, I haven't been through your things,' he said, reading her mind. 'Kate packed it. She brought it all over yesterday. Good job she had the spare key to your flat.'

Emily was speechless. Had he really gone to all this trouble?

'Are you okay, Em? I don't want to force this on you. If you don't want to come to Paris with me, we can have a walk round Hyde Park or the Natural History Museum, then get the train home this evening.'

'Of course I want to come. I just can't believe it.' She looked out of the window at the countryside flashing by. 'But where will we stay?'

'I booked a hotel. Two rooms as I didn't want to presume. But that doesn't mean we have to use both. Although you'd have to be gentle with me as I haven't quite healed yet.'

Paris. With Ludek. Dinner by the Seine. A hotel, and an invitation – that had sounded like an invitation – to share his room and be gentle with him. And she was finally going to visit those little cafés in Montmartre. So much to take in and the train hadn't even reached Pontefract.

'I've been very wary of getting involved with someone new,' said Ludek as they approached Doncaster. 'I know it's early days, Em, that we've got to get to know each other, but my relationships always go wrong when it gets to the moving-in stage. I've never met a woman yet who was willing to put up with a house full of board games.'

'But you've never dated a woman who owned a board game café before.'

'True. And I've got a proposition for you.'

'Aren't you supposed to wait till we're actually in Paris for that?' Emily said before she could stop herself. Kate would kill her. You weren't supposed to drop hints about marriage. Especially not at the very start of a relationship.

'A proposition, not a proposal, you numpty,' said Ludek, laughing. He wasn't running for the hills then. Not that he could run far at the moment; he was still walking with a limp and they were on a speeding train. 'I know you've bought quite a selection of board games for the café, but I was wondering if there'd be room for some more. For mine, in fact. Or at least, some of them.'

'You mean, for customers to use?'

'Why not? That way, you could offer loads of choice.'

'Why not? Because they could get damaged. And you like to keep them in pristine condition.'

'Games are meant to be played, to be enjoyed. I'm willing to take the risk.'

Their eyes met. He reached across the table and took her hand. 'I mean it, Em. I'm willing to take the risk.'

She was willing to take the risk too. To let herself fall hook, line and sinker for this beautiful man. And if that meant that she'd be heartbroken one day... Well, that was the way it was. The way it had to be.

'That morning...' she began. Ludek stroked her hand with his thumb. Just gently. Caressing. 'You know, the morning I walked out on you.'

'You don't need to explain.'

'I do. I do need to explain. I think it was fear. Fear of falling for you. I've always kept men at arm's length before – at least, that's what Kate and Dad say, and I think they're right. It's just ...'

Emily paused, unsure of how to continue, how to explain. His eyes met hers again. 'Is this because of losing your mum?'

She nodded. 'Dad was head over heels in love with Mum, and he fell apart when she died. It was terrible losing her. I never wanted to feel grief like that again so I never let myself fall in love with someone like that. Well, I did once, but then I got scared and I dumped him. I still feel bad about that, looking back, even though he's happily married to someone else now.'

Emily paused, glancing at Ludek. He nodded, tilting his head slightly as if to emphasise that he was listening. She wondered if he did that at work, to encourage his patients to talk.

'I mean, it wasn't a conscious decision,' she said, looking down at his hand, still stroking hers. 'It just happened that way. That's why I was comfortable with Peter. I liked him. I cared about him – I still do. But I wasn't besotted with him. Then I met you, and we spent the night together, and I knew I wouldn't be able to help myself. That a couple more nights like that, and I *would* be besotted.'

She looked up at him. Kate said you shouldn't tell a man something like that. You should stay a little aloof, let him declare his feelings first. But Ludek seemed unfazed.

'Thanks for explaining,' he said. 'For the record, I already *am* besotted. I don't need another night like that. Though, of course, it would be nice.'

Emily was just wondering about breaking another of Kate's rules and leaning across the table to press her lips against his, when Ludek glanced down at their hands, intertwined on the table. And then he looked at his watch.

'I see there's still over an hour till we reach King's Cross,' he said. 'I don't suppose…'

She knew exactly what he was about to say.

'Yes,' she said. 'Yes, I *do* fancy a game of Dinner in Paris.'

Acknowledgements

I began writing fiction whilst shielding during the Covid-19 pandemic as I'm immuno-suppressed. I never expected to be published, although it was, of course, the dream.

The road to this dream becoming reality began with a tweet from the wonderful writer Philippa Ashley – thank you, Philippa – which led me to a Books for Ukraine charity auction where I won a feedback session with Rachel Faulkner-Willcocks at Aria. I was very nervous during that zoom call with Rachel – a real-life editor reading my work! – but she put me at ease and was really encouraging. I was overjoyed when two months later, she offered me a book deal. Thank you, Rachel, for being so generous to offer your time in that charity auction and for your patience and guidance ever since.

Thank you too to the rest of the team at Aria, especially Bianca Gillam for answering my millions of questions.

Many thanks to Rebecca Ritchie at AM Heath Literary Agency for reading my work in record time, for agreeing to take me on as a client and for your emotional support and encouragement.

I was surprised and delighted to discover how wonderfully

supportive the writing community is. So many established authors have made time to help and encourage a newbie like me, but special thanks go to Pam Rhodes, Trisha Ashley, Amita Murray, Kitty Wilson and Katherine Mezzacappa.

I enjoyed some excellent writing courses online during lockdown, but particular thanks go to all at CBC Creative, not only for the courses but also their support and encouragement, and to Sophie MacKenzie from CityLit who is as brilliant a teacher as she is a writer.

I'm grateful to the many fellow students from these courses who have stayed in touch and offered ongoing support and feedback, but especially Neil James, Richard Williams, Nicola Port, Judith Hansell, Alex Welton and Tara Jenkins. A special mention goes to Helen Hawkins; the title of this novel was her inspired suggestion – thank you, Helen.

Thank you to my many friends, who put up with me rambling on about my plot for hours on end, but in particular Mikaela Brand Mills, whose positive comments on the very earliest draft of this book really spurred me on, and Fiona Christian who gave me useful feedback on a slightly later version. Thanks also to Marysia Hermaszewska, Dorota Kępińska and Gosia Patyjewicz for checking my Polish sentences.

I'm one of those people who always loses her glasses and forgets something at the supermarket – scatty, in other words – so I'm sure to have omitted someone. If that's you, then humblest apologies. I did contemplate listing everyone I know to be on the safe side, but this acknowledgement section would then resemble one of those long, boring speeches at the Oscars and nobody wants that.

But one person I haven't forgotten. Last, but not least, my heartfelt thanks to my wonderful husband, Hermi, for cheering me on, bringing me mugs of coffee and his unofficial proof-reading services. The long road to meeting him – 13 years on internet dating – was what inspired me to pick up a pen to write romance in the first place, and if he hadn't introduced me to the wonderful world of board games, Emily's little café would have been very ordinary indeed.

About the Author

JENNIFER PAGE wrote her first novel – a book about ponies – when she was eight. These days she prefers to write romance. When she isn't writing, Jennifer can usually be found playing board games which are the inspiration for her first novel. She has worked as a television producer, a music teacher and has even run a children's opera company. She now lives near Hebden Bridge in West Yorkshire with her husband and his large collection of games.